英文閱讀

Know it ALL

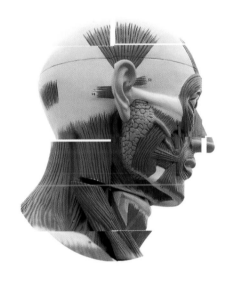

目錄 Contents

V Vocabulary Bank

1) **critic** [ˈkrɪtɪk] (n.) 評論家，批評家
Thomas is a restaurant critic for a local paper.

2) **preliminary** [prɪˈlɪməˌnɛrɪ] (a./n.) 初步的，預備的
The police are conducting a preliminary investigation of the case.

3) **seascape** [ˈsiˌskep] (n.) 海景畫
(n.) landscape [ˈlændˌskep]（陸上的）風景畫，山水畫
The artist is famous for his seascapes.

4) **movement** [ˈmuvmənt] (n.)（社會）運動，活動
The feminist movement began in the 19th century.

5) **career** [kəˈrɪr] (n.) 職業，生涯
After a long career in journalism, James will be retiring in August.

6) **charcoal** [ˈtʃɑrˌkol] (n.) 炭筆，木炭畫
The museum owns several of the artist's early charcoals.

7) **academy** [əˈkædəmɪ] (n.) 學院，藝術院
Pauline is studying at an art academy in France.

8) **resume** [rɪˈzum] (v.) 重新開始，繼續
After getting out of the army, Elvis resumed his singing career.

9) **contemporary** [kənˈtɛmpəˌrɛrɪ] (n.) 同時期或年齡的人
Tolstoy and Dickens were contemporaries.

進階字彙

10) **aspiring** [əˈspaɪrɪŋ] (a.) 有抱負的，有志氣的；有意成為…的
Many aspiring actors move to Hollywood to try to get into the movies.

11) **wallpaper** [ˈwɔlˌpepə] (n.) 壁紙
The wallpaper with the flowers will look nice in the living room.

Language Guide

Impressionism 印象派

簡而言之就是描繪光影瞬間在腦海留下印象的畫作。文中的幾位法國畫家簡介如下：

Eugene Boudin 歐仁布丹（1824–1898 年）
歐仁布丹是最早一批從事戶外寫生的法國風景畫家 (landscape painter)，善於描繪海面及海邊的景色。年輕時在家族經營的文具店及裱褙店工作，因而認識一批當地畫家，啟發他進行藝術創作。

Édouard Manet 愛德華馬內（1832–1883 年）
馬內出身富裕，一八五〇年開始習畫。儘管馬內始終與印象派維持疏離的關係，仍受到印象派技法的影響，使得他一八七〇年代的色彩運用更為豐富明亮。馬內經常將古典畫作中的元素重新組裝拼合，因此成為前衛藝術家的指標性人物。

Claude Monet
印象派大師 莫內

《印象，日出》
© commons. wikimedia.org

課文朗讀 MP3 1　單字朗讀 MP3 2　英文文章導讀 MP3 3

　　In April 1874, a review of an exhibition of paintings by a group of [10]**aspiring** French artists appeared in a Paris newspaper. "Impression—I was certain of it," wrote the [1]**critic**. "A [2]**preliminary** drawing for a [11]**wallpaper** pattern is more finished than this [3]**seascape**." He was referring to a painting titled *Impression, Sunrise*, from which he also borrowed the title of his review, "Exhibition of the Impressionists." Although the term "Impressionist" was meant to ❶ **poke fun at** the rough, unfinished style of the young artists, they nevertheless adopted the name for themselves. The art [4]**movement** known as Impressionism was thus born, along with the [5]**career** of one of its brightest lights: the painter of *Impression, Sunrise*, Claude Monet.

　　Monet was born in Paris in 1840, but moved with his family to Normandy at the age of five. There he began drawing [6]**charcoal** sketches that he later sold to his

neighbors for a few francs. In 1858, he met Eugene Boudin, who encouraged his interest in art and introduced him to the techniques of painting outdoors, or, as the French

《阿讓特伊的紅船》Red Boats At Argenteuil
© Deror avi / commons.wikimedia.org

say, "en plein air." A year later, Monet moved back to Paris to pursue his art studies, enrolling at the Swiss ⁷⁾**Academy** and ❷ **paying regular visits** to the Louvre. ⓖAfter serving in the French army in Algeria for two years, he returned to Paris in 1862 to ⁸⁾**resume** his training. Monet ❸ **fell in with** ⁹⁾**contemporaries** like Pierre-Auguste Renoir and Édouard Manet, and together they began experimenting with new artistic techniques.

Mini Quiz 閱讀測驗

❶ What does the newspaper critic think of *Impression, Sunrise*?
(A) He thinks that it is a masterpiece.
(B) He finds it very impressive.
(C) He isn't impressed by it.
(D) It is a good example of a seascape.

❷ According to the passage, what is true about Eugene Boudin?
(A) He invented "en plein air" techniques.
(B) He taught Monet how to paint outdoors.
(C) He lived and worked in Paris.
(D) He was a famous landscape painter.

中 Translation

一八七四年四月，巴黎一份報紙刊出一篇關於一場畫展的評論，那些畫作出於一群雄心萬丈的法國藝術家之手。「印象──我十分確定，」那位評論家寫道。「壁紙圖案的初步構圖完成度都比這幅海景畫還要高。」他指的是一幅名為《印象，日出》的畫，他那篇評論的標題〈印象派畫家之展〉，也借自這幅畫。雖然「印象派畫家」一詞原是要挖苦那群年輕畫家粗糙、不加潤飾的風格，但那群畫家卻以此自居。一場稱為「印象派」的藝術運動於焉誕生，而其中最耀眼的一道光芒──《印象，日出》的作者莫內──也就此展開他的繪畫生涯。

莫內在一八四〇年生於巴黎，但五歲和家人移居諾曼第，他在那裡開始畫炭筆素描，並將作品賣給鄰居換取幾法郎。一八五八年他認識歐仁布丹，布丹鼓勵他對藝術的興趣，並指導他戶外繪畫的技巧──即法國人所謂的 en plein air（在戶外）。一年後，莫內搬回巴黎學習美術，進入瑞士學院就讀，並經常造訪羅浮宮。赴阿爾及利亞服役兩年後，他在一八六二年回到巴黎，繼續接受訓練。莫內偶然認識雷諾瓦及馬內等同期畫家，一同實驗新的美術技巧。

Tongue-tied No More

❶ poke fun at... 取笑，嘲諷

每個人身上總有幾個癢處，一被碰到就渾身不自在，但看到別人被戳到癢處哭笑不得的表情，卻又會覺得好笑。poke fun at... 字面的意思「用手指戳（某處）來取樂」，也就是「（拿別人的某一點來）取笑」。
A: People are always poking fun at my accent.
大家老是取笑我的口音。
B: Don't let it get to you. Your English is getting better all the time.
別放在心上。你的英文一直在進步。

❷ pay a visit 拜訪

visit 在這個片語裡當名詞用，而 visit 本身也可以當動詞，因此下面對話中的第一句也可以說 What do you say we visit Aunt Ellie while we're in San Francisco?
A: What do you say we pay a visit to Aunt Ellie while we're in San Francisco?
我們到舊金山時去探望愛麗阿姨如何？
B: That's a great idea. We haven't seen her in ages.
好主意。我們好久沒見到她了。

❸ fall in with... （偶然）認識

fall in with 表示在沒有特意安排的情況下認識。
A: How come Michelle started taking drugs?
蜜雪兒怎麼會開始吸毒？
B: She fell in with a fast crowd in college.
她在大學認識了一群豬朋狗友。

Grammar Master

保留連接詞的分詞構句

連接詞的功用在於連接兩個動詞，若是句子裡有兩個動詞，卻沒有連接詞，我們就必須把其中一個動詞改為 Ving（表主動）或 Ved（表被動）的形式，這就稱為「分詞構句」。有時候就算有連接詞，但兩個動作的主詞相同，也可用「連接詞 + Ving/Ved」將主詞省略，沒有緊接連接詞的另一個動詞則維持原來的時態。
例 I always brush my teeth **before going** to bed.
我睡前都會刷牙。

閱讀測驗解答：❶ (C) ❷ (B)

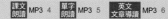

課文朗讀 MP3 4　單字朗讀 MP3 5　英文文章導讀 MP3 6

Vocabulary Bank

1) **extensively** [ɪk`stɛnsɪvlɪ] (adv.) 廣泛地
The drug is used extensively to treat infections.

2) **diverse** [dɪ`vɜs /daɪ`vɜs] (a.) 各式各樣的，不同的
San Francisco is a culturally diverse city.

3) **flee** [fli] (v.) 逃，逃離
The robber fled from the scene of the crime.

4) **marine** [mə`rin] (a.) 海洋的
Jack decided to study marine biology because he loves the ocean.

5) **property** [`prɑpətɪ] (n.) 房產，地產；資產
The landlord owns several properties.

6) **orchard** [`ɔrtʃəd] (n.) 果園
My family owns an apple orchard.

7) **estate** [ɪ`stet] (n.) 地產，莊園
The estate includes a big house, a tennis court and a swimming pool.

8) **early on** [`ɜlɪ ɑn] (phr.) 早期
The singer switched styles early on in her career.

9) **expand** [ɪk`spænd] (v.) 擴展
We decided to expand the house when I got pregnant.

10) **fond of** [fɑnd əv] (phr.) 喜歡
Susan is fond of chocolate.

11) **arched** [ɑrtʃt] (a.) 拱形的
(n.) arch [ɑrtʃ] 拱門，拱形
The church has an arched ceiling.

12) **span** [spæn] (v.) （橋、拱等）橫越，跨越
Several bridges span the river that runs through the town.

Monet traveled [1)]**extensively** during the 1860s, and the ❶ **travel bug** would stay with him throughout his life. He studied the different effects of light on the [2)]**diverse** landscapes he encountered on his journeys,

5　developing the style that would later become known as Impressionism. Many of his early works feature the figure of Camille Doncieux, and the two were married in 1870. Almost immediately, though, they had to [3)]**flee** France due to the Franco-Prussian War. The couple settled in

10　Argenteuil, a village near Paris, on their return in 1871. Monet, an accomplished sailor himself, loved to watch

ᴳthe sailboats floating along on the Seine there, as depicted in his 1875 works *Red Boats at Argenteuil* and [4)]*Marine View with a Sunset*.

15　　In 1883, Monet moved to Giverny, a small village 40 miles northwest of Paris. He rented a house on a two-acre [5)]**property** that included a small garden, [6)]**orchards**, and a barn that he used as a studio. He purchased the [7)]**estate** in 1890 with profits from the sale of his paintings,

20　and would live there for the rest of his life. [8)]**Early on**, he

《撐傘的女人》Woman with a Parasol - Madame Monet and Her Son
© National Gallery of Art

莫內早期畫作中常見妻子卡蜜兒的身影
《卡蜜兒公園小憩》繪於 1873 年，紐約大都會博物館收藏

《日落稻草堆》Graystaks
© Museum of Fine Arts, Boston

began digging a pond for water lilies and ⁹⁾**expanding** the gardens. Although he employed a team of gardeners, Monet was their chief designer, and the designed landscape at Giverny inspired many of his later works.

25 The water lilies there became his most famous subject, appearing in approximately 250 works. He was also ¹⁰⁾**fond of** the ¹¹⁾**arched** Japanese bridge ¹²⁾**spanning** the pond, and captured it in different lights and seasons as well.

Mini Quiz 閱讀測驗

❶ ____ What does "travel bug" mean?
(A) A disease caught while traveling
(B) A type of flying insect
(C) A fear of traveling
(D) A strong interest in traveling

❷ ____ What did Monet and his wife do right after they got married?
(A) They left France.
(B) They fought in a war.
(C) They settled in Argenteuil.
(D) They escaped to France.

中 Translation

莫內在一八六○年代常四處旅行，對旅行的熱愛也跟了他一輩子。旅途中，他一路研究光映照在各種地貌上的不同效果，發展出後來被稱為「印象派」的風格。他早期許多作品都見到卡蜜兒唐斯約的身影，兩人在一八七○年結為連理，但幾乎一完婚就因普法戰爭爆發而不得不逃離法國。一八七一年回國後，夫婦倆在巴黎附近的阿讓特伊村落腳。本身也是技術嫺熟水手的莫內，喜歡在那裡觀賞點點帆船漂過塞納河，一如他一八七五年所繪的《阿讓特伊的紅船》和《日落的海景》。

一八八三年，莫內搬到巴黎西北方四十哩的小村莊吉維尼。他租了一棟房子，位在占地兩英畝的土地上，還有一座小花園、果園以及他拿來當畫室用的穀倉。他在一八九○年拿賣畫所得把這座莊園買下來，在那裡度過餘生。剛遷入之初，他就開始挖掘池塘種植睡蓮，並擴建花園。雖然聘了一群園丁，莫內卻是花園的首席設計師，而在吉維尼設計出的造景也成為他後期許多作品的靈感來源。那兒的睡蓮成為他最知名的主題，出現在近二百五十幅畫作中。他也喜歡橫跨池塘的日式拱橋，並捕捉了不同光線和季節之下的拱橋景色。

.Know itALL 英文閱讀

V Vocabulary Bank

1) **prime** [praɪm] (a.) 主要的，最佳的
The woman's husband is the prime suspect in her murder.

2) **cathedral** [kə`θidrəl] (n.) 大教堂
Notre Dame is France's tallest cathedral.

3) **parliament** [`pɑrləmənt] (n.)（英國）國會
Parliament is debating a new immigration law.

4) **proceed** [prə`sid] (v.) 開始進行，繼續進行
Mary sat down and proceeded to tell me about her weekend.

5) **perspective** [pə`spɛktɪv] (n.) 角度，觀點
The mountain looks taller from this perspective.

6) **emphasis** [`ɛmfəsɪs] (n.) 強調，重點
The English teacher puts a lot of emphasis on pronunciation.

7) **abstract** [`æbstrækt] (a.) 抽象（派）的
In my opinion, Picasso's abstract paintings are terrific.

8) **despite** [dɪ`spaɪt] (prep.) 儘管
We enjoyed our vacation despite the bad weather.

9) **enthusiast** [ɪn`θuzɪˌəst] (n.) 熱中者
Car enthusiasts from all over the world attended the car show.

10) **collector** [kə`lɛktə] (n.) 收藏家
My uncle is an antique collector.

11) **auction** [`ɔkʃən] (n./v.) 拍賣
We bought our car at a police auction.

進階字彙

12) **cataract** [`kætəˌrækt] (n.)（醫）白內障
The vet removed our cat's cataracts.

13) **reddish** [`rɛdəʃ] (a.) 帶紅色的
The sand on the beach is a reddish-brown.

《日本橋下的睡蓮》© Metropolitan Museum of Art

課文朗讀 MP3 7　單字朗讀 MP3 8　英文文章導讀 MP3 9

The Water Lilies at Giverny are a ⁱ⁾**prime** example of Monet's famous "series" paintings, which he painted from the 1880s into his old age. In series paintings, Monet started with a subject, like a haystack in the French countryside, the ²⁾**cathedral** at Rouen, or the ³⁾**Parliament** building in London. He then ⁴⁾**proceeded** to paint it from the same ⁵⁾**perspective** at different times of day, ⒢whatever the weather. The different natural light created a variety of colors and shades, which he tried to capture. In fact, the light cast upon Monet's subject became just ⒢as important to the painting as the subject itself. The short brushstrokes he and his fellow Impressionists used, and their ⁶⁾**emphasis** on mood over subject, helped ❶ **pave the way for** ⁷⁾**abstract** art.

⁸⁾**Despite** suffering from health problems and double ¹²⁾**cataracts**, which gave his later paintings a ¹³⁾**reddish** tone, Monet continued to paint tirelessly until his death in 1926.

《睡蓮》Water Lilies
© Museum of Fine Arts, Boston

..

Today, Monet's paintings are prized by art [9]**enthusiasts**
20 and [10]**collectors** alike. Notably, a painting from his Water Lilies series was sold at [11]**auction** for US$71.8 million in 2008, a record for
25 a Monet.

莫內和他的花園
Étienne Clémentel 攝於 1917 年

© commons.wikimedia.org

Mini Quiz 閱讀測驗

❶ _____ **In Monet's series paintings, each painting** _____.
(A) has a different subject
(B) is painted from a different angle
(C) is painted from the same angle
(D) contains a building

30

❷ _____ **Why did Monet's later paintings have a reddish tone?**
(A) Because of his mental illness
(B) Because of an eye disease
(C) Due to weather conditions
(D) Because he was fond of red

中 Translation

《國會大廈的日落》
The Houses of Parliament, Sunset cliff1066™/ficker.com

吉維尼的睡蓮是莫內著名「系列」畫作的最佳代表，他從一八八〇年代開始畫系列畫，直到年邁。在系列畫中，莫內先從一個主題著手，例如法國鄉村的一疊乾草堆、盧倫的教堂，或倫敦的國會大廈，接下來他會在一天的不同時刻（不論天氣為何），從同樣的角度作畫。不同的自然光會創造出種種顏色和色調，他試著一一捕捉。事實上，在莫內畫作上，投射到主題上的光，和主題本身一樣重要。他和其他印象派畫家所用的短筆法，以及他們強調氣氛勝於主題，皆替抽象藝術奠定了基礎。

雖然飽受健康問題和雙重白內障折磨（後者使他晚期的畫作呈現偏紅的色調），莫內仍持續不孜不倦地作畫，直到一九二六年與世長辭。如今，莫內的畫作備受藝術愛好者和收藏家喜愛。值得一提的是，二〇〇八年，他的睡蓮系列畫其中的一幅，在拍賣會上以七千一百八十萬美元的天價賣出，刷新莫內名作的紀錄。

Vocabulary Bank

1) **charity** [ˈtʃærətɪ] (n.) 慈善，慈善事業
   John donates 15% of his annual salary to charity.

2) **celebrity** [səˈlɛbrɪtɪ] (n.) 名人，名氣
   Have you heard the latest gossip about that celebrity?

3) **establish** [ɪˈstæblɪʃ] (v.) 創辦，建立
   Our university was established in 1926.

4) **eliminate** [ɪˈlɪməˌnet] (v.) 消除，消滅
   The drug gang is trying to eliminate its rivals.

5) **convince** [kənˈvɪns] (v.) 說服，使人信服
   The kids convinced their parents to let them have pizza for dinner.

6) **ultimate** [ˈʌltəmɪt] (a.) 極致的，終極的
   Hawaii is the ultimate vacation destination.

7) **foundation** [faʊnˈdeʃən] (n.) 基金會，
   The billionaire established a foundation to support cancer research.

8) **dedicated** [ˈdɛdɪˌketɪd] (a.) 專注的，投入的
   John is a dedicated and diligent student.

9) **affordable** [əˈfɔrdəbl] (a.) 負擔得起的
   The store sells fashionable clothes at affordable prices.

10) **refugee** [ˌrɛfjʊˈdʒi] (n.) 難民
    Thousands of refugees fled across the border.

11) **orphanage** [ˈɔrfənɪdʒ] (n.) 孤兒院
    We donated clothes and toys to the local orphanage.

Language Guide

Give Till It Hurts 付出直到成傷

德蕾莎修女 (Mother Teresa) 是著名的天主教慈善家，致力於服務印度加爾各答的貧民，在西元一九七九年得到諾貝爾和平獎。她曾經在演說中強調 "give until it hurts"，並以耶穌最終死於十字架上為例，說明祂放棄了一切甚至犧牲自己的性命以拯救人類的罪，所以如果人類不互相幫助，罪惡仍無法消除。德雷莎修女也曾說過 "love until it hurts"——"I have found the paradox, that if you love until it hurts, there can be no more hurt, only more love." (愛至成傷時，就不會再有傷害，只有更多的愛。)

U2 主唱 Bono

Brad Pitt 及 Angelina Jolie 夫婦

Give Till It Hurts

捨己成傷在所不惜

課文朗讀 MP3 10　單字朗讀 MP3 11　英文文章導讀 MP3 12

When it comes to [1]**charity** work, for many people the first thing that comes to mind is [2]**celebrity** do-gooders. Bono, the rock star so famous he doesn't need a last name, is probably the best known. In addition to performing with

5　U2 at countless charity concerts, he also [3]**established** the DATA organization, which aims to [4]**eliminate** poverty and HIV/AIDS in Africa, and ⓖeven [5]**convinced** the leaders of the world's richest countries to forgive $40 billion in debt owed by the poorest. And then there's Brangelina—

10　the [6]**ultimate** power couple. Brad was so moved when he visited New Orleans after Hurricane Katrina that he decided to move there. But ⓖinstead of just buying a house, he established the Make It Right [7]**foundation**, which is [8]**dedicated** to rebuilding the city and creating

15　[9]**affordable** housing for low-income residents.

　　And Angelina 🔳 **is no slouch** either. She's visited [10]**refugee** camps in 20 countries in her role as Goodwill Ambassador for the United Nations High Commission for Refugees, and is actively involved with charities like

20　UNICEF, Doctors Without Borders and the Afghanistan

卡崔娜風災肆虐後的
紐奧良市區

©AP Photo U.S. Coast Guard, Petty Officer 2nd Class Kyle

Relief Organization. The couple has also taken their charity work to a more personal level—

25 in addition to their own children, they've adopted kids from Cambodia, Vietnam and Ethiopia. Madonna decided to

2 follow in their footsteps, but things didn't go so

30 smoothly for her. When she adopted a baby from Malawi, the media accused her of taking the boy away from his father—even though he was living in an [11]**orphanage**— and stressed that the money she'd spend raising him would be enough to feed a whole village in Africa.

Mini Quiz 閱讀測驗

① **According to the article, what do the celebrities all have in common?**
(A) They are all concerned with earning more money.
(B) They are all known by only their first names.
(C) They all give their time and money to help people.
(D) They all know what it is like to be poor and hungry.

② **Why was Madonna criticized after she adopted a baby from Malawi?**
(A) She only adopted one child instead of more.
(B) She didn't spend enough money raising him.
(C) She didn't visit the place where the baby lived.
(D) She took the boy away from his father.

Translation

說到慈善工作，許多人第一個會想到的就是做善事的名人。波諾——出名到不需要姓的搖滾明星——大概是其中最負盛名者。除了和 U2 樂團在無數慈善演唱會上演出，他還成立了以消滅非洲貧窮及愛滋為宗旨的 DATA 組織，甚至說服世界最富裕國家的領導人豁免最貧窮國家積欠的四百億美元債務。再來還有「布裘」——影響力無遠弗屆的情侶。布萊德曾於卡崔娜颶風過後造訪紐奧良，深受當地災情震撼而決定移居該地。但他不是只買一間房子，而是成立「把事做對」基金會，致力於重建當地、為低收入居民興建買得起的住宅。

安潔莉娜也不遑多讓。她為聯合國難民事務高級專員公署擔任親善大使期間，拜訪過二十個國家的難民營，目前也積極參與聯合國兒童基金會、無國界醫師及阿富汗救援組織等慈善團體的活動。這對情侶也將慈善工作跨到私人領域——除了自己親生的子女，他們還領養柬埔寨、越南和衣索匹亞等國的孩童。瑪丹娜決定追隨他們的腳步，但她的際遇就沒那麼順遂了。她領養一名馬拉威孩童時，媒體指控她強行把男童從父親身邊帶走——儘管他住在孤兒院——並強調她養育他所花的金錢，足以供養一整個非洲村落。

Tongue-tied No More

1 be no slouch 不遑多讓
slouch [slautʃ] 是指頭低低、肩膀下垂、無精打采的行走或坐著的姿勢，可當動詞和名詞使用。be no slouch 是口語上用來表達某人對某件事情非常在行，就算不是最出色的，也算箇中好手，意思類似「不是省油的燈」、「不遑多讓」。
A: Wow! Kathy's front yard looks great!
哇！凱西的前院看來真棒！
B: Yeah. She's no slouch when it comes to gardening.
對啊，說到園藝她可是箇中好手。

2 follow in someone's footsteps 步某人後塵，效法某人
footstep 顧名思義即為「腳步，步伐」，而 follow in someone's footsteps 就是追隨某人的腳步、步上某人的後塵。
A: You're going to art school? I thought your dad wanted you to study medicine.
你要去讀美術？你老爸不是要你去念醫科。
B: Yeah, but I don't want to follow in his footsteps.
是沒錯，但我不想要跟他走一樣的路。

Grammar Master

even 的用法
even 常用來形容意料之外的事情，做「甚至」、「連……」解釋。
例 **Even** my mother came to the party.
連我媽媽都來參加這場派對。

如果要用來連接兩個子句，則須使用 even if、even though 或 even when。
例 I wouldn't marry him **even if** he were a millionaire.
就算他是百萬富翁我也不會嫁給他。

instead of 沒有……反而
instead of 是用在表示後者應被前者替代，或是應該做的事是後者而不是前者。
句型 Instead of ..., S + V....
注意 instead of 後面要接名詞或動名詞片語。
如果要單獨使用副詞 instead 的話，則須改成：
句型 ...not ... Instead, S + V.
例 We **didn't** vacation in Europe this summer. **Instead**, we went on a road trip.
我們今年夏天沒有去歐洲度假，而是進行了一趟公路之旅。

翻譯練習
1. 潘 (Pam) 晚上待在咖啡館裡，沒有去看電影。

_____

2. 就算電視關上還是會耗電。

_____

閱讀測驗解答：**①** (C) **②** (D)
2. TVs use electricity even when they're turned off.
at a café.
1. Instead of going to a movie, Pam spent the evening
翻譯練習解答

Know it ALL 英文閱讀

V Vocabulary Bank

1) **immerse** [ɪˋmɜs] (v.) 沉浸於
The best way to learn a language is to immerse yourself in it.

2) **developing** [dɪˋvɛləpɪŋ] (a.) 開發中的
There are a lot of investment opportunities in the developing world.

3) **unrest** [ʌnˋrɛst] (n.) 不安，動盪
There are rumors of unrest in the border region.

4) **corps** [kɔr] (n.)（經專門訓練或有特種使命的）隊、組、團；兵團，部隊
The journalist is a member of the White House press corps.

5) **volunteer** [ˌvɑlənˋtɪr] (n./v.) 志工；當志工
Jack works as a volunteer at the local hospital.

6) **chairman** [ˋtʃɛrmən] (n.)主席，主任，董事長
The chairman called a meeting of the committee.

7) **disaster** [dɪˋzæstə] (n.) 災難，災害
Taiwan is frequently hit by natural disasters.

進階字彙

8) **idealistic** [aɪˌdiəˋlɪstɪk] (a.) 滿懷理想的，理想主義的
People tend to be more idealistic when they are younger.

9) **workforce** [ˋwɜkˌfors] (n.) 勞動力
More and more young people are joining the workforce each year.

Of course, it's easy for ᴳthe rich and famous to do charity work. But what about ordinary young people who want to make a difference? For 8)**idealistic** young Americans, the Peace Corps has long been the best way

5　to 1)**immerse** themselves in a new culture, learn a foreign language, and put their skills to work helping people in 2)**developing** countries. ᴳConcerned with growing 3)**unrest** and poverty in the Third World, President Kennedy founded the Peace Corps in 1961 to provide

10　development assistance and promote world peace and friendship. ᴳSince that time, over 200,000 Americans have joined the Peace 4)**Corps**, serving in 139 countries around the

15　world.Famous Peace Corps 5)**volunteers** include author Paul Theroux, Senator Chris Dodd and former AIT 6)**chairman** Raymond Burghardt.

Unfortunately, the Peace Corps is only open to Americans with college degrees. But not to worry—

20　there are plenty of charities and other NGOs that provide volunteering opportunities. One of the oldest and largest is the Red Cross, which started in Geneva in the 1800s as a movement to provide relief to war victims. The mission of the Red Cross gradually expanded to include

25　emergency and 7)**disaster** relief, and there are now Red

© wiki_Julius kusuma_Croixrouge

位於瑞士日內瓦的紅十字會總部
（CICR 為法文名稱縮寫）

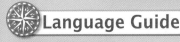

一九六一年，
美國甘迺迪與和平工作團

Cross societies in nearly every country in the world. Volunteers make up over 90% of the American Red
30 Cross [9)]**workforce**, so there are plenty of opportunities to get involved in relief work, blood drives and first aid training. And for those who don't have time to volunteer, the easiest way to contribute is
35 to give blood—over half of America's blood supply is collected by the Red Cross!

© c_Abbie_Rowe_Kennedy_greeting

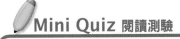

Mini Quiz 閱讀測驗

① **What kind of people are attracted to serve in the Peace Corps?**
(A) People who want to be rich and famous someday.
(B) Recent graduates who want to change people's lives.
(C) Fans of the late President John F. Kennedy.
(D) People who are fluent in foreign languages.

② **According to the passage, which of the following statements is true?**
(A) Over 200,000 Americans have served in the Peace Corps in the U.S.
(B) The Red Cross started out providing help to victims of natural disasters.
(C) Blood drives are a big part of volunteering with the Peace Corps.
(D) It is easier to volunteer with the Red Cross than it is with the Peace Corps.

中 Translation

當然，富商名流做慈善工作是輕而易舉之事，但想改變現狀的平凡年輕人呢？對於滿懷理想的美國青年來說，和平工作團長期以來一直是浸淫新文化、學習外國語言和發揮所長幫助開發中國家人民的最佳方式。有感於第三世界日益嚴重的動亂與貧窮，甘迺迪總統在一九六一年成立和平工作團，協助開發、促進世界和平及友好。自此之後，已有超過二十萬名美國人參加過和平工作團，在全球各地一百三十九個國家服務。和平工作團有名的志工包括作家保羅索魯斯、參議員克里斯達德及前美國在台協會主席薄瑞光。

可惜，和平工作團僅開放給有大學學歷的美國人參加，但別擔心──還有很多慈善機構以及其他非政府組織提供志願服務的機會。紅十字會便是其中歷史最久、規模最大的組織之一，它在十九世紀成立於日內瓦，當時是為戰爭受難者提供救助的一項運動。後來紅十字會的使命逐漸擴大到涵蓋緊急救援及災害救助，目前全球幾乎每個國家都有紅十字會的社團。美國紅十字會的成員有九成以上是志工，因此有很多機會可以參與救助工作、捐血及急救訓練。而對那些沒時間擔任志工的人來說，最簡單的奉獻方式就是捐血──美國有超過一半的血液供給是紅十字會收集的！

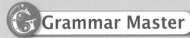

Language Guide

NGO 非政府組織
是 non-governmental organization 的縮寫。這些不屬於政府或國家的非營利組織，一般致力於推廣某些政治理念或社會目標。常見的有人權團體、環境或動物保護組織，以及社會福利團體。

紅十字會 (ICRC，International Committee of the Red Cross) 是早期發展的 NGO 之一，於西元一八六三年創立於日內瓦。一名瑞士商人亨利杜南有感於戰場上的傷亡人員無法受到妥善照顧，因此積極建立在戰時可以幫忙照顧傷兵的志願組織。隨著越來越多國家參與，紅十字會在國際上廣受尊重且蓬勃發展，且三次獲得諾貝爾和平獎。而中華民國紅十字會則是於西元一九○四年草創，一路經歷日俄戰爭到隨著政府遷台，先後執行各種醫療服務與急難救助，足跡遍及九二一大地震、四川地震、八八水災及海地地震等。

Grammar Master

形容詞前加 the 形成的名詞
rich 是「富有的」，famous 是「有名聲的」，在這兩個形容詞前面加上 the 就是指「具有 rich and famous 這兩種特性的人」也就是富商名流。其他常見的用法還有 the old/young 、blind/deaf、living/dead 等。

concern 的常見句型
● be concerned with/about + something 非常關注或擔心某事
● be concerned for + someone 非常關心某人
例 Jimmy's parents **are concerned about/with** his grades.
吉米的父母很擔心他的成績。
● concern 也可當名詞使用，當「關懷，關心」解釋，常與 show 和 feel 連用。
例 My relationship with my wife is none of your **concern**.
我與我太太之間的關係不關你的事。
例 Business owners should **show concern** for their employees.
企業主應關懷他們的員工。
● concern 當動詞也可表示「涉及，與……相關」解釋：
例 The problem of global warming **concerns** us all.
地球暖化的問題與我們都有關係。

since 自從……起
since 的常用句型是 since + 時間點，後面再加上現在完成式 (have + p.p.) 或現在完成進行式 (have + been Ving)
例 Michael has lived in Taiwan **since 2002**.
麥可從2002年起就住在台灣了。
例 Pam has been studying French **since last October**.
潘從去年十月開始學法文。

課文 朗讀 MP3 16　單字 朗讀 MP3 17　英文 文章導讀 MP3 18

Vocabulary Bank

1) **habitat** [ˈhæbɪˌtæt] (n.) 棲息地
   The panda's natural habitat is in the mountains of Sichuan, China.

2) **humanity** [hjuˈmænətɪ] (n.) 人類、人道
   What are the biggest issues facing humanity today?

3) **shelter** [ˈʃɛltə] (n.) 避難所，遮蔽處
   Margaret volunteers at a shelter for abused women.

4) **version** [ˈvɜʒən] (n.) 版本
   Which version of Windows do you have on your computer?

5) **prosperity** [prɑˈspɛrətɪ] (n.) 繁榮
   The railroad brought prosperity to the town.

6) **relevant** [ˈrɛləvənt] (a.) 相關的
   Your comment isn't relevant to the discussion.

7) **sponsor** [ˈspɑnsə] (v.) 贊助，資助
   This baseball team is sponsored by a local bank.

進階字彙

8) **carpentry** [ˈkɑrpəntrɪ] (n.) 木工，木匠業
   Fred learned basic carpentry skills in high school.

9) **impoverished** [ɪmˈpɑvərɪʃt] (a.) 窮困的
   Haiti became even more impoverished after the earthquake.

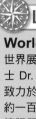

Language Guide

World Vision 世界展望會

世界展望會是由一位曾在中國傳教的美國傳教士 Dr. Bob Pierce 於一九五〇年成立，致力於兒童福利工作，據點分佈全球約一百個國家，是全球最大的兒童關懷照顧機構之一。台灣世界展望會成立於一九六四年，除了致力於推動認養、資助國內外貧童，也發起「飢餓三十」30 Hour Famine 活動，解救遭受急難的飢餓災民。

For people who enjoy working with their hands, [1]**Habitat** for [2]**Humanity** may be the perfect volunteering choice. Established in Georgia in 1976 to build affordable housing for the underprivileged, the organization now

5　sends volunteer teams all over the world. Best of all, you don't need any [8]**carpentry** skills to get involved—you just need to be in good shape and willing to work hard. To date, Habitat for Humanity has built over 300,000 houses in more than 100 countries. Of course, people

10　aren't the only ones who need help, and there are lots of opportunities for animal lovers to volunteer at their local SPCA or animal [3]**shelter**. It's not only a great way to help out our four-legged friends, but also to make two-legged ones as well.

15　For young Taiwanese who want to make a difference, Taiwan has its own [4]**version** of the Peace Corps: the ICDF's Taiwan Overseas Volunteers Program. In operation since 1993, this program was designed to promote progress and [5]**prosperity** around the world and

20　ⓒprovide development assistance to friendly developing

重返孟加拉
哈林庚澄慶見證資助
兒童計畫全人關懷
台灣世界展望會提供

志工正在為即將完工的房屋粉刷

nations. As of the end of 2009, 451 volunteers have served in 30 nations in Africa, Latin America and the Asia-Pacific region.

25 ⑤ To participate, you need to be 20 or older, have a college degree or five years of ⁶⁾**relevant** work experience, and ability in English or other foreign languages. And if you want to help but don't have the time to volunteer, why not do like pop singer Harlem Yu and ⁷⁾**sponsor** a child through World Vision

30 Taiwan. For only NT$700 a month, you can provide food, healthcare and education to an ⁹⁾**impoverished** child in a developing country. So what are you waiting for?

Mini Quiz 閱讀測驗

❶ ___ **What is the main goal of Habitat for Humanity?**
(A) To feed hungry people around the world
(B) To build homes for poor people
(C) To make sure animals are protected
(D) To teach children how to read and write

❷ ___ **What is NOT true about the ICDF's Taiwan Overseas Volunteers Program?**
(A) It has been in operation for over a decade.
(B) It was inspired by the US Peace Corps program.
(C) You must have a college degree in order to join.
(D) Volunteers serve in Africa, Latin America or Asia.

中 Translation

對喜歡親自動手的人來說，仁人家園或許是志工服務的最佳選擇。仁人家園在一九七六年成立於美國喬治亞州，旨在為貧困者興建買得起的住家，現在該組織把志工團隊送往世界各地。最棒的是，你不必具備木工技術就能參與──只要身體健康、願意努力工作就可以。到目前為止，仁人家園已在百餘國建造超過三十萬間房屋。當然，不是只有人類需要幫助，愛護動物者在自己當地的愛護動物協會或動物收容所也有許多服務機會，不僅是協助四腳朋友的絕好方法，也能結交兩條腿的朋友。

對想改變現狀的台灣青年而言，也有台灣版的和平工作團：財團法人國際合作發展基金會海外志工計畫。這項計畫自一九九三年開始運作，旨在促進全球進步繁榮，為友好的開發中國家提供開發協助。截至二○○九年年底，已有四百五十一位志工遠赴非洲、拉丁美洲和亞太地區服務。加入條件為年滿二十歲、大專學歷或五年相關工作經驗、具備英語或其他外語能力。如果你想幫助人但沒有時間擔任志工，何不仿效流行歌手庾澄慶，透過台灣世界展望會資助一個孩子。每月只需七百元，你就能為開發中國家的貧苦孩童提供食物、醫療和教育。你還在等什麼？

閱讀測驗解答：❶ (B) ❷ (C)
翻譯練習解答
The government provides social services for poor families./
The government provides poor families with social services.

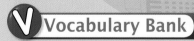

Vocabulary Bank

1) **scraping** [ˋskrepɪŋ] (n.) 刮磨的聲音。動詞為 scrape
   I think I need to get my brakes fixed—they keep making this scraping sound.

2) **awake** [əˋwek] (v.) 喚醒
   (phr.) awake to… 意識到，文中指「因為…而醒來」
   When we lived in the country, we awoke each morning to the sound of roosters.

3) **escort** [ˋɛskɔrt] (v.) 陪同，護送
   After you check in, one of our porters will escort you to your room.

4) **hood** [hʊd] (n.) 汽車引擎蓋
   The mechanic checked under the hood for loose connections.

5) **sway** [swe] (v.) 搖擺
   The crowd at the concert swayed to the music.

6) **version** [ˋvɝʒən] (n.)（一種事物的）變體，（不同）版本
   The new version of the software is much better than the old one.

7) **folklore** [ˋfok‚lor] (n.) 民間傳說，字尾的 lore 是「口頭傳說」的意思，4/30 文中的 Cokelore 一字即為「關於可口可樂的傳說」
   Michael is taking a class on Chinese folklore.

8) **moralize** [ˋmɔrə‚laɪz] (v.) 教化，說教
   I always fall asleep in church when the preacher starts moralizing.

9) **moral** [ˋmɔrəl] (n.) 道德訓示，寓意
   Most fairy tales have a moral.

補充字彙

* **secluded** [sɪˋkludɪd] (a.) 隱蔽的，僻靜的

* **siren** [ˋsaɪrən] (n.) 警報笛聲或鈴聲

* **secondhand** [ˋsɛkənd‚hænd] (a.) 間接的，二手的

* **plausible** [ˋplɔzəbl] (a.) 聽起來有道理的

* **poodle** [ˋpudl] (n.) 貴賓狗

URBAN LEGENDS: FACT OR FANTASY?

越傳越離譜的都市傳奇

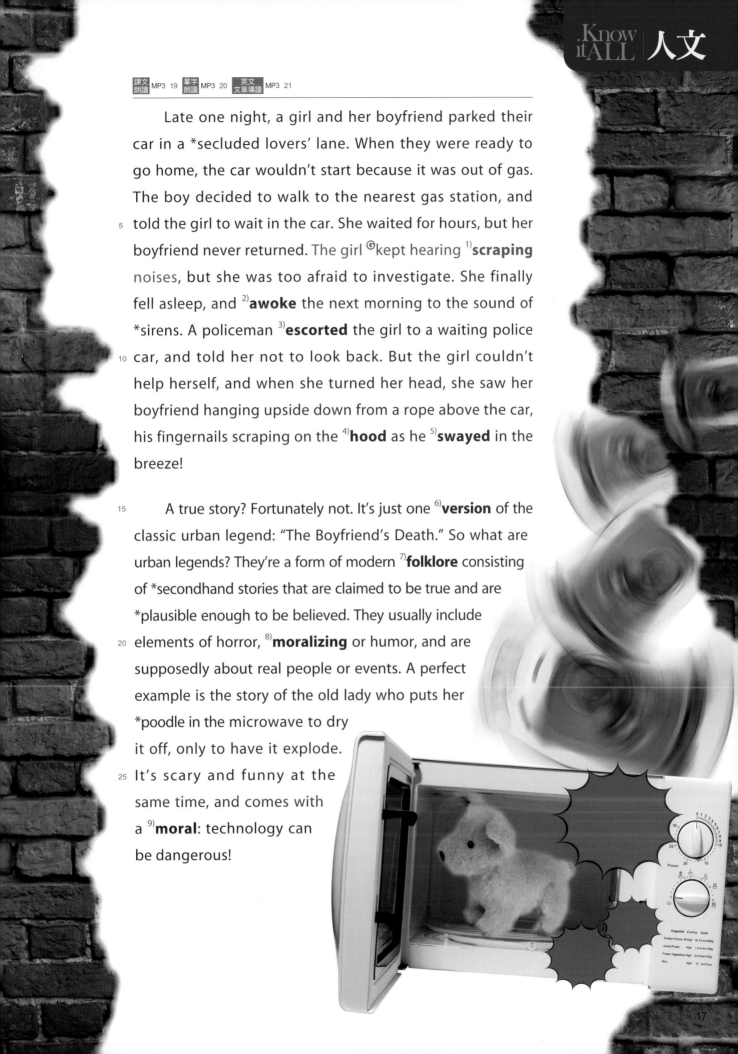

課文朗讀 MP3 19　單字朗讀 MP3 20　英文文章導讀 MP3 21

Late one night, a girl and her boyfriend parked their car in a *secluded lovers' lane. When they were ready to go home, the car wouldn't start because it was out of gas. The boy decided to walk to the nearest gas station, and
5　told the girl to wait in the car. She waited for hours, but her boyfriend never returned. The girl ⒼkepT hearing ¹⁾**scraping** noises, but she was too afraid to investigate. She finally fell asleep, and ²⁾**awoke** the next morning to the sound of *sirens. A policeman ³⁾**escorted** the girl to a waiting police
10　car, and told her not to look back. But the girl couldn't help herself, and when she turned her head, she saw her boyfriend hanging upside down from a rope above the car, his fingernails scraping on the ⁴⁾**hood** as he ⁵⁾**swayed** in the breeze!

15　A true story? Fortunately not. It's just one ⁶⁾**version** of the classic urban legend: "The Boyfriend's Death." So what are urban legends? They're a form of modern ⁷⁾**folklore** consisting of *secondhand stories that are claimed to be true and are *plausible enough to be believed. They usually include
20　elements of horror, ⁸⁾**moralizing** or humor, and are supposedly about real people or events. A perfect example is the story of the old lady who puts her *poodle in the microwave to dry it off, only to have it explode.
25　It's scary and funny at the same time, and comes with a ⁹⁾**moral**: technology can be dangerous!

Know it ALL 英文閱讀

Language Guide

lovers' lane 情侶幽會地點

lane 這個字在這裡並不是「巷弄」或「車道」的意思。lovers' lane 是一個固定的詞，專指情侶喜歡停下車來，並在車上幽會的地點。在美國人心目中，典型的 lovers' lane 包括郊區僻靜的小巷弄、停車場，或是景致優美（尤其是夜景）的隱密地方。

網路曾經盛傳一時的 urban legend

現在網路發達，幾乎所有的 urban legend 都是靠網路上一再轉寄而傳開來。以下就是幾則粉恐怖（或神奇）的 urban legends。

1 A college student got drunk and took drugs at a party, and woke up the next day to find that his kidneys had been stolen.
一個大學生參加派對時飲酒又嗑藥，隔天醒來發現自己的腎臟被偷走了。 *(假的)*

2 There's a man who puts kittens in bottles and sells them on the Internet as "bonsai" kittens.
有人把小貓塞進瓶子裡，上網當「盆栽貓」販售。 *(假的)*

3 A famous multinational fried chicken chain serves meat from genetically modified chickens with four legs and no head.
一家知名跨國連鎖炸雞店的雞肉是基因改造的雞隻，有四條腿，但沒有頭。 *(假的)*

4 The healthy twin embraced her sister, and saved her life as a result.
健康的寶寶伸手抱她的妹妹，因此挽救了妹妹的生命。 *(真的)*

Translation

都市傳奇：事實還是幻想？

某天深夜，一個女孩和她的男友將車停在一個僻靜的幽會地點。他們準備回家的時候，車子因為沒油而發不動，男孩決定步行到最近的加油站，並且要女孩在車裡等他。她等了幾個小時，但男友一直沒有回來。女孩一直聽到刺耳的刮擦聲，但她太害怕，不敢查看。她最後睡著了，第二天早晨被警車的警笛聲吵醒。一位警察護送女孩走到一輛在旁等候的警車，並告訴她不要回頭看。但女孩忍不住，當她轉頭，她看見男友被繩子倒吊在車子上方，他隨著微風搖擺的時候，指甲會刮著車蓋！

這是真實的故事嗎？幸好不是，這只是經典都市傳說「男友之死」的其中一個版本。那麼，什麼是都市傳說？這是一種現代民間傳說，由宣稱真實且看似可信的二手故事所構成。都市傳說通常會包括恐怖、道德教化或是幽默等元素，而且據說是真人真事。一個典型的例子是，有個老太太把貴賓狗放進微波爐烘乾，結果卻讓狗炸了開來。這故事既可怕又好笑，而且帶有一個寓意：科技可能是危險的！

Grammar Master

keep+V-ing

若動詞跟在介係詞之後，須變成動名詞 V-ing 的模式，keep 在這邊是 keep on「持續」的意思，雖然介係詞 on 大多會被省略掉，還是別忘記要用動名詞喔！

在此，順便複習一下其他幾個與動名詞連用的常見動詞：

❶ enjoy	（享受）	
❷ quit	（戒除；停止）	
❸ mind	（介意）	
❹ postpone	（延期）	+ Ving
❺ discuss	（討論）	
❻ avoid	（避免）	
❼ finish	（結束、完成）	
❽ consider	（考慮）	

V Vocabulary Bank

1) **contrary to**〔ˋkɑntrɛrɪ tu〕(phr.) 與…相反
Contrary to expectations, the company managed to survive the recession.

2) **plunge**〔plʌndʒ〕(v.) 跳（入），墜（入）
(phr.) plunge to one's death 墜樓身亡
The diver made a big splash when he plunged into the water.

3) **demonstrate**〔ˋdɛmən͵stret〕(v.) 示範，（用實例）說明
The salesman demonstrated how to use the vacuum cleaner.

4) **soar**〔sor〕(v.) 飛上去，高飛
On our hike, we saw a pair of eagles soaring in the sky.

5) **descend**〔drˋsɛnd〕(v.) 下降，下來
It took the hikers four hours to descend the mountain.

6) **alligator**〔ˋælə͵getə〕(n.)（產於美國及中國的）短吻鱷，gator 為其簡稱
That swamp is infested with alligators.

7) **sewer**〔ˋsuə〕(n.) 污水下水道，陰溝
The sewers here sometimes overflow

8) **vacation**〔veˋkeʃən〕(v.) 度假
We usually vacation in the Caribbean.

補充字彙

* pellet〔ˋpɛlɪt〕(n.) 彈丸。pellet gun即「空氣槍」

* outgrow〔͵autˋgro〕(v.) 長大以致不再適用

* cuteness〔ˋkjutnɪs〕(n.) 嬌小可愛。這個字是cute (a.) 可愛的 + -ness（名詞字尾）

* sighting〔ˋsaɪtɪŋ〕(n.) 目擊

課文朗讀 MP3 22　單字朗讀 MP3 23　英文文章導讀 MP3 24

　　[1)]**Contrary to** popular belief, urban legends aren't necessarily false. For example, the legend about a man falling to his death while testing a skyscraper window is true. In 1993, Gary Hoy, a lawyer at a Toronto law office,

5　[2)]**plunged** 24 stories to his death while [3)]**demonstrating** the safety of the office's windows to a group of visiting law students. The legend about the man who [4)]**soared** into the sky in a chair tied to a bunch of balloons is also true! In 1982, Larry Walters, a Los Angeles truck driver,

10　took flight in a lawn chair with 45 weather balloons tied to it. He rose to a height of 16,000 feet, and later [5)]**descended** by shooting several of the balloons with a *pellet gun.

　　Other urban legends, while not entirely true, are based on real events. It's long been rumored that there

15　are [6)]**alligators** living in the [7)]**sewers** of New York. Supposedly, New Yorkers [G8)]**vacationing** in Florida bring back baby alligators to keep as pets. When the [6)]**gators** *outgrow their *cuteness, however, their owners flush them down the toilet. Some of these creatures survive

20　and breed, creating colonies of alligators that live in the

Know it ALL 英文閱讀

Language Guide

各式各樣的「故事」與「傳說」

story 是各種「故事」的統稱,而「傳奇」 **legend** 經常是與歷史名人有關的故事,一般是真有其事的「歷史」history,但以訛傳訛,越講越離譜,到最後名人變偉人,偉人變成神。 **epic** 是「(希臘、羅馬)史詩」,歌頌人物的豐功偉蹟。**myth** 則是追溯遠古的「神話」,內容是在講述開天闢地、人類起源。

tale 指「捏造出來的謠言或故事」,**folk tale** 就是所謂「民間故事」,像本地的「二十四孝」、「梁山伯與祝英台」。專門寫給小孩看的「幻想故事,童話」則是 **fairy tale**,像是《安徒生童話》*Hans Anderson's Fairy Tales*。**fable** 是有道德訓示的「寓言」,好比家喻戶曉的《伊索寓言》*Aesop's Fables*。

Grammar Master

形容詞片語的用法

❶ New Yorkers vacationing in Florida…

N. ↵　↰形容詞片語

❷ New Yorkers who are vacationing in Florida…

N. ↵　↰形容詞子句

❶ 和 ❷ 同義,形容詞片語是由形容詞子句省簡化而來的,只有含有 who, which 或 that 的形容詞子句才可簡化為修飾前面名詞的形容詞片語喔!

sewers. Indeed, there is a documented case of an alligator being found in a New York sewer, and many *sightings have been reported over the years. According to experts, however, it would be impossible for alligators to actually
25 live and breed in the city's sewers because they need warmth and sunlight year-round to survive.

中 Translation

不同於普遍的看法,都市傳說未必是假的。例如,有個傳說是一個男人在測試摩天大樓窗戶時墜樓身亡,就是真的。一九九三年,多倫多律師事務所的律師加里霍伊,在對一群來訪的法律系學生展示辦公室窗戶安全性的時候,落下二十四層樓而死。有個傳說是一個男人坐在綁著一堆氣球的椅子上,上升到天空,也是真實的!一九八二年,洛杉磯卡車司機萊瑞華,坐在綁著四十五個氣象探測氣球的庭園折疊椅上飛行,他上升到高度一萬六千英尺,然後用空氣槍射破幾個氣球下降。

還有些都市傳說雖然不完全是真的,但卻是根據真實事件。長期以來一直有傳言說,紐約下水道有鱷魚住在裡面。據說,去佛羅里達州度假的紐約人將幼鱷帶回,當作寵物,鱷魚長大、不再可愛之後,主人就將它們沖入馬桶。其中幾隻存活了下來並且繁殖,創造出生活在下水道的鱷魚群。事實上,確實有一宗實據證明的案例記錄一隻鱷魚在紐約下水道被發現,而且多年下來也有許多目擊事件。不過,根據專家的說法,鱷魚不可能真的在該城市下水道生存和繁殖,因為它們全年需要溫暖和日照才能生存。

課文朗讀 MP3 25　單字朗讀 MP3 26　英文文章導讀 MP3 27

Considering the consumer culture we live in, it's not surprising that popular products are the subject of many urban legends. And as the most popular product of all, Coca-Cola is the subject of so many legends that

5　a special term has been [1]**coined**: "Cokelore." While the story that Coke used to contain *cocaine is actually true (the "Coca" in Coca-Cola [2]**refers to** *coca leaves, from which cocaine is made), most legends about the [3]**fizzy** drink are simply [4]**tall tales**. One of the most common

10　is that a combination of Coke and Pop Rocks (a brand of *carbonated candy that pops in your mouth) can cause your stomach to explode. Although this has never happened in real life, the rumors became so *rampant that General Mills, the manufacturer of Pop Rocks, spent

15　millions of dollars on an ad campaign to [5]**dispel** them.

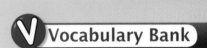

Vocabulary Bank

1) **coin** [kɔɪn] (v.) 造新字
Many new slang words are coined by teenagers.

2) **refer to** [rɪˋfɝ tu] (phr.) 指的是
When you talked about employees coming in late, who were you referring to?

3) **fizzy** [ˋfɪzɪ] (a.)（口）有氣泡的，發出嘶嘶聲的
Some people think fizzy drinks are good for an upset stomach.

4) **tall tale** [tɔl tel] (phr.) 鬼扯的故事，胡說八道
The old man liked to entertain his grandchildren with tall tales.

5) **dispel** [dɪˋspɛl] (v.) 消除，驅散
Many myths have been dispelled by science.

6) **filler** [ˋfɪlɚ] (n.) 填料
Oatmeal is often used as a filler for meatloaf.

7) **patty** [ˋpætɪ] (n.)（美）肉餅，hamburger patty 即「漢堡肉」
I like to season hamburger patties with salt, pepper and garlic.

8) **fluffy** [ˋflʌfɪ] (a.) 蓬鬆的，絨毛狀的
Brenda likes to sleep on fluffy pillows.

9) **paranoid** [ˋpærənɔɪd] (a.) 偏執狂的，神經兮兮的
Everybody is paranoid about losing their jobs these days.

補充字彙

* cocaine [koˋken] (n.) 古柯鹼，coca leaf 即「古柯葉」

* carbonated [ˋkɑrbə͵netɪd] (a.) 含有二氧化碳的，carbonated candy 即為「跳跳糖」

* rampant [ˋræmpənt] (a.) 蔓延的，猖獗的

* Styrofoam [ˋstaɪrə͵fom] (n.) 泡沫塑料，聚苯乙烯即「保麗龍」

Tongue-tied No More

1 pound for pound 以等重來說

pound 是指重量單位「磅」。pound for pound 字面上是「一磅對上一磅」，也就是「用相同的重量做為比較基準」的意思。

A: Wow, I never realized saffron was so expensive!
哇，我都不知道番紅花這麼貴！

B: Yeah. Pound for pound, it's more valuable than gold.
是啊。以同等重量來看，它比黃金還珍貴。

Grammar Master

Neither of these stories is true either
這個句子是對的嗎？

這是一個正確的句子。因為 neither 和 either 都有兩個不同用法：

neither：「兩者皆非」或「沒有任何一個」

either：「兩者其一是」或「也」（與否定句連用，不同於 also）

今天第一段提到可口可樂的不實謠言，第二段又提到兩個關於麥當勞的謠言，neither of 為否定兩個與麥當勞相關謠言的真實性，而 either 只是單純當作「也不是」來解釋，表示「可口可樂的謠言是假的，麥當的謠言也不是真的。」

Mini Quiz 閱讀測驗

1 Which of the following is true about urban legends?
(A) They are never true.
(B) They sound like they could be true.
(C) They are a form of traditional folklore.
(D) They are all about real people.

2 Why is the legend about alligators in the New York sewers not entirely false?
(A) Because some alligators survive and breed in the sewers
(B) Because alligators need warmth and sunlight to survive
(C) Because New Yorkers bring back alligators to keep as pets
(D) Because there is a proven case of an alligator found in a New York sewer

閱讀測驗解答：**1** (B) **2** (D)

As the world's largest restaurant chain, McDonalds is also the target of a number of urban legends. Fortunately, the stories about McDonalds using worms or cow eyeballs as [6]**filler** in their
20 hamburger [7]**patties** are false. These stories don't even make sense, because **1 pound for pound**, worms and cow eyeballs are actually more expensive
25 than beef! There have also been rumors that McDonalds calls their milkshakes "shakes" because they don't actually contain milk
30 (using *Styrofoam instead), and that McFlurries are so [8]**fluffy** because they're made with feathers. [G]Neither of these stories is true either, so
35 there's no need to get [9]**paranoid** next time you order a Happy Meal. Right?

中 Translation

想到我們周遭的消費文化，流行商品成為許多都市傳說的主題就不足以為奇了。身為最流行的產品，可口可樂自然會成為眾多傳說的主題，因而有了「可樂傳說」這個特別名詞。雖然可樂曾經含有古柯鹼的故事實際上是真的（可口可樂的「可口」是指古柯葉，是提煉古柯鹼的原料），然而有關這個碳酸飲料的傳說大多只是子虛烏有。最常見的傳說之一是，可口可樂和跳跳糖一起吃（跳跳糖是一種二氧化碳糖果的品牌，會在嘴巴裡劈歷叭啦跳動）會導致胃爆炸。雖然這種事從未在現實生活中發生，但謠言十分猖獗，生產跳跳糖的通用磨坊公司因而花了數百萬美元登廣告闢謠。

身為世界上最大的餐廳連鎖店，麥當勞也是不少都市傳說的目標。幸好，麥當勞用蟲或牛眼球當做漢堡填料的故事是假的。這些故事甚至說不通，因為以同樣的重量計算，蠕蟲和牛眼球其實比牛肉更貴！也有傳聞說，麥當勞將奶昔稱為「昔克」，是因為實際上不含牛奶（改用「保麗龍」），還說冰炫風那麼蓬鬆，是因為是用羽毛製成的。這兩個故事也沒有一個是真實的，所以下次點快樂兒童餐的時候不需要疑神疑鬼，是吧？

V Vocabulary Bank

1) **uncertain** [ʌnˋsɝtn] (a.) 不穩定的，不確定的
America's auto industry faces an uncertain future.

2) **unconventional** [ˌʌnkənˋvɛnʃənl] (a.) 不依慣例的；不合常規的
Drew Barrymore had a very unconventional upbringing.

3) **click** [klɪk] (v.) 發出卡嚓聲，此指按滑鼠的動作
You can now pay your bills with the click of a button.

4) **clue** [klu] (n.) 線索
The police had no clues about the identity of the killer.

5) **exposure** [ɪkˋspoʒɚ] (n.) 曝露，接觸
The exposure of children to pornography is a serious problem.

6) **tournament** [ˋtɝnəmənt] (n.) 比賽，錦標賽
Did you watch the tennis tournament on TV last night?

7) **series** [ˋsiriz] (n.) 連賽，系列賽
The two teams played a four-game series.

Tongue-tied No More

1 get/be bitten by the…bug 對……上癮

形容對某物或某事愛不釋手，就像中毒或上癮一樣。
A: I'm thinking of setting up my own darkroom.
我在考慮弄個自己的暗房。
B: Wow, you've really been bitten by the photography bug!
哇，你對攝影真是上癮！

2 beginner's luck 初學者的好運

初次接觸某遊戲或運動就可以玩得很不錯的人，我們就會形容他有很好的 beginner's luck，但也可能在暗示你小時了了，大未必佳喔！
A: I can't believe you beat me at chess!
我不敢相信你居然下棋贏我！
B: It's just beginner's luck.
只是初學者的好運而已。

3 big score 大勝利

score [skor] 是「勝利」的意思。big score 用來形容贏到大獎或高額獎金。
A: Where did you get all that money?
這些錢你從哪來的？
B: I made a big score at the track.
我在賽馬會中贏到大獎！

Terry Fan, Poker Prodigy

撲克天才——范雲翔

課文 朗讀 MP3 28　單字 朗讀 MP3 29　英文 文章導讀 MP3 30

Are you a junior or senior in college and worrying about your future in these [1)]**uncertain** economic times? While most people his age are just out of school and beginning their careers in the 9 to 5 world, Terry Fan has taken a much different path. Yet in spite of his highly [2)]**unconventional** career choice, Terry is making $15,000 a month by just [3)]**clicking** mouse buttons and doing what he loves to do best!

When Terry Fan graduated from Tamkang University with a B.A. in English Literature, he had no [4)]**clue** about what he wanted to do with his life. So in 2006, he decided to take a year off and travel around the world. After making stops in Japan, Guam, and Saipan, he **1 got bitten by the poker bug** while visiting the United States. But that wasn't his first [5)]**exposure** to the game. "I first learned Texas hold'em in 2004 when I was an exchange student at Indiana University of Pennsylvania," says Terry. "My friends needed one more guy to start a $5 dollar game, so I jumped in. I had no **2 beginner's luck** and lost my 5 dollars. I thought this game was stupid back then." A few months later, after reading a couple of poker books, Terry made his first **3 big score**, winning $14,000 in an online [6)]**tournament**. He continued his winning streak the following year, winning over $16,000 in the *World* [7)]*Series* *of Poker*.

Texas Hold'em Poker

中 Translation

你是大三或大四的學生，在這個經濟不穩定的時代擔心自己的未來嗎？當大多數跟他一樣大的人都才剛離開學校、在朝九晚五的世界開始他們的職業生涯，范雲翔已經踏上一條非常不同的道路。然而，儘管選擇了非常異於傳統的職業，范雲翔只要按一按滑鼠按鍵、做他最喜歡的事，就可以每月賺一萬五千美金！

范雲翔從淡江大學英文系畢業後，對自己想怎麼安排人生毫無頭緒。因此，在二○○六年，他決定放空一年周遊世界。遊歷了日本、關島、塞班島之後，他在造訪美國的時候迷上了撲克牌。但是，這並不是他第一次接觸撲克遊戲。「我第一次學德州撲克，是在二○○四年，當時我在賓州印第安那大學當交換學生」，范雲翔說，「我的朋友們需要多找一個人來開啟五美元的賽局，所以我就加入了。我沒有新手的好運氣，輸了五美元。當時我認為這種遊戲很蠢。」幾個月後，閱讀了一些撲克書籍，范雲翔首次旗開得勝，在一場網路比賽中贏得了一萬四千美元。隔年他繼續連勝，在世界撲克系列賽中贏得了超過一萬六千美元。

德州撲克牌——風靡全球的鬥智大賽

德州撲克牌玩法很像在電影賭神系列中常看到的梭哈，規則還蠻簡單的。如果你認為這只是另一種賭博的遊戲，那你可就大錯特錯了！英國《衛報》的撲克牌戲專欄作家維多利亞科蘭曾寫道：「撲克牌戲是一種充滿刺激的心理挑戰，結合了膽識勇氣與偵察能力，現金只不過是籌碼，是交易的工具，就像釣魚客手中的釣竿。撲克牌戲繞著金錢打轉，但是又與金錢毫不相干。」

學術圈與教育界可是對撲克牌戲興致勃勃。現在高學歷的職業玩家越來越多，他們在大學往往主修數學、統計學，上牌桌只不過是學以致用。哈佛大學法學院教授查爾斯奈森認為，撲克牌戲可以用來教導學生邏輯構思與運用的策略，並且能學習管理金錢，以及在壓力下保持耐性。

許多家長也開始鼓勵孩子玩牌，認為這種娛樂比電玩來得健康，不但可以鍛鍊腦力，還具有多種認知與生活技能的教育功能。

德州撲克牌有多紅？就現在美國有線電視的運動節目而言，撲克牌戲的收視率僅次於 NASCAR 賽車和美式足球，甚至還高過職業籃球 NBA。 EZ TALK 不推崇賭博，但若你是個喜歡享受下棋樂趣的人，這個遊戲絕對是你另一個最佳的選擇！

Poker Talk 撲克牌美語

Suits [suts] 花色（由大至小）

1 spades
[speds] 黑桃

2 hearts
[hɑrts] 紅心

3 diamonds
[ˈdaɪəmənds] 方塊

4 clubs
[clʌbs] 梅花

Rank of Hands 牌型（由大至小）

1 Royal Flush [ˈrɔɪəl flʌʃ] 同花大順

2 Straight Flush [stret flʌʃ] 同花順

3 Four of a Kind [for əv ə kaɪnd] 鐵支

4 Full House [fʊl haʊs] 葫蘆

5 Flush [flʌʃ] 同花

6 Straight [stret] 順子

7 Three of a Kind [θri əv ə kaɪnd] 三條

8 Two Pairs [tu pɛrz] 兩對

World Series of Poker
世界撲克牌系列賽

　　英文縮寫為 WSOP，是每年春夏季舉行的全球撲克大賽，通常為一個月，最刺激的是為期五天的總決賽。第一屆 WSOP 是於一九七〇年舉辦，到七〇年代末，WSOP 已經引起媒體的關注並開始有電視媒體爭相報導。除了巨額的獎金，WSOP 的冠軍還能得到一只冠軍手鐲，而這就是所有選手們心中至高無上的榮耀。

對 Texas Hold'em 有興趣？想跟 Terry Fan 討教戰術？
請上 FIVE OF A KIND：http://fiveofakind.net/

V Vocabulary Bank

1) **accomplish** [ə`kɑmplɪʃ] (v.) 完成，實現
I didn't accomplish anything at work today.

2) **attain** [ə`ten] (v.) 達到，獲得
You need to work hard to attain success.

3) **desperately** [`dɛspərɪtlɪ] (adv.) 拼命地，不顧一切地
The young couple was desperately in love.

4) **expense** [ɪk`spɛns] (n.) 開支
You need to cut down on your expenses if you want to save money.

5) **strategy** [`strætədʒɪ] (n.) 戰略，攻略
Our company is trying a new marketing strategy.

6) **management** [`mænɪdʒmənt] (n.) 管理
Dale wants to pursue a career in management.

7) **gambler** [`gæmblə] (n.) 賭徒
More and more gamblers are betting online these days.

8) **professional** [prə`fɛʃən]] (a.) 專業的
When I was a kid, I dreamed of becoming a professional athlete.

9) **pursue** [pə`su] (v.) 追求
I wish I had time to pursue a hobby.

✂ Tongue-tied No More

1 on the side 另外

on the side 可以用來表示「工作之餘兼差」、「其他興趣」或「另有交往對象」，也就是「劈腿」。點菜的時候，則用來表示「主菜之外另加配菜」或「醬料另外放」。

A: How come Ron and Karen haven't been getting along lately?
榮恩跟凱倫最近為什麼處得不太好？

B: I hear Ron's dating another girl on the side.
我聽說榮恩另外在跟別的女生約會！

⏱ Grammar Master

the reason (why / that) S + V...is that...

主體，表「……的理由」　　主體補語（名詞子句）

本文中用了兩次表說明理由的句型，唯一不同的是在補充說明主語的地方，一句是用 the reason... is because...，另一句則是用 the reason is that...。一般來說，is that...是較合乎文法邏輯的用法，is because...則較口語。

課文朗讀 MP3 31　單字朗讀 MP3 32　英文文章導讀 MP3 33

"I actually wasn't that interested in poker when I won that 16k," says Terry. "I just wanted to use that money to 1)**accomplish** my goal of completing a master's degree at a top U.S. grad

5　school." He was accepted to Northwestern University in 2006, where he 2)**attained** an MA in Learning Sciences. After graduation, he was 3)**desperately** looking for a full-time job so he could stay in the U.S. During his job hunt, he was playing online poker

10　**1 on the side** to cover his living 4)**expenses**. "I did finally get a job at a consulting firm," says Terry. "But after only 4 months, I realized that working in an office for someone else wasn't for me." So he quit his full-time job and decided to

15　play poker full time.

"One of ^Gthe reasons why I'm successful at poker is not because it makes money for me, but because I love the game itself," Terry stresses.

20 "I spend at least four hours every day reading poker ⁵⁾**strategy** *forums and watching videos to improve my game. I take it very seriously—it's my career. It's all about capital ⁶⁾**management**—

25 that's what separates ⁷⁾**gamblers** from ⁸⁾**professional** poker players. One of ^Gthe main reasons people succeed at what they do is that they don't follow the crowd. If you ⁹⁾**pursue** your interest

30 and put your heart into it, eventually the money and success will follow. I think that's really important during this time of economic recession when people are losing their jobs and it's

35 hard for young adults to find a career."

中 Translation

「我贏得一萬六千美元獎金那時候，其實對撲克的興趣不大」，范雲翔說，「我只是想用這筆錢完成我的目標，在美國頂尖研究所取得碩士學位。」他在二○○六年獲得美國西北大學的入學許可，在那裡取得了學習科學碩士學位。畢業後，為了留在美國，他拼命尋找全職工作。找工作期間，他一邊玩線上撲克來支付生活開銷。「我最後真的找到一份在顧問公司的工作」，范雲翔說，「但才四個月後，我就了解到，在辦公室替別人工作不適合我。」所以他辭去全職工作，決定全職玩撲克牌。

「我之所以能在撲克方面獲得成功，原因之一並不是因為它替我賺錢，而是因為我喜歡遊戲本身」，范雲翔強調，「我每天至少花四個小時閱讀撲克戰略論壇，並觀看影片改善我的賽局。我非常認真看待這件事——這是我的事業。撲克遊戲的重點在於資金管理，這也是賭徒和專業撲克玩家不同之處。有人能取得成功的主要原因之一，就是他們不隨波逐流。如果你依興趣發展，全心投入，金錢與成功最後都會隨之而來。我認為在現在許多人失業、年輕人找不到工作的經濟衰退之際，這真的很重要。」

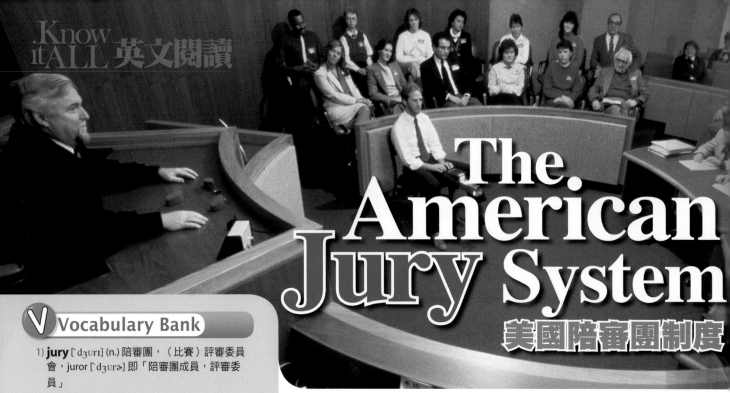

The American Jury System
美國陪審團制度

1) **jury** [`dʒʊrɪ] (n.) 陪審團，，（比賽）評審委員會，juror [`dʒʊrə] 即「陪審團成員，評審委員」
How many jurors are there on the jury?

2) **pillar** [`pɪlə] (n.) 樑柱，支柱
Mr. Jackson is a pillar of the community.

3) **democracy** [dɪ`mɑkrəsɪ] (n.) 民主制度，民主國家。形容詞為 democratic [ˌdɛmə`krætɪk]
The number of democracies in the world is on the rise.

4) **ultimately** [`ʌltəmɪtlɪ] (adv.) 最終，最後
Robert ultimately decided not to take the job.

5) **trial** [`traɪəl] (n.) 審判，審問，動詞為 try
(phr.) be tried by... 受到…的審判，be tried for... 因…受到審判
A former congressman is on trial for murder.

6) **entitle** [ɪn`taɪtl] (v.) 賦予…的權力、資格
All citizens over the age of 18 are entitled to vote.

7) **peer** [pɪr] (n.) 同儕，地位、能力相當的人
Teenagers are easily influenced by their peers.

8) **summon** [`sʌmən] (v.) 召喚，傳喚
Have you ever been summoned for jury duty?

9) **consensus** [kən`sɛnsəs] (n.) 共識
The jury took two days to reach a consensus.

10) **gradually** [`grædʒuəlɪ] (adv.) 逐步地，漸漸地
Global temperatures are gradually rising.

11) **evolve** [ɪ`vɑlv] (v.) 演進，逐步形成
Humans and apes evolved from a common ancestor.

補充字彙

* **verdict** [`vɝdɪkt] (n.) （陪審團的）裁定，裁決

* **defendant** [dɪ`fɛndənt] (n.) 被告

課文朗讀 MP3 34　單字朗讀 MP3 35　英文文章導讀 MP3 36

The jury system is a 2)**pillar** of the U.S. justice system. It's also at the heart of American 3)**democracy**. ⓒThis system, however, is not restricted to the United States, nor was it invented there. Juries are used in
5　courts around the world, and their history can be traced back to ancient times. Although they don't receive the same attention as judges and lawyers, court decisions 4)**ultimately** rest on 1)**jurors'** shoulders.

By definition, a jury is a group of people that
10　determines guilt or innocence in a 5)**trial**. In the U.S., a jury is generally made up of 12 people. The law states that people are 6)**entitled** to be 5)**tried** by a jury of their 7)**peers**. Jurors are supposed to be ordinary citizens, the same as the people being
15　tried. In fact, almost every adult is required to be available for jury duty. **1 Hence**, while it is their right to be judged by their peers, it is also their duty to serve in
20　court if 8)**summoned**.

©達志 / UPI PHOTO

Tongue-tied No More

1 hence的用法

hence [hɛns] 是副詞，表示「因此」的句型
為：S + V and hence....
例 The fruit is fresh and **hence** delicious.
這個水果很新鮮，也因此很好吃。

hence 用來表示「從此」時，則放在句尾。
例 He will begin his new job a month **hence**.
他從一個月後就任新工作。

Language Guide

陪審團——法庭戲最佳配角

「審判過程」trial process 是許多好萊塢電影
及電視影集的主軸，眾多主題嚴肅的電影就不
提了，但連輕鬆喜劇如《金法尤物》*Legally
Blonde* 都以法庭戲為主，就知道美國人對於上
法院爭個對錯有多著迷了。

但在這些電影或影集中，主角不是律師，就是
被告、原告，甚至證人，鮮少見到對陪審團
有所著墨的。最大的例外，要算是《十二怒
漢》*12 Angry Men* 這部經典電影了（Sidney
Lumet 執導，Henry Fonda 主演，榮獲四座奧
斯卡獎）。本片詳實描繪陪審團辯論審議、討
論證物，最後達成共識的經過；可惜的是這部
電影目前租不到，只能透過網路購買 DVD。
無緣欣賞此片的讀者也不必扼腕，因為近年*12
Angry Men* 被俄國導演 Nikita Mikhalkov重拍
（台灣發行片名《十二怒漢：大審判》），亦
曾入圍 2008 年奧斯卡最佳外語片，這部片在
台灣的連鎖 DVD 店就租得到了。

While juries around the world come in many
different forms, most have their roots in ancient
Greece. It was there that juries were first organized
to determine *verdicts. In fact, ancient juries were
25 often made up of thousands of people! It wasn't just
*defendants' peers who determined their fate, but
their entire community. Since it's hard
for thousands of people to come to a
9)**consensus**, the system 10)**gradually**
30 11)**evolved** over the years.

Grammar Master

雙重否定：nor 的用法

nor 是個連接詞，是否定句中的「也…」，放
在第二個否定子句的句首，且後面要接**倒裝句**
（先放 be 動詞或助動詞，再放主詞及適當動
詞）。注意因為 nor 本身就是連接詞，故不像
用 neither 時要在前面加連接詞 and。

- I will not lend you the money, nor will I help
  you borrow money.
  = I will not lend you the money, and neither
  will I help you borrow money.
- He didn't see the sign, nor did he notice
  that no one was sitting in that area.
  = He didn't see the sign, and neither did he
  notice that no one was sitting in that area.

Translation

陪審團制度是美國司法體系的支柱，也是美國民主體制的核心。不過，陪審團
制度並非只有美國才有，也並非美國所創。世界各地的法庭都有陪審團，其淵
源可追溯至古代。雖然陪審團不像法官和律師那麼受矚目，法庭最終判決卻落
在他們肩上。

顧名思義，陪審團就是一群在審判時決定受審者有罪或無罪的人。美國的陪審
團一般由十二個人組成。法律規定，人民有權由和他們身份地位相同的陪審團
來做審判。陪審團應該和受審者一樣是普通公民。事實上，幾乎每個成年人都
必須履行擔任陪審團的義務。因此，雖然人民有被同儕審判的權利，但法院傳
喚時也有擔任陪審員的義務。

雖然世界各地的陪審團制度不盡相同，但大部份都源自古希臘。最早的陪審團
就是在希臘組成以做出判決。事實上，古代的陪審團成員經常達數千人！決定
被告命運的不只是他們的同儕，而是整個社群。由於數千人很難達成共識，因
此陪審團制度隨著時間逐漸演變。

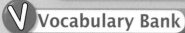 Vocabulary Bank

1) **explanation** [ˌɛkspləˋneʃən] (n.) 解釋，說明。注意動詞的拼法為 explain

Did you understand the teacher's explanation?

2) **practice** [ˋpræktɪs] (n.) 實行，慣例，常規

You should make a practice of being punctual.

3) **prejudice** [ˋprɛdʒədɪs] (n.) 偏見，偏袒

Martin Luther King, Jr. fought tirelessly against racial prejudice.

4) **corruption** [kəˋrʌpʃən] (n.) 腐敗，貪污

Many political leaders have been tried for corruption.

5) **take the place of** [tek ðə ples əv] (phr.) 取代，代替

Nothing can take the place of hard work and perseverance.

6) **transparency** [trænsˋpɛrənsɪ] (n.) 透明公開

Government transparency is vital to a democracy.

7) **come to mind** [kʌm tu maɪnd] (phr.) 想到，想起，想出

I'm trying to think of a good restaurant, but nothing comes to mind.

8) **get out of...** [gɛt aut əv] (phr.) 逃避，擺脫（責任、合約，邀請等）

Is there any way I can get out of this lease?

9) **make it** [mek ɪt] (phr.) 到達，達到（目標）

I'm sorry I couldn't make it to your party.

10) **agreement** [əˋgrimənt] (n.) 同意，協議

I'm glad we're in agreement about this issue.

補充字彙

* whim [wɪm] (n.) 一時的念頭，興致

* mandatory [ˋmændəˌtorɪ] (a.) 義務的，強制的

* exempt [ɪgˋzɛmpt] (v.) 免除，豁免

* plaintiff [ˋplentɪf] (n.) 起訴人，原告

課文朗讀 MP3 37　單字朗讀 MP3 38　英文文章導讀 MP3 39

Why do democracies like the United States value the jury system so highly? In days gone by, guilt or innocence could be determined by a single official. The fate of someone's life could be decided by the *whim of one person. No 1)**explanation** was needed, and the trial—if there was one—could be held in secret. In countries where such 2)**practices** still exist, 3)**prejudice** and 4)**corruption** 5)**take the place of** justice and 6)**transparency**.

11 Sadly, many people in the U.S. don't realize what an honor it is to serve on a jury. ⓖWhen a jury duty notice arrives in the mail, the first thing that [7]**comes to mind** is often how to [8]**get out of** it. While jury duty is *mandatory, people who are too ill or in financial

15 difficulty may be *exempted. In fact, however, the chances of actually being picked to serve on a jury are quite small. When trials are about to begin, hundreds of people are often called to court in the search for just 12 jurors. Often enough, cases don't even [9]**make**

20 **it** to trial. In a civil case, for example, the *plaintiff and defendant may reach an [10]**agreement** outside of court. When this happens, everyone brought in for jury duty is immediately sent home.

中 Translation

美國這樣的民主國家為什麼會如此重視陪審團制度？在過去，有罪或無罪可能只由一名官員定奪，一個人的命運可能取決於某個人一時的念頭，不需任何解釋，而且就算有審判，也可能是秘密進行的。在一些仍採用這種做法的國家，偏見和腐敗取代了正義和透明化。

令人遺憾的是，許多美國人並不了解擔任陪審員是何等光榮。當收到陪審通知的郵件時，第一個想到的通常是如何規避。雖然擔任陪審員是強制履行的義務，但生重病或經濟有困難的人可以免責。然而，真正被選為陪審員的機率其實很低。在審判快開始前，通常會有數百人被法庭傳喚，只為選出其中十二人擔任陪審員。案件也經常根本沒有進入審判階段。以民事案件為例，原告和被告可能庭外和解。當這種情況發生時，被傳喚前來擔任陪審員的人就可以立刻回家了。

Language Guide

civil case 是什麼？

civil case是「民事案件」，而「刑事案件」則為 criminal case。在美國，陪審團會參與刑事案件和部分民事案件，審理過程中，法官的職責不在於評判是非，而是控制訴訟程序，並根據陪審團的認定判斷適用的法律。然而「軍事法庭」military court 在美國則是例外，在這裡是由法官做最後裁決，不必有陪審團參與，而且就算有陪審團，也是由軍官組成。

在電影中，陪審團好像到最後都能順利做出判決，但其實他們並非一定能達成最後共識，hung jury 是有可能發生的情況（但發生機率很小）。hung jury 是指「未能作出裁定的陪審團」，陪審團十二人當中只要有一人堅決反對，就會形成 hung jury 的僵局，法官此時要宣布「審判無效」mistrial，必須重新選出一批陪審團，從頭開始審理。

Grammar Master

when 或 if 所引導之條件子句

when 或 if 所連接的兩個子句，若指的是固定的常態，則兩句都用現在簡單式。若指未來某事發生的條件，則 when / if 後面的子句用現在簡單式，另一個子句用未來簡單式。

● When / If water hits 100℃, it boils.
● When / If he gets here, I'll let you know.

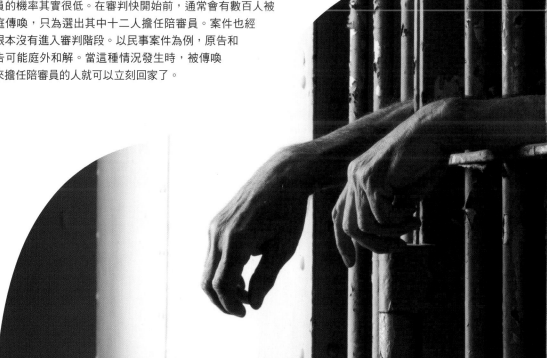

Know it ALL 英文閱讀

©達志 / UPI PHOTO

Vocabulary Bank

1) **question** [ˋkwɛstʃən] (v.) 訊問，探究
Several suspects were questioned at the police station.
2) **prosecution** [ˌprɑsɪˋkjuʃən] (n.) 原告（及其律師），檢察官這一方
The prosecution called a surprise witness.
3) **eliminate** [ɪˋlɪməˌnet] (v.) 排除，淘汰
Two contestants were eliminated from the competition today.
4) **biased** [ˋbaɪəst] (a.) 有偏見的，
bias [ˋbaɪəs] (n.) 偏見，傾向
(phr.) be biased against…有不利…的傾向，be biased towards…有利於…的傾向
Parents are always biased towards their own children.
5) **defense** [dɪˋfɛns] (n.) 被告（及其辯護律師），辯護
The lawyer met with the defendant to plan his defense.
6) **evidence** [ˋɛvədəns] (n.) 證據，物證
The police were accused of destroying evidence.
7) **witness** [ˋwɪtnɪs] (n.) 目擊者，證人
A key witness in the mob trial turned up dead.
8) **weigh** [we] (v.) 權衡，考慮
You should weigh all your options before you make a decision.
9) **unanimous** [juˋnænəməs] (a.) 一致的，無異議的
Members of the board were unanimous in rejecting the merger.
10) **courtroom** [ˋkortˌrʊm] (n.) 法庭，審判室
court (n.) 法院 + room (n.) 房間
Cameras aren't allowed in the courtroom.

補充字彙

* adjourn [əˋdʒɝn] (v.) 換地方，休會
* deliberation [dɪˌlɪbəˋreʃən] (n.) 審議，商討
* impartial [ɪmˋpɑrʃəl] (a.) 公正的，不偏不倚的

34 • Know it all

課文朗讀 MP3 40　單字朗讀 MP3 41　英文文章導讀 MP3 42

However, if a case ᴳdoes go to trial, it is then the lawyers' job to ¹⁾**question** and select jurors. In this process, the ²⁾**prosecution** tries to ³⁾**eliminate** jurors who are ⁴⁾**biased** against the plaintiff, and the ⁵⁾**defense** tries to get rid of those biased against the defendant. Each side is allowed to reject a certain number of jurors, and no reason is necessary for their choices. Ultimately, though, they must decide on 12 people.

When the trial begins, the jury is presented with ⁶⁾**evidence** and ⁷⁾**witnesses**. Arguments are made both ❶ **for and against** the defendant. Usually, the trial process lasts no more than a few days, and can often be completed in a single afternoon. Occasionally, however, the process can last weeks or even months.

Once the trial is over, the jurors then *adjourn to the jury room for *deliberation. A jury captain is chosen to lead the discussions. Jurors are required to remain as *impartial as possible while ⁸⁾**weighing** the evidence. Deliberation continues until a ⁹⁾**unanimous** decision is reached. The jury is then brought back to the ¹⁰⁾**courtroom**, and the jury captain reads the verdict: guilty or innocent.

Juries don't receive much attention; in fact, they're not supposed to. However, it is these humble citizens who decide the fate of both the guilty and the innocent. It may not be a perfect system, but it is one that continues a tradition of justice and democracy.

25

中 Translation

然而，要是案子真的進入審判階段，律師就要負責提問、挑選陪審員。在這個過程中，檢方會試著剔除對原告懷有偏見的陪審員，而辯方律師也會試著淘汰對被告懷有偏見的陪審員。雙方都可以剔除一些陪審員，不需任何理由，不過，最終他們必須共同選出十二個人。

審判一開始，證據和證人一一呈現給陪審團，然後對被告有利和不利的論點都會陳述。審判通常只會持續幾天，也經常一個下午就可以完成。不過，偶爾也會持續數周或甚至好幾個月。

審判一旦終結，陪審團就會移轉到陪審室討論判決。他們會選出陪審團長來主持討論。在衡量證據時，陪審團被要求要盡量保持公正。直到達成全體一致決議，討論才結束。然後陪審團會被帶回法庭，由團長宣讀判決：有罪或無罪。

陪審團不太受到注意，事實上，他們也不該受到注意。然而，這群平凡百姓卻要決定有罪和無罪的命運。這個制度也許不完美，但卻延續了正義和民主的傳統。

✂ Tongue-tied No More

1 for and against 支持與反對的

for and against 是一個固定聯用的介係詞片語，因為「分別支持與反對（某議題）的正反雙方」針對的主體是相同的，只需要在 for and against 後面說一次就好了。

Demonstrators for and against abortion gathered outside the clinic.
支持與反對墮胎的抗議群眾聚集在診所外。

At the Pentagon, military experts made the case for and against war.
美國五角大廈中，軍事專家提出支持與反對宣戰的論點。

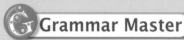

✎ Grammar Master

加強語氣

助動詞 do, does, did 等原本應該是否定和疑問句才用的，但肯定句中「 do / does / did + 原形動詞」是加強語氣，表示「真的…」、「的確…」。

● He **does** love you.
● I **did** see that movie.

✏ Mini Quiz 閱讀測驗

❶ In the United States, a jury is usually composed of _____.
(A) 8 people
(B) 10 people
(C) 12 people
(D) 2,500 people

❷ The modern jury system has its origins in _____.
(A) ancient Greece
(B) the French Revolution
(C) the American Revolution
(D) none of the above

❸ True or False
When a jury makes their final decision, everyone must be in agreement.

閱讀測驗解答 ❶ (C) ❷ (A) ❸ True

V Vocabulary Bank

1) **up front** [ʌp frʌnt] (phr.) 一開始，在最前面，預先地
You must pay for this television up front—we don't offer a payment plan.

2) **essentially** [ɪˋsɛnʃəlɪ] (adv.) 基本上
(a.) essential [ɪˋsɛnʃəl] 必要的，基本的
This car is essentially the same as your old car.

3) **financial** [faɪˋnænʃəl] (a.) 金融的，財務的
The rumor is that this company may be experiencing some financial difficulties.

4) **institution** [ˌɪnstəˋtuʃən] (n.) 機構
This university is the largest educational institution in the country.

5) **calculate** [ˋkælkjəˌlet] (v.) 計算，估計
(n.) calculation [ˌkælkjəˋleʃən] 計算，估計
She can help you calculate your monthly payments.

6) **consideration** [kənˌsɪdəˋreʃən] (n.) 考慮，考量
When purchasing a used car, the age of the vehicle is an important consideration.

7) **accurately** [ˋækjərətlɪ] (adv.) 精確地
(a.) accurate [ˋækjərɪt] 精確的
She has accurately described the problem.

8) **assess** [əˋsɛs] (v.) 對…進行估算，評估價值
It's wise to assess the real estate market before buying a house.

9) **previous** [ˋprivɪəs] (a.) 先前的，以往的
His previous girlfriend is now living in Japan.

10) **obligation** [ˌɑbləˋgeʃən] (n.) 清償債務的款項，（道義、法律）責任
He has an obligation to inform us of any changes to the contract.

11) **utility** [juˋtɪlɪtɪ] (n.) 公用事業（水、電、瓦斯等）
The power utility here is owned by the state.

12) **numerical** [nuˋmɛrɪk] (a.) 以數字表現的，數值的
Many numerical statistics are used in baseball.

13) **representation** [ˌrɛprɪˌzɛnˋteʃən] (n.) 表示，表現
This chart shows a visual representation of the nation's economy.

Raising Your Credit Score 提高個人信用評分

課文朗讀 MP3 43　單字朗讀 MP3 44　英文文章導讀 MP3 45

How and why credit scores are used

Most people don't have enough cash in the bank to pay for large purchases all [1]**up front**. Instead, it's common practice for buyers of expensive things like homes and cars to make purchases using credit. ⓒBuying something with

5　credit is [2]**essentially ▉ taking a loan from** a bank, credit card company or other [3]**financial** [4]**institution**. The loan is used to pay for the purchase, and the buyer ▉ **is** then **indebted to** the lender for the amount of the purchase plus interest. The interest rate of the loan is [5]**calculated**

10　using the borrower's credit history, and it has a huge effect on the total amount of money the person will need to pay. For this reason, a person's credit history is a very important [6]**consideration** in most large purchases.

However, [7]**accurately** [8]**assessing** a person's credit
15 history can be very complicated. This [5]**calculation**
needs to ❸ **take into consideration** all of the person's
[9]**previous** financial [10]**obligations**, including credit card
purchases, home, car and student loans, payments on [11]**utility**
bills and even unpaid parking tickets. Any kind of debt will
20 affect a person's creditworthiness. A personal credit score is a
number calculated from a person's credit history. It's a simple
[12]**numerical** [13]**representation** of a person's creditworthiness,
ranging from low (300) to high (850). Credit scores make it
easier for a lender to decide on an interest rate, or to decide
25 whether to even offer a loan in the first place.

中 Translation

信用評分怎麼使用，為什麼要使用

多數人在銀行並沒有足夠的現金可以預先付清所有大筆消費，買家購買如房子和汽車等昂貴物品的常見做法反而是：利用信用來購買。以信用購物基本上就是向銀行、信用卡公司或其他金融機構借錢。貸款是用來支付購物消費，於是買方便賒欠貸方購物的金額加利息。貸款利率的計算視借方的信用紀錄而定，這會大大影響借方必須支付的總金額。基於這個理由，在進行大筆消費時，一個人的信用紀錄是非常重要的考量。

然而，精確評估一個人的信用紀錄可是非常複雜的。其計算必須考量那個人先前的所有財務負債，包括：信用卡購物、房屋、汽車及就學貸款、水電瓦斯帳單繳款，甚至是未繳納的違規停車罰單等等。任何形式的債務都會影響一個人的信用評等。信用評分是依據一個人的信用紀錄計算得出的一個數字，簡單用數字來代表一個人的信用評等，分數從低（300）到高（850）不等（編註：信用分數會因採取不同計算系統得出不同數字，本文採取 FICO score，是美國最普遍採用的系統）。信用評分可以讓貸方更容易決定利率，甚至一開始就用來決定要不要提供貸款。

❀ Tongue-tied No More

❶ take a loan from...
向（某人）借錢

loan [lon] 是「貸款」，take a loan from the bank 是「向銀行借錢」，如果要說「銀行借錢給某人」則是 the bank made a loan to...。
A: How did you afford the down payment for the new house?
你怎麼付得起新房子的頭期款？
B: I had to take a loan from my brother.
我得跟我老哥借錢。

❷ be indebted to...
欠（某人）錢，欠（某人）一份情

indebted [ɪnˋdɛtɪd] 是形容詞「負債的」，而其中的 debt [dɛt] 即「債，借款」，也可引申為「恩惠，情意」的意思。因此 be indebted to... 也有「欠某人一份情」的意思。要注意 to 在這裡是介系詞，所以後面接名詞。
A: I'm indebted to you for all the help you've given me.
你幫我這麼多，我欠你一份情。
B: Don't mention it. That's what friends are for.
別這麼說。朋友就是要這樣啊。

❸ take into consideration...
將……列入考慮

take into consideration sb./sth. 就是「將……考慮在內」，表示那是做決定時必須顧慮的重要因素。consideration 換成 account（估算），意思也差不多，只是 account 更強調數字上的表現。sb./sth. 也可以調到 into 的前面：take sb./sth. into consideration、take sth. into account。
A: Is the stock market always a good investment?
股票市場一直是好的投資標的嗎？
B: Not always. You need to take into consideration the possibility that it will go down.
不盡然。你必須考慮到下跌的可能性。
A: Why do you owe so much on your house?
你為什麼房貸這麼重？
B: We didn't really take the variable interest rate into account.
我們當初沒把浮動利率算進去。

❀ Grammar Master

「動名詞」作為主詞時的用法

動詞不能當作主詞，若要用動作當主詞就必須改成「動詞 + V-ing」，也就是所謂的「動名詞」。
● V-ing...+ is/Vs + ...
例 **Buying** a house **is** an important decision.
買房子是項重要的決定。
例 **Breaking** up with Kate **took** a toll on Darren.
與凱特分手使得達倫受創極深。

課文朗讀 MP3 46　單字朗讀 MP3 47　英文文章導讀 MP3 48

Vocabulary Bank

1) **obtain** [əb`ten] (v.) 取得，獲得
You can obtain this form from the head office.

2) **profit** [`prɑfɪt] (n.) 利潤，盈利
This company has made a profit every quarter since it was founded.

3) **sponsor** [`spɑnsə] (v.) 贊助，主辦
government-sponsored 即「政府出資建立的」
This baseball team is sponsored by a local bank.

4) **shuffle** [`ʃʌfl̩] (v.) 交錯，把…移來移去
The people shuffled around quite frequently during the party.

5) **distribute** [dɪ`strɪbjut] (v.) 分佈，分配
These checks need to be distributed among all the employees.

6) **balance** [`bæləns] (n.) 結餘，欠款
She keeps a low balance on all of her credit cards.

7) **minimum** [`mɪnəməm] (a.) 最低限度的，最小量的
The minimum purchase to qualify for the rebate is $100.

8) **disastrous** [dɪ`zæstrəs] (a.) 悲慘的，災難性的
The fire at the hospital was truly disastrous.

9) **classify** [`klæsə‚faɪ] (v.) 將…歸入某類 / 等級
These stones are all classified according to their value.

進階字彙

10) **out to** [aut tu] (phr.) 就為了，以…為目的
That car salesman sounds like he's out to take your money.

口語補充

11) **savvy** [`sævɪ] (a.) 精明的
The savvy traveler knows the best time to travel to save money.

What to do about a low credit score

Apart from always paying your bills on time, there are many things a person can do to actively raise their credit score. The very first thing you need to do is [1]**obtain** a copy of your credit report from one of the many online credit

5　reporting agencies. Most of these agencies are [10]**out to** make a [2]**profit**, so more [11]**savvy** consumers use the government-[3]**sponsored** website annualcreditreport.com, which provides reports for free. After getting a copy of the report, it's wise to examine it carefully for errors. Mistakes on credit reports

10　are much more common than you might expect. Fixing them is not easy, but it's well worth the effort, as even a small increase in one's credit score can result in big savings on a loan.

It's also wise to [4]**shuffle** any outstanding credit card debts to avoid having any one card maxed out. If a

15　card is maxed out, that means you've used up all of the available credit on the card. This has a very negative effect on your credit score. It's better to [5]**distribute**

Please pay £116.53

your debt among several cards so that no single card is kept at its upper limit. A good **1 rule of thumb** is

20 to never use more than 50% of the available credit on any one card. And of course, always pay your ⁶⁾**balance** ^{G)}in full every month. If that isn't possible, then be sure to at least pay the ⁷⁾**minimum** amount. Ignoring your credit card bills, even for a very short time, can have a ⁸⁾**disastrous** effect

25 on your score. On the other hand, if you always pay your balance at the end of the month and never pay interest, you will be ⁹⁾**classified** as not having a credit history. Lenders, after all, still want to make money.

中 Translation

信用評分低，該怎麼辦
除了一定要準時繳納帳單，還有許多辦法可以有效提高信用評分。你的首要之務是在眾多網路信用報告機構中擇一，透過該機構取得信用報告。這類機構多半是為了營利，所以越來越多精明的消費者會向政府贊助的網站 annualcreditreport. com （年度信用報告網）免費申請報告。拿到報告後，明智的作法是仔細檢查是否有誤。信用報告出錯的機率比你預期高很多。修正錯誤並不容易，但絕對值得投注心力，因為區區提高些許信用分數就可能替你在貸款時省下大筆金錢。

交錯使用多張卡來分散未清償的信用卡債務，以避免任何一張信用卡刷爆，也是明智之舉。信用卡刷爆了就表示你已經用盡該卡所有可用的信用額度，這對你的信用評分有非常不利的影響。最好將你的債務分散在數張信用卡，以免哪一張卡刷到最高額度。一個不錯的經驗法則是，任何一張卡絕對不要動用到百分之五十以上的信用額度。當然，每個月一定要全額繳納欠款，如果做不到，至少也一定要繳納最低應繳金額。忽略信用卡帳單──就算時間非常短──可能會對你的評分造成非常嚴重的的後果。話說回來，如果你總是在月底準時繳清，從來不須支付利息，那你會被歸類為「沒有信用紀錄」。貸方畢竟還是想賺錢。

Language Guide

在台灣要如何取得個人信用紀錄？
只要連上財團法人金融聯合徵信中心網站 www.jcic.org.tw 進入「社會大眾專區」，即可下載申請書表。由於金融聯合徵信中心屬財團法人，並非營利單位，任何人只要繳交 100 元手續費，附上雙證件，即可取得聯徵紀錄。

聯徵紀錄是銀行及信用卡公司提供的資料彙總，金融聯合徵信中心只是保管資料，資料正確與否並不負責，因此大家應該養成定時調閱訂正的習慣，以免影響未來申請貸款的利率。

Tongue-tied No More

1 rule of thumb
　經驗法則，一般來說（做好是…）
rule of thumb 是指依照過去經驗所歸納出來的最好作法，或是最可信的答案。
A: Do you know when the rainy months in California are?
　你知道加州的雨季是什麼時候嗎？
B: As a rule of thumb, it's rainier in the winter.
　一般來說，冬天比較多雨。

Grammar Master

in full 完全地
副詞片語的用法與類型
副詞主要是修飾動詞、形容詞或副詞。最基本的副詞是單一英文字，如 quickly、truly、mentally 等等。而兩個字以上的就稱為副詞片語，如加上介系詞的 next door、without a word 與接不定詞的 work(s) hard to support the family、get(s) close to the house 等。副詞片語 in full 等於 completely、fully、entirely。

● 加上介系詞的副詞片語
例 Peter <u>answered</u> the teacher's question **in a rude manner**.
　彼得用無理的態度回答老師的問題。
● 加上不定詞的副詞片語
例 Mark <u>dressed</u> nicely **to impress** Tina.
　馬克盛裝打扮好給蒂娜好印象。

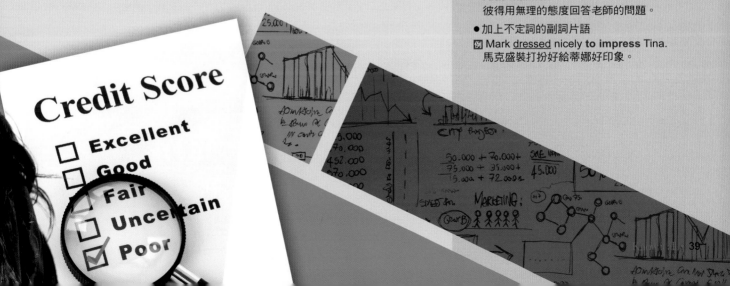

Know it ALL 英文閱讀

Vocabulary Bank

1) **mention** [ˈmɛnʃən] (v.) 提到，說起
He mentioned that he'll be driving through Chicago on his way home.

2) **counterintuitive** [ˌkaʊntəɪnˈtjuətɪv] (a.) 與直覺相反的，違背常理的
counter 相反的 + intuitive 直覺的
Steering the boat is counterintuitive– you push to the left to turn the boat to the right.

3) **gauge** [gedʒ] (v.) 估量，評斷
It's hard to gauge when he's telling the truth and when he's lying.

4) **opposite** [ˈɑpəzɪt] (a.) 相反的，對立的，
opposite effect 即「反效果」
Day is the opposite of night.

5) **negotiate** [nɪˈgoʃɪˌet] (v.) 協商，談判
Our company can help you negotiate a better price.

6) **repayment** [rɪˈpemənt] (n.) 付款償還
The repayment of this loan is expected to take ten years.

7) **specialize** [ˈspɛʃəˌlaɪz] (v.) 專攻，專門從事或研究
She plans to specialize in marine biology.

8) **ensure** [ɪnˈʃʊr] (v.) 確保，保證
We try to ensure that all of our customers leave the store satisfied.

進階字彙

9) **track record** [træk ˈrɛkəd] (phr.) 過去的業績、工作紀錄
You should examine the track record of a new employee before hiring him or her.

Building your credit score

⑤It's necessary to ¹⁾**mention** that a person's credit score is something that needs to be built up. If, for example, you've never had a credit card and have never taken out any sort of loan, then your credit score will
5　actually be quite low. This may seem ²⁾**counterintuitive** at first. But consider that, without any kind of credit history, the lender has no way of ³⁾**gauging** your creditworthiness. For this reason, it's important to have and occasionally use your credit cards, as long as you're
10　going to pay them off on time. A long history of on-time credit card payments is one of the best ways to maintain a high credit score. Frequently canceling and applying for new credit cards has the ⁴⁾**opposite** effect.

Lastly, you should understand that most lenders are
15　willing to work with customers who have large amounts of debt. Credit card companies are sometimes willing to ⁵⁾**negotiate** better ⁶⁾**repayment** terms for
20　large debts. There are also professionals who

[7)]**specialize** in fixing bad credit scores. Consumers need to research these professionals carefully to [8)]**ensure** that they have a good [9)]**track record**.

25 **1 All in all**, building and maintaining a high credit score is not difficult, but it does take time and a little planning. If your credit score is currently high, then you need to make sure it stays that way. If it's currently on the low side, then you should work on raising it before 30 you make that next big purchase.

中 Translation

累積信用評分

必須一提的是,個人信用評分是必須累積的東西。舉例來說,如果你從未辦過信用卡,也從來沒申請過任何種類的貸款,那麼你的信用評分其實會相當低。乍看之下這似乎有違常理,但你想想看:沒有任何信用紀錄,貸方就無從判斷你的信用價值。基於這個理由,擁有並偶爾使用信用卡是重要的,只要你能準時償還。長期準時繳納信用卡帳單,是維持高信用評分的最好辦法之一,時常取消信用卡以及申請新卡則有反效果。

最後,你應該了解,多數貸方都願意和有大筆債務的顧客合作。信用卡公司有時也願意為龐大債務協商更好的償還條件。坊間也有專門挽救不良信用評分的專業人士,消費者必須仔細研究這些專業人士,確定他們紀錄優良。

總的來說,累積及維持高信用評分並不困難,但需要時間和一些規畫。如果你目前的信用評分很高,那麼就必須努力維持下去。如果目前偏低,那你應該在下一次進行高額消費之前先努力提高分數。

Tongue-tied No More

1 all in all... 總而言之,總括來說

in all 是「總計」,all + in all 字面上的意思就是「全部加起來」,也就是用來表示各方面考量之後的結論。all in all 若置於句首,後面要加逗號。

A: So how was the conference?
那場會議進行得如何?

B: Boring at times, but all in all it was quite good.
有些時候滿無聊的,但整體來說還不錯。

Grammar Master

it 當作虛主詞的用法

當一個英文句子的主詞是動名詞或是不定詞但又過長時,就會用 it 放在句首作為虛主詞,以避免頭重腳輕的感覺。it 的後面可接 be 動詞、一般動詞或助動詞。

● it 當作虛主詞 + 助動詞

例 Taking a walk in an open area for ten minutes after dinner every day will improve your health.

= **It will improve** your health to take a walk in an open area for ten minutes after dinner every day.
每天晚餐後到開放的空間散步十分鐘對你的健康有益。

● it 當作虛主詞 + be 動詞

例 Avoiding confrontations all the time is not a good way of living.

= **It is** not a good way of living avoiding confrontations all the time.
一味避免衝突不是好的生活方式。

Mini Quiz 閱讀測驗

1 Which of the following is NOT a wise way to use your credit card?
(A) Maxing out all your credit cards every month.
(B) Shuffling any outstanding credit card debts to avoid maxing out any one card.
(C) Always paying your balance in full every month.
(D) Distributing your debt among several credit cards.

2 Buyers are indebted _____ lenders for the amount of the purchase plus interest.
(A) of   (B) to
(C) in   (D) with

3 Fixing mistakes on your credit reports is not easy, but it's well _____ the effort.
(A) worthless   (B) worthy
(C) worse   (D) worth

閱讀測驗解答 1 (A) 2 (B) 3 (D)

太陽塔 (Tower of the Sun)
1970 Expo '70
日本，大阪

©John Robertson

東方之冠 (The Crown of the East)
2010 Expo 2010
中國，上海

世界級博覽會
A World of Fairs

Vocabulary Bank

1) **facilitate** [fəˋsɪlə͵tet] (v.) 促進，使便利
Some think cutting taxes will facilitate economic recovery.

2) **reputation** [͵rɛpjəˋteʃən] (n.) 名譽，名聲
The scandal destroyed the senator's reputation.

3) **diverse** [dɪˋvɝs] (a.) 多元的，不同的
(n.) diversity [dɪˋvɝsətɪ] 多元性，不同
San Francisco is a culturally diverse city.

4) **headquarter** [ˋhɛd͵kɔrtɚ] (v.) 設立總部
(n.) headquarters [ˋhɛd͵kɔrtɚz] 總部
Where is your company headquartered?

5) **manufactured** [͵mænjəˋfæktʃɚd] (a.) 製造的
(v.) manufacture [͵mænjəˋfæktʃɚ]
The country mainly exports manufactured goods.

進階字彙

6) **exposition** [͵ɛkspəˋzɪʃən] (n.) 博覽會，展覽會，常簡稱為 expo
Are you planning on going to the trade exposition?

7) **horticulture** [ˋhɔrtɪ͵kʌltʃə] (n.) 園藝
Thousands of horticulture enthusiasts attended the flower show.

8) **focal point** [ˋfok! ͵pɔɪnt] (phr.) 焦點，中心
The woman's children are the focal point of her life.

9) **fast-forward** [ˋfæst͵fɔrwəd] (v.) 快進，快轉
Let's fast-forward through the commercials.

10) **under way** [ˋʌndɚ ͵we] (phr.) 正在進行中的
Preparations for the wedding are already under way.

11) **urban greening** [ˋɝbən ˋgrinɪŋ] (phr.) 城市綠化
The urban greening project will include several new parks.

課文朗讀 MP3 52　單字朗讀 MP3 53　英文文章導讀 MP3 54

World's Fairs, known today as World [6]**Expositions** (or Expos for short), are large public exhibitions held regularly around the world. Expos serve a number of purposes: they give host cities the opportunity to stage a world-class
5　event; they [1]**facilitate** international cultural exchange and understanding; and allow participating countries to enhance their [2]**reputations** through a process called "nation branding." Expos are international exhibitions organized around [3]**diverse** themes like transportation, technology
10　and [7]**horticulture**. The governing body of these events is the Bureau of International Exhibitions, founded in 1928 and [4]**headquartered** in Paris.

World Expos date all the way back to 1851, when the first World's Fair was held in London. The Great Exhibition, as
15　it is known today, was the first-ever international exhibition of [5]**manufactured** products. Subsequent Fairs focused on industry and inventions up until the 1930s, when a shift to more human themes took place. Cultural exchange, the future, and man's place in the world replaced industry as the
20　[8]**focal point** of World's Fairs.

[9]**Fast-forward** to the present day and another international exhibition, the 2010 Taipei International

巴黎鐵塔 (The Eiffel Tower)
1889 Paris International
法國，巴黎

太空針 (Space Needle)
1962 Century 21 Exposition
美國，西雅圖

菲力斯摩天輪 (Ferris Wheel)
1893 World's Columbian
美國，芝加哥

原子塔 (Atomium)
1958 Brussels World's Fair
比利時，布魯塞爾

Flora Expo, is [10)]**under way** ◼ **in our very own backyard**. While somewhat smaller in scope than a World Expo, the

25 Flora Expo hopes to draw 6 million visitors, who will have a chance to learn about green technology, [11)]**urban greening** efforts, and the amazing [3)]**diversity** of Taiwan's plants and flowers. If you haven't been yet, it's the perfect opportunity to experience an international exhibition firsthand.

Mini Quiz 閱讀測驗

❶ ███ **According to the article, which of the following is true about World Expos?**
(A) They used to be called World Expos.
(B) They used to be called World's Fairs.
(C) They are all organized around the same themes.
(D) They are held every year in a different city.

❷ ███ **What happened in the 1930s?**
(A) World's Fair themes began to change.
(B) Industry became the focal point of World's Fairs.
(C) World's Fairs began to focus on industry and inventions.
(D) They became known as World Expos.

Translation

萬國博覽會，現名世界博覽會（或簡稱世博會 (Expo)），是定期於世界各地舉辦的大型公開展覽。舉辦世博會有數種目的：給予主辦城市策畫世界級盛事的機會、促進國際文化交流與了解、也讓參與國得以透過所謂的「國家品牌行銷」過程來提高聲譽。世博會是依多元主題規畫的國際展覽會，如交通運輸、科技和園藝。其主管機構為國際博覽總局，該局成立於一九二八年，總部設於巴黎。

世界博覽會的源起可回溯至一八五一年，當時在倫敦舉行首屆萬國博覽會。這項如今俗稱「大博覽會」的盛會，是史上第一場工業製品的國際展覽會。之後幾屆萬博會的焦點都擺在工業與發明，直到一九三〇年代才趨向更人文的主題，文化交流、未來世界，以及人類在世界的位置，取代工業成為萬國博覽會的焦點。

快轉至今日，另一場國際博覽會，二〇一〇年台北國際花卉博覽會，正在我國進行。雖然規模比起世博會是小了點，但花博仍可望吸引六百萬名遊客，他們將有機會認識環保科技、城市綠化工作，以及琳瑯滿目的台灣植物和花卉。如果你還沒去過，這是親自體驗國際博覽會的絕佳良機。

Tongue-tied No More

◼ **in one's own backyard**
自己國內 / 城市內，在自家附近

backyard ['bæk`jɑrd] 是家中的「後院」，但 in one's own backyard 通常不是真的指一座後院花園，而是引申為國內 / 城市內，或是距離自己很近、經常遊走的地方。

A: I can't believe how many houses were destroyed in the hurricane.
我真是不敢相信這次的颶風毀了多少房子。

B: Yeah. I never imagined such a major disaster could happen in our own backyard.
是啊。我從沒有想像過這種大災難竟然會發生在自家附近。

Language Guide

Flora 花神芙羅拉
看到台北花博會的英文名稱 (Taipei International Flora Expo)，會不會對 Flora 這個字感到很陌生？或是很驚訝自己的名字怎麼變成花博標題了？這 Flora 其實是羅馬女神——花神芙羅拉，但有趣的是，在希臘羅馬神話的記載中，花神祭 (Flora Rites) 的慶祝方式通常是以粗糙不雅的鬧劇 (farce) 進行。這個現象和羅馬務實的民族性或多或少有關；一切和浪漫、想像有關的事物，其實都不是他們關注的焦點。雖然最早的花神芙羅拉祭典不是那麼符合我們的想像，但至少我們現在可以確定：人們對於 Flora 這個典故 (allusion) 的想像，如今已經因時空的不同而改變了許多，此外，flora 這個字在英文也中有「植物」的意思。

(A) 2 (B) 1 答解題測讀閱

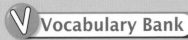

Vocabulary Bank

1) **construct** [kən`strʌkt] (v.) 建造
   The city plans to construct a new library.

2) **elaborate** [ɪ`læbərɪt] (a.) 製作精巧的，裝飾華麗的
   Michael Jackson was famous for his elaborate outfits.

3) **tourism** [`turɪzəm] (n.) 旅遊（業），觀光（業）
   The town makes most of its money from tourism.

4) **revenue** [`rɛvə,nu] (n.) 收入，稅收
   The factory lost revenue during the strike.

5) **immune** [ɪ`mjun] (a.) 不受影響的，免疫的
   Few people are immune to criticism.

6) **displace** [dɪs`ples] (v.) 迫使…離開家園，（從原來的地方）移開
   Millions of people were displaced by the war.

7) **symbol** [`sɪmbḷ] (n.) 象徵
   Luxury cars are status symbols.

8) **tribute** [`trɪbjut] (n.) 證明，體現
   The painting is a tribute to the artist's genius.

進階字彙

9) **draw** [drɔ] (n.) 吸引人的人事物，(v.) draw 吸引，招攬
   The orcas are the aquariums main draw.

10) **showcase** [`ʃo,kes] (v.) 展示
    The singing contest showcases talented young singers.

11) **infrastructure** [`ɪnfrə,strʌktʃə] (n.) 基本設施
    The country's infrastructure was severely damaged in the war.

12) **urban renewal** [`ɝbən rɪ`nuəl] (phr.) 都市更新
    The city center is undergoing urban renewal.

13) **sustainability** [sə,stenə`bɪlɪtɪ] (n.) 永續性，持續性
    Many cities now have sustainability plans.

14) **everlasting** [,ɛvə`læstɪŋ] (a.) 永久的，歷久不衰的
    The general's victory won him everlasting fame.

As everyone who has attended a recent World Expo knows, the biggest [9]**draws** are, of course, the national pavilions. Participating countries spend millions of dollars designing and [1]**constructing** [2]**elaborate**
5　structures to [10]**showcase** their products and unique culture. While the costs may be high, the potential returns from increased foreign investment and higher tourist numbers justify the expense. Speaking of costs, host cities also spend huge sums preparing for World
10　Expos. This money goes to site construction, improved transportation [11]**infrastructure**, and [12]**urban renewal**. This not only helps make the Expo a success in the short run, but also benefits citizens in the long run.

Although there are significant economic benefits
15　to hosting a World Expo, such as increased [3]**tourism** [4]**revenue**, Expos are not [5]**immune** to criticism. The Shanghai Expo 2010 planners, for example, [6]**displaced** 18,000 families to clear land for the 5.28 square km exposition site, the largest on record. And when the
20　Expo ended last October, more than fifty pavilions had to be torn down—that's a lot of leftover concrete and steel to deal with, which raises questions about Expo [13]**sustainability**. **1** **On the plus side**, however, World Expos can leave a valuable legacy for
25　host cities. One of the world's most beloved landmarks, the

沙烏地阿拉伯館

韓國館

2010
上海世博

2010
上海世博

荷蘭館

台灣館

澳洲館

Eiffel Tower, was constructed for the Universal Exposition of 1889. Similarly, Seattle's famed Space Needle was originally the [7)]**symbol** of the 1962 World's Fair. These are [14)]**everlasting** [8)]**tributes** to the wonderful world of Expos.

Mini Quiz 閱讀測驗

❶ According to the article, which of the following is true about the national pavilions at a World Expo?
(A) They are all built by the host country.
(B) They are the most expensive structures.
(C) They are the only attractions.
(D) They are the most popular attractions.

❷ Which of the following is true about the Shanghai Expo?
(A) The site for it was nearly five square kilometers.
(B) Most of the structures on the site are still there.
(C) Many families were forced to move because of it.
(D) It is a model for sustainability.

Translation

每個去過近幾屆世博會的人都知道，最精彩的當然是各國的主題館。各參與國都會砸下重金設計及建造精美的建築，來展示該國的產品和獨特文化。雖然成本或許很高，但吸引更多外國投資或觀光客帶來的潛在收益，會讓那些錢花得值得。說到成本，主辦城市也會不惜血本籌備世博會。這些經費用於場地興建、改善交通基礎建設以及都市更新，這不僅短期有利於世博圓滿成功，長期來看也造福市民。

雖然主辦世界博覽會有龐大的經濟利益，諸如提升觀光收入，但世博會也不能免於批評，例如，二〇一〇上海世博的規畫者就強迫一萬八千戶人家遷徙，以清出五點二八平方公里的土地供博覽會使用——創下史上占地最大紀錄。而世博會於去年十月落幕時，有超過五十座場館必須拆除——留下大量混凝土和鋼鐵亟待處理，這也替世博會引發了有關永續性的問題。不過，從好的一面來看，世博會可為主辦城市留下彌足珍貴的遺產。全世界最受遊客喜愛的地標之一，巴黎鐵塔，就是一八八九年為世界博覽會興建的。同樣地，西雅圖名聞遐邇的太空針塔原本是一九六二年萬國博覽會的象徵。這些都是對世博會奧妙世界的永恆證明。

Language Guide

The Origin of World's Fairs
世界博覽會起源

十九世紀正值西方殖民蓬勃階段，英國可謂當時殖民國的龍頭。為了展現雄厚國力，並與一八四四年法國在巴黎舉辦的「法國工業展」(French Industrial Exposition) 相互較勁，世界博覽會 (World's Fair) 在維多利亞女王 (Queen Victoria) 的全力支持下於一八五一年舉辦，取名為「各國工業大展」(The Great Exhibition of the Works of Industry of All Nations)，簡稱為「大博覽會」(The Great Exhibition)。參展品多來自英國，及當時的英國殖民地（澳洲、印度、紐西蘭），其次才是法國、丹麥、瑞士等等西方國家。

當 The Great Exhibition 舉辦地點為倫敦海德公園 (Hyde Park) 中的水晶宮 (The Crystal Palace)。以代表進步工業的鋼鐵與玻璃建造的水晶宮內巨木參天，暗示當時「人定勝天」戰勝自然的意識型態，為十九世紀的建築奇觀，也是工業革命的重要象徵建築。

水晶宮

Shaolin Temple

少林武功蓋天下
少林武功蓋天下

本單元圖片由中國少林寺提供

Vocabulary Bank

1) **monk** [mʌŋk] (n.) 和尚，修道士
A group of monks prayed at the temple.

2) **Buddhist** [ˋbudɪst] (a./n.) 佛教的；佛教徒
(n.) Buddhism [ˋbudɪzəm] 佛教
Thailand is famous for its Buddhist temples.

3) **feat** [fit] (n.) 技藝，武藝
The acrobats performed amazing feats of balance.

4) **endurance** [ɪnˋdʊrəns] (n.) 耐力
(v.) endure [ɪnˋdur] 忍耐，忍受
Running in a marathon takes great endurance.

5) **emphasis** [ˋɛmfəsɪs] (n.) 重點
(v.) emphasize [ˋɛmfə͵saɪz] 強調，注重
Schools should place more emphasis on math and science.

6) **compassion** [kəmˋpæʃən] (n.) 同情，慈悲
The doctor had great compassion for his patients.

7) **preach** [pritʃ] (v.) 講道，說教
The priest preached for over an hour last Sunday.

8) **dynasty** [ˋdaɪnəstɪ] (n.) 朝代
The Tang Dynasty lasted for nearly 300 years.

9) **meditation** [͵mɛdɪˋteʃən] (n.) 冥想，打坐
(v.) meditate [ˋmɛdɪ͵tet] 打坐
The Beatles traveled to India to learn meditation.

10) **demanding** [dɪˋmændɪŋ] (a.) 苛求的，高要求的
Teaching is very demanding work.

11) **foundation** [faʊnˋdeʃən] (n.) 基礎，根據
The course provides the foundation necessary for advanced study.

進階字彙

12) **monastery** [ˋmɑnə͵stɛrɪ] (n.) 僧院，男修道院
Monks still live at the ancient monastery.

13) **abbot** [ˋæbət] (n.) 住持，方丈；男修道院院長
The monks at the monastery gathered to elect a new abbot.

14) **enlightenment** [ɪnˋlaɪtņmənt] (n.) 頓悟，開化
The ultimate goal of Buddhism is enlightenment.

15) **stamina** [ˋstæmənə] (n.) 耐力，韌性
The boxer didn't have the stamina to last 12 rounds.

課文朗讀 MP3 58　單字朗讀 MP3 59　英文文章導讀 MP3 60

The Shaolin Temple, with its orange-robed fighting 1)**monks**, is perhaps the most famous 2)**Buddhist** 12)**monastery** in the world. By performing amazing 3)**feats** of skill, strength and 4)**endurance**, the Shaolin
5 monks have created a reputation as the ultimate kung fu fighters. And yet 2)**Buddhism** is generally considered a peaceful religion, with 5)**emphasis** on principles like non-violence and 6)**compassion**. Why, then, did the monks of Shaolin Temple become fighters?

10 According to legend, an Indian monk named Batuo came to China to 7)**preach** Buddhism in 480 A.D. Emperor Xiaowen of the Northern Wei 8)**Dynasty** was impressed with Batuo, and in 495 gave him land to build a monastery at Mt. Shaoshi, 30 miles from the capital
15 at Luoyang. He named it Shaolin Temple, which means "temple in the woods of Mt. Shaoshi." Thirty years later, another Indian monk, Bodhidharma, came to China to teach Buddhist 9)**meditation**. When the Shaolin 13)**abbot** turned him away, he went to live in a nearby
20 cave, where he 9)**meditated** for nine years until he achieved 14)**enlightenment**. Bodhidharma then returned to Shaolin Temple and founded Zen Buddhism, which 5)**emphasizes** meditation as a path to enlightenment.

When Bodhidharma began teaching meditation, he found that the monks were **① out of shape** from lack of exercise. As his meditation techniques were very [10]**demanding**, he designed a series of exercises to help them develop mental and physical [15]**stamina**. These exercises, which were based on the movements of animals, would later become the [11]**foundation** of Shaolin kung fu.

Mini Quiz 閱讀測驗

❶ ▨▨ When did Bodhidharma come to China?
(A) In 480
(B) In 495
(C) In 510
(D) In 525

❷ ▨▨ Why did Bodhidharma design a series of exercises?
(A) To teach the monks kung fu
(B) To get the monks in shape
(C) To study the movements of animals
(D) Because he was out of shape

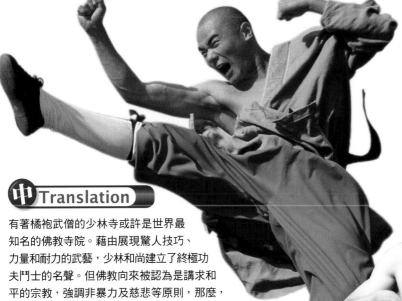

Tongue-tied No More

① out of shape 體能欠佳

shape 在這邊的意思不是「形狀」，而是指「經過鍛鍊的好體能」，若要形容某人體能狀況極佳，就可以用 in (good) shape 來表示，反之，out of shape 則表示體能欠佳。

A: How would you like to come hiking with us this Saturday?
你這星期六要跟我們一起去健行嗎？

B: I'd like to, but I'm really out of shape.
我想去，但我體力很差。

Language Guide

少林武功

天下武術源出少林，這「中國武術」Chinese martial arts 現在已經簡稱為 kung fu（功夫）了。想要介紹派別給外國人了解時，「門派」可用 sect 或 school。

少林拳法光是小說中就有七十二技（根據中國大陸官方網站，這個「技」英文是 unique skill），至於我們常說的「招式」可以用 move 或「技巧」technique 來表示。

另外，少林拳法講究內外兼修，所謂「內功」internal 就是指「氣」qi 的修練，有助於「外功」external 的力量。外功是有形的招式，而許多招式大多都是觀察動物行為演變而來，好比鶴形拳或蛇形拳。某某形拳可以用 style 這個字，虎形拳即稱 tiger style。至於少林的十八般武藝則是指十八種「兵器」weapon。

閱讀測驗解答 **❶ (B) ❷ (D)**

Translation

有著橘袍武僧的少林寺或許是世界最知名的佛教寺院。藉由展現驚人技巧、力量和耐力的武藝，少林和尚建立了終極功夫鬥士的名聲。但佛教向來被認為是講求和平的宗教，強調非暴力及慈悲等原則，那麼，為什麼少林寺的和尚會涉足武林呢？

根據傳說，一位名叫跋陀的印度僧侶在西元四八〇年來到中國宣揚佛教。北魏孝文帝對跋陀很敬佩，於西元四九五年賜給他一塊土地，在距離首都洛陽三十哩的少室山興建寺院。他替寺院取名為少林寺，意為「在少室山樹林間的寺院」。三十年後，另一位印度僧侶達摩來中國傳授佛教打坐。被少林方丈拒於門外後，他住在附近的洞穴，在此打坐九年直到頓悟，然後達摩回到少林寺，成立了禪宗，強調打坐為頓悟的途徑。

當達摩開始傳授打坐，他發現那些僧侶因缺乏運動而體力欠佳。由於他的打坐技巧極費心力，於是他設計了一套運動，幫助他們培養身心耐力。這一套以動物的動作為本的運動，後來便成為少林功夫的基礎。

Vocabulary Bank

1) **chaos** [ˋkeɑs] (n.) 混亂，雜亂
The country was in chaos after the war.

2) **evolve** [ɪˋvɑlv] (v.) 演變，演化
Is it true that humans evolved from apes?

3) **martial art** [ˋmɑrʃəl ɑrt] (n.) 武術
Tae kwon do is the most popular martial art in the world.

4) **defeat** [dɪˋfit] (v./n.) 戰勝，擊敗
The Americans defeated the Japanese in World War II.

5) **grateful** [ˋgretfəl] (a.) 感謝的，感激的
We felt grateful to be alive after the earthquake.

6) **fortune** [ˋfɔrtʃən] (n.) 命運，運氣。fortunes 為「運氣隨著時間的起伏」
The recession affected the fortunes of both political parties.

7) **destroy** [dɪˋstrɔɪ] (v.) 毀滅，破壞
The town was destroyed in the flood.

8) **rebellion** [rɪˋbɛljən] (n.) 叛亂，起義
The government sent in troops to put down the rebellion.

9) **pirate** [ˋpaɪrət] (n.) 海盜，盜版者
Many ships have been attacked by pirates in the Indian Ocean.

10) **revolution** [ˌrɛvəˋluʃən] (n.) 革命
Millions of people died during the Russian Revolution.

11) **promote** [prəˋmot] (v.) 促銷，宣傳
The band is on tour to promote their new album.

Tongue-tied No More

1 reach its/one's peak 達到巔峰

peak 是指「山頂，尖峰」，reach its/one's peak 可以用在表示某事物達到巔峰，或是某人處在最佳狀態，處於最高峰。

A: I think LeBron is the best player in the NBA.
我認為小皇帝詹姆斯是 NBA 最佳球員。

B: Yeah, and he hasn't even reached his peak yet.
對啊，而且他還沒達到巔峰。

The following century was a time of war and [1]**chaos,** and the Shaolin monks were often forced to fight to protect their temple. Over the years, their peaceful exercises [2]**evolved** into a [3]**martial art**, and they 5 became famous for their fighting skills. Early in the Tang Dynasty, a group of Shaolin monks helped the emperor's son, Li Shiming, [4]**defeat** an enemy general. Li Shiming was [5]**grateful** for their help, and when he later became emperor, he gave the monks land and even made one a 10 general in his army. The Shaolin Temple **1 reached its peak** during the Tang—at one point, it was home to over a thousand monks!

After the fall of the Tang, the [6]**fortunes** of Shaolin Temple rose and fell with the dynasties. The temple was 15 finally [7]**destroyed** during the Red Turban [8]**Rebellion** at the end of the Yuan Dynasty. By the Ming, though, the monks were back in business and helping the army fight Japanese [9]**pirates** on China's coast. Shaolin Temple was burned down again at the end of the Ming Dynasty, and 20 then destroyed and rebuilt several more times during the Qing.

Shaolin Temple's greatest challenge, however, came in modern times. Religion and martial arts were banned by the CCP, and Shaolin monks were beaten and jailed during the Cultural [10]**Revolution**. By the early '80s, there

25 were only a few monks left. But kung fu was becoming popular again, thanks to stars like Jackie Chan and Jet Li, whose *Shaolin Temple* was a huge hit in China. Under the current abbot, Shi Yongxin, the temple is more famous than ever. He's been so successful at [11]**promoting** the
30 Shaolin brand that he's even known as the "CEO monk."

Mini Quiz 閱讀測驗

❶ ▨ **Why were the Shaolin monks given land during the Tang Dynasty?**
(A) Because their temple was destroyed
(B) Because they dåeveloped a martial art
(C) Because Li Shiming was grateful for their help
(D) Because they were grateful for the emperor's help

❷ ▨ **In which dynasty was Shaolin Temple destroyed more than once?**
(A) The Tang
(B) The Yuan
(C) The Ming
(D) The Qing

中 Translation

接下來的世紀戰亂頻仍，少林僧侶常被迫動手來保衛他們的寺院。久而久之，他們平和的運動逐步演化成一門武術，他們也因對戰技巧聞名天下。唐朝初年，一群少林和尚幫助皇帝之子李世民擊敗敵人的將軍。李世民感激他們的協助，於是在他即位後賜予少林僧侶土地，甚至封其中一位為軍隊中的將軍。少林寺在唐朝攀達高峰——一度有上千名僧侶之多！

唐朝衰亡後，少林寺的命運隨朝代更迭而起落。寺院最後在元朝末年紅巾軍起義時遭摧毀。但僧侶們於明朝重起爐灶，協助軍隊在中國沿海抵禦日本倭寇。少林寺在明朝末年再度遭到焚毀，清朝期間則又歷經數度摧毀及重建。

但少林寺最大的挑戰出現於現代。中國共產黨嚴禁宗教及武術，少林僧侶也在文化大革命期間遭到毆打和囚禁。到了八〇年代初期，少林寺所剩的和尚寥寥無幾。所幸拜成龍和李連杰等明星之賜（李連杰的電影《少林寺》在中國十分賣座），中國功夫再次蔚為流行。在目前方丈釋永信領導下，少林寺比以往更為出名。他非常成功地推廣「少林品牌」，甚至被稱為「和尚 CEO」。

Language Guide

進入少林不是夢

想到少林寺學武術，並非一定得皈依佛門，不想剃度出家者，少林寺山腳下數十間的武術學校其實也是不錯的選擇，這些私人經營的武術學校雖然非直屬於少林寺，但練武生活一樣艱苦，學生必須住校、按表操課，除了修習武藝之外，還有電腦、語文等課程，每年學費約一至兩萬人民幣不等。

近年來，參觀少林寺也是相當熱門的旅遊行程，開放時間為早上八點至下午五點，門票一百元人民幣，民眾還可在門口自費找專業導遊為您進行沿路導覽。在這裡除了能欣賞每日固定的武術表演，還能到少林藥局買藥，少林寺特製的禪果和酥餅也是人手一袋的必備紀念品。

現任少林方丈——釋永信

釋永信一九六五年出生，俗名劉應成，十七歲即剃度出家，拜師少林；二十二歲承師衣缽，擔任少林寺管理委員會主任；三十六歲榮膺少林寺第三十代方丈，獲賜法號「永信」，成為少林寺史上最年輕的方丈。此外，釋永信也是中國首位取得 MBA 學位（Master of Business Administration，企業管理碩士）的僧人。他致力於推動少林文化，不但成立少林寺武僧團、少林影視公司等機構，為少林註冊商標，還跨足多項領域，如架設網站、經營素餐館、開發紀念品、舉辦中國功夫之星全球電視大賽等等，成功地將少林經營成一個品牌，並積極造訪世界各國推廣少林文化，目前已設立數十間少林寺海外中心。

《千年少林出世入世》一書收錄釋永信不為人知的少林智慧經營哲學（日月大好書屋提供）

閱讀測驗解答 ❶ (C) ❷ (D)

Human Resources

Managing the Human Side of Business

搞定員工大小事的 人力資源部

To the outside world, many companies appear to be large, faceless, and sometimes uncaring [1]**organizations**. This, of course, can be bad for business. To [2]**combat** this problem, companies spend millions on advertising [3]**campaigns** that [4]**portray** to [5]**consumers** a more positive, friendly [6]**corporate** image. But what about the people within those companies, the actual [7]**employees**, who may sometimes feel as though they work for an uncaring organization? This, too, can be bad for business. And to fight this problem, many companies have a special position: the Director of Human Resources.

At its most basic level, a human resources department is the [12]**intermediary** between a company's upper management and its employees. If employees have problems with other employees, or with the company itself, they can take the [8]**issue** up with someone in HR. It's the HR professional's job to [9]**ensure** that the problem is solved according to the company's policies. And this, hopefully, allows business to proceed as usual. But there's much more to an HR job than just that!

HR professionals wear many hats. Exactly which hats they wear depends largely on the size of the company they work for. In a small company, the HR professional will usually handle many

35 [10)**aspects** of employee relations: from hiring and firing, to questions about pay and company policies, and even disputes between coworkers. In short, the goal of the HR department is to keep employees happy and [11)**productive**.

中 Translation

對外界而言，許多公司看來都是規模龐大、沒有特色，有時甚至是冷漠的組織。這當然對公司不好。為了對抗這個問題，許多公司花了數百萬做廣告，向消費者描繪一個較正面、親切的企業形象。但這些公司裡面的人又是如何？這些公司的員工有時會覺得是在替冷漠的組織工作。這也對公司不好。而要對付這個問題，許多公司都設立了一個特別的職務：人力資源部主任。

人力資源部門最基本的工作是擔任公司管理高層和員工之間的橋梁。如果員工和其他員工，或與公司之間發生問題，他們可以找人力資源部的同仁商量，而人資人員的工作是確保問題會按照公司政策來解決，力求公司如常運作。不過，人力資源的工作不僅於此！

人資人員身負多重角色。至於到底有哪些角色，主要取決於公司的規模。在小公司，人資人員通常會處理許多跟員工關係相關的事務：從聘用、解雇，到處理薪資與公司政策相關問題，甚至是員工之間的糾紛。簡單說，人力資源部的目標是讓員工保持心情愉快、工作有效率。

V Vocabulary Bank

1) **organization** [ˌɔrgənəˋzeʃən] (n.) 組織，機構，團體
There are many aid organizations working in Africa.

2) **combat** [kəmˋbæt] (v.) 打擊，對抗
(n.) combat [ˋkɑmbæt] 戰鬥，反對
The candidate has promised to combat crime if elected.

3) **campaign** [kæmˋpen] (n.) 運動，活動
The government launched a campaign against drunk driving.

4) **portray** [porˋtre] (v.) 描寫，描繪
The book portrays the soldier as a hero.

5) **consumer** [kənˋsumə/kənˋsjumə] (n.) 消費者
Consumers are spending less during the recession.

6) **corporate** [ˋkɔrpərɪt] (a.) 企業的，公司的
Apple's corporate headquarters is in California.

7) **employee** [ɛmˋplɔɪi] (n.) 員工，受雇者
All full-time employees at the company receive health insurance.

8) **issue** [ˋɪʃu] (n.) 問題，爭議
We have several issues to discuss at today's meeting.

9) **ensure** [ɪnˋʃur] (v.) 確保，保證
Companies are required to ensure the safety of their products.

10) **aspect** [ˋæspɛkt] (n.) 方面
We must consider the various aspects of the problem.

11) **productive** [prəˋdʌktɪv] (a.) 有生產力的，多產的
Some employees are more productive than others.

進階字彙

12) **intermediary** [ˌɪntəˋmidɪˌɛrɪ] (n.) 中間者，媒介者
The diplomat acted as an intermediary between the two leaders.

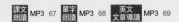 Vocabulary Bank

1) **correspondingly** [͵kɔrəˋspɑndɪŋlɪ] (adv.)
相應地
(v.) correspond [͵kɔrəˋspɑnd] 相應，符合
Real estate prices in wealthy countries are correspondingly high.

2) **specialist** [ˋspɛʃəlɪst] (n.) 專家，專員
(v.) specialize in [ˋspɛʃə͵laɪz ɪn] 專門從事
(n.) specialty [ˋspɛʃəltɪ] 專長，專業
The company hired a network specialist to set up its computer network.

3) **recruitment** [rɪˋkrutmənt] (n.) 聘用，徵募
(v.) recruit [rɪˋkrut] 聘用，徵募
Many companies are worried about rising recruitment costs.

4) **background** [ˋbæk͵graund] (n.) 背景，經歷
Does your company perform background checks on new employees?

5) **psychology** [saɪˋkɑlədʒɪ] (n.) 心理學，心理特質
It's important for coaches to have an understanding of sports psychology.

6) **asset** [ˋæsɛt] (n.) 才能，資產，有價值的條件
Richard's leadership skills are his greatest asset.

進階字彙

7) **multinational** [͵mʌltɪˋnæʃən]] (n./a.)
跨國公司；多國的，跨國公司的
Many multinationals are headquartered in the United States.

8) **Knack** [næk] (n.) 本領；訣竅
Daniel has a knack for finding simple solutions to complicated problems.

Tongue-tied No More

❶ divide sth. up 將……分類

divide 原本是「切割」的意思，根據某個準則切割事物，即為「分類」的意思，類似的表達也可以用 sort sth. 或是 classify/categorize sth.。
A: How should we organize all of these papers?
我們應該如何分類這些文件？
B: Let's divide them up by topic.
我們以主題來分類吧。

Large companies have ¹⁾**correspondingly** large HR departments, with many HR ²⁾**specialists** serving in different roles. It's not uncommon for a very large company, such as a ⁷⁾**multinational**, to have an HR department
5　❶ **divided up** into many smaller units, for example: ³⁾**Recruitment**, Training and Organizational Development.

Since most HR jobs are centered around working with people, those looking to enter the field should have a ⁸⁾**knack** for, or at least enjoy, this kind of work.
10　It's also a great field for people with varied interests, as ⁴⁾**backgrounds** in education, ⁵⁾**psychology**, business and management can all be considered ⁶⁾**assets**. Many students are attracted to the HR field for just this reason; they can ²⁾**specialize** in one or several fields, and then put
15　their ²⁾**specialties** to work helping a business show a more caring, human face to its workers.

中 Translation

大公司通常也有規模較大的人力資源部，由多位人資專員扮演不同角色。規模非常大的公司，如跨國企業，人資部門常分成許多較小單位，例如：召募、訓練及組織發展等。

由於人資工作大多牽涉人際互動，想進入這個領域的人應該具備這類工作的本領，或至少要喜歡作。對於興趣廣泛的人來說，這也是個很棒的領域，諸如教育、心理學、商業和管理等背景都被視為有利條件，許多學生就是因為如此才受到人資領域的吸引，他們可以專精一個或多個領域，然後將他們的專長應用於工作上，協助公司向員工展現更體貼、更有人性的面容。

Interview

What kind of person is suited to a career in HR?
Of course you need to enjoy working with people. But you also need to be able to handle conflict.

問：什麼樣的人適合走人資這條路？

答：當然你必須喜歡和人互動，但你也必須能夠處理衝突。

What advice would you give to a person wanting a career in HR?
Actually, I'd like to advise that more people consider entering the field! It seems many HR people only find their careers after trying to do other stuff first. For many students, aiming for an HR career is a perfect match for their skills and interests, even if they've never considered one.

問：你會給想走人資這行的人什麼建議？

答：其實，我希望有更多人考慮進入這個領域！許多人資人才似乎都先嘗試別的工作才進入人資這一行。對許多學生來說，以人資生涯為目標非常切合他們的技能和興趣，即使他們沒想過。

What's the most difficult part of your job?
Settling commission disputes. When two or more employees help to make a sale, it's not always clear who should get the commission or how it should be divided. Having money on the table sometimes brings out the worst in people. You just can't let it get to you.

問：你的工作最困難的部分是什麼？

答：解決佣金糾紛。如果一筆銷售有兩個以上的員工都有功勞，有時很難釐清誰該拿到佣金或佣金該怎麼分。談到錢，有時會帶出人性最黑暗的一面。只是能不讓自己受影響。

Did You Know? 人資行業知多少？

- HR professionals are sought for their strong communication and interpersonal skills. Backgrounds or experience in business administration, corporate organizational structure and mediation are also desired.
  人力資源專業人員必須有很強的溝通技巧和人際技巧，企業管理、企業組織架構及斡旋相關的背景或經驗，也是受青睞的條件。

- Entry-level HR jobs usually pay between $35,000 and $45,000. Those who've been in the field for many years can expect to make $70,000 or more a year.
  基層人資工作的年薪通常在三萬五千至四萬五千美元之間，在這個領域服務多年的人，年薪可望七萬美元以上。

- Level of education is a very important factor in the field. Many HR specialists suggest that an undergraduate degree is no longer adequate for the more competitive positions. They recommend Master's degrees.
  這個領域很重視教育程度。許多人資專家建議，大學文憑已不足以應徵競爭較激烈的職務，他們建議應具備碩士學歷。

V Vocabulary Bank

1) **impact** [`ɪmpækt] (v./n.) 影響，衝擊
High oil prices are impacting the economy.

2) **notable** [`notəbḷ] (a.) 著名的，顯要的，值得注意的
The collection includes stories by many notable authors.

3) **converted** [kən`vɜtɪd] (a.) 改變形態、用途的，改變信仰的
(v.) convert [kən`vɜt] 改變，轉換
The nightclub is located in a converted warehouse.

4) **modest** [`mɑdɪst] (a.) 不太大（多、顯眼的），適度的
It's hard to support a family on such a modest salary.

5) **negative** [`nɛgətɪv] (a.)〔數〕負的；負面的。positive [`pɑzətɪv] 即「正的，正面的」
We're learning about negative numbers in math class.

6) **influential** [ˌɪnflu`ɛnʃəl] (a.) 有影響力的，有支配力的
The reporter got a job at an influential newspaper.

7) **remotely** [rɪ`motlɪ] (adv.) 遠距地，遠端地
(a.) remote [rɪ`mot] 遠距的，遠端的
Surgeons are now able to perform operations remotely.

8) **random** [`rændəm] (a.) 隨機的
The results of this survey are based on a random sample of college students.

9) **access** [`æksɛs] (n.)（可以）使用，（可以）取得
Few students in Africa have access to computers.

10) **unrealistic** [ˌʌnriə`lɪstɪk] (a.) 不切實際的，不真實的
It's unrealistic to expect children to behave well all the time.

進階字彙

11) **lucrative** [`lukrətɪv] (a.) 賺錢的，有利可圖的
Real estate investing can be very lucrative.

12) **tutorial** [tu`tɔrɪəl] (n.) 教學單元，個別指導
(v./n.) tutor [`tutɚ] 教導；家教
Lots of free tutorials are available online.

The Power of Ideas
Youth Will Be Served!
用創意改變世界的青年創業家

課文朗讀 MP3 70　單字朗讀 MP3 71　英文文章導讀 MP3 72

More and more, young people are [1)]**impacting** the way we live and learn. Here are the stories and ideas of two of today's most [2)]**notable** young entrepreneurs.

Only a few years ago, Salman Khan was a successful hedge fund manager. With degrees from MIT and an MBA from Harvard, Khan had a bright—and [11)]**lucrative**—future ahead of him. Today, however, he spends his days in a [3)]**converted** closet at his [4)]**modest** California home posting video [12)]**tutorials** to his Khan Academy website. He doesn't get paid for this, and jokes that he's " **1** cash flow [5)]**negative**," but he's changing the world for hundreds of thousands of students worldwide. "It was a good day when his wife let him quit his job," said Bill Gates, one of Khan's more [6)]**influential** fans.

Khan's second career happened by accident. In 2004, his cousin Nadia was having trouble in her seventh-grade math class, so he volunteered to [12)]**tutor** her [7)]**remotely**. After encountering scheduling problems, Khan began putting short videos on YouTube that Nadia could watch on her own time. As luck would have it, 8)**random** people **2 stumbled upon** them and began watching. Encouraged by the positive feedback he received, Khan kept adding new videos.

Today, the site hosts over 1,800 free videos on math, science and economics that have been watched over 30 million times by people all around the globe. Khan's hope is that anyone in the world with a computer and 9)**access** to the Internet can go to the Khan Academy and get a world-class education. Given Khan's success so far, this goal may not be as 10)**unrealistic** as it seems.

Mini Quiz 閱讀測驗

❶ ▢▢ **Which of the following is true about Salman Khan?**
(A) He lives in a fancy house.
(B) He spends more money than he makes.
(C) He works as a hedge fund manager.
(D) He is Nadia's uncle.

❷ ▢▢ **Which of the following best describes the Khan Academy?**
(A) A public university
(B) A video tutorial
(C) A private prep school
(D) An educational website

🀄 Translation

年輕人來愈來愈影響我們的生活和學習方式。以下是其中兩位當今最知名年輕創業家的故事和理念。

不過才幾年前,薩曼罕是成功的避險基金經理人,擁有麻省理工學院的學位及哈佛企管碩士的他,前途——以及「錢」途——似錦。但如今,他每天都窩在加州簡樸的家中一個改裝過的更衣間裡,把教學影片上傳到他的罕學院網站。他這麼做並沒有酬勞,還打趣說他的「現金流量是負的」,但他正在改變全球數十萬學生的世界。「他妻子讓他辭職是大家的福氣,」比爾蓋茲說,他是薩曼罕最有權勢的粉絲之一。

薩曼罕的第二個事業是偶然發生的。二○○四年,他表妹娜迪雅的七年級數學課聽不懂,所以他自願提供遠距教學。由於時間兜不上,薩曼罕開始把短片上傳到 YouTube,讓娜迪雅可以自己利用時間看。碰巧,隨機點選的網友偶然發現這些短片,開始觀看。受到正面回應的鼓舞,薩曼罕不斷增加新影片。

如今,那個網站收錄了一千八百多段免費影片,數學、科學和經濟學都有,全球各地已有超過三千萬人次觀看。薩曼罕的願望是,世上任何一個有電腦、能上網的人都能前往罕學院,接受世界級的教育。從薩曼罕目前為止的成就看來,這個目標或許沒有乍看下那麼不切實際。

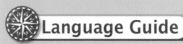

☠ Tongue-tied No More

1 cash flow negative
入不敷出,赤字虧損
cash flow 表示「現金流量」,也就是一連串的現金收入與支出,negative 表示「負數的」,所以 cash flow negative 即表示支出大於收入的賠錢狀態,也可以寫成 (a) negative cash flow。
A: How's your store doing these days? Is business picking up?
你的店最近還好嗎?生意有起色了嗎?
B: Well, business is better than before, but we're still cash flow negative.
嗯,生意比之前好,但我們還在虧損。

2 stumble upon/on/across/into
偶然碰見,偶然發現
stumble 原意是「不小心絆倒,失足」,引申解釋為「無意間偶然發現」,後面介系詞 upon、on、across、into 可相互替換。
A: This book is really rare! Where did you find it?
這本書很稀少!你在哪找到的?
B: I stumbled on it at a used book store.
我在二手書店偶然發現的。

🧭 Language Guide

hedge fund 避險基金
所謂的「基金」fund 就是大眾集資,這筆由一群投資人集資的錢會交給基金公司,由基金公司的理財專家投資管理此筆金錢,投資獲利時會讓投資大眾分享,賠錢時也由大眾分擔。

基金的種類繁多,「避險基金」hedge fund 即為其中一種,也稱為對沖基金或套利基金,hedge 表示「防護,保衛」,但其實避險基金並非如字面上所言毫無風險,只不過它是利用一些投資策略來規避大部分市場風險,與完全取決於市場走勢的一般基金不同,但也由於避險基金的發展彈性極廣,所以必須相當仰賴經理人的專業操作技術以及經驗,風險不小。一般的基金經理人是依基金淨值收取固定比例的管理費,但避險基金經理人則是由操作利潤中賺取管理費,績效良好時收入可觀。

閱讀測驗解答 ❶ (B) ❷ (D)

Know it ALL 英文閱讀

Vocabulary Bank

1) **revolutionize** [ˌrɛvəˈluʃəˌnaɪz] (v.) 徹底變革
(n.) revolution [ˌrɛvəˈluʃən] 革命
Cell phones have revolutionized the way people communicate.

2) **dorm** [dɔrm] (n.) 宿舍，為 dormitory
[ˈdɔrmɪˌtori] 的簡稱
Would you rather live in the dorms or rent an apartment?

3) **inspiration** [ˌɪnspəˈreʃən] (n.) 靈感，啟發
Where do you get the inspiration for your songs?

4) **directory** [dəˈrɛktəri] (n.) 名冊簿
Employees' extension numbers and e-mail addresses are listed in the personnel directory.

5) **registered** [ˈrɛgɪstəd] (a.) 註冊的，登記過的
(v.) register [ˈrɛgɪstə] 註冊，登記
Are you a registered voter?

6) **dispute** [dɪˈspjut] (n./v.) 爭論，爭端
Negotiations were held to resolve the international dispute.

7) **breakup** [ˈbrek.ʌp] (n.) 分手，（婚姻）破裂
Paul and Teresa haven't spoken since their breakup.

8) **promotion** [prəˈmoʃən] (n.) 升遷，促銷
Did you get the promotion you were hoping for?

9) **trivial** [ˈtrɪvɪəl] (a.) 不重要的，瑣碎的
You shouldn't get upset about such a trivial matter.

進階字彙

10) **co-founder** [ˈkoˌfaʊndə] (n.) 共同創辦人，
也可寫作 cofounder
Bill Gates is a co-founder of Microsoft.

11) **networking** [ˈnɛt.wɝkɪŋ] (n.) 建立人脈網絡
Megan found her job through networking.

12) **skyrocket** [ˈskaɪˌrɑkɪt] (v.) 飛漲，猛漲
The cost of healthcare is skyrocketing.

13) **headshot** [ˈhɛd.ʃɑt] (n.) 大頭照
Should I attach a headshot to my résumé?

Tongue-tied No More

1 go public（公司）股票上市
go public 除了解釋為「將祕密公開」，還可以表示某公司股票正式掛牌上市，開放讓一般民眾投資購買該公司股票，巨額的資金湧入，將會為公司帶來可觀的財富。
A: Why did the company go public?
為什麼這間公司要股票上市？
B: They wanted to raise money to expand their operations.
他們想募資金擴大營運。

課文朗讀 MP3 73　單字朗讀 MP3 74　英文文章導讀 MP3 75

At the same time that Salman Khan is helping change the way people learn, Mark Zuckerberg, [10]**co-founder** and CEO of social [11]**networking** site Facebook, is [1]**revolutionizing** the way people connect. At just 26, Zuckerberg is the world's
5　youngest billionaire, and should Facebook **1 go public**, his wealth would [12]**skyrocket**. Despite his youth, Zuckerberg was ranked No. 1 on *Vanity Fair*'s recent list of the most influential people of the Information Age.

While Google and Apple were famously started in
10　garages, the idea for Facebook was hatched in a Harvard [2]**dorm**. [3]**Inspiration** likely came from the student [4]**directory** published by Phillips Exeter Academy, the elite boarding school Zuckerberg attended for two years. It included [13]**headshots** alongside students' personal
15　information, and was commonly called the "Face Book." At Harvard, Zuckerberg and his friends adapted the concept and put it online in early 2004. At first limited to Harvard students, the site quickly spread to other schools. Now, six short years later, Facebook has become the second most popular site on
20　the Internet (after Google), with over 500 million [5]**registered** users.

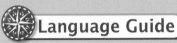

These days, the influence and impact of Facebook is **❷ beyond** [6)]**dispute**. Ordinary people everywhere, both young and old, log in to announce major events like births,

25 marriages, [7)]**breakups** and [8)]**promotions**, as well as [9)]**trivial** information like what they had for breakfast that day, or what happened at school or work. We have Mark Zuckerberg to thank for this current trend of sharing (or over-sharing as the case may be). So, perhaps the most appropriate question

30 now is, what will he come up with next?

Mini Quiz 閱讀測驗

❶ ___ **Which of the following is true about Mark Zuckerberg?**
(A) He published a student directory at boarding school.
(B) He is the world's youngest millionaire.
(C) He went to Phillips Exeter Academy.
(D) He is the sole founder of Facebook.

❷ ___ **What do Khan and Zuckerberg have in common?**
(A) They are both young and wealthy.
(B) They are both Harvard graduates.
(C) They both started influential websites.
(D) They both went to boarding school.

中 Translation

在薩曼罕協助改變人們學習方式的同時，社群網站臉書的共同創辦人和執行長馬克佐克柏，也徹底改變人們聯繫的方式。年僅二十六歲，佐克柏已經是全球最年輕的億萬富翁，如果臉書股票上市，他的財富更將一飛沖天。儘管還這麼年輕，佐克柏已經榮登《浮華世界》雜誌最近評選的資訊時代最具影響力人士第一名。

眾所皆知，Google 及蘋果公司都是在車庫裡誕生的，臉書的概念則是在哈佛宿舍裡孵化出來，靈感可能來自菲立普艾克瑟特學院出版的學生名冊──佐克柏曾在那所菁英寄宿學校兩年。名冊中除了學生的個人資訊，還有每個人的大頭照，因此常被稱為「臉書」。就讀於哈佛時，佐克柏和友人應用了這個概念，在二〇〇四年初放上網路，一開始僅限哈佛學生使用，但隨即快速擴展至其他學校。如今，短短六年後，臉書已成為網際網路第二受歡迎的網站（僅次於 Google），註冊會員人數超過五億。

如今，臉書的影響力和衝擊毋庸置疑。全球各地的老百姓，不分老少，都登入臉書宣布大事，例如生小孩、結婚、分手和升遷等，還有瑣碎的小事，例如他們那天早餐吃什麼，學校或公司發生了什麼等。我們要感謝佐克柏創造了這股分享的趨勢（或許有點過度分享），因此，或許現在最適合的問題是，他接下來會想出什麼點子？

🧭 Language Guide

***Vanity Fair* 雜誌**
Vanity Fair《浮華世界》（或稱《名利場》）於一九一三年由康得納斯出版公司 (Condé Nast Publications Inc.) 出版，旗下尚有 *Vogue*、*GQ* 等知名時尚雜誌。最初的《浮華世界》以報導上流社會的生活、宴會、藝術等內容為主，如今《浮華世界》轉型更趨多樣化，結合了美國文化、時尚、娛樂和政治等多元主題，也曾多次被評選為「最暢銷雜誌」，《浮華世界》不僅是明星幕後推手、華府政客必讀刊物，也是追名逐利的芸芸眾生展望世界的重要窗口。

車庫傳奇
市值高達千億美元的 Google 是在一九九六年由當時年僅二十五歲的兩位史丹福大學博士候選人布林 (Sergey Brin) 和佩吉 (Larry Page) 在車庫所創立，這棟位於舊金山西岸門洛公園市 (Menlo Park) 的房子目前已被 Google 公司買下，而當年房東現在是 Google 的產品管理部副總裁。雖然 Google 的創業車庫還不算是歷史古蹟，但已有不少遊客特地到此拍照留念。

同樣從車庫起家而為人津津樂道的傳奇還有惠普與蘋果公司。惠普出自加州帕羅奧多市 (Palo Alto) 一間車庫，不遠的洛斯阿圖斯市 (Los Altos) 則有賈伯斯 (Steve Jobs) 與沃茲尼克 (Steve Wozniak) 用數條電纜和簡易配備創立蘋果電腦時的車庫。

Google 的創辦倉庫

Add as Friend

A World in 3D

虛擬 3D 世界

課文朗讀 MP3 76　單字朗讀 MP3 77　英文文章導讀 MP3 78

What is 3D?

Imagine that you're sitting in a cool, ᶜair-conditioned ¹⁾**cinema** eating popcorn and sipping a soda. The lights ⁶⁾**dim** and the movie starts. Suddenly, a car speeds toward you and just about hits you! A monster appears to jump
5　out of the screen, making you jump out of your seat! The action is so amazing that you feel like you're not just watching the movie; you're somehow *in* the movie! Welcome to the thrilling world of 3D.

3D is short for the three ²⁾**dimensions**: height, width
10　and depth. This is how most people see the world. We can tell how tall or wide an object is, as well as how thick or far away it may be. However, this is not always the case when watching a movie or TV. Since screens are flat, it isn't easy to judge depth or distance. So movie directors and studios

began considering the problem of ⁶how to make movies

15 more ³⁾**realistic**.

The answer, of course, was to ⁴⁾**integrate** technology to create the illusion of depth. Starting in the 1950s, directors used special cameras to record images from two perspectives. Theaters then showed the movie using

20 special projectors, and the audience even wore special glasses with red and blue lenses to ⁵⁾**filter** the images on the screen. While the technology was not exactly new— ⁷⁾**stereoscopic** photography, on which it is based, had been invented over one hundred years earlier—audiences found

25 watching movies in 3D ⁸⁾**incredibly** exciting.

Mini Quiz 閱讀測驗

❶ ____ **Which extra dimension do 3D movies have?**
(A) height
(B) width
(C) depth
(D) time

❷ ____ **What did directors do to create the illusion of depth?**
(A) Wear glasses with red and blue lenses
(B) Show movies with special projectors
(C) Make movies more realistic
(D) Film images from different angles

中 Translation

什麼是 3D

想像你正坐在一間涼爽有冷氣的電影院，吃著爆米花、喝著汽水。燈光暗下來，電影開始。忽然，一部汽車飛快朝你衝過來，差點撞到你！一隻怪獸看似跳出銀幕，讓你嚇得從椅子上跳起來！這些動作如此驚心動魄，讓你覺得自己不只是在看電影，而是人在電影中！歡迎來到刺激的 3D 世界。

3D 是 three dimensions（三度空間）的簡稱：高度、寬度和深度。這是多數人感受世界的方式。我們可以分辨一個物體有多高或多寬，以及多厚或可能距離多遠。不過，看電影或電視時可見不得如此。因為銀幕是平的，我們不容易判斷深度或距離。於是電影導演和電影公司開始思考如何讓電影更逼真的問題。

答案當然就是整合科技來創造深度的錯覺。一九五〇年代開始，導演開始運用特殊的攝影機，從兩種角度錄下影像，接著戲院會用特殊的投影機來播放電影，觀眾甚至得戴上紅、藍鏡片的特殊眼鏡來過濾銀幕上的影像。雖然這種技術不算新——它的基礎「立體攝影」在一百多年之前便已發明——但觀眾仍覺得觀賞 3D 電影分外令人興奮。

Grammar Master

複合形容詞：「名詞＋過去分詞」

複合形容詞就是由兩個字中間加上連字號而成的形容詞，複合形容詞的兩個字有幾種固定的組合方式，課文第一句使用的是 air（空氣）＋ conditioned（被調節）＝「有空調的」這種組合。

例 a **remote-controlled** robot
遙控機器人

例 a **self-centered** person
自我中心的人

注意有一些複合形容詞因為使用頻率非常高，所以把連字號拿掉，直接兩個字變成一個字：

例 a **handmade** cabinet
手工的櫃子

例 a **heartbroken** girl
心碎的女孩

名詞片語：疑問詞＋不定詞

名詞片語的功能就像是名詞，可以是句子的主詞、受詞或接在 be 動詞後面做補語。要注意疑問詞若是 how、when、where，不定詞後面要有另外的受詞，疑問詞若是 what、which、whom，不定詞後面則不能有另外的受詞。

例 Do you know **how to ride** a horse?
你會騎馬嗎？

例 Don't tell me **what to do**.
不要命令我。

翻譯練習

1. Rick 是個非常有自信的人。

_____

2. 我無法決定要去哪度假。

_____

閱讀測驗解答 ❶ (D) ❷ (C)
翻譯練習解答
1. Rick is a very self-confident person.
2. I can't decide where to go on my vacation.

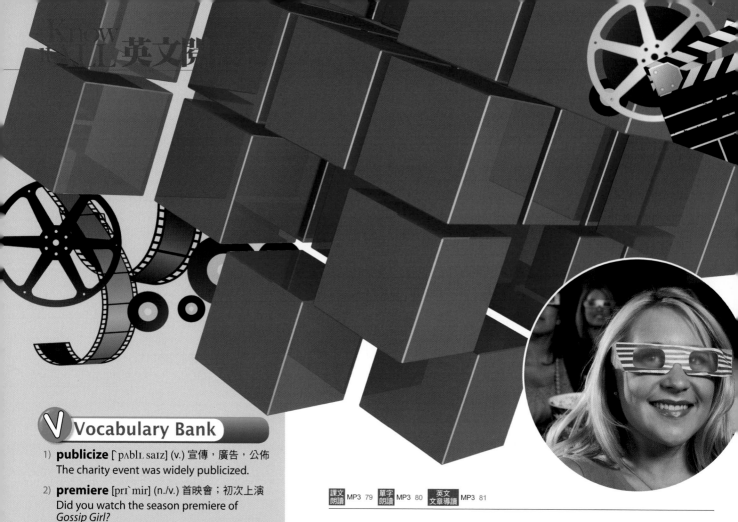

Vocabulary Bank

1) **publicize** [ˋpʌblɪˌsaɪz] (v.) 宣傳，廣告，公佈
The charity event was widely publicized.

2) **premiere** [prɪˋmɪr] (n./v.) 首映會；初次上演
Did you watch the season premiere of *Gossip Girl?*

3) **flicker out** [ˋflɪkɚ aʊt] (phr.) 逐漸熄滅，逐漸消失
The candle flickered out, leaving the room in darkness.

4) **subsequent** [ˋsʌbsɪˌkwənt] (a.) 隨後的，後續的
We'll keep you informed about subsequent developments.

5) **occasional** [əˋkeʒən!] (a.) 偶爾的
Most people have occasional headaches.

6) **mainstream** [ˋmenˌstrim] (n./a.) 主流（的）
The singer's music is popular with mainstream audiences.

7) **innovative** [ˋɪnəˌvetɪv] (a.) 創新的
Apple is famous for its innovative products.

8) **visual** [ˋvɪʒuəl] (a.) 視覺的
Did you use visual materials in your presentation?

9) **prompt** [prɑmpt] (v.) 引發，促使
What prompted Sarah to change her mind?

進階字彙

10) **craze** [krez] (n.) 風潮，熱潮
3D TV is the latest craze.

11) **hit** [hɪt] (n.) 成功而風行一時的事物
The band had a string of hits in the 1990s.

12) **mining** [ˋmaɪnɪŋ] (n.) 採礦
Copper mining is Chile's largest industry.

課文朗讀 MP3 79　單字朗讀 MP3 80　英文文章導讀 MP3 81

The History of 3D

The 1952 film *Bwana Devil* ᴳis widely considered to be the first American 3D motion picture. To [1]**publicize** the realism of 3D, the poster read, "A LION in your lap! A LOVER in your arms!" *Bwana Devil* started a wave of 3D
5 moviemaking, and a photograph of the audience wearing 3D glasses taken at the [2]**premiere** is one of the most famous images of the 1950s.

Studios rushed to ᴳcash in. 1953 saw the release of 27 full-length 3D films, including Vincent Price's *House*
10 *of Wax*, a masterpiece of horror. *Creature from the Black Lagoon*, another great 3D horror movie, came out a year later. But as quickly as the [10]**craze** began, it [3]**flickered out**. Only one 3D movie came out in 1955, and [4]**subsequent** years saw only [5]**occasional** releases. 3D comics enjoyed a
15 similar, brief success in the early 1950s, but like 3D films, never caught on completely. After showing initial promise, 3D had become a niche market.

Fast-forward to 2009 when the sci-fi ¹¹⁾**hit** *Avatar* brought 3D back into the ⁶⁾**mainstream**. Directed by

20 James Cameron, *Avatar* is set in the year 2154 and tells the story of how man's ¹²⁾**mining** activities on a distant planet threaten the native Na'vi people. The ⁷⁾**innovative** 3D effects were created by shooting each scene with two cameras, resulting in a stereo image. The stunning ⁸⁾**visual**

25 effects, which won the movie an Oscar, ⁹⁾**prompted** critics to suggest that after *Avatar*, filmmaking would never be the same.

Mini Quiz 閱讀測驗

❶ **According to the passage, which of the following is true about *Bwana Devil*?**
(A) It started a 3D movie trend.
(B) It was the first 3D film ever made.
(C) It was one of the most famous films of the 1950s.
(D) It was based on a true story.

❷ **When were 3D films probably the most popular?**
(A) In the late 1950s
(B) In 2009
(C) In the early 1950s
(D) In the mid-1950s

中 Translation

3D 歷史

一九五二年的電影《布瓦納魔鬼》被公認為是美國 3D 電影的鼻祖。為宣傳 3D 的逼真效果，電影海報上寫著：「獅子坐在你腿上！愛人躺在你懷中！」《布瓦納魔鬼》開啟了製作 3D 電影的浪潮，一九五○年代最著名的影像之一，正是觀眾戴著 3D 眼鏡參加電影首映的照片。

電影公司趕著大撈一票。一九五三年共有二十七部 3D 劇情長片上映，包括文生普萊斯的驚悚大作《恐怖蠟像館》。另一部出色的 3D 恐怖片《黑湖妖潭》則在一年後問世。但這股熱潮來得急，去得也快。一九五五年只推出一部 3D 電影，之後多年更只有零星的片子上映。3D 漫畫在一九五○年代初期也享有同樣短暫的成功，但就像 3D 電影一樣，從來沒有蔚為流行。在最初的熱潮消退後，3D 已成為小眾市場。

快轉到二○○九年，科幻賣作片《阿凡達》將 3D 帶回主流。由詹姆士卡麥隆執導的《阿凡達》，場景設在二一五四年，敘述人類在一座遙遠星球的採礦活動如何威脅當地娜美人的生活。該片用兩部攝影機拍攝每一個場景，形成立體影像，創造出創新的 3D 特效。令人驚豔的視覺效果為本片拿下奧斯卡獎，也讓影評人認為在《阿凡達》之後，電影製作已進入嶄新境界。

Ⓥ Vocabulary Bank

1) **cardboard** [ˋkɑrd͵bord] (a./n.) 硬紙板（的）
We packed all our belongings in cardboard boxes.

2) **update** [ʌpˋdet] (v.) 更新
[ˋʌp͵det] (n.) 更新
The website is updated once a week.

3) **enhance** [ɪnˋhæns] (v.) 提高（價值），提升（品質）
The government is working to enhance water quality.

4) **logical** [ˋlɑdʒɪkl] (a.) 有邏輯的，合理的
Children should be taught logical thinking in school.

5) **content** [ˋkɑntɛnt] (n.) 內容
The film contains adult content.

6) **revitalize** [riˋvaɪt͵aɪz] (v.)
使恢復生氣，使復甦
(a.) vital [ˋvaɪtl] 充滿活力的，不可或缺的
The government hopes the stimulus plan will revitalize the economy.

7) **realization** [͵riələˋzeʃən] (n.) 實現，體現
The realization of the plan took nearly a year.

進階字彙

8) **gimmick** [ˋgɪmɪk] (n.) 噱頭
The contest is just a sales gimmick.

傳統紅藍3D眼鏡 cardboard glasses with red and blue lenses
© Snaily / commons.wikimedia.org

課文朗讀 MP3 82　單字朗讀 MP3 83　英文文章導讀 MP3 84

The Future of 3D

3D technology ⓖhas come a long way since the 1950s. The original ¹⁾**cardboard** glasses ⓖhave been ²⁾**updated**, and now computers can significantly ³⁾**enhance** or even create 3D effects. IMAX theaters, with their impressive
5　sound systems and huge screens, ⓖhave also helped make 3D popular again. In fact, studios are planning to release dozens of new 3D movies in the near future, including *Transformers 3* (2011) and *Men in Black III* (2012).

Following the success of *Avatar*, media companies
10　are looking to ❶ **ride this** second 3D **wave**, and ⓖhave expanded well beyond the movies. Last season, Sky TV in the U.K. broadcast Premier League soccer matches in 3D, and Taiwanese fans were treated to select 2010 FIFA World Cup games in 3D as well. Musicians ⓖhave also ❷ **gotten**
15　**into the act**. The Irish rock band U2 released a concert film, *U2 3D*, in 2008, and pop stars like Lady Gaga and the Jonas Brothers are among the many artists experimenting with 3D.

So what does the future hold for 3D? Now that pretty much everyone has high-definition TV, 3D HDTV seems like

20 the next 4)**logical** step. The next generation of the Internet also promises to be 3D-ready. Perhaps introducing 3D 5)**content** is a way to 6)**revitalize** the troubled newspaper industry. It's still possible, though, that 3D may return to being just a 8)**gimmick**—the idea of it being superior to

25 the 7)**realization**. Time will tell, but don't be shocked if you see people wearing 3D glasses on the street one day soon.

Mini Quiz 閱讀測驗

❶ ___ **According to the passage, which of the following are NOT taking advantage of the new popularity of 3D?**
(A) Pop entertainers
(B) Taiwanese soccer players
(C) Media companies
(D) A British television network

❷ ___ **Which of the following does the author think will most likely happen in the future?**
(A) People will wear 3D glasses on the street.
(B) 3D will return to being just an idea.
(C) Newspapers will be published in 3D.
(D) There will be 3D high-definition televisions.

中 Translation

3D 未來發展

自一九五〇年代以來，3D 技術已有長足進步。原有的紙板眼鏡已經更新，現在電腦也能大幅提升甚至創造 3D 效果。以驚人音響系統和超大銀幕著稱的 IMAX 劇院，也有助於 3D 東山再起。事實上，電影公司正計畫在不久的未來推出數十部新的 3D 電影，包括《變形金剛 3》（二〇一一年上映）及《星際戰警 3》（二〇一二年上映）。

《阿凡達》成功之後，媒體公司期待搭上這第二波的 3D 浪潮，並拓展至電影以外的領域。上個球季，英國天空衛視用 3D 播出英國超級足球聯賽，台灣球迷也能以 3D 觀看二〇一〇年世界盃足球賽的精選。音樂家也參上一腳。愛爾蘭搖滾樂團 U2 在二〇〇八年推出演唱會影片《U2 3D》，流行巨星女神卡卡和強納斯兄弟等等諸多藝人也正「以身試 3D」。

那麼，3D 的前景究竟如何？現在幾乎人人家裡都有高畫質電視，3D 的高畫質電視似乎就是合理的下一步了。下一代國際網路也可望具備 3D 功能。或許推出 3D 內容也是振興低迷報紙產業的一條途徑。不過，3D 也有可能到最後只是個噱頭——它的概念勝於實現。時間會給我們答案，但如果你不久之後在街上看到有人戴 3D 眼鏡，可別太驚訝就是了。

😛 Tongue-tied No More

1 ride the wave 趁勢而起

所謂「時勢造英雄」，「時勢」就是這裡的 wave，「站上浪頭」ride the wave 的人就能借浪推升向上而成功，ride (on) the wave of... 就是「參與……的熱潮」。而 catch the wave 則表示「試著趕上……的熱潮」。

A: Oh, no! Not another stupid reality show!
糟了！別又來一個愚蠢的真人實境秀！
B: Yeah, it seems like all the networks are riding the reality wave.
沒錯，似乎各家電視網都搭上這股實境秀熱潮了。

2 get into the act 中途加入

act 當名詞是「行動」，get into the act 表示中途加入進行中的活動或計畫，也可以說 get in on the act。

A: Wow! All these phones look just like iPhones.
哇！這些手機看起來都跟 iPhone 好像。
B: Yeah, everybody's trying to get into the smart phone act.
對啊，大家都想進入智慧型手機市場。

Grammar Master

現在完成式

「現在完成式」是指截至目前為止，目前仍在繼續的情況。

句型 主詞＋ have/has ＋ p.p. ...

例 A man **has fallen** into the well.
有一個男人掉進井裡了。

易混淆句型

● 詢問過去的經驗
Have you ever been to...?
你是否曾去過……？

● 陳述既有的經驗
S+ has + been to....
某人已經去過……。

例 **Have** you **ever been** to London?
你去過倫敦嗎？

例 **I've been** to London twice.
我去過倫敦兩次了。

翻譯練習

Tom 住在這裡八年了。

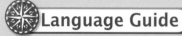 Vocabulary Bank

1) **explanation** [ˌɛkspləˋneʃən] (n.) 說明，解釋
(v.) explain [ɪksˋplen]
Did you understand the teacher's explanation?

2) **evolutionary** [ˌɛvəˋluʃəˌnɛrɪ] (a.) 發展的，進化的 (n.) evolution [ˌɛvəˋluʃən] 發展，演化，進化
The researcher is an expert in evolutionary biology.

3) **descend from** [dɪˋsɛnd frʌm] (phr.) 起源於，是…的後裔
It has been proven that birds are descended from dinosaurs.

4) **hatch** [hætʃ] (v.) 孵化
It takes about a month for duck eggs to hatch.

5) **riddle** [ˋrɪdḷ] (n.) 謎，謎語
Scientists are working to solve the riddle of why bees are disappearing.

6) **protein** [ˋprotin] (n.) 蛋白質
Most Americans have a high protein diet.

7) **crystal** [ˋkrɪstḷ] (n.) 結晶體，水晶
Some clouds are made of tiny ice crystals.

8) **clamp** [klæmp] (n./v.) 夾子；夾住
The lamp is attached to the desk with a clamp.

9) **particle** [ˋpartɪkḷ] (n.) 微粒，粒子
Smoke contains tiny particles of ash.

10) **calcium carbonate** [ˋkælsiəm ˋkarbəˌnet] (phr.) 碳酸鈣
Calcium carbonate is used as a toothpaste ingredient.

11) **formation** [fɔrˋmeʃən] (n.) 形成，組成
The formation of snowflakes is a complex process.

進階字彙

12) **theological** [ˌθiəˋladʒɪkḷ] (n.) 神學的
Father Reilly teaches at a local theological college.

13) **prior to** [ˋpraɪɚ tə] (n.) 在…以前
Prior to moving here, Lisa lived in Colorado.

14) **simulate** [ˋsɪmjəˌlet] (v.) 模擬，模仿
Scientists use computer models to simulate climate change.

15) **ovary** [ˋovərɪ] (n.) 卵巢
Women's ovaries release one egg each month.

Language Guide

calcite 方解石
calcite [ˋkælsaɪt] 是狀態最穩定的碳酸鹽 (CaCO₃) 礦物，舉凡石灰岩、大理石和鐘乳石的主要成分均為方解石。方解石透過生物學作用，能形成貝殼、珊瑚礁及蛋殼。

calcite

Which Came First, the Chicken or the Egg?

雞生蛋？蛋生雞？

課文朗讀 MP3 85　單字朗讀 MP3 86　英文文章導讀 MP3 87

This mystery of life ©has been the focus of debate for centuries. Arguments include the 12)**theological** 1)**explanation** that God created all animals in seven days, not eggs; and the 2)**evolutionary** argument that
5　chickens 3)**descended from** dinosaurs, which also 4)**hatched** from eggs. At last, researchers at the University of Warwick and the University of Sheffield in England have found an answer to the 5)**riddle** based on scientific findings.

By using a supercomputer and a powerful computing
10　tool called metadynamics, the researchers were able

to observe the role that the [6)]**protein** ovocledidin-17 (OC-17) plays in the development of the egg's hard shell. [13)]**Prior to** this research, it was unclear how OC-17 encouraged the growth of calcite [7)]**crystals** to

15 form an actual eggshell in such a short amount of time (eggshells are formed literally overnight). The information from the supercomputer helped the researchers [14)]**simulate** [G)]**the way OC-17** acts as a chemical [8)]**clamp**, holding [9)]**particles** of [10)]**calcium carbonate**

20 together to encourage the [11)]**formation** of calcite crystals.

OC-17 can only be found in a chicken's [15)]**ovaries**, and without this protein, the eggshell can't form. Therefore, the egg can only exist if it has been created inside a chicken. Perhaps the 21st century version of the question should be

25 "Which came first, the chicken or the OC-17?"

Mini Quiz 閱讀測驗

❶ [ ] **Which of the following can be concluded from the article?**
(A) The egg came before the chicken.
(B) The chicken came before the egg.
(C) Egg shells are made out of OC-17.
(D) The chicken came before the OC-17.

中 Translation

千百年來，這個生命之謎向來是人們辯論的焦點。各類論述包括神學論——是上帝在七天內創造所有動物，不是卵；以及進化論——雞是從恐龍演化而來，而恐龍也是從蛋孵化的。終於，英國瓦威克及薛菲德大學的研究人員根據科學發現，找到了這道謎題的答案。

運用一部超級電腦和一部名為「元動力學」的強大計算工具，研究人員觀察到蛋白質 OC-17 在堅硬蛋殼形成過程中扮演的角色。在此研究之前，我們仍不了解 OC-17 是如何促進方解石晶體成長，而短短時間內就形成真正的蛋殼（蛋殼確實是在一夕之間形成的）。從超級電腦得來的這些資訊，協助研究人員模擬 OC-17 如何像個化學鉗一樣，將碳酸鈣的分子聚合起來，形成方解石晶體。

只有雞的卵巢內才有 OC-17，若沒有這種蛋白質，蛋殼就不可能生成。因此，唯有在雞的體內形成，蛋才有可能存在。或許二十一世紀版的雞蛋問題應改成「是先有雞，還是先有 OC-17 ？」

Grammar Master

S + have/has been... 一直都是……

現在完成式 have/has been 用來表示從過去一直到現在為止持續的狀態。

This mystery of life has been the focus of debate for centuries.
now

been 是表示狀態 be 動詞的 p.p.。在這樣的描述中，狀態或許會持續到未來，因此通常和不明確的時間連用（例：文中的 for + 一段時間、not yet「尚未」、already「已經」、just「剛剛」……）。

例 Archeologists have long been fascinated by the mysteries of the pyramids.
考古學家一直深受金字塔之謎的吸引。

過去的某時間點　　now

這類的表達也可以用「since + 過去簡單式 / 過去時間」來說明狀態是由過去的何時開始。

例 I've been living in Taipei since I graduated from university.
我自從大學畢業後就一直住在台北。

the way S +V... ……的方式 / 狀態

the way S+V 可以用來描述主詞 (OC-17) 的狀態 (acts as a chemical clamp)。我們可以把它看作是一個名詞 (The way OC-17 acts as a chemical clamp)，再進行補述。

例 The way she does things annoys her co-workers.
她的行事作風已經惹惱了她的同事。

翻譯練習

1. 她已經學法文三年了。

_____

_____

2. 他開車的方式很恐怖。

_____

_____

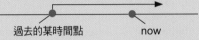

Beyond Your Wildest Dreams

作夢也想不到

Ⓥ Vocabulary Bank

1) **relevant** [ˋrɛləvənt] (a.) 有關的，切題的，有意義的
(phr.) relevant to... 與…有關
Your comment isn't relevant to the discussion.

2) **spectrum** [ˋspɛktrəm] (n.)（物理）光譜；幅度，範圍
The new policy has wide support across the political spectrum.

3) **arbitrary** [ˋɑrbə͵trɛrɪ] (a.) 任意的，隨便的
If you can't make up your mind, just make an arbitrary choice.

4) **random** [ˋrændəm] (a.) 隨機的，無規則的
The company is carrying out random drug testing.

5) **static** [ˋstætɪk] (n.) 訊號受阻所產生的噪音、雜訊
The radio is picking up nothing but static.

6) **interpretation** [ɪn͵tɝprɪˋteʃən] (n.) 解釋
(v.) interpret [ɪnˋtɝprɪt] 詮釋，說明
What's your interpretation of the poem?

7) **scenario** [sɪˋnɛrɪ͵o] (n.) 情節，情境
The worst-case scenario is a worldwide economic depression.

8) **signify** [ˋsɪgnə͵faɪ] (v.) 表示，意味著
What does the man's strange behavior signify?

9) **underlying** [ˋʌndɚ͵laɪɪŋ] (a.) 潛藏的，根本的
There's no consensus about the underlying cause of the crisis.

補充字彙

* **gruesome** [ˋgrusəm] (a.) 可怕的，痛苦的
The paper published gruesome photos of the accident.

* **decidedly** [dɪˋsaɪdɪdlɪ] (adv.) 確定地，毫無疑問地
Voters are decidedly opposed to higher taxes.

* **manifestation** [͵mænəfɛsˋteʃən] (n.) 表現形式，顯示
The demonstration was a manifestation of public discontent.

課文朗讀 MP3 88　單字朗讀 MP3 89　英文文章導讀 MP3 90

Dreams can be very strange. Even stranger, perhaps, are the explanations people give for them. Some people believe that all dreams are full of hidden
5 meaning. Each element of every dream, they say, contains a message [1]**relevant** to one's waking life. On the other end of the [2]**spectrum** are those who believe that dreams are just [3]**arbitrary** thoughts and
10 images produced by an unconscious mind. In other words, they're little more than [4]**random** brain [5]**static**.

Have you ever had a dream about your teeth falling out? Yes, it's quite
15 *gruesome, but it's also one of the most commonly reported types of dreams. Let's take a look at the various [6]**interpretations** of this kind of dream
20 and see just how widely the interpretations vary.

The most common, obvious interpretation of this dream is that the dreamers are overly concerned about their looks. Certainly your teeth form an
25 important part of your overall appearance, and losing them all, as often happens in this nightmare [7]**scenario**, is the last thing you'd want. So why would the brain dream about it? Perhaps, in some cases, it
30 [8]**signifies** an [9]**underlying** anxiety about one's appearance. ©Yet even people who are *decidedly unconcerned with appearances report having this dream. In these cases, it's more likely that the
35 dream is a *manifestation of some other underlying anxiety.

中 Translation

夢有時很奇怪，更奇怪的也許是人們對夢的解釋。有些人認為每個夢都充滿隱含的意義，他們說，夢的每個元素都含有與一個人日常生活有關的訊息。另一派的人認為，夢只是無意識的心智所產生的難以捉摸思維和圖像，換句話說，夢只不過是隨機的腦波干擾。

你曾夢過你掉牙齒嗎？沒錯，是滿可怕的，但也是最常見的夢之一。我們來檢視各種對這種夢的詮釋，看看這些解釋的差異有多大。

這個夢最普遍、最理所當然的解釋是，作夢者太過於擔心自己的外貌。當然，牙齒是構成整體外表很重要的一部份，牙齒掉光（就像常見於此惡夢情境一樣），是你最不想發生的事。那大腦為什麼會作這種夢呢？也許，在某些情況下，它意味著對外表潛在的焦慮。但就連完全不擔心外表的人也說會作這種夢，就這些例子來說，夢比較可能是其他潛在焦慮的表現。

Grammar Master

限定及非限定關係代名詞子句

關係代名詞子句是用來形容和說明先行詞的句子，故也稱做形容詞子句。以文中此句為例：

> 限定說明
>
> 例 Yet even people <u>who are decidedly unconcerned with</u>
>   先行詞
>   <u>appearances</u> report having this dream.

people 是人，所以後面用關係代名詞 who 帶出子句，說明此句的「人」不是全部的人，而是那些不在乎自己外貌的人。此句話除了說明作用外，也給了先行詞一個「界定」，所以稱為「限定關係代名詞子句」，句中若少了這個子句，我們便無法得知 people 指的是哪種人，句意也不一樣，會變成「全體人類宣稱作過這種夢」，完全扭曲了原句所要表達的。

另外還有一種在閱讀及寫作時常見到的關係代名詞子句，也就是在先行詞和關係代名詞中間多了一組逗號的「非限定關係代名詞子句」則沒有句意被扭曲或不完整的問題，而是對先行詞作「補充說明」用。

> 補充說明
>
> 例 Mrs. Rogers, <u>who is a retired nurse,</u> does volunteer work at
>   先行詞
>   the community day-care center.

此句若直接以 Mrs. Rogers 當主詞，連接逗號後的動詞 does 之句子，便是一完整句子：Mrs. Rogers does volunteer work at the community day-care center.（羅傑斯太太在社區的托兒所當義工）此處的關係代名詞子句補充說明 Mrs. Rogers 的身份，與整個句意無直接關係。

和 Dream 有關的英文說法

beyond one's wildest dreams
超乎某人的想像

wildest dreams 是指想像不受限、期待無上限的事物，beyond one's wildest dreams 即「超乎某人的想像」。 另一個類似的說法是 never in one's wildest dreams「想都沒想過，連想都不敢想」。

A: If you could have one wish, what would it be?
如果你可以許一個願望，你會許什麼？

B: I'd want to be rich beyond my wildest dreams.
我會想要有錢得不得了。

A: Wow, I can't believe you actually won the lottery!
哇，真不敢相信你真的中樂透了！

B: I know. Never in my wildest dreams did I think I'd be this lucky.
對啊。我想都沒想過自己會這麼幸運。

pipe dream 白日夢

pipe 是指「菸管」，而 pipe dream 表示不可能實現的空想，這個說法是從抽鴉片之後的恍惚、產生幻覺而來。「白日夢」的另一種說法是 daydream。

A: Kyle is always talking about becoming an author, but I doubt it's going to happen.
凱爾老是說要當作家，但我懷疑那會實現。

B: Yeah. It's just a pipe dream.
是啊，不過是個白日夢而已。

déjà vu 似曾相識

這是個法文字，意思是 already seen（曾經見過）。這是在描述一種眼前景物已經歷過的特殊感覺。也引申為「一再重演的歷史」。

A: Whoa! I'm experiencing serious déjà vu here.
嘩！我覺得似曾相識。

B: Are you sure you haven't been here before?
你確定從來沒來過這裡？

wet dream 春夢，夢寐以求的東西

wet 是由男性夢遺造成的結果（濕濕的）而來，在俚語中引申為「能帶來極大愉悅、興奮的事物」。

A: Have you played the new Halo game yet?
你玩過新推出的《最後一戰》電玩遊戲了嗎？

B: No, but I can't wait to try it. Everybody says it's a gamer's wet dream.
還沒，但我等不及要玩玩看了。大家都說那是電玩玩家夢寐以求的遊戲。

American dream 美國夢

指每個美國人只要肯努力，都有平等機會獲得自由、富裕的理想生活。

A: Why do so many people immigrate to the U.S.?
為什麼那麼多人移民美國？

B: They all want to live the American dream.
他們都想實現美國夢囉。

like a dream 如夢般美好

雖然夢有好夢 (good dream)、惡夢 (bad dream/nightmare) 之分，但當我們說某樣東西 like a dream 的時候，都是指好的、美妙的。

A: Did you try that antivirus software I told you about?
你試過我跟你說的那套防毒軟體了嗎？

B: Yeah. It works like a dream!
試了，真是太好用了！

a dream come true 美夢成真

come true 是「成真，實現」，a dream come true 又是一個把 dream 當美夢的說法，表示長久以來渴望的事終於發生。

A: I never thought we'd own our own home.
我從來沒想過我們能擁有自己的家。

B: Me neither. It's really a dream come true.
我也想不到，真的是美夢成真啊。

a dream ticket 一組（政治）夢幻組合

這是和選舉有關的說法，當兩個政治人物合作之後能起互相加成的作用，使選舉的贏面大增，就會說他們是 a dream ticket。

A: Obama and Hillary would have been a dream ticket.
歐巴馬和希拉蕊當初實在會是夢幻組合。

B: For sure. I don't know why Obama chose Biden.
沒錯，我想不透歐巴馬到底為何選拜登。

be/live in a dream world 懷有不切實際的想法

這個說法經常用進行式，表示一直在作夢的持續狀態。

A: Rebecca keeps waiting for Doug to ask her to marry him.
瑞貝卡一直在等道格向她求婚。

B: Not gonna happen. She's living in a dream world.
不可能的啦，她在作夢。

broken dream 幻滅的美夢

broken 是「破碎的」，broken dream 即「幻滅的美夢」。

A: It seems like my life's been nothing but disappointments.
我這輩子似乎只有失望。

B: Hey, we all have our share of broken dreams.
嘿，大家都有幻滅的美夢啊。

dream about/of someone or something 夢見某人、物

A: I had a dream about you last night.
我昨天晚上夢到你。

B: I hope it was a good dream.
希望是個好夢。

dream of doing something 夢想做某件事

如果要講「夢見做某件事」，介系詞就要用 of。常見的說法是 wouldn't dream of doing something，表示「想都不會去想，所以根本不會去做」。

A: Maybe your parents will lend you the money.
或許你爸媽會借你錢喔。

B: Oh, no—I wouldn't dream of asking them for money.
不可能——我根本不指望去跟他們借錢。

dream up something 編織某個美夢

A: It seems like Earl is always dreaming up get-rich-quick schemes.
厄爾好像老是在想一些快速致富的方法。

B: Yeah. He needs to stop dreaming and get a real job.
啊，他該停止作夢，去找個實在的工作。

Dream on. 想得美。

當有人發白日夢時，你就可以用這句回他，表示那是不可能發生的事。也可以說 In your dreams!

A: Do you think Patricia would go out with me?
你覺得派翠莎會跟我出去約會嗎？

B: Dream on, dude.
想得美啊，老兄。

the man/woman/something of your dreams 夢中情人，夢幻事物

A: I think I've finally found the house of my dreams.
我好像終於找到夢想中的房子了。

B: Yes, but can you afford it?
是啊，但你買得起嗎？

Vocabulary Bank

1) **approach** [əˋprotʃ] (n.) 方法，態度
Different problems require different approaches.

2) **relative** [ˋrɛlətɪv] (n.) 親屬
(v.) relate [rɪˋlet] 有關連
How often do you get together with your relatives?

3) **evolution** [ˌɛvəˋluʃən] (n.) 生物進化，進化論
(a.) evolutionary [ˌɛvəˋluʃəˌnɛrɪ] 進化的
Many Christians don't believe in evolution.

4) **species** [ˋspiʃiz] (n.) 物種（單複數同形）
There are thousands of different species of ants.

5) **spell** [spɛl] (v.) 意味著，招致
Warming oceans spell trouble for coral reefs.

6) **starvation** [stɑrˋveʃən] (n.) 饑饉，餓死
Millions of people die of starvation every year.

7) **primitive** [ˋprɪmətɪv] (a.) 原始的，遠古的
Primitive people lived in caves.

補充字彙

* **prophetic** [prəˋfɛtɪk] (a.) 預言性的
The Bible is full of prophetic stories.

* **foretell** [forˋtɛl] (v.) 預言
It's impossible to foretell the future.

* **head** [hɛd] (v.)（朝特定方向）前往，head your way 即「朝你而來」
Where are you headed?

* **vestigial** [vɛsˋtɪdʒɪəl] (n.) 殘餘的，退化的
The appendix is a vestigial organ.

* **cautionary** [ˋkɔʃəˌnɛrɪ] (a.) 警告的
The Boy Who Cried Wolf is a cautionary tale.

* **denture** [ˋdɛntʃɚ] (n.)（整副）假牙
Both of my grandparents wear dentures.

課文朗讀 MP3 91　單字朗讀 MP3 92　英文文章導讀 MP3 93

But hey, you're not the center of the universe—©maybe your dreams aren't even about you! ©The Greeks, for example, take a very different 1)**approach** to interpreting this same dream. They claim that a dream 5 about one's teeth falling out is a warning that a close 2)**relative** or friend will soon have health issues. Dreams often have a *prophetic quality to them, and the Greeks aren't alone in believing that dreams can *foretell the future.

10   Now for something near and dear to all of our hearts: money. Yes, some Americans will tell you that dreaming of your teeth falling out is a sure sign that money is *headed your way. It's hard to see the connection between teeth and money, but it [G]may be

15 [2)]**related** to the myth of the Tooth Fairy, who gives money to children when they leave their newly fallen teeth under their pillows at night.

    There's another interesting interpretation of this dream based on the [3)]**evolution** of our [4)]**species**. For

20 most animals, the loss of a significant number of teeth usually [5)]**spells** death by [6)]**starvation**. This was also the case for most of man's [3)]**evolutionary** history. So maybe this is some sort of *vestigial dream; it served a *cautionary function to [7)]**primitive** man, but is no longer

25 relevant in our modern world of dentists and *dentures.

牙仙子
Tooth Fairy
歐美各地都有與 Tooth Fairy 相關的習俗，每當小孩的乳牙 (baby tooth) 脫落，父母就會教他們睡前把牙齒放在枕頭下，隔天就會發現 Tooth Fairy 已將牙齒帶走、並留下一枚嶄新的銅板。

中 Translation

不過醒醒吧！宇宙又不是繞著你轉，也許你的夢和你一點關係也沒有！以希臘人來說，他們就用截然不同的方法來解釋這種夢。他們聲稱，夢到掉牙齒是預警一位近親或朋友很快會有健康問題。夢通常帶有預言的味道，而且不是只有希臘人相信夢可預言未來。

接下來談談每個人都很喜歡的東西：錢。是的，有些美國人會告訴你，夢見掉牙齒是錢財會進口袋的預兆。很難看出牙齒與金錢的關聯，但可能和牙仙子的神話有關。小孩子在夜裡把剛脫落的牙齒放在枕頭下，牙仙子就會給他們錢。

另一種有趣的解釋是根據人類的進化。對大部份動物而言，大量掉牙通常意味著餓死。人類進化歷史大致也是如此。所以也許這是某種殘餘的夢，對原始人類有預警功能，但是在有牙醫和假牙的現代社會已不再具有意義。

G Grammar Master

may be 和 maybe
may be 與 maybe 只有一個空格之差，但用法與意思不同。

may 是助動詞，後面接原形動詞，表示推量、推測。
例 I may go to the store later.

maybe 是副詞，意為「也許、可能」
例 Maybe I'll go to the store later.

定冠詞 + 複數名詞之總括用法
定冠詞+複數名詞（或集合名詞）可表示該名詞所代表的事物全體：

the Greeks 全希臘人 Greek 是單數，加上 s 形成複數，前面的定冠詞使它成為全希臘人的意思。

例如：

the Americans	全體美國人
the Chinese	全體中國人
the Japanese	全體日本人

其中 Chinese 和 Japanese 是單複數同形，所以不用加上 s。

Vocabulary Bank

1) **identify** [aɪˋdɛntəˌfaɪ] (v.) 確認，識別，發現
The police identified the suspect by his tattoo.

2) **resemble** [rɪˋzɛmbḷ] (v.) 相似，類似
Everyone says I resemble my mother.

3) **involve** [ɪnˋvɑlv] (v.) 使專注於，忙於
I was so involved in writing my report that I forgot to return the book.

4) **storage** [ˋstorɪdʒ] (n.) 儲存，記憶，倉庫
We put our furniture in storage when we went overseas.

5) **sensitivity** [ˌsɛnsəˋtɪvətɪ] (n.) 敏感性
People vary greatly in their sensitivity to pain.

6) **plot** [plɑt] (n.) 情節，劇情
I don't understand the plot of this movie.

7) **encounter** [ɪnˋkaʊntɚ] (v.) 意外遇見，遭遇（困境）
Matthew encountered an old friend on the street.

8) **rescue** [ˋrɛskju] (n.) 營救，解圍
(phr.) come to the/one's rescue 解救某事（或某人）
I was about to get mugged, but a policeman came to my rescue.

9) **shed** [ʃɛd] (v.) 散發，放射
(phr.) shed light on 照亮，使…明朗，曝光
The investigation shed light on government corruption.

補充字彙

* **housekeeping** [ˋhaʊsˌkipɪŋ] (n.) 家務，家事
My wife and I share the housekeeping duties.

* **neurotransmitter** [ˌnjʊroˋtrænsmɪtɚ] (n.) 神經傳導素
Neurotransmitters are chemicals that transmit signals from one nerve cell to another.

* **dopamine** [ˋdopəˌmin] (n.)（生化）多巴胺
Dopamine is a neurotransmitter that occurs in a wide variety of animals.

* **receptor** [rɪˋsɛptɚ] (n.) 受體，感受器
Painkillers work by blocking the pain receptors in the brain and spine.

* **inactivity** [ˌɪnækˋtɪvətɪ] (n.) 靜止，不活動
Overeating and inactivity can lead to obesity.

Modern dream research began in the 1950s when REM sleep was first [1)]**identified**. REM (rapid eye movement) sleep is a stage of sleep in which the eyes move rapidly behind the closed eyelids and the brain shows surprising amounts of activity. Indeed, this activity closely [2)]**resembles** the brain's activity when awake, and it's during this phase of sleep that most dreams occur.

Some dream researchers believe that dreams are the result of the brain organizing information. [G]When awake, our brains are so [3)]**involved** in real-world tasks that they don't have the time to properly form memories or place them in long-term [4)]**storage**. By doing this important *housekeeping at night, our brains allow us to be more productive during the day.

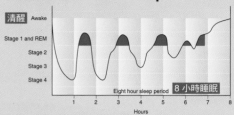
15　Another possibility is that dreams are the result of certain *neurotransmitters shutting down at night. Chemicals in the brain such as *dopamine are used to send signals within the brain, and the *receptors for these signals need periods of *inactivity to recover [5]

20　**sensitivity**. Their inactivity may cause the mind to run wild, which could be responsible for the crazy [6]**plots** we [7]**encounter** in our dreams.

　　And so modern science has come to the [8]**rescue** once again, [9]**shedding** light on something that was once a

25　complete mystery. But, to be fair, much of the mystery still remains. We may now have an idea about what the brain is doing when it dreams,

30　but we're still a long way from understanding why it dreams of the things it does.

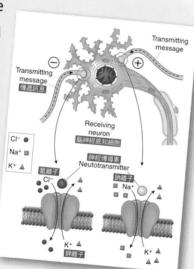

中 Translation

現代的夢研究始於一九五〇年代，當時 REM 睡眠期首次被發現。REM（快速動眼）睡眠是睡眠的一個階段，在這個階段，眼球在闔上的眼皮下快速運動，腦部也呈現驚人的活動量。事實上，腦部活動和大腦在清醒時的活動很相似，而且大多數的夢都在此階段產生。

有些研究夢的研究人員認為，夢是大腦整理資訊的結果。當我們醒著時，大腦非常專注於真實世界的工作，沒有時間好好形成記憶，或將記憶長久保存。在晚間進行這項重要的整理工作，大腦可以讓我們白天更有生產力。

還有一種可能，夢是一些神經傳導素晚間停止作用所造成。多巴胺之類的腦中化學物質是用來傳遞訊號，而接收訊號的受體需要有靜止期來恢復感受力。靜止期可能會使心智失去控制，也就是為什麼夢境情節會很瘋狂的原因。

於是現代科學又再次出手解圍，讓原本完全難以理解的事物更明朗，但平心而論，仍然有很多謎團存在。現在我們或許了解作夢時大腦在做什麼，但仍然不了解大腦為什麼會夢到這些東西。

✵ Language Guide

快速動眼睡眠 REM sleep

REM sleep 是在 1953 年由美國芝加哥大學研究生 Eugene Aserinsky 發現，他與他的博士指導教授 Nathaniel Kleitman 對睡眠時腦部活動的研究，使兩人成為現代睡眠研究的先驅。

一般成人睡眠大約有四分之一的時間屬於 REM sleep（上圖紅色區），新生兒則八成睡眠時間都在進行 REM sleep。在正常睡眠的情況下，一夜會經歷四至五次 REM sleep，至於未進行 REM sleep 的時間，就稱為 non-REM sleep (NREM)。

G Grammar Master

When 子句

When 所引導的子句，主詞若與主要子句之主詞相同，可完全省略主詞和 be 動詞。

第 9～12 行的這句：

When awake, our brains are so involved in real-world tasks that they don't have the time to properly form memories or place them in long-term storage.

原句應為：

When our brains are awake, our brains are so involved in real-world tasks that they don't have the time to properly form memories or place them in long-term storage.

When 子句中的主詞 our brains 和主要子句中的主詞 our brains 相同，所以可以將 when 子句中的 our brains 和 are 省略。

✎ Mini Quiz 閱讀測驗

❶ Which of the following is NOT mentioned as a possible interpretation of a dream about one's teeth falling out?
(A) a warning about health problems
(B) a prediction of losing one's teeth
(C) concern about one's appearance
(D) a sign that money is coming

❷ Evan _____ going to Paris this summer to study French.
(A) will　　　　(B) perhaps
(C) may be　　 (D) maybe

The E-books Are Coming!

電子書 時代降臨！

Vocabulary Bank

1) **commuter** [kə`mjutɚ] (n.) 通勤者
The train into the city was full of commuters.

2) **stain** [sten] (v.) 玷污，污染
My parents said they'd kill me if I stained the couch.

3) **grumble** [`grʌmbl̩] (v.) 咕噥，發牢騷
Maureen is always grumbling about her job.

4) **device** [dɪ`vaɪs] (n.) 設備，裝置
Our store sells all the latest wireless devices.

5) **popularity** [ˌpɑpjə`lærətɪ] (n.) 普及，流行，廣受歡迎
The popularity of video games continues to grow.

6) **retailer** [`ritelɚ] (n.) 零售商
(n./a./v.) retail [`ritel] 零售
Retailers are doing better than expected this quarter.

7) **digital** [`dɪdʒɪtl̩] (a.) 數位的
(v.) digitize [`dɪdʒɪˌtaɪz] 數位化
How do you like my new digital watch?

8) **portable** [`pɔrtəbl̩] (a.) 可攜式的，手提的
Do you sell portable hard drives?

9) **storage** [`storɪdʒ] (n.) 儲存（空間）
How much storage space does your iPod have?

10) **capacity** [kə`pæsətɪ] (n.) 容量，容積
The stadium has a capacity of 30 thousand.

11) **usher in** [`ʌʃɚ ɪn] (phr.) 開創，預示⋯的來臨
The Internet has ushered in a new age of communication.

進階字彙

12) **disgruntled** [dɪs`grʌntl̩d] (a.) 不滿的，不高興的
A disgruntled employee has threatened to sue the company.

13) **sleek** [slik] (a.) 造型優美的，流線型的
Have you seen the ad for that sleek new cell phone?

課文朗讀 MP3 97　單字朗讀 MP3 98　英文文章導讀 MP3 99

The ABC's of E-books

One rainy morning, a man gets on a crowded subway train to go to work. He manages to find a seat and settles down to read his newspaper. While he's unfolding it, however, it **1 brushes up** against a fellow ¹⁾**commuter's** wet umbrella.
5　Now, he has to be careful that the ink doesn't ²⁾**stain** his pants. He sits there ³⁾**grumbling** and holding his damp newspaper. Surely, there must be another way for him to enjoy his morning paper. Well, in fact, there is!

Electronic books (or e-books) and the ⁴⁾**devices** people
10　use to read them, called e-readers, are growing in ⁵⁾**popularity**. The online ⁶⁾**retailer** Amazon.com announced in July 2010 that sales of e-books for its own Kindle e-reader had surpassed those of new hardcover books for the first time. And with the recent release of Apple's iPad (which serves, among other things, as an
15　e-reader), the market **2 is primed for** continued growth. Books are not the only traditional print media getting the ⁷⁾**digital** treatment—electronic versions of magazines and newspapers are now available for e-readers as well. Perhaps even the daily paper favored by our ¹²⁾**disgruntled** commuter above.

20　E-books began appearing way back in 1971 as part of the Gutenberg Project, ©named after the inventor of moveable type, Johannes Gutenberg. The basic idea behind e-books is simple: instead of paper and ink, e-books are electronic files (Adobe's PDF being the most common) that you can read on

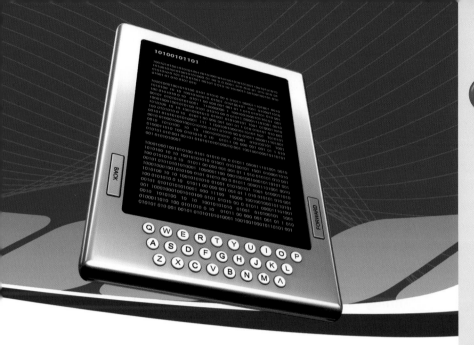

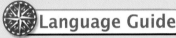
Tongue-tied No More

1 brush (up) against... 輕拂，碰到
是指人或物品輕拂或碰觸到身旁的他人或其它東西。
A: Do you know who stole your wallet?
你知道是誰偷走你的皮夾嗎？
B: I think it may have been this guy that
brushed up against me on the bus.
我覺得可能是在公車上和我擦身而過的一個男的。

2 be primed for (事先) 做好準備
當前面主詞是人，意思為某人準備好做某事，或
被事先指點該做的事或說的話；當主詞是事物，
則代表其已經做好準備。
例 The local team is primed for the big game.
當地隊伍準備好要迎戰大賽。

25 a screen. While computers can handle this job well enough, [13]**sleek**, lightweight [8]**portable** e-readers with backlit screens and large [9]**storage** [10]**capacities** may [11]**usher in** the next revolution in reading.

Mini Quiz 閱讀測驗

❶ ■■ **How many types of print media are mentioned in the article?**
(A) 1
(B) 2
(C) 3
(D) 4

❷ ■■ **What do the Kindle and the iPod have in common?**
(A) They are both electronic books.
(B) They can both be used to read e-books.
(C) They are both sold by the same company.
(D) They can only be used to read e-books.

Translation

電子書起源
一個下雨的早上，一名男子搭上擁擠的地下鐵去上班。他好不容易找到一個座位，坐下來看報。然而，正當他攤開報紙時，報紙卻擦到另一位通勤者濕淋淋的雨傘。現在，他必須提防墨水弄髒他的長褲。他拿著濕掉的報紙，坐在那裡咕噥著。總有其他方式可以讓他享受早報。嗯，事實上是有的！

電子書，以及人們用來讀電子書的裝置——電子書閱讀器——正愈來愈受歡迎。網路零售業者亞馬遜書店在二〇一〇年七月宣布，其自有品牌 Kindle 閱讀器銷售的電子書，營業額首度超越精裝本新書。而隨著蘋果公司的 iPad 在最近上市（閱讀電子書也是 iPad 的功能之一），這個市場已做好持續成長的準備。書不是唯一一種進入數位化的傳統印刷媒體——電子書閱讀器現在也有電子版的雜誌和報紙可讀。或許前述那位不悅的通勤者喜歡看的日報也在其中。

電子書早在一九七一年即已問世，當時是古騰堡計畫的一部分（以活字版印刷術發明人約翰內斯古騰堡為名）。電子書背後的基本概念很簡單：代替紙、墨，電子書是可以在螢幕上閱讀的電子檔（Adobe 的 PDF 檔是最常見的檔案）。雖然電腦可以把這項工作處理得夠好，但美型、輕巧、有背光源螢幕和超大記憶容量的可攜式電子書閱讀器，或許會帶來下一場閱讀革命。

Language Guide

Gutenberg Project 古騰堡計畫
古騰堡計畫由麥克哈特 (Michael Hart) 於一九七一年啟動，當時還是伊利諾伊大學 (University of Illinois) 學生的哈特，獲得了學校材料研究實驗室中 Xerox Sigma V 大型計算機的使用權，他想藉此做一些有價值的事情，於是便決定將書籍電子化以供更多人閱讀，而他背包中的美國獨立宣言也就成為古騰堡計畫第一個電子文本。此計畫以約翰內斯古騰堡 (Johannes Gutenberg, 1398-1468) 命名，用來紀念這位西方活字印刷術的發明人。

九〇年代中期，有許多志工加入手工輸入的行列，西元二〇〇〇年也成立了古騰堡計畫文獻建檔基金會 (The Project Gutenberg Literary Archive Foundation) 處理相關事務。隨著科技進步，書籍也可以更有效率地透過掃描或其他相關軟體建檔。收錄作品除了有西方文學、期刊外，也有樂譜或是食譜等。主要以英文作品為大宗，也有相當數量的法文、德文、義大利文、西班牙文及中文等著作。

Grammar Master

be named after... 以……來命名
name after... 是「為了紀念某人／事而命名」的意思，是一個不可分的動詞片語。通常這個片語會用被動式，表示句子裡的主詞是「根據……被命名」的。
文章中第 21 行的這句直接用 named after，是省略了 Gutenberg Project 後面的 which was。
例 New York **is named after** the city of York in England.
紐約是以英國的約克市來命名。

（翻譯練習）
這座學校是以國家首位總統來命名。

（B）② （C）① 答案慧贝题测
The school is named after the country's first president.
答案慧真練習翻
Know it all • 75

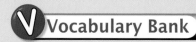

Vocabulary Bank

1) **degrade** [dɪ`gred] (v.)（使）退化
The environment has been degraded by industrial pollution.

2) **backpack** [`bæk͵pæk] (n.) 背包，旅行包
Will these books fit in your backpack?

3) **take up** [tek ʌp] (phr.) 佔據（空間或時間）
I'm sorry to take up so much of your time.

4) **steep** [stip] (a.)（價格）過高
The prices at that store are too steep for me.

5) **consumer** [kən`sumɚ] (n.) 消費者，顧客
Consumers are spending less during the recession.

6) **corresponding** [͵kɔrə`spɑndɪŋ] (a.) 相應的
Sales are higher than in the corresponding period last year.

7) **academic** [͵ækə`dɛmɪk] (a.) 學術的
Shelly has a good academic record.

8) **specialized** [`spɛʃə͵laɪzd] (a.) 專業的，專門的
Becoming a surgeon requires years of specialized training.

進階字彙

9) **moldy** [`moldɪ] (a.) 發霉的
You should throw away bread if it gets moldy.

10) **brittle** [`brɪtl̩] (a.) 脆弱的，易碎的
Your bones become brittle as you age.

11) **lug** [lʌg] (v.) 使勁地提、搬
Could you help me lug this suitcase upstairs?

12) **clutter (up)** [`klʌtɚ] (v.) 使零亂、堆滿
The desk was cluttered up with papers.

13) **outlay** [`aʊt͵le] (n./v.) 花費，開支
For a small outlay, you can start your own website.

14) **balk** [bɔk] (v.) 卻步，猶豫
Most people balk at the thought of eating insects.

口語補充

15) **dirt cheap** [dɝt tʃip] (a./adv.) 非常便宜
The apartment is small, but the rent is dirt cheap.

Tongue-tied No More

❶ breathe a sigh of relief 鬆一口氣
因解除擔憂害怕而鬆了一口氣，也就是中文常說的「如釋重負」。

例 Local residents breathed a sigh of relief when the killer was finally caught.
殺人犯終於被捕，當地居民鬆了一口氣。

The Benefits

©Besides avoiding damp newsprint, e-books and e-readers have a number of other benefits to consider. Huge amounts of paper are used to print books, newspapers and magazines each year, and since e-books are paper-free,
5 the world's trees can ❶ **breathe a sigh of relief**. Speaking of paper, while a traditional book's pages may become 9)**moldy** or 10)**brittle** with age if not properly cared for, you don't have to worry about e-book files 1)**degrading**.

We all have memories of 11)**lugging** a 2)**backpack**
10 full of heavy textbooks to class. Now imagine instead having all your textbooks as e-books. That's literally a huge weight off your shoulders. Some people don't like books 12)**cluttering** up their shelves either, and a library of thousands of e-books 3)**takes up** hardly any space at all.
15 And you don't need to waste time going to a bookstore, as e-books can be conveniently downloaded directly from the Internet.

While the initial 13)**outlay** for an e-reader is a little 4)**steep** (the most popular versions cost around US$200),
20 they may save the 5)**consumer** a lot of money ❷ **in the**

long run. A new hardcover bestseller typically retails for $25 to $35, but the [6)]**corresponding** e-book may cost just half that, and most classics are either free or [15)]**dirt cheap**. E-books can also give new life to books that are

25 long out of print. Publishers may [14)]**balk** at reprinting an old book, especially an [7)]**academic** or [8)]**specialized** title, but digitizing costs next to nothing. No wonder people are ⓒcomparing e-books to Gutenberg's invention of the printing press.

Mini Quiz 閱讀測驗

❶ ▓▓ **Which of the following is NOT an advantage of e-books?**
(A) They are environmentally friendly.
(B) They can save you time.
(C) They are mostly free.
(D) They can save you money.

❷ ▓▓ **What is the most likely price for a bestselling e-book?**
(A) $5
(B) $15
(C) $25
(D) $35

Translation

優點

除了新聞用紙不會沾濕之外,電子書和電子書閱讀器還有許多其他好處。每年用在印刷書本、報紙和雜誌的紙量非常大,而電子書不會用到紙,全球的樹木可鬆一口氣。說到紙張,傳統書籍的紙張若未適當照料,久而久之可能會發霉、易碎,而電子書檔案就不必擔心品質變差的問題。

我們全都有扛著滿滿一背包厚重課本進教室的回憶。現在,想像一下課本全變成電子書的情景。真的是名副其實「卸下肩膀的重擔」。有些人也不喜歡書本亂糟糟地塞滿書架,而數千本電子書的藏書幾乎完全不佔空間。你也不必浪費時間去書店,因為電子書可直接從網路下載,方便極了。

儘管電子書閱讀器一開始的費用有點高(最受歡迎的版本要價約兩百美元),長久來看卻可能替消費者省下不少錢。一本精裝暢銷新書的零售價通常在二十五至三十五美元,但電子書版本的價格可能只要實體書的一半,而且大多數經典作品不是免費,就是非常便宜。電子書也可以賦予絕版已久的書籍新生命。出版社可能不敢貿然重印舊書,特別是學術或專業書籍,但數位版本幾乎不需成本。也難怪人們會把電子書比喻成古騰堡發明了印刷機。

Tongue-tied No More

❷ in the long run 從長遠來看
不從事情表面或現今狀態來衡量,而是從長遠的觀點或角度來看待某件事。

A: Why should I buy energy-saving light bulbs? They're more expensive.
為什麼我應該買省電燈泡?這比較貴耶。

B: They are a little more expensive, but they'll save you money in the long run.
雖然貴了點,但長遠來看能幫你省荷包。

Grammar Master

Besides + N/Ving, ... 除了⋯⋯,還有
besides 是一個介系詞,意義和 in addition to... 相近,表示「除了⋯⋯之外,還有」。besides 和 except 容易混淆,besides 後方接的是「加上去」的概念,except 後方接的是則是「減掉」的概念。

例 **Besides** Dan, Tom and Michael are also coming on the trip.
除了丹,湯姆和麥可也會參加這次旅遊。

例 Everyone is coming on the trip **except** Dan.
除了丹之外,所有人都會參加這次旅遊。

besides 也可以當副詞來使用,意思等同於「此外」in addition、moreover、furthermore,放在句首時,後面記得要加上逗號。

例 We don't need a new car. **Besides**, we can't even afford one.
我們不需要新車,更何況,我們也買不起。

compare 的兩種用法
compare 有兩種解釋,一為「比較,對照」,另一個則是「比喻為⋯⋯,比作⋯⋯」,雖然都可寫成 compare A to B,但其實語意上有些不同。

● compare A to B 將 A 比喻成 B

例 The poet **compared** his lover's smile **to** the sun.
這位詩人將情人的微笑比喻為太陽。

● compare A to/with B 比較 A 和 B

例 The teacher asked me to **compare** the American government **with** the British government.
老師要我比較美國政府和英國政府。

翻譯練習

1. 除了葡萄酒,我們也喝了啤酒。

_____

2. 科學家常常把人腦比喻為電腦。

_____

Vocabulary Bank

1) **drawback** [ˋdrɔˏbæk] (n.) 缺點，不利條件
   The main drawback to living in Chicago is the weather.

2) **curl up** [kɝl ʌp] (phr.) 蜷曲著坐 / 躺
   Elaine likes to curl up with a good book when it rains.

3) **toxic** [ˋtɑksɪk] (a.) 有毒的
   The company was fined for dumping toxic chemicals in the river.

4) **contribute (to)** [kənˋtrɪbjut] (v.) 促成，加重
   Air pollution contributes to global warming.

5) **abandon** [əˋbændən] (v.) 丟棄，遺棄
   It is illegal to abandon or abuse a pet.

進階字彙

6) **sterile** [ˋstɛrəl] (a.) 無生氣的，冰冷無味的
   Vicky left the bank because she hated working in such a sterile environment.

7) **instill (in)** [ɪnˋstɪl] (v.) 灌輸，徐徐地教導
   We hope to instill good values in our children.

8) **mindless** [ˋmaɪndləs] (a.) 無需動腦筋的，愚蠢的，毫無意義的
   How can you listen to that mindless pop music?

9) **contraption** [kənˋtræpʃən] (n.) 裝置，玩意
   What does this contraption do?

10) **obsolete** [ˏɑbsəˋlit] (a.) 淘汰的，過時的
    Typewriters are becoming obsolete.

口語補充

11) **wind up** [waɪnd ʌp] (phr.) 落得，結果變成
    If you drink and drive, you may wind up in jail.

Tongue-tied No More

1 be no substitute for sth. 無可替代

substitute 是「取代，替代」的意思，be no substitute for sth. 也就是說某事物的功能是無法用其它東西取代的。

A: How's that instant coffee? Is it drinkable?
那種即溶咖啡喝起來如何？能喝嗎？

B: It's better than nothing, but it's no substitute for freshly brewed coffee.
有總比沒有好，但還是無法取代現煮咖啡。

課文朗讀 MP3 103　單字朗讀 MP3 104　英文文章導讀 MP3 105

The ¹⁾Drawbacks

There's perhaps nothing better than ²⁾**curling up** on the couch on a rainy day with a hot cup of coffee and a good book. The experience just isn't the same with an e-book though. The ⁶⁾**sterile** touch of a plastic e-reader
5　in your hands **1 is no substitute** for the smell and feel of a real book, and the latter never runs out of batteries. Bookshelves full of books not only give a room character, they reveal a lot about their owner—something e-books simply can't do. As the American educator Horace Mann
10　once said, "A house without books is like a room without windows."

It would be most unfortunate if public libraries and local bookshops had to close because only e-books were being "published." These places not only provide jobs for
15　our neighbors, they serve as meeting places and centers of knowledge for our communities. Give children a library card and you'll ⁷⁾**instill** in them a love of reading; put them in front of a computer screen, however, and they'll likely ¹¹⁾**wind up** playing ⁸⁾**mindless** video games.

20 　　With respect to the environment, e-books may indeed save trees, but there are a number of 3)**toxic** chemicals in e-book readers. As these 9)**contraptions** become 10)**obsolete**, they'll only 4)**contribute** to the world's growing e-waste problem. Just imagine if people 25 5)**abandon** e-readers at the same rate they do cell phones— it's unthinkable! 6)Despite the many benefits of e-books, it would be hard to imagine a world without traditional paperback and hardcover books. Will they still have a place after the e-book revolution? Only time will tell.

Mini Quiz 閱讀測驗

❶ ▇ **What does the author imply about e-readers?**
(A) They can run out of batteries.
(B) They contain toxic chemicals.
(C) They reveal a lot about their owner.
(D) They are used to play video games.

❷ ▇ **What does the word "contraptions" refer to?**
(A) E-waste
(B) Toxic chemicals
(C) E-books
(D) E-book readers

Translation

缺點
或許沒有什麼事比得上雨天裡蜷在沙發、喝杯熱咖啡、看本好書。電子書就無法帶給人們這種體驗。塑膠閱讀器握在手裡的冷冰冰的觸感，完全無法取代實體書的氣味和感覺，而且後者絕不會有電池用完的問題。堆滿書本的書架不僅賦予房間特色，也充分透露屋主的性格——這是電子書辦不到的。誠如美國教育家侯瑞斯曼恩所言：「沒有書的屋子就像沒有窗戶的房間。」

如果因為只「出版」電子書而導致公立圖書館和當地書店必須關門大吉，這是非常可惜的事。這些地方不僅為我們的鄰居提供就業，也是社區的聚會地點和知識中心。給孩子一張圖書館借閱證，就能灌輸他們對閱讀的喜愛；但如果讓他們坐在電腦螢幕前，他們最後很可能會玩起不須動腦的電玩遊戲。

就環保而言，電子書或許真的能拯救樹木，但閱讀器本身也含有不少有毒化學物質。當這些玩意兒變得過時，只會助長全球日益嚴重的電子廢棄物問題，只要想一想，如果人們丟棄電子閱讀器的速度和汰換手機一樣快——後果真是不堪設想！電子書固然有許多好處，但我們仍然難以想像一個沒有傳統平裝和精裝書籍的世界。在歷經電子書革命後，實體書仍能占有一席之地嗎？只有時間能給我們答案。

Language Guide

各種書的類型
paperback 平裝書
也稱為 softcover，用來指以紙或薄紙板為封面的書。當出版商不想花高成本投資一本作品或不期待其成為暢銷作時，就會用平裝書的方式發行。平裝書可以分為兩種：商業平裝本 (trade paperback) 與大眾市場平裝本 (mass-market paperback)。商業平裝本的尺寸通常等同於精裝書的大小，紙質也優於大眾市場平裝本，價格也相對高一點。大眾市場平裝本尺寸較小，沒有多餘的包裝與插圖，通常於傳統書店或超市販售。

hardcover 精裝書
也稱為 hardback 或 hardbound，顧名思義就是指封面較厚且硬的書。因為封面具有保護的作用，所以比平裝書耐用，設計也比較精美，相對的製作成本價格較昂貴。精裝書的書脊通常富有彈性，使書本翻開時能攤平。

audio book 有聲書
用聲音來呈現書的內容，也就是以聲音為媒介，用朗讀、對話、廣播劇或報導等方式讓聽眾「閱讀」，格式有錄音帶、CD、或是數位檔（如 mp3）。常見於語言學習、童話故事，近年來也有商業資訊及名人演講的相關作品。除了可以下載或轉檔至個人的隨身聽的便利之外，透過配音員及後製也能使內容更活潑多元。

Grammar Master

despite... 儘管……
despite 是一個介系詞，後方可以直接接名詞片語，像文章第 26 行，後面直接加 the many benefits of e-books。另外，in spite of... 也是儘管的意思，用法和 despite... 相同。
例 **Despite** the bad weather, we had fun on our vacation.
= We had fun on our vacation **despite** the bad weather.
儘管天候不佳，我們還是開心度過了假期。

如果要表達「儘管」，但後方又必須接子句來描述事件時，可以用 although 來表示。
句型 Although (Though) S+V, S+V.
例 **Although** the weather was bad, we still had fun on our trip.
儘管天候不佳，我們還是開心度過了假期。

（翻譯練習）
儘管受傷，這名選手還是贏得了比賽。

閱讀測驗解答 ❶ (A) ❷ (D)
= Despite his injury, the player won the game.
The player won the game despite his injury.
翻譯測驗解答

V Vocabulary Bank

1) **embrace** [ɪmˋbres] (v./n.) 信奉，全心接納
It's difficult for old people to embrace new ideas.

2) **consciousness** [ˋkɑnʃəsnɪs] (n.) 意識，知覺
Meditation can be used to reach a higher state of consciousness.

3) **rebel (against)** [rɪˋbɛl] (v.) 叛逆，反抗
(a.) rebellious [rɪˋbɛljəs] 叛逆的
It's normal for teenagers to rebel against their parents.

4) **suffocating** [ˋsʌfəˏketɪŋ] (a.) 令人窒息的，壓制的
The woman was trapped in a suffocating marriage.

5) **hypocrisy** [hɪˋpɑkrəsɪ] (n.) 虛偽，偽善
(n.) hypocrite [ˋhɪpəkrɪt] 偽善者，偽君子
Critics are accusing the politician of hypocrisy.

6) **prosperity** [prɑsˋpɛrətɪ] (n.) 繁榮
The railroads brought prosperity to the American West.

7) **migration** [ˏmaɪˋgreʃən] (n.) 遷移，遷徙
(n.) migrant [ˋmaɪgrənt] 移民，immigrant [ˋɪmɪgrənt] 移入者，emigrant [ˋɛməgrənt] 移出者
The biologist is studying bird migration.

8) **rally** [ˋrælɪ] (n.)（政治）集會，大會
The opposition party is holding a rally tonight.

9) **resistance** [rɪˋzɪstəns] (n.) 抵制，反抗
Gandhi advocated peaceful resistance against the British.

補充字彙

* **oppressive** [əˋprɛsɪv] (a.) 壓抑的，專制的
The oppressive military government has been in power for over 50 years.

* **conformity** [kənˋfɔrmətɪ] (n.) 順從（規範），一致
Ryan couldn't stand the conformity of small-town life.

* **worldly** [ˋwɝldlɪ] (a.) 世故的，涉世的
David was much more worldly after returning from studying abroad.

* **marijuana** [ˏmærəˋwɑnə] (n.) 大麻
Marijuana is the most commonly used illegal drug in the U.S.

嬉皮 The Rise and Fall of the 運動的興衰 Hippie Movement

PEACE

課文朗讀 MP3 106　單字朗讀 MP3 107　英文文章導讀 MP3 108

The hippies were an influential youth subculture that began in the United States during the mid-1960s and gradually spread around the world. The word "hippie" comes
5　from "hipster," which was originally used to describe beatniks who [G]had moved from New York to San Francisco's Haight-Ashbury district. Inspired by the countercultural values of the Beat Generation, the hippies
10　went on to create their own forms of expression, including psychedelic rock, ethnic clothing and free love. They also [1]embraced Eastern religion and philosophy, and used soft drugs to expand
15　their [2]consciousness. For nearly a decade, the hippie movement attracted many young people who were [3]rebelling against what they felt were society's [4]suffocating standards and [5]hypocrisies.

In America, the 1960s were a decade of
21　unprecedented economic [6]prosperity but also *oppressive social *conformity. During the Great Depression and WWII, there had been a mass [7]migration to the
25　cities. These economic [7]migrants had children who grew up more *worldly and open-minded than their parents. By the early 1960s, they were
30　listening to rock & roll and jazz, and many were experimenting with *marijuana. By the mid-60s, student activists were organizing mass [8]rallies in

35　support of free speech, while Martin Luther King, Jr. and the Freedom Riders fought against racial segregation. What united these and other [3]rebellious youth into a mass counterculture was the Summer of Love
40　in Haight-Ashbury, The Beatles' [1]embrace of hippie culture, and [9]resistance to the Vietnam War.

中 Translation

嬉皮是一種影響深遠的青年次文化，一九六〇年代中期始於美國，然後逐漸散布到全世界。「嬉皮」一詞源自 hipster（意為「趕時髦的人」），原本是用來形容從紐約搬到舊金山海特阿胥巴利區的「垮掉的一代追隨者」。受到「垮掉的一代」反文化價值觀的啟發，嬉皮繼續創造自己新的表達方式，包括迷幻搖滾、民俗服飾和自由性愛。他們也接受東方宗教和哲學，並使用軟性毒品擴展他們的意識。有將近十年，嬉皮運動吸引了許多年輕人，這群年輕人擁有共同的特質：反抗他們心目中叫人窒息的社會標準和偽善。

在美國，一九六〇年代是經濟空前繁榮的十年，但社會規範的壓力很大。在經濟大蕭條和第二次世界大戰期間，美國有大批民眾遷居城市。這些經濟移民的子女，長大後皆較父母更世故、更能接受新思潮。一九六〇年代初期，他們聆聽搖滾及爵士樂，也有很多人嘗試抽大麻。至六〇年代中葉，學運人士紛紛發動大規模集會，支持言論自由，當時正值馬丁路德金恩和「自由行示威者」挺身對抗種族隔離。讓這些人與其他叛逆青年結合成大眾次文化的是海特阿胥巴利區的「愛之夏」、披頭四對嬉皮文化的接納，以及反越戰運動。

G Grammar Master

過去完成式：主詞 + had p.p. 的用法
過去完成式通常用來強調在過去某件事之前「就已經」發生的事，或已持續一段時間的狀態。

例 ● They **had dated** for three years <u>before they got married.</u>
　　　已經交往　　　　　　　　　　結婚之前
　　他們在婚前已交往三年。

● <u>Before he quit his job,</u> he **had been unhappy** for quite
　　　辭職之前　　　　　　　　　已經不快樂
　　some time.
　　在他辭職前就已經不快樂好一陣子了。

本文第一段出現了 subculture（次文化）、counterculture（反文化）這兩個字，那麼 1960 年代當時的主流文化到底是什麼呢？請見 1-4 說明。

❸ Beat Generation
嬉皮的偶像

這群被稱作「垮掉的一代」Beat Generation 的作家一開始以詩人Allen Ginsberg（艾倫金斯伯格，詩作 Howl）、作家 William S. Burroughs（威廉波羅斯，小說 Naked Lunch）及作家 Jack Kerouac（傑克凱魯雅克，小說 On the Road）為首，他們原本聚集在紐約，於 1950 年代中期陸續移居舊金山，與當地的文化人結交，形成一波新文學運動。

Beat Generation 文人（或被簡稱為 the Beats）的註冊商標——波西米亞式的生活、狂放不羈的行為、使用軟性毒品以「追求創作靈感」——成為許多中產階級家庭的青年爭相模仿的對象，媒體開始稱這群跟風的年輕人為 beatnik、hipster，這股風潮持續發酵，最後形成 1960 年代中期蔚為大觀的 hippie 風潮！

1920	1930	1940	1950

1929~1940 初 經濟大蕭條

1940末~1950末 恐共時期

1939~1945
第二次世界大戰

❶

Great Depression
經濟大蕭條

1960 年代正值壯年的人，童年都遭逢 Great Depression（經濟大蕭條），因為隨著小羅斯福總統的 New Deal（新政）漸漸走出陰霾，這群人從小就培養出強烈的愛國心，剛成年又碰上第二次世界大戰，更是全國動員參戰，上下一心追隨政府領導。第二次大戰後經濟快速起飛的同時，政府的控制隨著冷戰開始而繼續擴張，這群 1920 年代出生的人經歷了十年的恐共時期（1940 年代末期至 1950 年代末期），美國人所受的言論及思想箝制前所未有，但經濟繁榮讓這群習慣相信統治者的人過著安分守己的生活。這就是當時的主流文化。

Freedom Riders 自由行示威者

racial segregation（種族隔離）直到 60 年代都還存在於美國南部各州，不論是餐廳、劇院，甚至是公車上，都對非裔美國人有所限制。Freedom Riders 是一群種族平權人士，他們於 1961 年 5 月 4 日展開一連串搭乘公車的抗議活動，刻意去坐白人專用座位、使用白人專用的車站設施，目的是要反抗種族隔離及種族歧視。

這群 Freedom Riders（7 名黑人，6 名白人，大多為四、五十歲）於華府分別登上公車，途經維吉尼亞州、南北卡羅萊納州、喬治亞州、阿拉巴馬州、密西西比州，預計 5 月 17 日在路易西安納州的紐奧良會師。但整個活動歷經三 K 黨攻擊、警方逮捕，一直到 5 月 24 才抵達密西西比州，此時已有更多人加入 Freedom Riders 的行列，公車一進車站，他們就全部被逮捕入獄，當地監獄因此人滿為患，這群 Freedom Riders 在獄中受到殘酷對待。

Freedom Riders 的抗議活動受到國際廣泛矚目，對當時的甘迺迪政府造成極大壓力。隨後加入 Freedom Riders 的人在接下來幾個月繼續抗議活動，超過 60 組黑白人種各半的抗議人士搭乘公車在南方各州縱橫。

Freedom Riders 的努力終於在 1961 年 11 月 1 日獲得勝利，當日新的行政命令公布，所有公車、火車上不再區分座位，車站內所有設施都不再進行種族隔離。而他們更大的貢獻，在於激起南部各州人民追求平等的思想，並帶動全美跨黑白種族加入推動平權運動的行列。據估計全部參與過這次抗議的 Freedom Riders 將近有 450 人，活動到了後期，大多數參與者的年齡小於三十歲，多位 Freedom Riders 後來成為種族平權運動領袖，在整個 60 年代抗議活動中扮演重要角色。

❹ Summer of Love
愛之夏

1967 年春假開始，全美各地大學生及高中生開始湧入舊金山的 Haight-Ashbury district（海特阿胥巴利區），到了夏天，全球聚集於此的人數高達十萬，同時間在全美及歐洲各大城市聚集的嬉皮更是不計其數！這群年輕嬉皮齊聚一堂，展開一場史無前例的社會實驗。

他們住在無政府組織免費提供的篷舍，自組義務醫療服務，與陌生人共享物資、欣賞南腔北調的音樂及創作、分食迷幻藥品、體驗性解放，用行動徹底表現對政治、思想箝制與商業文化的反抗。那個夏天，就是所謂的 Summer of Love。但反諷的是，當嬉皮高唱愛與和平的同時，爭取種族平等的活動也進入空前暴力的階段，多個城市發生血腥衝突，因此有人稱那年夏天是 The Long, Hot Summer（漫長炎熱的夏天）。

 1967
蒙特瑞音樂節
 1969
胡士托音樂節

1970 　 1980

1959~1975 越戰

❷ Vietnam War 越戰

但這群認分的美國人在 1940 年代生養的下一代，從小過的是富裕生活（尤其是在都市長大的中產階級子女），聽的是深受黑人文化影響的爵士樂、藍調音樂及搖滾樂，他們剛成年時，面臨 Vietnam War（越戰，1959 年開戰）徵召入伍，養尊處優的他們不想接受父母當年參戰的命運，但是當乖乖牌的主流文化壓力無孔不入、令人窒息，這時一群 1950 年代崛起的美國作家成了他們的明燈。

soft drugs 是什麼？

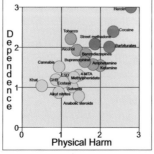

soft drugs（軟性毒品）一般是指大麻（也稱為 cannabis），但也包括 psilocybin mushrooms（魔菇）、LSD（一粒沙，或稱搖腳丸）……等等。

有 soft drugs 就有 hard drugs（硬性毒品），如 heroin（海洛因）、cocaine（古柯鹼）、methamphetamine（甲基安非他命，即台灣所謂的安非他命）……等等。一般對兩者差別的判定在於成癮性（dependence）及對身體傷害（physical harm）程度的高低，但界定標準很有爭議性（例如酒精及尼古丁的成癮性及對身體的傷害其實高過大麻，見右表），且各國對於麻醉藥物的分類方式也不相同。

© Wikipedia/Apartmento2

---

psychedelic rock 迷幻搖滾

60 年代初期的搖滾樂壇是由英國好男孩團體披頭四（The Beatles）及壞男孩團體滾石合唱團 (The Rolling Stones) 稱霸，相對於這兩個團體的流行搖滾 (pop rock)、搖滾 (rock & roll) 及節奏藍調（rhythm and blues，或稱 R&B）樂風，一股反映嬉皮風潮的搖滾型態漸漸形成。

psychedelic [ˌsaɪkəˋdɛlɪk] rock（或稱 acid rock）興起於 60 年代中期的英國及美國，psychedelic 是「迷幻藥（的）」，尤指當時盛行的 LSD，psychedelic rock 顧名思義是一種表現吸食 LSD 感官經驗的音樂形式。姑且不論吸毒的對錯，但 psychedelic rock 音樂人在嘗試以音樂抒發迷幻經驗的同時，拋開音樂就是要「好聽、朗朗上口」的呆板印象，讓搖滾樂廣納各種藝術形式及東方樂器（如印度西塔琴），帶動前衛搖滾（progressive rock，常以一個主題創作概念專輯）、藝術搖滾（art rock，或稱 classical rock，常以組曲 (suites) 而非單曲 (songs) 形式呈現，跨界採用音樂及文學作品）……等等以提升搖滾樂藝術層次為目的的創作，對於晚近的硬式搖滾 (hard rock) 及重金屬音樂 (heavy metal) 發展功不可沒。

以下為 60 年代中期至 70 年代重要搖滾團體（成軍時間／地點）：

psychedelic rock 迷幻搖滾

The Doors
門戶合唱團
1965年，美國

Jefferson Airplane
傑佛森飛船合唱團
1965年，美國
Grateful Dead

死之華合唱團
1965年，美國

progressive rock 前衛搖滾

The Moody Blues
憂鬱藍調合唱團
1964年，英國

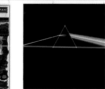
Pink Floyd
平克佛洛伊德合唱團
1965年，英國

Yes
Yes 合唱團
1968年，英國

art rock 藝術搖滾

The Who
何許人合唱團
1965年，英國

The Velvet Underground
非法利益合唱團
1965年，美國

Roxy Music
羅西音樂合唱團
1970年代初期，英國

Know it ALL 英文閱讀

V Vocabulary Bank

1) **advocate** [ˈædvəˌket] (v.) 擁護，主張
The presidential candidate advocated lowering taxes.

2) **recreational** [ˌrɛkriˈeʃən]] (a.) 消遣的，（藥物）非醫療用途的
(phr.) recreational drug use 為消遣（而非醫療）目的使用藥物
Marijuana and cocaine are popular recreational drugs.

3) **restriction** [rɪˈstrɪkʃən] (n.) 約束，限制
Cheap air tickets usually have lots of restrictions.

4) **withdrawal** [wɪθˈdrɔəl] (n.) 撤退
The government has decided to accelerate troop withdrawal.

5) **momentum** [moˈmɛntəm] (n.) 動力，能量
The economic recovery is gaining momentum.

6) **scatter** [ˈskætə] (v.) 分散，散開
The birds scattered at the sound of the rifle.

補充字彙

* **career-oriented** [kəˈrɪrˈorɪəntɪd] (a.)
以追求事業為目的的
Kate wants to date a guy who is career-oriented.

* **rat race** [ræt res] (phr.)（俚）（喻）擔心落後會被取代而天天辛苦奔波的工作（像籠中老鼠不斷在滾輪中奔跑）
I can't wait to retire and get out of the rat race.

* **commune** [ˈkɑmjun] (n.) 公社，嬉皮村
(a.) communal [kəˈmjʊn]] 共有的
Summer's parents lived in a commune in the 60s.

* **identify with** [aɪˈdɛntəˌfaɪ wɪθ] (phr.)
認同，產生共鳴
Most readers identify with the novel's hero.

* **anarchy** [ˈænəkɪ] (n.) 無法無天，無政府的混亂狀態
The civil war threw the country into anarchy.

課文朗讀 MP3 109　單字朗讀 MP3 110　英文文章導讀 MP3 111

Hippie culture was instantly recognizable. The mainstream was conservatively dressed, *career-oriented, and focused on **1 keeping up with the Joneses**. In contrast, the colorfully-clothed, long-haired hippies
5 ¹⁾**advocated** ²⁾**recreational** drug use, open relationships and dropping out of the *rat race. As the culture matured, hippies began going back to nature and living in *communes. Makeup, shoes, and even bathing were seen as unnecessary ³⁾**restrictions**. Corporations were seen
10 as enemies of peace and a clean environment. Hippies dropped out of school and abandoned careers for long pilgrimages to San Francisco, Mexico, and India. They *identified with minority cultures around the world, and thought being all-American was narrow-minded and
15 limiting. For a while it seemed like hippie culture was here to stay.

But the hippie movement **2 lost steam** in the early 1970s. ⓒWith American ⁴⁾**withdrawal** from Vietnam, the protest movement collapsed. The music scene lost ⁵⁾**momentum**

20 with the breakup of The Beatles and the death of several rock stars from drug overdoses. While communes

25 sounded great in theory, their stress on personal freedom often led to *anarchy. And as hippies got older, they began to settle down and raise families. Needing money, they returned to mainstream careers. The younger generation thought hippies were old-fashioned and

30 rebelled against them by reembracing mainstream culture. The remaining hippies ⁶⁾**scattered**. Some moved abroad, while others dropped out of the movement and just did their own thing. Others opened businesses specializing in health food or natural skin products. One hippie even founded Apple

35 Computer.

中 Translation

嬉皮文化很容易辨識。當時的社會主流是穿著保守、事業取向，並把焦點擺在如何與鄰居一較高下。相對地，穿著鮮艷、一頭長髮的嬉皮族提倡消遣藥物使用、開放的男女關係以及脫離永無休止的繁忙工作生活。隨著這種文化成熟，嬉皮族開始回歸自然，並且以「公社」型態居住。化妝、鞋子、甚至洗澡都視為不必要的約束，企業被視為和平與乾淨環境的大敵。嬉皮族紛紛輟學或放棄事業，展開往舊金山、墨西哥和印度的長途朝聖之旅。他們認同世界各地的少數民族文化，認為當「純正的美國人」是心胸狹隘、畫地自限的。一時之間，嬉皮文化看似就要落地生根。

不過，嬉皮運動在一九七〇年代初期失去動力。隨著美國從越南撤兵，抗議運動也戛然而止。隨著披頭四解散和多位搖滾巨星因藥物過量致死，嬉皮在音樂上也失去動力。「公社」乍聽下是很棒的概念，但它們著重個人自由的做法常造成混亂失序。而且嬉皮族年歲漸長，他們開始安身立命、養家活口。由於需要金錢，他們陸續回到主流職業。年輕的一代則認為嬉皮族已經過氣，而以重新擁抱主流文化來反抗。碩果僅存的嬉皮四散各地，有些移居海外，有些退出運動，做他們自己的事，還有人開起健康食品或天然護膚產品的專賣店。有一位嬉皮甚至創立了蘋果電腦。

蘋果電腦創辦人 Steve Jobs

Tongue-tied No More

1 keep up with the Joneses
輸人不輸陣

Jones 是一個非常普遍的英文姓氏，就像我們說的「張三李四」，所以 keep up with the Joneses 是泛指許多人，而非特定姓 Jones 的人。keep up with the Joneses 是指為了能與鄰居較勁而維持生活水準，打腫臉充胖子購買非必要的虛榮物品。
A: Did you get that raise you asked for?
你要求加薪如願了嗎？
B: No. Now I'll never be able to keep up with the Joneses.
沒。我以後出門都抬不起頭來了。

2 lose steam 失去動力、驅力
也可以說 run out of steam。steam 就是推動引擎的「蒸汽」，當外在情勢改變，或是人們失去興趣，讓一件事無法推動下去，就會用 lose steam 或 run out of steam 來形容。
A: Do you think Stinson is going to win the election?
你認為史丁遜會勝選嗎？
B: I used to, but it seems like his campaign is losing steam.
我以前是這樣認為，但他目前的競選活動似乎欲振乏力。

Language Guide

pilgrimage 朝聖之旅
pilgrimage [ˋpɪlgrəmɪdʒ] 原指各種宗教信徒長途跋涉到聖地朝拜的「朝聖之旅」，如回教徒一生要去一次麥加、猶太人造訪耶路撒冷，而這些「朝聖者」就是 pilgrim [ˋpɪlgrɪm]。這樣的說法後來引申為與宗教無關的用法，如熱愛電影的人前往好萊塢或坎城，也可以說是去朝聖。但對 60-70 年代的年輕嬉皮而言，展開 pilgrimage 最主要的目的是拖延離家的時間，在經費拮据的情況下，絕大多數都是靠搭便車 (hitchhiking) 或搭公車完成旅程。
Thousands of fans make the pilgrimage to Jim Morrison's grave in Paris each year.
每年有成千上萬吉姆莫里森（The Doors 主唱，吸毒身亡）的樂迷前往他在巴黎的墳墓朝聖。

Grammar Master

with + 名詞／名詞片語 → 由於……
例 ● With the expansion of the education system, a college education is no longer reserved for the rich.
由於教育的普及，大學教育不再是有錢人的專利。
● With all his savings tied up in investments, he had to borrow money from his parents to pay for the operation.
由於他所有存款都拿去投資了，他得向父母借錢來支付手術費用。

V Vocabulary Bank

1) **fascination** [ˌfæsəˋneʃən] (n.) 陶醉，迷戀
I don't understand Roger's fascination with stamps.

2) **meditation** [ˌmɛdɪˋteʃən] (n.) 冥想，打坐
The Beatles traveled to India to learn meditation.

3) **acceptance** [əkˋsɛptəns] (n.) 接受，承認
The biologist's theory quickly won acceptance in the scientific community.

4) **encyclopedia** [ɪnˌsaɪkləˋpidɪə] (n.)
百科全書。Wikipedia 即「維基百科，自由的百科全書」
The encyclopedia has an excellent article on the Industrial Revolution.

5) **attendance** [əˋtɛndəns] (n.) 出席（人數）
The concert set a new attendance record.

6) **glimpse** [glɪmps] (n.) 一瞥
I caught a glimpse of the Golden Gate Bridge from the plane.

補充字彙

* **popularize** [ˋpɑpjələˌraɪz] (v.) 普及
Elvis Presley played a key role in popularizing rock music.

* **idealism** [aɪˋdiəˌlɪzəm] (n.) 理想主義
The 1960s were a decade of idealism.

* **open-source** [ˋopənˋsors] (a.) （電腦）公開
軟體的原始程式碼 (source code)（供其他程式設計人員免費使用），共享資源
Linux is the most popular open-source operating system.

* **empathy** [ˋɛmpəθɪ] (n.) 移情，同理心
The man's empathy for the poor led him to start a charity.

* **globalization** [ˌglobəlɪˋzeʃən] (n.)
全球化
Globalization is an inevitable trend.

* **exploitation** [ˌɛksplɔɪˋteʃən] (n.) 剝削
The exploitation of migrant workers is becoming a serious problem.

* **revitalize** [riˋvaɪtˌlˌaɪz] (v.) 重振
The government has announced a new plan to revitalize the economy.

* **arena rock** [əˋrinə rɑk] (phr.)
舞台搖滾，濫觴於七〇年代重金屬、搖滾及前衛搖滾樂團在大型活動場館 (arena) 舉辦現場演唱會的音樂表演形式，特色在於歌曲中會特意安插現場聽眾容易配合演唱的副歌、引爆現場情緒的大音量、舞台燈光、煙霧爆破等視覺效果
Led Zeppelin was one of the first arena rock bands.

課文朗讀 MP3 112　單字朗讀 MP3 113　英文文章導讀 MP3 114

Though the hippie movement ended nearly forty years ago, it has had a lasting impact on mainstream culture. Hippies' 1)**fascination** with Asian culture helped *popularize Buddhism, 2)**meditation** and yoga. And
5 their love of nature, open-mindedness and emphasis on healthy living gave birth to the environmental movement, 3)**acceptance** of gays and lesbians, medical marijuana, and alternative medicine. The hippie communal spirit even inspired the sharing and *idealism
10 of the Internet seen today in file sharing, *open-source software, and 4)**Wikipedia**, a free 4)**encyclopedia** where all content is created and edited by users. And hippie *empathy for foreign societies and passion for peaceful resistance has inspired large-scale protests
15 against *globalization, the *exploitation of Third World countries, and the recent Iraq War.

Hippies also *revitalized the music industry through mass 5)**attendance** of events like the Monterey Pop Festival. ⒼIn 1969, 450,000 people came together for the
20 world's most famous rock concert: Woodstock. It lasted three days, featured superstar acts, and when too many fans arrived, the management made it a "free concert" in true hippie fashion. It was a popular and commercial success, and paved the way for the *arena rock of Ⓖthe 70s
25 and 80s. Woodstock continues to inspire artists, dreamers, and even movie directors. *Taking Woodstock*, director Ang Lee's 2009 comedy-drama film, is based on the book, *Taking Woodstock: A True Story of a Riot, a Concert, and a Life*. It follows the life of Elliot Tiber, the gay New
30 Yorker who helped organized Woodstock. See the movie and you'll get a 6)**glimpse** of the hippie spirit that has affected our lives in so many ways.

中 Translation

雖然嬉皮運動已在近四十年前畫下句點，它對主流文化有了深遠的影響。嬉皮對亞洲文化的迷戀有助於佛教、冥想和瑜伽的普及，而他們對大自然的愛、開放的心胸以及對健康生活的注重，也催生出環保運動、接納男女同性戀、藥用大麻和另類醫療。嬉皮的公社精神甚至啟發了網際網路的分享和理想主義，現今的檔案分享、開放原始碼軟體和維基百科（免費的網路百科全書，所有內容皆由使用者撰寫及編輯）等皆為例證。而嬉皮對外國社會的同理心以及對平和式抵抗運動的熱忱，也喚起了反對全球化、剝削第三世界國家和最近之伊拉克戰爭的大規模抗議。

嬉皮也透過蒙特瑞流行音樂節等大規模參與的活動，振興了音樂產業。一九六九年，四十五萬人齊聚世界最知名的搖滾音樂會：胡士托。盛會持續三天，演出的都是超級巨星，到場的粉絲實在太多，主辦單位遂秉持真正的嬉皮精神，將之改為「免費音樂會」。音樂會大受歡迎，也在商業上大獲成功，更為七〇及八〇年代的舞台搖滾奠定基礎。胡士托持續啟發藝人、夢想家甚至電影導演的靈感。導演李安二〇〇九年推出的喜劇／劇情片《胡士托風波》是以《胡士托風波》一書為本，本片細述紐約同性戀者以利特泰柏的一生，他是胡士托的推手之一。觀賞這部電影，你將能一窺至今在多方面影響我們生活的嬉皮精神。

✦ Language Guide

Monterey Pop Festival
蒙特瑞流行音樂節

1967 年 6 月 16 日到 18 日於美國加州蒙特瑞市舉辦的音樂節，是史上首場強力造勢的大型搖滾音樂活動，估計有 20 萬人參與這場盛會，到場表演的黑人樂手 Jimi Hendrix、Otis Redding、女歌手 Janis Joplin、英國樂團 The Who……都就此在美國聲名大噪，Jimi Hendrix 在舞台上放火燒吉他，更成為搖滾樂史的經典畫面。這場連續三天的音樂會被視為 Summer of Love 的濫觴之一，也成為日後舉辦大型搖滾音樂會（如 Woodstock Festival）的範本。

Woodstock Festival
胡士托音樂節

1969 年 8 月 15 日到 18 日於美國紐約州近郊的貝瑟爾 (Bethel) 舉辦的音樂節，在這個陰雨連綿、間歇雷雨的週末，近五十萬人聚集在泥濘不堪的農場上欣賞 32 個音樂團體／個人的表演（其中包括 Joan Baez、Santana、Grateful Dead、Jefferson Airplane，詳細節目流程見 🔗http://en.wikipedia.org/wiki/Woodstock，共同締造流行音樂史劃時代的一頁。

Ⓖ Grammar Master

(in) the + 幾十年代數字 + s
（在）……幾十年代（的十年中）

在沒有特別說明的情況下，是指二十世紀 (19X0) 年代

例 ● He was a famous movie star **in the 1960s.**
　　他在 1960 年代是知名影星。

● **The 70s** was the age of Disco music.
　 70 年代是迪斯可音樂的年代。

專指19X0那一年則不必加 the。

● Alfred Hitchcock passed away **in 1980.**
　大導演希區考克於 1980 年去世。

✎ Mini Quiz 閱讀測驗

❶ According to the article, which of the following contributed to the decline of the hippie movement?
(A) The Beatles' embrace of hippie culture
(B) the American withdrawal from Vietnam
(C) dropping out of the rat race
(D) recreational drug use

❷ By the time Ron and Jackie got married, they _____ together for six years.
(A) was (B) were
(C) has been (D) had been

Vocabulary Bank

1) **wander** [ˋwɑndɚ] (v.) 流浪，閒逛
We spent the day wandering around the town.

2) **exotic** [ɪgˋzɑtɪk] (a.) 異國（情調）的，奇特的
The soup was seasoned with exotic spices.

3) **fortune-telling** [ˋfɔrtʃən͵tɛlɪŋ] (n.) 算命
Tea leaves have long been used for fortune-telling.

4) **traditionally** [trəˋdɪʃənlɪ] (adv.) 傳統上，習慣上
Turkey is traditionally eaten on Thanksgiving.

5) **odd** [ɑd] (a.) 臨時的，不固定的。odd job即「零工，雜活」
Peter was only able to find odd jobs during the recession.

6) **property** [ˋprɑpɚtɪ] (n.) 房屋及院落，房地產
Get off my property or I'll call the cops!

7) **squat (on/in)** [skwɑt] (v.) 偷住，擅自佔用
(n.) squatter [ˋskwɑtɚ] 未經允許即住下來的人
Many homeless people squatted in the abandoned building.

8) **accuse** [əˋkjuz] (v.) 指控，指責
Scott's wife accused him of cheating.

9) **persuade** [pɚˋswed] (v.) 說服，勸說
Bella persuaded her parents to let her get a tattoo.

10) **laborer** [ˋlebərɚ] (n.) 勞動者，勞工
In Taiwan, foreign laborers are paid the minimum wage.

11) **popularity** [͵pɑpjəˋlærətɪ] (n.) 普及，流行，受歡迎程度
The popularity of video games continues to grow.

進階字彙

12) **nomad** [ˋnomæd] (n.) 游牧民族，流浪者
(a.) nomadic [noˋmædɪk] 游牧的，流浪的
The nomads travel through the desert on camels.

13) **Egypt** [ˋidʒɪpt] (n.) 埃及
I've always wanted to see the pyramids of Egypt.

14) **banish** [ˋbænɪʃ] (v.) 趕走，驅逐
Adam and Eve were banished from the Garden of Eden.

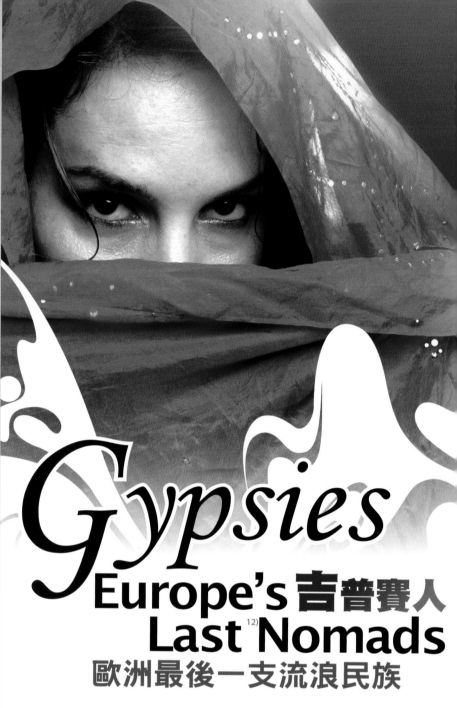

Gypsies
Europe's 吉普賽人
Last [12]Nomads
歐洲最後一支流浪民族

課文朗讀 MP3 115　單字朗讀 MP3 116　英文文章導讀 MP3 117

While everyone has heard of Gypsies, most people don't really know much about them. The Gypsies, who are also known as Travelers because they spend their lives [1]**wandering** from place to place, are Europe's last [12]**nomadic**
5　people. The word Gypsy is short for [13]**Egypt**, which is where Europeans thought they came from originally. They were thought to be Egyptians because of their dark skin, [2]**exotic** clothing and reputation for [3]**fortune-telling** and black magic. In fact, the Gypsies came from northern India over a

10 from northern India over a thousand years ago. At present, there are around six million gypsies in Europe. Most of them live in Central and Eastern Europe, and large numbers are also found in France, 15 Russia and Spain.

Gypsies ⁴⁾**traditionally** made a living as ❶**jacks-of-all-trades**. They mended pots and pans, repaired clothes and leather, told people's fortunes and did useful ⁵⁾**odd** jobs. But they also gained a reputation for not respecting private 20 ⁶⁾**property**. They ⁷⁾**squatted** on people's land, and were often ⁸⁾**accused** of stealing. For centuries, governments tried to ⁹⁾**persuade** them to become farmers or ¹⁰⁾**laborers**. But because they refused to settle down, they were ¹⁴⁾**banished** from entire countries and even murdered. Although Gypsies 25 aren't feared like they used to be, wandering hippies and New Age ⁷⁾**squatters** are giving them a bad name today. This is because most people don't even know what a real Gypsy looks like. But the good news is that the growing ¹¹⁾**popularity** of flamenco music and dance is slowly 30 ᴳhelping to improve their image.

中 Translation

雖然大家都聽過吉普賽人，但多數人對他們所知並不多。吉普賽人亦有「游居者」之稱，因為他們終其一生都在各地流浪，是歐洲最後一支流浪民族。吉普賽（Gypsy）一詞是埃及（Egypt）的縮寫，因為歐洲人認為他們最初是來自埃及。吉普賽人會被認為是埃及人，係因他們皮膚黑、服裝奇特，且以算命及巫術聞名。其實，吉普賽人一千多年前來自印度北部，目前歐洲大約有六百萬名吉普賽人，其中大多數住在中歐及東歐，法國、俄羅斯和西班牙也有為數不少的吉普賽人。

傳統上，吉普賽人以「萬事通」謀生。他們會修理鍋壺、修補衣服和皮革、幫人算命和做做實用的零工。但他們也是出了名的不尊重私人財產。他們會擅自佔據他人土地，也常被指控偷竊。幾百年來，各國政府試著說服他們成為農民或勞工，但因為他們拒絕定居下來而屢遭驅逐離境，甚至遭到殺害。今天，雖然吉普賽人已不像過去那樣為人所恐懼，但四處為家的嬉皮和新世紀佔地者今日仍給他們帶來惡名。這是因為多數人甚至不知道吉普賽人究竟長什麼樣子，所幸，人氣漸高的佛朗明哥音樂和舞蹈正慢慢改善他們的形象。

吉普賽旅行拖車 Gipsy caravan

✦ Language Guide

Gypsies 吉普賽人

吉普賽人自稱羅姆人（Romani 或 Roma），這個古老的游居民族，使用的語言是羅姆語 (Romany)。據說吉普賽人源自印度北部，但因屢次遷徙，所以也講各居住國的主要語言，現遍佈世界各地，尤以歐洲為主。會以「吉普賽」稱之是因為當時的歐洲人誤以為黑眼、深色皮膚的羅姆人來自埃及，於是稱他們為「埃及人」(Egyptian)，而吉普賽 (Gypsy) 是埃及 (Egypt) 的變音。吉普賽人有許許多多名稱，包括卡爾德拉什人 (Kalderash)、吉坦人 (Gitanos)、金加利人 (Zingari)、辛堤人 (Sinti) 等。因「吉普賽」含有貶義，現在有些英國人會以「游居者」(Traveler) 代稱。第二次世界大戰時，約有四十萬吉普賽人和猶太人一樣被關進集中營進行種族屠殺。

✦ Tongue-tied No More

1 jack-of-all-trades 萬事通

jack-of-all-trades 源自於十七世紀流行的諺語 Jack of all trades, master of none.「樣樣通、樣樣鬆」。當時 Jack 這個名字很普遍，所以成了一般人的代稱，而 trades「手藝」在這裡引申為各行各業。jack-of-all-trades 是指什麼都懂、什麼都會做的人，是正面的用法。但若是加上後面的 master of none「沒一樣專精」，就變成了負面用法，指一個人看來樣樣精通，卻沒有一樣真正專長。

A: Wow, I didn't know Jim knew how to fix cars!
哇，我之前都不知道吉姆會修車！

B: Yeah. He's a jack-of-all-trades.
是啊，他可是個萬事通呢！

✦ Grammar Master

help 的用法

help 這個字有許多用法，有時候接 Ving，有時候接 to+V，也可以直接加原形動詞。若以 help 表達「幫助做某事」來看，有下列幾種說法：

● （事情）help + (to) 原形 V
例 本課最後一句：
…the growing popularity of flamenco music and dance is slowly **helping to improve** their image.（to 可省略，但習慣有 to）

● （人）help + 原形 V（help 和原形 V 之間通常沒有 to）
例 Mandy **helped organize** the party.
曼蒂幫忙籌辦晚會。

● help（人）in + N / Ving
例 Reading that book really **helped me in my career**.
讀那本書真的對我的職業生涯有所幫助。

例 The customer service rep **helped me in solving my problems**.
這位客服人員幫我解決了我的問題。

● help（人）with + N
例 Can you **help me with the laundry**?
你可以幫我洗那些衣服嗎？

佛朗明哥舞蹈

佛朗明哥音樂以及舞蹈被認為是西班牙文化重要的一部份，然而如同文章中所說的，它最早的發源地是安達魯西亞。佛朗明哥的音樂及舞蹈是阿拉伯、安達魯西亞、塞法迪猶太人 (Sephardic Jews) 和吉普賽等各種文化的大融合 (fusion)。Flamenco 這個字一直到十九世紀時才開始出現，在此之前並無史料記載。

除了發源地安達魯西亞外，佛朗明哥另一個主要發展地區為西班牙的埃斯特雷馬杜拉 (Extremadura) 和莫夕亞 (Murcia)。有許多精通佛朗明哥舞蹈與音樂的表演者並非僅限於西班牙，像是拉丁美洲地區 (Latin America)，尤其是古巴 (Cuba)，對此舞蹈及音樂的影響甚鉅。

cajon

佛朗明哥表演的場合

發展至今的佛朗明哥常會出現在以下三種場合：

最傳統的表演場合是佛朗明哥歡宴（juerga [ˈhwɛrga]），這是吉普賽人聚集在一起時一種非正式 (informal) 且隨性的 (spontaneous) 慶祝歡宴。包含了舞蹈、歌唱、拍掌 (palmas)，亦或只是簡單地利用木箱 (crate) 或桌子拍打節奏，是一種最自然 (organic) 也最具活力 (dynamic) 的表演，整個氣氛會隨著現場觀眾而更顯熱鬧。佛朗明哥歌者（cantaores [ˈkɔntroɾəs]）是表演的主軸。

專業的表演會就比較正式了。傳統的歌唱表演只有一位歌者與一位吉他手，而舞蹈表演時通常包含了二到三位的吉他手，一至多位的歌者以及舞者。其中一位歌者會打擊一種叫做木箱鼓（cajon [kɑˈhon]）的樂器，其他人會以手掌聲附和。而所謂新世代的佛朗明哥還會有長笛 (flute)、薩克斯風、鋼琴甚至是電吉他等樂器的伴奏。已故的西班牙國寶級佛朗明哥歌手 Camarón de la Isla 就是成功推廣此種方式的重要推手。

最後一種表演場合是佛朗明哥的戲劇表演 (theatrical presentation)，是一種藉由佛朗明哥的技巧與音樂來呈現的戲劇演出，近似於芭蕾舞表演 (ballet performance)，會有樂隊席 (orchestra pit)、佈景 (scenery) 與燈光等等。

對其他舞蹈也有興趣嗎？
除了熱情的佛朗明哥舞，還有一些大家耳熟能詳的舞蹈類型，一起學學英文的說法吧！

Ballroom Dance
社交舞
● **waltz** [ˈwɔlts] 華爾滋
● **tango** [ˈtæŋɡo] 探戈
● **fox trot** [fɑks trɑt] 狐步舞
● **quickstep** [ˈkwɪkˌstɛp] 快步舞

Latin Dance
拉丁舞
● **mambo** [ˈmɑmbo] 曼波舞
● **rumba** [ˈrʌmbə] 倫巴舞
● **cha-cha** [ˈtʃɑˌtʃɑ] 恰恰
● **salsa** [ˈsɑlsə] 騷莎舞

Hip Hop Dance
嘻哈舞
● **breaking** [ˈbrekɪŋ] 地板街舞
● **popping** [ˈpɑpɪŋ] 機械舞
● **locking** [ˈlɑkɪŋ] 鎖舞

Vocabulary Bank

1) **fable** [ˈfebḷ] (n.) 傳說，寓言
The Fox and the Grapes is my favorite fable.

2) **descend (from)** [dɪˈsɛnd] (v.) 是…的後裔
It has been proven that birds are descended from dinosaurs.

3) **written** [ˈrɪtṇ] (a.) 書面的，寫下的
Carl's written English is better than his spoken English.

4) **combine** [kəmˈbaɪn] (v.) 結合，兼備
Cuban music combines Spanish and African influences.

5) **strength** [strɛŋθ] (n.) 力量，力氣
It took him months to regain his strength after the surgery.

6) **expression** [ɪkˈsprɛʃən] (n.) 表情，臉色
I can tell by Sam's expression that he's in a bad mood.

7) **performance** [pəˈfɔrməns] (n.) 表演，演出
The man won an Oscar for his performance in the film.

8) **extended** [ɪkˈstɛndɪd] (a.) 延伸的，伸展的
The alligator was sixteen feet long with its tail extended.

9) **bow** [baʊ] (v.) 鞠躬，低頭
All the actors bowed at the end of the performance.

10) **snap up** [snæp ʌp] (phr.) 猛然往上
Everyone's heads snapped up when they heard the explosion.

11) **thrust** [θrʌst] (v.) 用力推，伸展
The boy thrust his hands into his pockets.

12) **grip** [ɡrɪp] (v.) 緊握，緊抓
We gripped the sides of the boat to keep from falling out.

進階字彙

13) **Jewish** [ˈdʒuɪʃ] (a.) 猶太人的，猶太教的
Israel is the first Jewish state in history.

14) **stomp** [stɑmp] (v.) 跺腳，重踩
The man was stomped to death by an elephant.

課文朗讀 MP3 118　單字朗讀 MP3 119　英文文章導讀 MP3 120

There is a European ¹⁾**fable** that says the Gypsies are ²⁾**descended** from 12,000 musicians sent by an Indian king to a Persian ruler. This story is still believed by some people, because the Gypsies did in fact come from India,

5 and are best known today for flamenco. While flamenco is considered an important part of Spain's national culture, it actually comes from just one region: Andalusia. Yet flamenco wasn't invented by Andalusian Gypsies alone. It is now believed to be a mix of Gypsy, Arab, Andalusian and

10 ¹³⁾**Jewish** cultures, although the full truth may never be known. The Gypsies didn't keep ³⁾**written** records, and the word flamenco is only about two hundred years old.

Flamenco is a unique art form that ⁴⁾**combines** dance, singing and guitar music. The arm and leg movements of

15 the flamenco dancer stress physical ⁵⁾**strength** and speed. Intense facial ⁶⁾**expressions** tell the story behind the music.

Although the music is provided by the singers and guitar players, the dancers ᴳadd to it by clapping their hands and ¹⁴⁾**stomping** their feet. As the ⁷⁾**performance** begins, the dancers stand perfectly straight with their arms ⁸⁾**extended** forward and their hands together. Their heads ⁹⁾**bow** as they wait for a burst of musical energy from the hands of the guitarists. Suddenly, their feet stomp powerfully, their heads ¹⁰⁾**snap up**, and they ¹¹⁾**thrust** their hands down and ¹²⁾**grip** their waists. Like beautiful birds putting on a display for their mates, the dancers strut proudly across the stage.

中 Translation

歐洲相傳吉普賽人是一位印度國王送給波斯君主的一萬兩千名樂師的後裔。至今仍有人相信這個故事，因為吉普賽人確實是來自印度，現今又以佛朗明哥最為知名。儘管佛朗明哥被視為西班牙國家文化的重要部分，但它其實僅源自一個地區：安達魯西亞。不過佛朗明哥並非安達魯西亞的吉普賽人獨創，現在一般認為，它是混合了吉普賽、阿拉伯、安達魯西亞和猶太文化的產物，但完整的真相或許永遠不得而知。吉普賽人並未留下文字紀錄，而「佛朗明哥」一詞也只問世兩百年左右。

佛朗明哥是一種獨一無二的藝術形式，結合了舞蹈、歌唱和吉他音樂。佛朗明哥舞者手臂及腿部的動作強調身體的力量與速度，強烈的臉部表情則訴說音樂背後的故事。雖然音樂是由歌手和吉他手展現，但舞者也以擊掌和跺腳來增添效果。表演開始時，舞者會站得直挺挺，兩臂向前延伸，雙手合十。他們低著頭，等待音樂的能量從吉他手的手中爆發。突然，他們的腳重重跺地，頭猛然揚起，然後用力放下雙手，插在腰際。就像美麗的鳥兒擺開求偶陣勢，舞者也驕傲地在舞台上昂首闊步。

Language Guide

Andalusia 安達魯西亞

Portugal
葡萄牙

Andalusia
安達魯西亞

Mediterranean Sea
地中海

Strait of Gibraltar
直布羅陀海峽

Morocco
摩洛哥

安達魯西亞是西班牙十七個自治區 (autonomous community) 其中之一，人口高達八百二十八萬五千人。以陸地面積來說，是西班牙第二大自治區。首都是賽維利亞 (Seville)。安達魯西亞位於伊比利亞半島 (Iberian Peninsula) 南部，地中海 (Mediterranean Sea) 與直布羅陀海峽 (Strait of Gibraltar) 以北，隔海與北非的摩洛哥 (Morocco) 相望。

此地區的音樂囊括了傳統與現代 (contemporary)，像是民謠 (folk) 與創作音樂，它的音樂範圍更從佛朗明哥到搖滾樂，而佛朗明哥是安達魯西亞最具代表性的音樂與舞蹈類型 (genre)。

Grammar Master

to 當介系詞的用法
動詞 add 表示「增加」，用法為 add something to something 或 add to something，注意這裡的 to 是介系詞，所以後面需接名詞／代名詞／動名詞。
例 The collector **added** a Picasso **to** her collection.
收藏家為她的收藏增添了一幅畢卡索的畫。
例 Tom's girlfriend's encouragement only **added to** his pressure.
湯姆女友的鼓勵只增加了他的壓力。
其他同樣以 to 當介系詞的動詞片語：
● look forward to 期待
● pay attention to 注意
● be addicted to 沉溺於
● appeal to 吸引
● lead to 導致

Vocabulary Bank

1) **imitate** [ˋɪmɪ.tet] (v.) 模仿，仿效
Larry is good at imitating foreign accents.

2) **professionally** [prəˋfɛʃənəlɪ] (adv.)
專業地，職業地
Tim used to play football professionally.

3) **pop up** [pɑp ʌp] (phr.) 突然出現
New problems keep popping up all the time.

4) **frequent** [ˋfrikwənt] (a.) 頻繁的，常發生的
Frequent earthquakes make the place dangerous.

5) **out of** [aut əv] (phr.) 出於（原因、動機）
Jessica stayed with her husband out of loyalty.

6) **witch** [wɪtʃ] (n.) 女巫，巫婆
Carrie dressed up as a witch for Halloween.

7) **concentration** [.kɑnsənˋtreʃən] (n.)
集中（資源、注意力等）
Silicon Valley has the highest concentration of high-tech companies in the world.

8) **generally** [ˋdʒɛnərəlɪ] (adv.) 大體上，通常
The weather here is generally warm and sunny all year round.

9) **tolerant** [ˋtɑlərənt] (a.) 寬容的，容忍的
Amsterdam is a very tolerant city.

10) **alternative** [ɔlˋtɜnətɪv] (a.) 非主流的，另類的
More and more doctors are beginning to practice alternative medicine.

11) **fortunately** [ˋfɔrtʃənɪtlɪ] (adv.) 幸運地，僥倖地
Fortunately, the weather was perfect during our vacation.

進階字彙

12) **Nazis** [ˋnɑtsɪz] (n.) 德國納粹黨，
單數為 Nazi
The Nazis came to power in 1933.

Earlier generations of flamenco artists didn't receive formal training. Instead, they learned to sing and dance by watching and [1]**imitating** talented relatives, friends and neighbors. These days, however, it is common for flamenco

5　dancers, singers and guitarists to be [2]**professionally** trained. Schools are [3]**popping up** all over, and as flamenco becomes more international in sound and style, its popularity is spreading around the world. Here in Taiwan, there are [4]**frequent** flamenco performances in pubs

10　near National Taiwan Normal University. There is even a famous flamenco center in Taipei whose instructors are professional performers from Spain. Students come from as far away as Hong Kong, Malaysia and Singapore just to take their classes.

15　The life of a Gypsy has never been an easy one. Ever since leaving India, they have been attacked for their wandering lifestyle and [5]**out of** fear that they were [6]**witches**. During World War II, the [12]**Nazis** put Gypsies in [7]**concentration** camps, and killed as many as they

20　could. Even today, Gypsies continue to be hated in some parts of Europe, and often live in poverty. However, people are [8]**generally** becoming more [9]**tolerant** of [10]**alternative** lifestyles, and government financial support is helping Gypsies find a place in modern society. Just a few decades

25　ago, it looked ᴳas if the Gypsies might disappear from the face of the earth forever. [11]**Fortunately**, the Gypsies and their rich cultural traditions are now stronger than ever. And that's good

30　news for everybody.

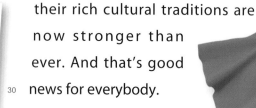

中 Translation

早期的佛朗明哥藝術家並未接受正式訓練，而是透過觀察及模仿有天分的親友和鄰居來學習歌舞。但時至今日，佛朗明哥舞者、歌手和吉他手接受專業訓練已稀鬆平常。學校四處林立，而且隨著佛朗明哥在聲音和風格上愈來愈國際化，普及度也於全球各地蔓延。在台灣這裡，國立台灣師範大學附近的酒吧常有佛朗明哥的表演。台北甚至有一間知名的佛朗明哥中心，指導老師是來自西班牙的專業表演者，有許多從香港、馬來西亞和新加坡遠道而來的學生專程來此上課。

吉普賽人的生活從不輕鬆。自從離開印度後，他們就一直因為流浪的生活方式，也因世人深怕他們是巫師而飽受攻擊。在二次世界大戰期間，納粹將吉普賽人抓進集中營，能殺多少就殺多少。甚至到今天，吉普賽人在歐洲某些地區仍持續遭到憎恨，往往過著貧苦的日子。不過，人們一般來說愈來愈能容忍另類的生活方式，政府的財務支援也幫助吉普賽人在現代社會找到容身之地。不過才數十年前，吉普賽人眼看似乎就要從地球永遠消失，幸好，如今吉普賽人和他們豐富的傳統比以往都要穩固，這對每個人來說都是好消息。

Language Guide

concentration camp 集中營

集中營原指監禁政治犯 (political prisoners)、戰俘 (prisoners of war) 以及難民 (refugees) 的地方，但德國納粹在柏林召開萬湖 (Wannsee) 會議，決定殲滅全歐洲的猶太人。之後，猶太人、吉普賽人等少數民族 (ethnic minorities) 被送往集中營集體屠殺，估計約有六百多萬猶太人遭到殺害。惡名昭彰的集中營包括《辛德勒的名單》所記錄的波蘭「奧許維茲集中營」Auschwitz Concentration Camp。

Grammar Master

as if、like 彷彿；好像

as if 跟 like 常與 look / sound / feel 等連綴動詞連用。雖然兩者都有「彷彿；好像」之意，且 as if 和 like 後面都可以接子句，但 like 在此當介系詞，所以後面可以接名詞或動名詞。

例 Ben took an umbrella with him because it **looked as if** it was going to rain.
班帶著雨傘，因為看來快要下雨了。

例 What a beautiful house! It **looks like** a palace.
多麼漂亮的房子啊! 看起來就像皇宮一樣。

此外，若 as if 後面子句的動詞為過去式時，通常表示非真實或不太可能會發生的情況（如本課課文）。

例 Mary spent money **as if** she had won the lottery.
瑪莉花錢的方式彷彿中了樂透一般。

Mini Quiz 閱讀測驗

1 Why are Gypsies also known as Travelers?
(A) Because they like to travel during vacations
(B) Because they live a wandering lifestyle
(C) Because they like to visit different countries
(D) Because they are daring people

2 The man was accused _____ stealing from the old woman.
(A) in
(B) with
(C) of
(D) to

3 Can you help me _____ the dishes?
(A) in
(B) for
(C) on
(D) with

閱讀測驗解答 1 (B) 2 (C) 3 (D)

Greek Mythology 101
希臘神話 從頭說起

V Vocabulary Bank

1) **mythology** [mɪˋθɑlədʒɪ] (n.) 神話，神話學
Indian mythology is full of fantastic characters.

2) **understandably** [ˌʌndəˋstændəblɪ]
(adv.) 可理解地，合理地
(a.) understandable [ˌʌndəˋstændəbl] 可理解的，合理的
Voters are understandably angry about rising taxes.

3) **theme** [θim] (n.) 主題
What is the theme of your essay?

4) **overthrow** [ˌovəˋθro] (v.) 推翻，打倒
The army is plotting to overthrow the government.

5) **parenting** [ˋpɛrəntɪŋ] (n.) 養兒育女，親職。
parenting skills 即「為人父母的能力」
The young couple is taking a parenting class.

6) **smuggle** [ˋsmʌgl] (v.) 走私，偷帶
Around 30 tons of heroin is smuggled into the U.K. each year.

進階字彙

7) **void** [vɔɪd] (n.) 混沌空無，天空，空間
In many myths, the universe was created out of the void.

8) **incest** [ˋɪnsɛst] (n.) 亂倫，近親通婚
The young girl is a victim of incest.

9) **castrate** [ˋkæstret] (v.) 閹割；割除卵巢
The farmer castrated the calves.

10) **sickle** [ˋsɪkl] (n.) 鐮刀
In ancient times, farmers used sickles to harvest their crops.

11) **genitals** [ˋdʒɛnɪtlz] (n.) 生殖器
(a.) genital 生殖（器）的
Men in the tribe cover their genitals with leaves.

12) **inbreeding** [ˋɪnbridɪŋ] (n) 近親繁殖，同系交配
(v.) inbreed [ˌɪnˋbrid] 近親繁殖，同系交配
The different breeds of dogs are a result of inbreeding.

13) **prophecy** [ˋprɑfəsɪ] (n.) 預言
According to a Mayan prophecy, the world will end in 2012.

14) **nymph** [nɪmf] (n.)（希臘、羅馬神話）山林水澤間的仙女
The ancient Greeks believed that nymphs lived in forests and rivers.

課文朗讀 MP3 124　單字朗讀 MP3 125　英文文章導讀 MP3 126

In Greek [1]**mythology**, just as in the Bible, in the beginning there was nothing. From this [7]**void** came Gaia, Goddess of the Earth. Without any male assistance, Gaia gave birth to Uranus, God of the Sky. Uranus became Gaia's mate (there were no [8]**incest** laws back then), and the couple gave birth to six sets of twins called the Titans. As if 12 kids weren't enough, the Titans were followed by three Cyclopes and three Hecatonchires, monsters with 50 heads and 100 hands. Uranus hated the Cyclopes and Hecatonchires, so he imprisoned them in Tartarus, a cave deep in the earth. Gaia, [2]**understandably**, wasn't too happy about that, and she convinced Cronus, the youngest Titan, to [9]**castrate** his father with a [10]**sickle**. From his spilled blood came the Giants, and from the sea where his [11]**genitals** fell came Aphrodite, goddess of love.

愛神阿芙蘿黛緹

With his father ❶ **out of the picture**, Cronus became ruler and married his twin sister Rhea (yes, [12]**inbreeding** is a popular [3]**theme** in Greek mythology). The two had six children: Hestia, Demeter, Hera, Hades, Poseidon and Zeus. Because of a [13]**prophecy** that one of his children would [4]**overthrow** him, Cronus swallowed each of them as they were born. Disappointed by her husband's poor [5]**parenting** skills, Rhea decided to ❷ **change tack** with

希臘雅典的地標 Parthenon（帕德嫩神殿）
奉祀雅典守護女神 Athena（雅典娜）

her sixth child, Zeus. Instead of handing Cronus the child, she gave him a rock wrapped in a blanket. Cronus swallowed it, believing it was the baby. Rhea then 6)**smuggled** Zeus to the island of Crete to be raised by 14)**nymphs**. ©Little did she know, he would one day become King of the Gods.

30

天神宙斯

✏️ Mini Quiz 閱讀測驗

❶ ▢▢ How many children did Uranus and Gaia have?
   (A) 6
   (B) 12
   (C) 15
   (D) 18

❷ ▢▢ What did Cronus and Uranus have in common?
   (A) They both married their sister.
   (B) They both committed incest.
   (C) They both tried to kill their children.
   (D) They were both Titans.

中 Translation

在希臘神話中（和《聖經》裡的記載一樣），世界的起源是一片虛無。渾沌之中出現了大地女神蓋亞。在沒有任何男性的協助下，蓋亞生出天空之神烏拉努斯。烏拉努斯成了蓋亞的伴侶（當時沒有禁止亂倫的律法），兩人生了六對雙胞胎，名為泰坦。彷彿十二個孩子還不夠似的，他們接著又生了三個獨眼巨人賽克羅普斯和三個有五十個頭、一百隻手的巨怪赫克頓蓋爾。烏拉努斯憎惡獨眼巨人和赫克頓蓋爾，因此將他們監禁在地底深淵塔特魯斯。可想而知，蓋亞對此不太高興，於是她說服克羅努斯（年紀最小的泰坦）拿鐮刀將父親去勢。從烏拉努斯四濺的血液中誕生了巨人，而他的生殖器墜入的大海則出現了愛神阿芙蘿黛緹。

父親已經不在，於是克羅努斯成為統治者，娶了雙胞胎妹妹蕾亞為妻（是的，近親交配是希臘神話一個普遍的主題）。兩人生了六個孩子：海絲蒂亞、笛美特、希拉、黑帝斯、波塞頓和宙斯。由於有預言說其中一個子女會推翻他，每個孩子一出生克羅努斯就把他們吞下肚。因為對丈夫欠佳的養育方式感到失望，蕾亞在第六個孩子宙斯出生時決定改弦易轍。她沒把宙斯交給克羅努斯，而是給他一塊包裹著毛毯的石頭。克羅努斯不疑有它，把石頭吞了下去。然後蕾亞將宙斯偷偷送往克里特島，由仙女撫養。當時她並不知道，宙斯日後會成為眾神之王。

🧭 Language Guide

希臘神話簡介

Greek mythology（希臘神話）最早是透過口述傳播，先民的傳說內容不外乎是透過故事闡述自然現象（開天闢地、四季的形成）、人生的奧祕（生與死、財富、智慧）。直到西元前七世紀才開始出現以文字編寫神話的作家。希臘神話相關著作當中，最有名的要算是將神話穿插於戰爭故事中的荷馬（Homer）史詩（一開始也是透過口述，西元前八世紀才文字化）；另一則是西元一世紀羅馬作家奧維德（Ovid）的《變形記》（*Metamorphoses*），他的故事特色在於會用人物變形來反映角色的心理變化，影響後世作家與藝術家的創作甚深。

✂️ Tongue-tied No More

1 out of the picture 出局

out of the picture 是指一個人從眼前消失，不必再顧慮他了。除了表示一個人「離開」，也可引申為「死亡」。

A: Did you hear that Stella got divorced?
   你聽說史黛拉離婚了嗎？
B: Yeah. She says she's much happier now that her husband's out of the picture.
   聽說了。她說她開心多了，因為現在沒有這個老公了。

2 change tack 改變戰略

tack [tæk] 是指「做事的方法、步驟」。當你發現一件事做了半天都在白忙，就是該 change tack 的時候了。也可以說 try a different/new tack。

A: I go to the gym five times a week, but I'm still not losing any weight.
   我一星期去健身房五次，但還是一兩肉也沒少。
B: Maybe it's time to change tack. How about going on a diet?
   或許該換個作法了。開始節食如何？

⏰ Grammar Master

否定字詞引導的倒裝句

句首為否定字或片語（scarcely、hardly「幾乎不」，by no means「絕不」，seldom、little、few「不，很少」……）時，後方的子句必須倒裝。若子句內是一般動詞，加上助動詞即能形成倒裝；若是 be 動詞，則直接對調主詞和動詞的詞序。

例 **Scarcely** <u>had we arrived</u> when it began to rain.
   我們到了沒多久就開始下雨。

例 **By no means** <u>is he</u> easy to get along with.
   他絕不是個好相處的人。

例 **Seldom** <u>has there been</u> such a serious crisis.
   很少發生如此嚴重的危機。

閱讀測驗解答 ❶ (D) ❷ (B)

V Vocabulary Bank

1) **feed on** [fid ɑn] (phr.) 以…為食物，以…餵食
The mosquitoes fed on me all night!

2) **devour** [dɪˋvaʊr] (v.) 狼吞虎嚥地吃，吃光
The hungry lions devoured the wildebeest.

3) **disguise** [dɪsˋgaɪz] (n./v.) 掩飾，用來偽裝的東西；假扮，偽裝
The star always wears a disguise when she goes shopping.

4) **spike** [spaɪk] (v.) （在飲料中）摻入烈酒或毒藥
The professor spiked his coffee with whiskey.

5) **grateful** [ˋgretfəl] (a.) 感激的
I'm so grateful for all your help.

6) **gratitude** [ˋgrætɪˌtud] (n.) 感恩，感激之意
We gave Kim a present to express our gratitude for her help.

7) **defeat** [dɪˋfit] (v./n.) 戰勝，擊敗
The Americans defeated the Japanese in World War II.

8) **eternity** [ɪˋtɜnətɪ] (n.) 永遠，（似乎）無止盡的時間
It seems like an eternity since we've seen each other.

9) **spoil** [spɔɪl] (n.) （常用複數）戰利品，贓物
The spoils of war go to the victor.

進階字彙

10) **sibling** [ˋsɪblɪŋ] (n.) 兄弟姊妹，手足
It's normal for siblings to fight.

11) **trident** [ˋtraɪdn̩t] (n.) 三叉戟，三齒魚叉
Poseidon created earthquakes with his trident.

12) **invisibility** [ɪnˌvɪzəˋbɪlətɪ] (n.) 無形 (a.) invisible [ɪnˋvɪzəbl̩] 無形的，看不見的
Ninjas are said to have the power of invisibility.

13) **boulder** [ˋboldɚ] (n.) 巨石，大圓石
The road was blocked by a large boulder.

14) **underworld** [ˋʌndɚˌwɜld] (n.) （首字母常大寫）陰間，冥府
During Ghost Month, the spirits are said to rise from the underworld.

在泰坦之戰中落敗，被罰永遠支撐天空的亞特拉斯

手持三叉戟的海神波塞頓

課文朗讀 MP3 127　單字朗讀 MP3 128　英文文章導讀 MP3 129

During his childhood on the island of Crete, the young god Zeus had no idea that his father was Cronus, King of the Titans. ¹⁾**Fed on** a strict diet of milk and honey, he grew up strong and brave. On learning that Cronus
5　ᴳhad ²⁾**devoured** his brothers and sisters, he swore revenge. Zeus visited his father in ³⁾**disguise** and ⁴⁾**spiked** his wine, causing him to throw up his ¹⁰⁾**siblings**. They were so ⁵⁾**grateful** to Zeus that they made him their leader. Fearing the rising power of Zeus, Cronus gathered
10　the Titans at Mount Othrys to prepare for battle. The Titans chose Atlas as their general. Zeus and his siblings made Mount Olympus their base, and the War of the Titans began.

　　The Titans and the Olympians fought for ten years
15　with neither side able to gain an advantage. At that point, Gaia advised Zeus to free the Cyclopes and Hecatonchires and persuade them to join his side. The mission was a success, and out of ⁶⁾**gratitude**, the Cyclopes gave lightning and thunder to Zeus, a ¹¹⁾**trident** to Poseidon
20　and a helmet of ¹²⁾**invisibility** to Hades. With the help of

天后赫拉頭像

冥王黑帝斯與三顆頭
的地獄看門犬

森林仙女試圖逃脫
好色的森林之神薩梯

these advanced weapons, and [13)]**boulders** thrown by the Hecatonchires, the Olympians were finally able to win the war. The [7)]**defeated** Titans were locked up in Tartarus, but Atlas, as their leader, was condemned to hold up the sky for [8)]**eternity**. [G]Now that the war was over, it was time to divide the [9)]**spoils**. Zeus, as King of the Gods, became ruler of the heavens, Poseidon was given the seas, and Hades became King of the [14)]**Underworld**.

Mini Quiz 閱讀測驗

1 ☐ **What did Zeus do when he visited Cronus?**
(A) He put alcohol in his drink.
(B) He killed him.
(C) He put poison in his drink.
(D) He told him to release his siblings.

2 ☐ **Who gave Zeus advice that helped him win the War of the Titans?**
(A) His grandmother
(B) His mother
(C) The Hecatonchires
(D) The Cyclopes

中 Translation

童年居住於克里特島期間，年輕的宙斯神並不知道自己的生父是泰坦王克羅努斯。在只喝牛奶與蜂蜜的嚴格飲食下，他長得強壯又勇敢。一獲悉克羅努斯吞食了他的兄姊之後，他誓言復仇。宙斯喬裝去拜訪他的父親，在他的葡萄酒裡下毒，致使克羅努斯吐出他的兄姊。兄姊們非常感謝宙斯，因此擁立他為領導者。畏懼於宙斯日益強大的勢力，克羅努斯將所有泰坦集合於奧西里斯山備戰，泰坦們挑選亞特拉斯做為將領。宙斯和其手足則以奧林帕斯山為基地，泰坦之戰於焉爆發。

泰坦們和奧林帕斯諸神交戰十年，雙方均占不到便宜。就在此時，蓋亞建議宙斯解救出獨眼巨人和赫克頓蓋爾，說服他們加入他的陣營。這次任務圓滿成功，出於感激，獨眼巨人給了宙斯雷電、給了波塞頓三叉戟、給了黑帝斯有隱形功用的頭盔。有了這些先進武器的幫助，再加上赫克頓蓋爾投擲巨礫，奧林帕斯諸神終於贏得戰爭。戰敗的泰坦們被囚在塔特魯斯，而其領導者亞特拉斯則被判處永遠支撐天空。戰爭既已結束，就是分發戰利品的時候了。諸神之王宙斯成為天庭統治者，波塞頓被賜予海洋，黑帝斯則封為冥王。

Language Guide

希臘、羅馬神話諸神名稱對照

希臘神話經過千百年的傳述、翻譯，直到進入羅馬帝國時期經過多位作家的改編，因此同一個神祇會有希臘及羅馬兩種名稱。

Greek 希臘	Roman 羅馬	職掌
Zeus	Jupiter	眾神之王
Hera	Juno	眾神之后
Poseidon	Neptune	海神
Hades	Pluto	死神
Persephone	Proserpina	死神之后
Demeter	Ceres	植物、農業女神
Dionysus	Bacchus	酒神；主司感官歡愉
Pan	Faunus	森林之神
Ares	Mars	戰神
Hermes	Mercury	眾神的信差
Hephaestus	Vulcan	火神；鐵工之神
Athena	Minerva	智慧女神；戰爭女神
Aphrodite	Venus	愛神；美麗女神
Apollo	Phoebus Apollo	太陽神；主司詩歌、音樂、舞蹈、醫藥及預言
Artemis	Diana	狩獵女神；月神；貞潔女神；主司動物及生育
Eros	Cupid	愛神
Hebe	Juventas	青春女神

🕐 Grammar Master

過去完成式

had + p.p. 表示某一個比過去時間 (he swore revenge) 更早發生的動作 (Cronus had devoured his brothers and sisters)。

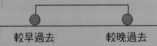

較早過去　　　較晚過去

例 By the time the police showed up, the criminals **had already fled.**
等到警方出現時，歹徒早已逃跑了。

例 He didn't have any money because he **had lost** his wallet.
他那時候沒錢，因為他的錢包丟了。

Now that... 由於／既然……

now that 引導的子句可以用來表示原因，意思類似 because now，通常用來描述關於現在和未來情況的原因。由於文中是講述故事的形式，所以時態全都用過去式。

例 **Now that** we've finished our homework, we can take it easy for a while.
既然我們已經做完功課了，我們可以好好放鬆一下。

例 **Now that** you're an adult, you should act like an adult.
你現在既然是大人了，就應該要有大人的樣子。

閱讀測驗解答 **1** (C) **2** (A)

Know it ALL 英文閱讀

Vocabulary Bank

1) **populate** [ˈpɑpjəˌlet] (v.) 殖民，居住
The American West was populated in the 19th century.

2) **trait** [tret] (n.) 特徵，特點
Scott's sense of humor is his best trait.

3) **hand out** [hænd aut] (phr.) 分發
The teacher asked Sally to hand out the test papers.

4) **sneak** [snik] (v.) 偷偷地走，溜
動詞三態：sneak; snuck; snuck
The boys snuck into the movie theater without paying.

5) **torch** [tɔrtʃ] (n.) 火把
The fisherman used torches to attract fish at night.

6) **rescue** [ˈrɛskju] (v./n.) 營救，解圍
The fireman rescued the girl from the burning building.

7) **blacksmith** [ˈblækˌsmɪθ] (n.) 鐵匠
The village blacksmith made tools and horseshoes.

8) **curiosity** [ˌkjʊrɪˈɑsətɪ] (n.) 好奇心
(a.) curious [ˈkjʊrɪəs] 好奇的
The book didn't satisfy my curiosity about the subject.

9) **refer (to)** [rɪˈfɜ] (v.) 表示，提到
Nick always refers to his wife as his "old lady."

進階字彙

10) **likeness** [ˈlaɪknɪs] (n.) 模樣，相像
The Bible says that God created man in his likeness.

11) **unforeseen** [ˌʌnforˈsin] (a.) 預料之外的
Insurance can protect you against unforeseen circumstances.

Language Guide

Prometheus 普羅米修斯與 Epimetheus 伊皮米修斯

Prometheus 盜給人類的天火是「人類智能」的象徵，他跟雙胞胎兄弟 Epimetheus 分別代表人類的智、愚（Prometheus 的字面意思為前瞻、遠見 foresight，Epimetheus 字面意思為後見之明 (hindsight)）。

嫁給 Epimetheus 的是希臘神話中的第一個女人 Pandora，她出於好奇心打開的 Pandora's box（潘朵拉的盒子）在現代英文中經常出現，用來代表一些原本立意甚佳，到頭來卻後患無窮的知識領域。

例 The Pandora's box of nuclear weapons should never have been opened.
核子武器的潘朵拉盒子打從一開始就不該被打開。

blacksmith 鐵匠姓史密斯？

After winning the War of the Titans, Zeus asked the Titans Prometheus and Epimetheus to create men and animals to [1]**populate** the earth. Prometheus formed men from clay in the [10]**likeness** of the gods, and Athena,

5　daughter of Zeus, breathed life into them. Meanwhile, Epimetheus created the animals, giving each the [2]**traits** Ⓖneeded for survival. Unfortunately, Epimetheus [3]**handed out** all the good traits, and there was nothing left for man. Prometheus therefore asked Zeus to give man the gift of

10　fire, but he refused. ❶ **Not one to take no for an answer**, Prometheus [4]**snuck** up to Mount Olympus, lit a [5]**torch** from the Sun, and brought it down to man. When Zeus found out, he was so mad that he chained Prometheus to a rock and had an eagle eat his liver every day (it grew back

15　at night). He was later [6]**rescued** by the hero Hercules, but that's another story.

To punish man for accepting the gift of fire, Zeus ordered Hephaestus, [7]**blacksmith** to the gods, to create woman. Pandora, the first woman, received gifts from each

20　of the gods: Aphrodite gave her beauty, Athena gave her

盜天火的普羅米修斯啟發了不計其數的藝術創作。紐約市洛克菲勒中心廣場上的金色雕像（下圖），及暢銷小說改編的電影《波西傑克森 神火之賊》（左圖）都與這個神話故事相關。

wisdom, and Hera gave her [8)]**curiosity**. Zeus then presented Pandora with a golden box that he told her never to open, and gave her to Epimetheus in marriage. Pandora just couldn't resist her curiosity, and when she opened the

25 box, evil and misery were released into the world. Pandora quickly shut the lid, trapping hope inside. Even today, the expression "Pandora's box" is often used to [9)]**refer** to a source of

30 [11)]**unforeseen** trouble.

大力士海克拉斯

Mini Quiz 閱讀測驗

❶ ▬▬ **Why did Prometheus ask Zeus to give man fire?**
    (A) Because he handed out all the good traits to animals
    (B) Because there were no good traits left for man
    (C) Because men were made out of clay
    (D) Because he made men in the likeness of the gods

❷ ▬▬ **Which of the following is NOT true about Pandora?**
    (A) She was an evil woman.
    (B) She was the first female.
    (C) She released evil into the world.
    (D) She was very curious.

中 Translation

贏得泰坦戰爭後，宙斯要泰坦神普羅米修斯及伊皮米修斯創造人類與動物來進住地球。普羅米修斯用陶土將人類塑成神的模樣，而宙斯的女兒雅典娜則將生命呼進他們體內。同時，伊皮米修斯創造動物，分別給牠們生存所需的特性。不幸的是，伊皮米修斯把所有好特性都給光了，沒有什麼可以賦予人類。於是普羅米修斯請求宙斯把火賜給人類，但宙斯拒絕。鍥而不捨的普羅米修斯便偷偷爬上奧林帕斯山，用太陽點燃一個火炬，然後把火炬帶下山給人類。當宙斯發現這件事，他氣得用鐵鏈把普羅米修斯鏈在一塊岩石上，命令一隻老鷹每天啄食他的肝（肝會在夜裡長回來）。後來他被英雄海克拉斯搭救出來，但那又是另一個故事了。

為了懲罰人類接受用火的天賦，宙斯命令諸神的鐵匠希費斯特斯打造出世界第一個女人潘朵拉，並讓她獲得眾神的禮物：阿芙蘿黛緹賜予她美貌，雅典娜賜予她智慧，赫拉則賜予她好奇心。接著宙斯送給潘朵拉一只金盒子，告訴她絕對不能打開，並將她許配給伊皮米修斯。潘朵拉抗拒不了好奇心，當她一開啟盒子，邪惡與苦難便被釋出進入這個世界。潘朵拉快速關上盒蓋，把希望關在裡面。直到今天，「潘朵拉的盒子」一語仍常被用來比喻預料之外困境的根源。

打開金盒子的潘朵拉

✂ Tongue-tied No More

這邊的 no 是名詞，整句字面上的意思就是「不接受 no 這個答覆」，也就是不讓人拒絕，說好聽一點是「不達目的、誓不罷休」，但其實經常用來抱怨死纏爛打、死皮賴臉的人。

A: You accepted Bob and Mary's dinner invitation? I thought you didn't want to go.
   你接受了鮑伯和瑪麗的晚餐邀請？我以為你不想去咧。
B: I tried to make excuses, but they just wouldn't take no for an answer.
   我想盡辦法找藉口，但他們就是不讓我拒絕。

✴ Grammar Master

形容詞子句的省略
形容詞子句中含有 be 動詞
可以直接省略關係代名詞（which、who、that）和 be 動詞。在本文中，needed 前方省略了 that are，而呈現 needed for survival 這個分詞型態來修飾前方的 traits。

例 They're staying at a hotel <u>that was</u> built in the Victorian era.
   = They're staying at a hotel built in the Victorian era.
   他們住在一間維多利亞時期建造的旅館中。

形容詞子句中不含 be 動詞
可以直接省略關代（which、who、that……），但後方的動詞必須改為分詞型態。

例 Do you know anybody <u>who</u> works at that company?
=Do you know anybody working at that company?
你認識任何一位在那間公司任職的員工嗎？

閱讀測驗解答 ❶ (B) ❷ (A)

Niche Photography 酷玩攝影

Vocabulary Bank

1) **photography** [fə`tɑgrəfɪ] (n.) 攝影
Robin learned how to develop film in her photography class.

2) **resolution** [ˌrɛzə`luʃən] (n.) 解析度
My cell phone only takes low resolution pictures.

3) **dedicated** [`dɛdəˌketɪd] (a.) 盡心盡力的，奉獻的，專注的
Robert and Marcie are dedicated parents.

4) **motto** [`mɑto] (n.) 座右銘，格言
My motto is, "live and let live."

5) **spontaneity** [ˌspɑntə`niətɪ] (n.) 自發性，即性
Jazz music is known for its spontaneity.

6) **straightforward** [ˌstret`fɔrwəd] (a.) 直接了當的，易懂的
The instructions for my MP3 player are pretty straightforward.

7) **vintage** [`vɪntɪdʒ] (a.) 老而經典的
My uncle collects vintage baseball cards.

8) **intense** [ɪn`tɛns] (a.) 強烈的
Firefighters wear special clothing to protect them from intense heat.

9) **accessory** [æk`sɛsərɪ] (n.) 附件，配件
Our company manufactures auto parts and accessories.

10) **offbeat** [`ɔf.bit] (a.) 不跟隨潮流的，特異的
Sally has an offbeat sense of humor.

11) **lens** [lɛnz] (n.) 鏡頭
I just bought a new wide-angle lens for my camera.

補充字彙

* niche [nɪtʃ] (a.)（在某領域中）特殊的，小眾的

* hobbyist [`hɑbɪɪst] (n.) 沉迷於某嗜好者

* blurring [`blɜrɪŋ] (n.) 模糊

* distortion [dɪs`tɔrʃən] (n.) 失真，扭曲

課文朗讀 MP3 133　單字朗讀 MP3 134　英文文章導讀 MP3 135

[G]The more things change with [1)]**photography**, the more they stay the same. For the photo *hobbyist, there are more tools now than ever
5　before. Most of them are high-tech: digital cameras, high [2)]**resolution** printers and instant file sharing. But there is also a small but [3)]**dedicated** group of niche photographers who enjoy
10　using old fashioned technology to achieve original results.

　　"Don't think, just shoot" is the [4)]**motto** of Lomography, a movement that is attempting to move photography forward by going backwards. The LOMO
15　is a simple camera that still uses 35mm film. The key to LOMO photography is [5)]**spontaneity**; shooting is simple and [6)]**straightforward**. The results, however, are quite unique. Photographs taken with the LOMO have a playful, [7)]**vintage** style to them. The controls
20　are simple, so that users can just point and shoot to create interesting shots. The resulting photos have [8)]**intense** colors and high contrast. Light leaks, *blurring

and other *distortions add to their
25 original look. LOMO cameras also come
with 9)**accessories** to help users take
10)**offbeat** photos. Fish eye 11)**lenses**
create extremely wide, round images.
Other tools, such as rainbow flashes, give
30 hobbyists a fun and simple way to create
highly unusual photographs.

Language Guide

與相機相關的字彙

aperture [ˈæpətʃə] 光圈

focus [ˈfokəs] 焦距

flash [flæʃ] 閃光燈

lens [lɛnz] 鏡頭

contrast [ˈkɑn͵træst] 對比，反差

light leak [laɪt lik] 漏光

pixel [ˈpɪksəl] 畫素

shutter [ˈʃʌtə] 快門

film [fɪlm] 底片

tripod [ˈtraɪpɑd] 三腳架

Grammar Master

The + 比較級 (1)…, the + 比較級 (2)…
「越…就越…」的句型

要表達「越…就越…」時，前後兩個子句都要
用「the + 比較級形容詞或副詞」開頭，再接
主詞和動詞。

● **The more** you give, **the more** you gain in
return.
付出的越多，收穫也越多。

● **The faster** he spoke, **the more confused**
the audience was.
他講得越快，聽眾們越感到困惑。

● **The darker** it gets, **the quieter** the streets
are.
天色越黑，街道就越安靜。

Translation

攝影這項技術改變得越多，就越保持不變。對攝影迷而言，現在的工具比以往任
何時候都還要多，其中大部分是高科技：數位相機、高解析度印表機和即時檔案
分享。但是也有一群人數不多但很投入的特殊攝影同好，他們喜歡使用老式的技
術來達到獨創的效果。

「不用想，拍就對了！」是 LOMO 攝影的座右銘，LOMO 是試圖藉由返璞歸
真來推展攝影藝術的運動。LOMO 是一種簡單的相機，仍使用 35 釐米底片。
LOMO 攝影的關鍵是隨興，拍照是簡單易懂的。然而，拍攝的成果卻相當獨一無
二。用 LOMO 相機拍攝的照片有種好玩的、懷舊的風格。操控很簡單，所以使
用者只要瞄準、拍攝，就能創造出有趣的相片，拍攝出的相片有飽滿的色彩和高
反差。漏光、模糊、以及其他影像變形功能可以加強獨創性的視覺效果。 LOMO
相機也有配件，協助用戶拍攝奇特的照片。魚眼鏡頭可以製造超廣角、圓弧形的
圖像。其他工具，例如彩虹閃光燈，可以提供愛好者一個有趣又簡單的方法，創
造出極不尋常的照片。

關於 LOMO 相機

圖片提供：Verycan

高科技時代中，數位相機帶給人們拍照的便利性以及精準性，但在同時，也有一群人繼續追求傳統底片銀鹽以及低科技相機所產生的效果。LOMO LC-A 正是這個數位時代中逆向操作的代表。

LOMO的全稱是（Leningradskoye Optiko Mechanichesckoye Obyedinenie 列寧格勒光學儀器廠），該儀器廠於 1982 年設計了一款小型自動相機 LC-A，希望蘇聯民眾利用這台相機記錄祖國的光榮。1991 年兩名維也納學生發現了這台已停產的相機，回國後展出所拍的照片，暗角和濃艷的色彩吸引了眾多年輕人的目光，使得 LC-A 聲名大噪。1996 年這兩名學生請求該製造廠重新生產 LC-A，隨即造成搶購，因此誕生了 Lomography（LOMO攝影）這一新詞。

今天 LOMO 一詞已經不僅僅是列寧格勒光學儀器廠的縮寫，還代表一種生活型態以及年輕與創造力。

目前市面上除了經典的 LC-A 之外，還有許許多多不同的 LOMO 相機。像是超廣角、可拍攝 170 度視角、並將照片壓縮成圓形影像的 Fisheye、可以改變不同閃燈顏色的 Colorsplash、把一秒內的事情一分為四的 Action Sampler、複刻六〇年代的相機 Diana、復古雙眼相機 Lubitel 166+ 等，每一台都各自擁有不同的風格，拍出來的照片更是千變萬化，讓照相不再只是照相，更是一種創作！！

LOMO 玩家黃金十誡 （摘自 Lomo 官網）

1 Take your camera everywhere you go.
機不離身。

2 Use it any time—day and night.
不分晝夜，隨時使用。

3 Lomography is not an interference in your life, but part of it.
LOMO 攝影不是你生活的干擾，它是你生活的一部分。

4 Try the shot from the hip.
試著把相機放在腰臀拍照。

5 Approach the objects of your lomographic desire as close as possible.
盡可能靠近你想拍攝的物件。

6 Don't think.
不要想。

7 Be fast.
動作要快。

8 You don't have to know beforehand what you captured on film.
不必事先想好要捕捉的影像。

9 Afterwards either.
也不用管最後拍出了什麼。

10 Don't worry about any rules.
把規則丟到一邊。

拍照常用英文

- Can you take our picture?
  能幫我們拍張合照嗎？

- Smile! / Say cheese!
  笑一個！

- Everybody stand closer together.
  大家站近一點！

- It's too dark here—you need to use the flash.
  這裡太暗了，你需要用閃光燈。

- The flash didn't go off.
  閃光燈沒閃。

- Take another shot!
  再拍一張！

購買相機常用英文

- Excuse me, how many megapixels is this camera?
  請問這台相機多少萬畫素？

- Excuse me, is this a grey market camera?
  請問這是水貨嗎？

- How long is the warranty?
  保固多久？

- Does it have auto focus?
  有自動對焦功能嗎？

- How many shooting modes does it have?
  有幾種拍攝模式可供選擇？

- What kind of memory card does this camera use?
  這台相機使用哪種記憶卡？

- Does it have an image stabilizer?
  有防手震功能嗎？

- Does it have a Chinese interface?
  有中文介面嗎？

- Is the manual in Chinese or English?
  說明書是中文還是英文？

- Do you have an installment plan? / Can I buy it on installment?
  能分期付款嗎？

課文朗讀 MP3 136　單字朗讀 MP3 137　英文文章導讀 MP3 138

Another group of niche photographers are dedicated to a more familiar form of *retro technology. At one time, *Polaroid cameras were the best way to create instant photos. As soon as you press the 1)**shutter**, a print shoots out from the camera and 2)**develops** right before your eyes. The *glossy images that result have a look straight from the past. Colors can be bold, while also feeling 3)**worn** and 4)**faded**. This is point-and-shoot photography in the extreme, with no fancy

10　controls to worry about. However, with the rise of digital photography, the popularity of Polaroid photography is 5)**on the decline**. ᴳLast year, the company announced that it planned to discontinue making its Polaroid film, leaving the future of this art form in doubt.

Perhaps one of the most interesting forms of niche

16　photography is *tilt-shift photography. This a 6)**complex** technique that makes actual places like parks and small towns look like 7)**miniature** landscapes. When you see a photo made with the tilt-shift process, it's hard

20　to believe that it's real. The results look exactly like a fake, mini version of the real thing. While this effect can be created

25　using a special lens, it is usually achieved on a computer with image processing software. For example, only a small part

30　of the image is kept in focus, while the rest of it is blurred. *Saturation can

© Hylo

Vocabulary Bank

1) **shutter** [ˈʃʌtə] (n.) 快門
Press the shutter halfway to focus the camera.

2) **develop** [dɪˈvɛləp] (v.) 沖洗（照片）
Where did you get your film developed?

3) **worn** [worn] (a.) 破舊的，磨損的
You should get those worn tires replaced.

4) **faded** [ˈfedɪd] (a.) 褪色的
Faded jeans are back in style again.

5) **on the decline** [ɑn ðə dɪˈklaɪn] (phr.) 走下坡的，衰退的
Statistics show that crime is on the decline.

6) **complex** [ˈkɑmplɛks] (a.) 複雜的
No one in the class was able to solve the complex math problem.

7) **miniature** [ˈmɪnətʃə] (a.) 小型的，模型的
Danny collects miniature cars.

8) **defy** [dɪˈfaɪ] (v.) 違背，抗拒
The movie's plot defies logic.

9) **enthusiast** [ɪnˈθjuzɪˌæst] (n.) 對…熱中的人
Matt is a model airplane enthusiast.

10) **ancient** [ˈenʃənt] (a.) 古代的，古老的
I studied ancient Greek in university.

補充字彙

* retro [ˈrɛtro] (a.) 復古的

* Polaroid [ˈpoləˌrɔɪd] (n.) 拍立得相機（或照片）

* glossy [ˈglɔsɪ] (a.) 光面的，光滑的

* tilt-shift photography [tɪlt ʃɪft fəˈtɑgrəfɪ] (n.) 移軸攝影

* saturation [ˌsætʃəˈreʃən] (n.) 飽和度

also be increased to make
the colors look more fake. When it all comes together,
35 the final picture will [8]**defy** your senses, and you won't
believe your eyes.

Whether having fun with the toy-like LOMO, or
mastering the fine art of tilt-shift photography, there are
plenty of options for photo [9]**enthusiasts** everywhere.
40 And who knows, perhaps in the not-too-distant future,
hobbyists will search for [10]**ancient** cell phone cameras to
create an entirely new style of niche photography!

中 Translation

還有一群特殊攝影迷致力於一種比較為人所知的復古技術。曾經，拍立得相機是製造即時照片的最好方法。一按下快門，相片就從相機射出，在你的眼前顯影，產生出的光滑圖像直接重現過往真貌。色彩可以大膽，同時也可以有破舊及褪色的感覺。這是瞄準即拍攝影的極致表現，沒有花俏的操控功能要擔心。然而，隨著數位攝影的崛起，拍立得攝影的人氣一直下滑。去年，該公司宣布計劃停止製造拍立得底片，使這種藝術形式的未來讓人存疑。

也許最有趣的特殊攝影形式之一是移軸攝影。這是一種複雜的技術，可以讓公園和小城鎮等真實地點看起來像是盆景一樣。當你看到經過移軸處理的照片，你很難會相信裡頭的景物是真的，成像看起來就像是實際物體的假造、迷你版。雖然這種效果可以用特殊鏡頭創造出來，但通常是用有影像處理軟體的電腦達成的。例如，只有一小部分的圖像是保持對焦的，而其餘部分則是模糊的。也可以增加飽和度，使顏色看起來比較假。把這些處理綜合起來，最後產生的相片就會違反你的感官，你將無法相信自己的眼睛。

不管是把玩玩具一般的 LOMO 相機，或是精進數位移軸攝影美術的技巧，各地的攝影愛好者都有很多選擇。誰知道，也許在不太遙遠的未來，攝影愛好者會尋找古老的照相手機，創造一種全新風格的特殊攝影！

Grammar Master

分詞構句

本句原本該用 and 連接，但如果是想表達時間先後或因果關係的兩個子句，可以將含有「先發生事件」或「表達結果」的其中一個子句中的主詞去掉，用分詞作為子句開頭。子句若為主動句用現在分詞 Ving，被動句則用過去分詞。

● 表達時間先後
Walking down the street, I saw an old friend.
先發生事件，主動，用 Ving

Hit by a car, the boy was taken to a hospital.
先發生事件，被動，用過去分詞

● 表達因果關係
He called me out of the blue, making me wonder what he was up to.
此句為前句的結果，用 Ving 表示

Mini Quiz 閱讀測驗

❶ Which of the following is true about LOMO cameras?
(A) They use advanced technology.
(B) They create unique photographs.
(C) They use instant film.
(D) They are vintage cameras.

❷ Which of the following can be used to create tilt-shift photography?
(A) special lenses
(B) image processing software
(C) increased saturation
(D) all of the above

❸ True or False
The Polaroid camera is a recent invention.

閱讀測驗解答 ❶ (B) ❷ (D) ❸ (False)

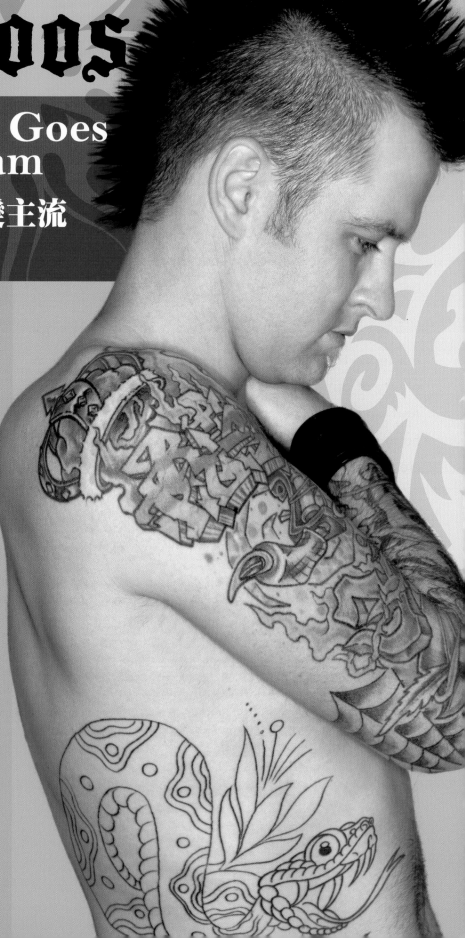

Tattoos

① Rebellion Goes ② Mainstream

刺青 叛逆變主流

V Vocabulary Bank

1) **rebellion** [rɪˋbɛljən] (n.) 反叛，叛逆
In American culture, the motorcycle has long been a symbol of rebellion.

2) **mainstream** [ˋmen͵strim] (a.) 主流的
Johnny never listens to mainstream music.

3) **nowadays** [ˋnauə͵dez] (adv.) 現今
Young people nowadays are spoiled and selfish.

4) **outlaw** [ˋaut͵lɔ] (n.) 歹徒，亡命之徒
Jesse James was one of the most famous outlaws of the Wild West.

5) **norm** [nɔrm] (n.) 規範，常態
Corruption is the norm in many countries.

6) **profile** [ˋprofaɪl] (n.) 輪廓，能見度
The company is working hard to raise the profile of its brand.

7) **taboo** [təˋbu] (a.) 禁忌的
Living together before marriage is still taboo in many countries.

8) **parlor** [ˋpɑrlə] (n.) 店舖（通常用來構成複合詞，如 tattoo parlor、massage parlor、funeral parlor、beauty parlor 等等）
My aunt works at a beauty parlor.

補充字彙

* **spur** [spɝ] (v.) 刺激，激勵
The government has announced a new program to spur economic growth.

* **individuality** [͵ɪndə͵vɪdʒuˋælətɪ] (n.) 個人特色，個體性
Teens are always looking for new ways to express their individuality.

課文 朗讀 MP3 139　單字 朗讀 MP3 140　英文 文章導讀 MP3 141

In the United States, there ^Gused to be only
two kinds of people who had tattoos:criminals
and sailors. But ³⁾**nowadays**, you're
as likely to see a tattoo on a prom queen
5　as you are on an ⁴⁾**outlaw**. Cultural ⁵⁾**norms**
have changed a lot, *spurred by the high-
⁶⁾**profile** rock stars of the 60s and 70s and
sports stars of the 80s and 90s, and the once
⁷⁾**taboo** tattoo has become an accepted form
10　of rebellion within mainstream culture.

But these days, is getting a tattoo still
about rebellion? Not really. "It's about
*individuality," says Diandra Lewis of Austin,
Texas. "This one here," she says, pointing to a
15　Celtic knot pattern on her upper arm, "I drew
and redrew this for months before finally
getting it done. It's my own design. Only I
have it." Many 20-somethings have similarly
unique tattoos, often with a background story
20　or event. Diandra's was done in memory of
her Irish grandfather.

Because individuality is so important to
people, tattoo artists have countless designs,
patterns, and images from which to choose.
25　The tattoo designs, or "flash," are displayed
around the ⁸⁾**parlor**, although quite often
customers will bring in their own designs.
People like to get tattoos that have a special,
personal meaning for them, and often the
30　best way to do that is to design it themselves.

中 Translation

在美國，以往只有兩種人的身上有刺青：罪犯和水手。不過時至今日，你在舞會皇后身上看到刺青的機會，和你在罪犯身上看到刺青的機會幾乎差不多。受到六、七O年代那些備受矚目的搖滾明星，以及八、九O年代的運動明星所刺激，文化規範改變了許多，曾經被視為禁忌的刺青，已經變成主流文化中一種可接受的叛逆形式。

不過這年頭，刺青還算是叛逆表現嗎？並不盡然。住在德州奧斯汀的黛恩卓路易斯表示：「都是為了個人風格」。「像這一個」，她指著自己上臂的凱爾特結圖案說，「我花了幾個月一畫再畫，終於將它完成。這是我自己設計的，專屬於我。」許多二十多歲的年輕人也有同樣獨一無二的刺青，通常背後都有個故事或某件事情。黛恩卓的刺青就是為了紀念她的愛爾蘭祖父。

由於個人風格對人們來說很重要，因此刺青師提供了無數設計、花樣和圖案供人選擇。店鋪裡展示了許多刺青設計圖（或稱 flash），儘管顧客常常會攜帶自己設計的圖案前來。人們喜愛刺上特殊、有個人意義的刺青，而通常最好的方法就是自己設計。

丙 Grammar Master

used to + V 從前…；過去…（現在已非如此）

主詞 + used to V 代表該主詞過去做某事或是某種狀態，但現在已不是如此。注意這裡的 used 是過去式動詞，因此要表達「過去不…」（但現在是如此）就要用過去式的否定：didn't use to+V，疑問句則是：Did 主詞 + use to + V…?

- I used to exercise every day, but now I hardly ever exercise.
  我以前每天運動，但是現在很少運動了。
- Linda didn't use to like coffee, but she does now.
  琳達以前不喜歡喝咖啡，但現在喜歡了。
- Did you use to live on Washington Street? You look familiar.
  你以前住在華盛頓街嗎？你看起來好面熟。

比較：be used to + 名詞 / Ving 習慣於…

- I'm used to living in Taipei. 我習慣住在台北。
- I used to live in Taipei. 我以前住在台北。

Language Guide

什麼是 Celtic knot？

「凱爾特結」Celtic knot [ˋkɛltɪk nɑt] 最大的特色為其無始無終的圖案設計，相傳這象徵永恆。關於凱爾特結的由來眾說紛紜，一個說法是，古時居住於愛爾蘭及蘇格蘭地區的凱爾特族嚴禁具象的圖樣，故以抽象的符號表示動物、植物及其他物件。凱爾特結總是帶有神祕的宗教色彩，早期常被裝飾於聖經或紀念碑上，現在則常用於珠寶設計及刺青圖騰。

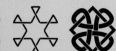

為什麼刺青叫 tattoo？

tattoo 這個字的由來已不可考，但一般推論其出處可能為波里尼西亞文裡的 tatao 一字，意思為「輕敲」，或是大溪地方言 tatu，有「做記號」的意思。

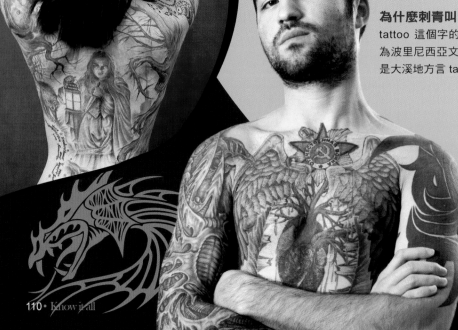

刺青流程

Step 1	選擇刺青圖案
Step 2	刺青師在紙上畫出刺青草圖
Step 3	將圖印在欲刺青的部位
Step 4	刺青師開始割線（刺青術語，表示在刺青圖案邊緣刺上大致輪廓）
Step 5	打霧（刺青術語，表示幫刺青圖案上色，並做出深淺的陰影及顏色變化）
Step 6	完成後，檢查顏色是否均勻

刺青前注意事項

- 須慎選衛生品質良好的刺青店。店家必須使用拋棄式手套和刺針，若使用紋身機，則以不鏽鋼材質為宜。

- 店家會請顧客出示身分證，須年滿十八歲才能刺青。其他如患有糖尿病、心臟病、癲癇病、皮膚病以及女性生理期間不宜刺青，若欲以紋身覆蓋傷疤者，則須等傷口完全癒合後才能刺青。

刺青後注意事項

- 刺青完幾天皮膚發癢、結痂、脫皮屬正常現象，切記千萬不可抓傷口，須塗抹專業紋身藥膏或醫用凡士林，以免感染或脫色。

- 避免穿著緊身衣物，洗澡後讓傷口風乾，避免讓肥皂或沐浴乳接觸傷口，盡量讓傷口保持通風乾燥。

- 刺青後一個月內禁止游泳、三溫暖、日曬、淋雨、飲酒以及刺激性飲食，否則恐引起傷口發炎。

- 若刺青位置在接近關節處，平日活動須多加留意，避免劇烈拉扯留下裂紋。

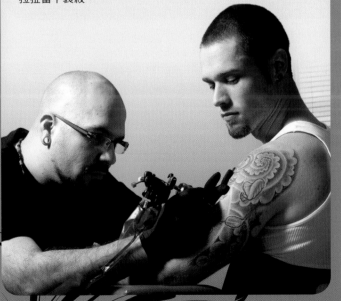

刺青異言堂

The older generation always seems to associate tattoos with criminals.
老一輩的人總把刺青和罪犯聯想在一起。

In the past, most people had a negative view of tattoos.
過去，大多數人對刺青的觀感是負面的。

Nowadays, people get tattoos for many different reasons.
現在，人們出於各種不同的理由去刺青。

Some people get tattoos to commemorate important events, and others get them to express their individuality.
有些人為了紀念重要事件而刺青，有些人則是藉此表現自我風格。

Some people even get tattoos on their private parts.
有些人甚至會在私密部位刺青。

My parents would kill me if I got a tattoo.
要是我去刺青，我爸媽一定會殺了我。

Does it hurt to get a tattoo?
刺青會痛嗎？

What designs are popular now?
最近流行什麼樣的圖案？

What part of my body should I get it on?
我應該刺在哪個部位？

You should think carefully before getting a tattoo.
決定刺青前，務必要三思。

Because once you get a tattoo, it's hard to get rid of.
因為一旦刺下去，是很難消除的。

You can get a tattoo removed with laser surgery.
你可以透過雷射手術來消除刺青。

V Vocabulary Bank

1) **definite** [ˋdɛfənɪt] (a.) 明確的，肯定的
We need a definite answer by Monday.

2) **atomic** [əˋtɑmɪk] (a.) 原子的
The first atomic bomb was dropped in 1945.

3) **segment** [ˋsɛgmənt] (n.) 部份，區隔
Which market segment is the product targeting?

4) **signify** [ˋsɪgnəˏfaɪ] (v.) 表示
What does that symbol on your shirt signify?

5) **distinction** [dɪˋstɪŋkʃən] (n.) 榮譽，成就
The professor received an award for distinction in teaching.

6) **medal** [ˋmɛdl̩] (n.) 獎章
The general's chest was covered with medals.

7) **feat** [fit] (n.) 功績
Michael Phelps achieved the historic feat of winning eight gold medals.

8) **permanent** [ˋpɜmənənt] (a.) 永久的
The accident caused permanent brain damage.

補充字彙

* **geisha** [ˋgeʃə] (n.) 日本藝伎
It takes years of training to become a geisha.

* **allegiance** [əˋlidʒəns] (n.) 忠誠
All the knights swore allegiance to the king.

* **adorn** [əˋdɔrn] (v.) 裝飾
The queen's crown was adorned with jewels.

* **sorority** [səˋrɔrətɪ] (n.) 姊妹會
I heard Amy is thinking of joining a sorority.

Maori tattoo design

課文朗讀 MP3 142　單字朗讀 MP3 143　英文文章導讀 MP3 144

But like everything else, there are trends in the world of tattoos. "There are [1]**definite** trends in tattoo design," says Doctor Shayne of [2]**Atomic** Tattoo. "For a while the Maori designs were popular; then it was

5　Celtic stuff. We were in a Chinese symbol phase for a while, but now that seems to be fading. It's hard to say what will come next, but I've had a lot of customers asking for Japanese *geisha girls."

Gang members are another ³⁾**segment** of society
that uses tattoos, though for a very different purpose.
Gang tattoos ⁴⁾**signify** *allegiance, and they're also
often given as marks of ⁵⁾**distinction** or service, much
as a soldier might receive a ⁶⁾**medal**. This is not a new
use for tattoos. In fact, some of the earliest people to
use tattoos were the Polynesians of the South Pacific,
and they were often given to mark ⁷⁾**feats** in battle. The
Mara Salvatrucha in the United States and the Yakuza
in Japan are two criminal organizations known for their
tattoos.

Over the years, tattoos have *adorned the skin of
people ranging from soldiers and sailors to sports stars and
*sorority sisters. People have wide-ranging opinions on
them. Only one thing is for certain: like the ⁸⁾**permanent**
ink ᴳ they're made with, tattoos are here to stay.

Grammar Master

be made with… / of… / from… 的區別

本文最後一句提到：…like the permanent ink they're made with, tattoos are here to say. 這裡指刺青是「用」墨水繪製而成，墨水只是刺青的工具之一，所以用 with。但在指製造某物的原料時，則要用 of… 或 from…。若從成品外觀看得出原本材質（如木桌、棉質襯衫），就用 be made of…；若從成品已完全看不出原料為何（如酒、藥品），則用 be made from…。

- The wedding dress is made with thin gold threads.
  這件結婚禮服以金線縫製而成。
- The suitcase is made of metal.
  這行李箱是金屬製成。
- The medicine is made from 20 different plants.
  這種藥是用二十種不同的植物製作而成。

Mini Quiz 閱讀測驗

❶ These days, tattoos have become _____.
(A) taboo
(B) rebellious
(C) mainstream
(D) flash

❷ What does the author think about the future of tattoos?
(A) They will be around for a long time.
(B) They will mostly be used by gang members.
(C) Tattoos of geisha girls will be most popular.
(D) They will become more accepted.

❸ What are those chess pieces made _____?
(A) from
(B) with
(C) for
(D) of

❹ I _____ live in Austin, but now I live in Dallas.
(A) was
(B) have
(C) used to
(D) use to

閱讀測驗解答 ❶ (C) ❷ (D) ❸ (A) ❹ (C)

Translation

不過就像其他所有事物一樣，刺青的世界也有趨勢。「刺青設計有明確的趨勢」，原子刺青店的夏恩博士表示，「有一陣子很流行毛利花紋，後來是凱爾特圖樣當道。中文符號曾經紅遍一時，不過似乎在逐漸退燒。很難預測接下來會流行什麼，不過最近我有許多客戶指定要刺日本藝伎圖樣。」

幫派份子是社會上另一群會刺青的族群，不過目的大不相同。幫派的刺青象徵忠誠，也常會因某種特殊榮或服務之後而被賜與，很類似軍人獲贈勳章。這並不是刺青的新用途，事實上，最早使用刺青的民族之一是南太平洋的波里尼西亞人，他們通常因為戰績彪炳而獲贈刺青表揚。美國的薩爾瓦多幫以及日本的黑道就是兩個以刺青聞名的犯罪集團。

多年來，刺青裝飾了各種人的皮膚：從軍人和水手到運動明星和姊妹會成員。人們對刺青的觀感也不盡相同，唯一可以確定的是：如同刺青所用的永久性油墨一樣，刺青就此留駐。

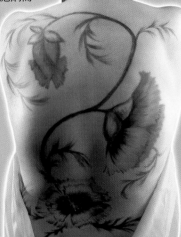

V Vocabulary Bank

1) **explosion** [ɪk`sploʒən] (n.) 爆炸；爆增，快速發展
(a./n.) explosive [ɪk`splosɪv] 有爆炸性的；炸藥
Government experts fear a population explosion.

2) **emerge** [ɪ`mɝdʒ] (v.) 浮現，出現
A new balance of power is emerging in Asia.

3) **ironic** [aɪ`rɑnɪk] (a.) 諷刺的，嘲諷的
(n.) irony [`aɪrənɪ] 有嘲諷意味的事、話語
Stephanie has an ironic sense of humor.

4) **graphic** [`græfɪk] (n.) 圖畫，圖像
(phr.) graphic design 平面設計
Could you scan this graphic for me?

5) **innovative** [`ɪno͵vetɪv] (a.) 創新的
Apple is famous for its stylish, innovative products.

6) **illegal** [ɪ`ligl̩] (a.) 非法的
Online gambling is illegal in some countries.

7) **stall** [stɔl] (n.) 小攤子
The night market is filled with food stalls.

8) **launch** [lɔntʃ] (v.) 將⋯投入市場，發表
We plan to launch our new product next month.

9) **state** [stet] (v.) 陳述，說明
Please state your name and address.

10) **harmless** [`hɑrmlɪs] (a.) 無傷大雅的，無害的
Most spiders are harmless to humans.

補充字彙

* **chic** [ʃik] (a.) 時髦的，精緻的
That boutique sells chic women's clothing and hats.

* **mass-market** [`mæs`mɑrkɪt] (a.) 行銷給一般大眾的；(v.) 以大眾為目標作銷售
Our publishing house specializes in mass-market fiction.

* **brainchild** [`bren͵tʃaɪld] (n.) 獨創的觀念，（某人的）創作
The electric light bulb was the brainchild of Thomas Edison.

* **uber** [`ubə] (a.) 特級的，超級的。此字源自德文，意同英文 super
Only the uber-rich can afford to stay at that resort.

* **fashionista** [fæʃə`nɪstɑ] (n.) 追求流行和時髦的人
What are all the fashionistas wearing this season?

Indie Design
創意隨意玩——獨立設計

TAIPEI BREMEN 圖片由CAMPOBAG提供

!!

ON'T LOOK BACK

UIDEBOOK OF INDIE BRAND "TAIPEI BREMEN"®

Stickers series 3.
ABNORMAL ANIMALS

The 3rd sticker series is "ABNORMAL ANIMALS". It's a fantasy about kinds of animals. And we add the corresponding comic in the back of package so each sticker can be an independent story.

BAD BUNNY | ↑ LEVEL UP ↑ | OH~OOPS! | BEAR AREA
BE STRONG! | LION KING | NEW ARRIVAL! | SAY CHEESE!
KEEP SWIMMING! | BULL SHIT! | NEVER GIVE UP | PUNKATTITUDE

課文朗讀 MP3 145　單字朗讀 MP3 146　英文文章導讀 MP3 147

TOMORROW'S DESIGNS TODAY

In the past, the *chicest and most modern designs all came from the big design houses in Milan, Paris and New York. But now, with the 1)**explosion** of indie design, cool new trends are 2)**emerging** all over the world, and Taiwan is no exception. From the 3)**ironic** 4)**graphics** of Taipei Bremen to the East-meets-West fashions of Drinkin Taipei Design Studio, you don't need to look far to find exciting and 5)**innovative** designs.

So what makes indie design different from the *mass-market variety we all grew up with? Well, for starters, it isn't mass-marketed. All indie—that's short for independent— designers start small. In many cases, they start very, very small. But the best ones don't stay small for long, and the Taipei Bremen studio is the perfect example.

Taipei Bremen began as the *brainchild of Taipei's *uber-creative Mickeyman. Back in 2004, he started selling some of his designs as stickers at an 6)**illegal** street 7)**stall** in Taipei. His designs quickly became popular with the city's young *fashionistas, and ■ **before long** he was selling his stickers at music festivals around the island. ©By 2005, he'd 8)**launched** his own brand in major department stores, although his designs, as he 9)**states**, "Still keep the original spirit to bring people surprise with both positive creativity and a little 10)**harmless** irony."

中 Translation

未來設計先睹為快

以往,最時髦、最摩登的設計全都出自米蘭、巴黎和紐約的大型設計工作室,但現在,隨著獨立設計爆增,酷炫的新潮流在世界各地崛起,台灣也不例外。從台北不來梅的反諷式平面設計,到北寅社東西合併的時尚,要尋找令人興奮的創新設計,你不必捨近求遠。

那麼,獨立設計究竟和伴隨我們成長的各類大眾市場產品有何不同?首先,獨立設計並未對大眾作行銷。所有獨立(indie 是 independent 的縮寫)設計師都是從小規模做起,而且往往是從非常、非常小開始做起。但最好的獨立設計師不會保持小規模太久,台北不來梅就是最好的例子。

台北不來梅源於住在台北的創意王米奇鰻的創作概念。二〇〇四年,他開始在台北街道違法設攤,銷售他設計的貼紙。他的設計很快就在台北那些追逐潮流的年輕人間大受歡迎,不久之後,他便開始在全島各地的音樂節販賣他的貼紙。到二〇〇五年,他的自創品牌已打進大型百貨公司,不過如他所說,他的設計「仍保持原創精神,以正面的創造力及少許無傷大雅的反諷,帶給人們驚喜。」

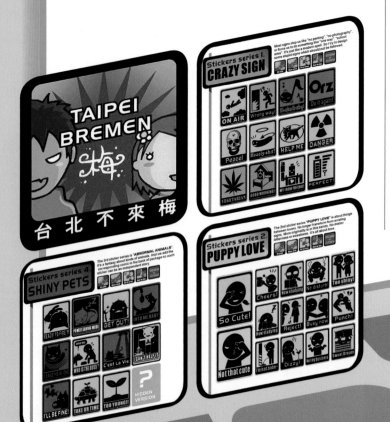

✂ Tongue-tied No More

1 before long 不久之後

這個慣用語的意思等同於 soon,但是 before long 的用法不太相同,通常放在句子的結尾,若置於句首,則須於 before long 之後加逗號。

例 She got used to her new life in New York before long.
= Before long, she got used to her new life in New York.
= She soon got used to her new life in New York.

A: Learning how to play the guitar is so hard.
學彈吉他好難喔!

B: Just keep practicing, and you'll be playing like a pro before long!
只要持續練習,不久之後你就可以彈得像個高手一樣啦!

⚙ Grammar Master

by＋時間:表達期限或重要時間點的句型

用「by＋時間」表達過去或未來的「期限」或「某個重要時間點」時,句子的時態有好幾種:

❶ 指未來的事,且動詞用的是 have to(必須)時,用現在簡單式:
We have to finish the project by Friday.

❷ 指未來的事,但動詞不是 have to 時,用未來完成式:
We will have finished the project by Friday.

❸ 指過去某個時間點的狀況,用過去完成式:
By last Friday, he had already lost 10 kg.

❹ 在假設語氣 if 的句型裡,則配合 if 的句型用法:
If he doesn't come back by noon, we will leave without him.

If we hadn't finished the project by May 30th, the boss would have been very upset.

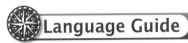

Language Guide

說新潮 講流行 12招

和朋友談論潮流、潮物、潮人時,你還是只會用 Wow, so cool. 嗎?EZ TALK 教你說出時髦有創意的表達法,讓你的英文不再老摳摳!

She always wears such **stylish** clothes!
她穿的衣服都好有型喔!

Have you been to that **hip** new boutique yet?
你去過那間新潮的精品店沒?

That star only wears clothes by **cutting-edge** designers.
那個明星只穿時尚尖端設計師的衣服。

The Japanese design such **ingenious** gadgets.
日本人設計的小玩意都很精巧。

That designer's accessories are really **original**.
那個設計師的飾品都很有創意。

French women are so **chic**.
法國女人都很時髦。

That designer has a really **unique** style.
那個設計師獨具風格。

That shop sells really **innovative** jewelry.
那間店賣的珠寶都很創新。

That design studio does some really **edgy** stuff.
那間設計工作室都做些很前衛的玩意。

Those are some **awesome** graphics on your skateboard!
你的滑板上那些圖案酷斃了!

That's a **wicked** tattoo!
那個刺青真炫!

What a **rad** sticker!
好讚的貼紙!

什麼都賣
什麼都好玩!

影藝小舖 Film Arts' Shop

想要瞭解更多獨立創作嗎?台北市西門町的 in89 豪華數位影院,裡面的影藝小舖陳列許多獨立創作的作品,主要分為三大類:

★ **創意商品**
提供平台讓創意能發聲
與藝術接觸點CAMPOBAG合作,提供獨家創意商品。

★ **獨立音樂**
專屬櫃位作為音樂創作者單曲EP發表平台
提供音樂創作者單曲EP的展售通路,並挑選優秀作品播放,

★ **獨立影像**
主流影片之外的創意發表處
電影上映正片前或電影院外的電視牆可欣賞獨立創作短片的輪播,另外也在店內販售獨立影像作品。

.Know it ALL 英文閱讀

V Vocabulary Bank

1) **strive** [staɪv] (v.) - to, for 奮鬥，努力；
   - against 反抗，鬥爭
   My parents taught me to strive for success.

2) **trendy** [ˈtrɛndɪ] (a.) 時髦的，流行的
   Where do all the trendy people hang out?

3) **teen** [tin] (n.) 青少年
   Car insurance for teens is very expensive.

4) **prescription** [prɪˈskrɪpʃən] (n.)
   藥方，處方
   In the U.S., it's illegal to buy antibiotics
   without a prescription.

5) **constraint** [kənˈstrent] (n.) 拘束，限制
   (v.) constrain
   John had trouble adapting to the
   constraints of military life.

6) **entirely** [ɪnˈtaɪrlɪ] (adv.) 完全地，徹底地
   The accident was entirely my fault.

7) **combine** [kəmˈbaɪn] (v.) 結合，連結
   Combine the ingredients in a large bowl
   and chill overnight.

8) **feature** [ˈfitʃɚ] (v.) 以…為特色
   Our restaurant features authentic Italian
   cuisine.

9) **theme** [θim] (n.) 主題，題材
   What are the major themes in the story?

Language Guide

第 14 行的 in short 是指長話短說，簡而言之
的意思，通常用在文章寫作或是演講中。可取
代此用語的英文還有 in brief 和 to sum up，這
些詞一出現就是在告訴別人接下來你要說話的
絕對是精華和重點，可別用了這些詞之後又繼
續長篇大論喔！

G Grammar Master

not + a / an / any + 名詞 = no + 名詞
not 和它前面的 be 動詞或助動詞是「一夥」
的，所以後面必須照名詞的文法規則，在名詞
前加上冠詞 a / an 或 any；no 則是用來修飾名
詞，取代了 a / an 或 any。

例 ● I don't have any money.
   = I have no money.
  ● There aren't any apples.
   = There are no apples.
  ● It is not an accident.
   = It is no accident.

課文朗讀 MP3 148　單字朗讀 MP3 149　英文文章導讀 MP3 150

Breaking with Tradition

The **1 common ground** shared by most successful indie designers is that they have a young fan base. This isn't a coincidence, as ^Git's no secret that young people [1]**strive** to be different, to set themselves apart from their parents' generation. Can you imagine a day when the [2]**trendiest** kids in Taipei's Ximending or New York's Greenwich Village are all seen walking around in their parents' clothes? Unless it's done for the sake of irony, it's not gonna happen! [3]**Teens** want, even need, to be different.

And indie designers are the best doctors to fill that [4]**prescription**. **2 Free from** the [5]**constraints** of the previous generation of designers, they're able to explore the humor and ideas of today's teens. In short, they give a voice to the younger generation, and it's a voice all their own.

But just as no man is an island, no designer can be [6]**entirely** independent. The best designers find ways to [7]**combine** old elements with new ideas. Take Drinkin

DTDS 圖片由CAMPOBAG提供

20 Taipei Design Studio (DTDS), for example. The designs of DTDS often 8)**feature** traditional Asian 9)**themes**, like dragons and samurai swords. But they then add modern images into the mix, like showing a bikini-clad, tattooed girl holding a samurai sword and wearing headphones.
25 DTDS is the perfect example of an indie design house that has one foot firmly planted in the past, and the other doing a full roundhouse kick into the future.

中 Translation

突破窠臼,跳脫傳統

多數成功獨立設計師的共同點是,他們都有一群年輕粉絲。這不是巧合,正如眾所周知的,年輕人總是努力要標新立異,讓自己有別於父母輩。你能想像有一天,台北西門町和紐約格林威治村最時髦的年輕人都穿著父母的衣服在街頭閒晃嗎?除非是為了表達諷刺,否則不會發生這種事!青少年想要(甚至需要)與眾不同。

獨立設計師是調配這種處方藥的最佳醫師。他們不會受到前一代設計師的桎梏,因此得以探索今日青少年的幽默和想法。簡而言之,他們替年輕一代發聲,而且是年輕人自己的聲音。

不過,沒有人是孤島,同樣的,也沒有設計師能夠完全獨立。最出色的設計師會尋求舊元素與新概念的結合之道。以北寅社為例,他們的設計常以龍和武士刀等傳統亞洲味的主題為主,但也會注入現代意象,譬如呈現一個身有刺青的比基尼女郎手持武士刀、戴著頭戴式耳機。北寅社就是獨立設計工坊一腳穩穩立足於過去、一腳全力迴旋踢向未來的絕佳例證。

Tongue-tied No More

1 common ground
共識,共通點

要注意作「共通點」解釋時的用法,只能用來形容「事件、狀況」的共通點,若要說「他們兩個有許多共通點」,英文則是 They have a lot in common.

A: These negotiations are going nowhere.
這些談判毫無結果。

B: Yeah. If we can't find common ground, we'll never reach an agreement.
是啊,如果我們再沒有共識,我們永遠也別想達成協議。

2 free from...
由……中解脫,免於……

這個片語是形容從某框架中跳脫出來,也可以用來形容因某原因而讓你不需要做某事,或得到豁免權,意同於 deliver [dɪ`lɪvə] from、exempt [ɪg`zəmpt] from。

A: I want a job that's free from stress.
我想要一個沒有壓力的工作。

B: Is there such a thing?
有這樣的工作嗎?

Mini Quiz 閱讀測驗

❶ According to the article, which of the following is NOT true?
 (A) New design trends are appearing worldwide.
 (B) Indie design isn't mass-marketed.
 (C) All indie designers start very, very small.
 (D) Taipei Bremen was started by Mickeyman.

❷ Why is indie design popular with young people?
 (A) Because it helps them express themselves
 (B) Because they have a young fan base
 (C) Because no designer is entirely independent
 (D) Because it provides doctors' prescriptions

❸ After lying down on the couch, Becky _____ fell asleep.
 (A) did
 (B) before long
 (C) quick
 (D) soon

閱讀測驗解答 ❶ (C) ❷ (A) ❸ (D)

Secrets of Symbols

符號的祕密

V Vocabulary Bank

1) **mysterious** [mɪsˋtɪrɪəs] (a.) 神祕的
   (n.) mystery [ˋmɪstərɪ] 神祕的事物，謎
   The coffin is covered with mysterious symbols.

2) **fluent** [ˋfluənt] (a.) 流利的，流暢的
   My brother is fluent in French.

3) **literate** [ˋlɪtərɪt] (a.) 具讀寫（解讀）能力的，有文化修養的
   The boy's parents are barely literate.

4) **purpose** [ˋpɝpəs] (n.) 目的，用途
   What is the purpose of your visit?

5) **merely** [ˋmɪrlɪ] (adv.) 僅僅，只是
   He was merely a child when his parents passed away.

6) **depiction** [dɪˋpɪkʃən] (n.) 描述
   The drawing is a depiction of village life.

7) **decoration** [ˌdɛkəˋreʃən] (n.) 裝飾品），裝潢
   (v.) decorate [ˋdɛkəˌret] 裝飾，修飾
   Where did you put the Christmas tree decorations?

8) **technique** [tɛkˋnik] (n.) 技巧，技術
   New scientific techniques are being used to study the brain.

9) **symbolism** [ˋsɪmbəˌlɪzəm] (n.) 象徵的使用），象徵主義
   (n.) symbol [ˋsɪmbḷ] 象徵，符號
   (v.) symbolize [ˋsɪmbəˌlaɪz] 象徵，用符號表示
   Symbolism is often used in literature.

10) **peak** [pik] (n.) 高峰，頂端
    Tiger Woods is at the peak of his career.

11) **persecution** [ˌpɝsɪˋkjuʃən] (n.) 迫害
    Our class watched a movie about the persecution of the Jews.

補充字彙

* **dramatize** [ˋdræməˌtaɪz] (v.) 戲劇化的描述，改編為戲劇
  The play dramatizes the life of Andy Warhol.

課文朗讀 MP3 151　單字朗讀 MP3 152　英文文章導讀 MP3 153

You ⑥may have seen *The Da Vinci Code*, the popular movie that *dramatizes European art and its ⁱ⁾**mysterious** language. But what hidden meanings does art really hold?
5　The answer to this question depends on how ²⁾**fluent** you are in the language of symbols. Sometimes the meanings of symbols are as plain as day; other times, however, they speak a secret language only understood by the most ³⁾**literate**.

　　From the beginning of history,
11　people used art for special ⁴⁾**purposes**. In what is now France, ancient humans painted animals such as horses and deer on the walls and ceilings of caves. Were these cave paintings ⁵⁾**merely**
15　simple ⁶⁾**depictions** of the natural world or early forms of ⁷⁾**decoration**? Many people believe that these were not just pictures, but magical symbols used to guarantee success in hunting.

　　While great advances in artistic ⁸⁾**techniques**
20　and materials were made over the centuries, the ⁹⁾**symbolism** used in art remained as mysterious as ever. European art reached a ¹⁰⁾**peak** during

the Renaissance. From the 14th to the 17th centuries, great advances were made in both science and art.
25 The Renaissance, however, was also a time of religious [11]**persecution**. Saying the wrong thing about the Christian religion could put you in jail—or worse. To protect themselves, artists used symbolism to hide the true meanings of their paintings from
30 the Church.

中 Translation

你也許已看過《達文西密碼》，這部人氣電影將歐洲藝術及其神祕語言生動地描繪出來。不過藝術真正隱含的意義究竟為何？此問題的答案端看你的符號語言有多流利。有時候，符號的意義顯而易見，不過有時傳達的是一種只有最博學的人才懂的祕密語言。

有史以來，人類就為特殊目的而使用藝術。在現今的法國，古代人在洞穴的壁面和壁頂上繪製馬和鹿等動物。這些洞穴壁畫只是單純描繪自然界，或者是早期的裝潢形式嗎？許多人認為這些不只是圖畫而已，而是用來確保狩獵成功的魔法符號。

數世紀以來，藝術技巧與素材雖然已經有重大進步，但藝術所使用的符號依然神祕如昔。歐洲藝術在文藝復興時期達到顛峰。從十四世紀到十七世紀，科學與藝術都有長足的進步，不過，文藝復興時期同時也是宗教迫害時期。說基督教的不是，可能會入獄——甚至更糟。為了保護自己，藝術家運用象徵符號來隱藏畫作的真實意涵，以免教會看出。

Language Guide

文藝復興時期是什麼？為什麼一提到文藝復興就有達文西？

文藝復興 (Renaissance) 是西方史上一個非常重要的時期，天文學家哥白尼 (Nicolaus Copernicus)、天文望遠鏡的發明者伽利略 (Galileo Galilei)、地理大發現的哥倫布 (Christopher Columbus) 及麥哲倫 (Ferdinand Magellan)、第一部揭露宗教腐敗的文學作品《神曲》Divine Comedy、大文豪莎士比亞……等，皆出自於文藝復興時期。這段科學和藝術上的革命使得十五、十六世紀的西洋文明大放異彩，其成就與影響深遠至今日。此時期不但被認為是中古時代的「神本主義」和現代「人文主義」的分界，馬克思學派更認為這是一個社會體系由封建制度轉變為資本主義的分界。

在不勝枚舉的藝術、科學名人中，達文西 (Leonardo da Vinci)、米開朗基羅 (Michelangelo Buonarroti) 以及拉斐爾 (Raffaello Sanzio) 號稱文藝復興三傑，但為什麼文藝復興鄙棄宗教，而這三傑 卻都以宗教藝術聞名？其實仔細觀察他們的藝術作品，不難發現在他們以宗教故事為主題的繪畫和雕刻中，所表現的都是凡人的場景，對神敬而遠之，強調人的地位和價值。尤其是達文西精確描繪的人體比例，最能表現文藝復興藝術與科學結合的特色。簡而言之，文藝復興精神就是以文學及藝術表達人的思想情感，以科學為人謀福利，而達文西則可說是將此精神藝術化、具象化的佼佼者。

Grammar Master

助動詞 ＋have (not) p.p. 表示「當時原本（不）……」或對過去事實的推測

can、may / might、will、must、should 等助動詞後面接原形動詞時，表達的是現在或未來的事情。但它們的後面接完成式 have p.p. 時，意思就變成和過去事實相反的「當時原本（不）……」，或是對過去所發生的事的推測。不過 can 和 will 這兩個有過去式的字就要改用 could 和 would 再接 have p.p.。

● could have p.p. →當時原本可以……
● would have p.p. →當時原本會……
● should have p.p. →當時原本應該……
● may / might have p.p. →當時也許是……
● must have p.p. →當時一定是……

例 ● Why didn't you tell me you were in trouble? I could have helped you.

● Rita didn't answer the phone. She must have been asleep when I called.

V Vocabulary Bank

1) **lap** [læp] (n.) 大腿上方
My cat likes to sit in my lap when I watch TV.

2) **portrait** [`portrɪt] (n.) 肖像，寫照
The rich merchant hired an artist to paint his portrait.

3) **frightening** [`fraɪtnɪŋ] (a.) 令人恐懼的
(v.) frighten [`fraɪtn] 嚇唬某人，使某人驚恐
Everyone wore frightening costumes to the Halloween party.

4) **in contrast with** [ɪn `kɑntræst wɪθ] (phr.) 對比於…，相對於…
In contrast with his brother, Michael is a good student.

5) **figure** [`fɪgjɚ] (n.) 人物
The event was attended by many important political figures.

6) **restrict (to)** [rɪ`strɪkt] (v.) 限制，約束
The government has decided to restrict imports of certain foreign products.

7) **communist** [`kɑmjənɪst] (n.) 共產黨
Cuba is one of the world's few remaining communist countries.

8) **alien** [`elɪən] (n.) 外星人
Do you believe in aliens?

9) **mob** [mɑb] (n.) 暴民，烏合之眾
An angry mob gathered outside the government building.

10) **turn on / upon** [tɚn ɑn] (phr.) （突然地）反目成仇，懷有敵意
The dog turned on its owner and bit him.

11) **grip** [grɪp] (v.) 緊握，緊咬
Many African countries are gripped by poverty.

12) **prejudice** [`prɛdʒədɪs] (n.) 偏見
Racial prejudice is still a serious problem.

補充字彙

* **blackout** [`blæk.aʊt] 停電
The blackout was caused by an explosion at the power plant.

圖片提供《圖騰的祕密》，山岳文化

課文朗讀 MP3 154　單字朗讀 MP3 155　英文文章導讀 MP3 156

An excellent example of hidden symbolism in Renaissance art is the drawing *The Virgin and Child with St. Anne* by Leonardo da Vinci. In it, we see the Virgin Mary with her mother, Saint Anne. ᴳIn Mary's 1)**lap** sits
5　the baby Jesus. Is this just a simple family 2)**portrait**? Look again. The eyes of Saint Anne are dark and 3)**frightening**. Anne's head also seems to be coming out of Mary's body. She thus seems to represent the dark side of human nature, 4)**in contrast with** the beauty and peace
10　of Mary's face. It is a powerful image, especially since showing anything negative about these religious 5)**figures** could get an artist killed.

Hidden symbolism, however, isn't
6)**restricted** to the distant past. In the
15　1950s, America was in the middle of a

[7)]**communist** scare. Many Americans accused of being communists lost their jobs or were even sent to jail. This was also the golden age of television, and Rod Serling wrote an episode [20] of *The Twilight Zone* to comment on what was going on around him. In "The Monsters are Due on Maple Street," a small town neighborhood becomes paranoid during a *blackout. People start believing that [25] [8)]**aliens** have come to earth, and they quickly turn into a fearful, violent [9)]**mob**. Neighbors become enemies, and everyone [10)]**turns on** each other.

It's not difficult to understand the symbolism here. [31] The fearful neighborhood represents a paranoid America. More broadly, it represents any community [11)]**gripped** by fear and [12)]**prejudice**. Today, this *Twilight Zone* episode is shown in classrooms to teach students about the dangers [35] of prejudice and paranoia.

中 Translation

文藝復興藝術品中隱含象徵的絕佳例子是達文西的畫作《聖母、聖嬰和聖安妮》。在此畫作中，我們看到聖母與她的母親聖安妮。聖母的大腿上坐著嬰兒時期的耶穌。這只是一幅單純的家庭肖像畫嗎？再看一次。聖安娜的雙眼陰鬱且令人感覺驚恐，她的頭部也好像是從聖母的身體中長出來似的。因此，她似乎代表人性的黑暗面，和聖母臉龐的美麗與安詳成為對比。這是一幅強而有力的圖像，特別是當時的藝術家可能會因為表現出這些宗教人物任何的負面形象而送命。

然而，隱藏的象徵並非只有遙遠的過去才有。一九五〇年代，美國正處於共產主義恐慌，許多被控是共產黨員的美國人紛紛失業或甚至入獄。當時也是電視的黃金年代，羅德瑟林為影集《陰陽魔界》寫了一集來評論他周遭發生的一切。在《怪物要來楓樹街》這集中，一座小鎮中的街坊鄰居因停電而變成偏執狂，人們開始相信外星人已經降臨地球，這些人很快就變成一群擔心受怕又兇暴的暴民。鄰居變成敵人，大家都互相攻擊。

這裡的象徵意義不難了解。擔心受怕的鄰里代表偏執的美國，更廣泛來說，代表任何受恐懼與偏見所控制的社群。現在，這一集《陰陽魔界》會在課堂上播映，教導學生偏見與偏執的危險。

Language Guide

冷戰與恐共時期

二次世界大戰結束後，世界兩大強權——自由世界（美國）和共產世界（蘇聯和其同盟）——之間仍存在嚴重的衝突及分歧，雙方為了避免再次造成全球性的戰爭，決定不訴諸武力，卻在科技、軍備及外交發展上竭力競爭，這段時期被稱為冷戰 Cold War，並且一直到九〇年蘇聯解體後才結束。

冷戰初期，美國參議員喬瑟夫麥卡錫 Joseph McCarthy 不設法安撫人心，反而利用美國人民對共產黨迅速擴張的恐懼，大肆渲染共產黨入侵滲透美國各階層的印象。「麥卡錫主義」McCarthyism 加上胡佛 (John Edgar Hoover) 領導下的 FBI 乘機大力掃蕩所有質疑或反對美國政府的言論，美國人開始互相揭發，數千人因此被扣上共產黨的紅帽子，衍生大量的逮捕監禁和暗殺慘案，許多藝文界名人被列入「黑名單」Hollywood blacklist，形成所謂「白色恐怖」White Terror。

麥卡錫主義盛行期間（四〇年代末期至五〇年代末期）迫使許多優秀人士出走他國，嚴重影響美國民主自由形象，為美國歷史上最黑暗的時期。

Grammar Master

表地點的副詞片語＋倒裝句型

In Mary's lap sits the baby Jesus. 這句話原本應該是：The baby Jesus sits in Mary's lap. 但這種用介系詞 + 名詞的地點副詞片語，可以搬到句首，後面先接動詞，再接主詞。這樣的寫法可以增加寫作時句型的變化性，讓文章不會太單調。注意在這種句型裡，通常進行式的動詞都要改為簡單式。

例 ● A present and a card lay in the box.
　　= In the box lay a present and a card.
　● A beautiful girl is standing under the tree.
　　= Under the tree stands a beautiful girl.

不過要是句子原本用的是 there＋be 動詞的句型時，地點片語的後面還是先接 there＋be 動詞（不倒裝），再接主詞。

例 ● There is a book on the table.
　　= On the table there is a book.
　● There is a girl standing under the tree.
　　= Under the tree there is a girl standing.

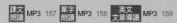

Vocabulary Bank

1) **era** [ˋɪrə] (n.) 時代，年代
The fall of the Berlin Wall marked the end of an era.

2) **conservatism** [kənˋsɝvə͵tɪzəm] (n.) 保守主義
(a.) conservative [kənˋsɝvətɪv] 保守的，守舊的
The Republican Party is the party of conservatism.

3) **strictly** [ˋstrɪktlɪ] (adv.) 嚴厲地，嚴格地
Traffic laws should be strictly enforced.

4) **prohibit** [prəˋhɪbɪt] (v.) 禁止
Smoking is prohibited inside the restaurant.

5) **embrace** [ɪmˋbres] (v.) 擁抱
The friends embraced and said goodbye.

6) **intimate** [ˋɪntəmɪt] (a.) 親密的，有性關係的
The couple has not yet been intimate.

7) **symbolic (of)** [sɪmˋbɑlɪk] (a.) 象徵性的，作為象徵的
The dove is symbolic of peace.

8) **evidence** [ˋɛvɪdəns] (of) (n.) 證據，跡象
There is no evidence that the man committed the crime.

9) **barefoot** [ˋbɛr͵fʊt] (adv./a.) 赤腳的
The family walked barefoot on the beach.

10) **ultimately** [ˋʌltəmɪtlɪ] (adv.) 最後，終極地
The enemy was ultimately defeated after a long battle.

During this same [1]**era** of American [2]**conservatism**, showing sexual images in films or on TV was [3]**strictly** [4]**prohibited**. Filmmakers, however, quickly learned to use symbols to let audiences know what was happening

5　behind closed doors. If a couple [5]**embraced** in a kiss and knocked over a glass of water, everyone knew that it meant they were getting [6]**intimate**. Similarly, if there was romance in the air between a man and a woman, and the woman put a cigarette in her mouth, it was also [7]**symbolic**

10　of a sexual act.

A decade later, The Beatles were the biggest rock band on the planet. Their albums sold millions, and [G]it wasn't

long before fans started seeing symbolism in their album artwork. What did the symbols say? To many fans, the

15 message was clear: Paul McCartney was dead. 8)**Evidence** of Paul's death ranged from him holding a black instrument on the cover of *Sgt. Pepper's Lonely Hearts Club Band*, to him walking 9)**barefoot** and out of step with the other Beatles on *Abbey Road*. Decades later, this "dead" Beatle continues

20 to record albums and play concerts. It just goes to show that, as Sigmund Freud said, sometimes a cigar is just a cigar.

10)**Ultimately**, symbols are open to many interpretations. We may never truly know the meaning

25 behind those ancient cave drawings in France, but we'll always enjoy guessing.

中 Translation

在美國盛行保守主義的同一時期，電影或電視嚴禁出現性畫面。然而，電影人很快就學會使用符號象徵來讓觀眾知道緊閉的門後發生的事情。如果一對伴侶擁吻並打翻一杯水，大家就知道這代表他們即將發生親密關係。同樣地，如果一對男女正處於曖昧不明時，女子嘴裡叼著一根菸，也是性行為的象徵。

十年之後，披頭四成為全球頭號搖滾樂團。他們的專輯銷售數百萬張，粉絲很快就從他們的專輯作品看出了象徵意義。這些象徵符號表達出哪些意涵呢？對許多粉絲來說，寓意很清楚：保羅麥卡尼死了。保羅死亡的證據從他在《比伯軍曹寂寞芳心俱樂部》唱片封面上手持一把黑色樂器，到《艾比路》封面上他光著腳走路，而且與其他披頭四成員步伐不一致可以看出。數十年後，這個「已死」的披頭四成員繼續灌錄唱片並開演唱會。這一切足以表示，正如佛洛伊德所說的，有時候，雪茄就只是雪茄而已。

畢竟，符號沒有既定解釋。我們也許永遠無法確知法國那些古老洞穴壁畫背後的意義，但我們永遠能享受猜謎的樂趣。

Language Guide

二十世紀影響力人物——佛洛伊德

出生於奧地利的佛洛伊德 Sigmund Freud (1856-1939) 是精神分析學 (psychoanalytic school) 的創始人。佛洛伊德的理論相當驚世駭俗，雖被譽為精神分析之父，但其理論直到今日仍非常有爭議性，甚至遭受抨擊。

在終其一生的研究中，佛洛伊德提出了夢境、人格結構和發展與「性」之間密不可分之關係，認為人的心理障礙皆出自於「原我」id、「自我」ego、「超我」super-ego 之間產生了衝突，而這些衝突極可能來自從嬰兒時期開始的人格發展中，「性」部分被壓抑或不滿足。他的夢境分析研究探討大量與性有關的象徵，文中所提到的香菸、水、雪茄即是其中幾個例子。

佛洛伊德對人類心理與行為分析的方式，不只讓精神醫科、人類學、刑罰學完全改觀，甚至哲學、美學、文學和教育都受到深刻的影響，也給小說家和劇作家提供無限的寫作資料，可謂二十世紀最具影響力的人物之一。

Grammar Master

It wasn't / won't be long before…
不久……

這個句型的意思是「不久」也就是 soon…。指已發生的事情時，用 It wasn't long before＋過去簡單式子句；指未來的事情時，用 It won't be long before＋現在簡單式子句。

例
- It wasn't long before I realized my mistake.
- It won't be long before James becomes a successful artist.

Mini Quiz 閱讀測驗

1 Why did Renaissance artists use symbolism in their paintings?
(A) To make their works mysterious
(B) To hide from the Church
(C) To protect themselves from persecution
(D) To express their religious faith

2 You _____ let me know you weren't coming to the party.
(A) have
(B) should have
(C) should
(D) hadn't

3 It _____ long before man lands on Mars.
(A) wasn't
(B) hasn't be
(C) isn't
(D) won't be

(D) 3 (B) 2 (C) 1 ：答解鼴測讀閱

Vocabulary Bank

1) **avert** [əˋvɝt] (v.) 防止，避開
Disaster was averted when a bomb was found aboard the plane.

2) **release** [rɪˋlis] (v.) 發表，發行
The band will release their new album in July.

3) **escalate** [ˋɛskə‚let] (v.) 上升
(n.) escalation [‚ɛskəˋleʃən] 上升、擴大
Tensions between the two countries continue to escalate.

4) **riot** [ˋraɪət] (n.) 暴動
A riot broke out when the home team lost the game.

5) **drought** [draut] (n.) 乾旱
Many rivers dried up during the drought.

6) **reduce** [rɪˋdjus] (v.) 減少，縮小，降低
The new government has promised to reduce poverty and hunger.

7) **loom** [lum] (v.) 陰影逼近，隱約呈現
The economist warned of a looming financial disaster.

8) **evidence** [ˋɛvədəns] (v.) 證明
Support for the war has fallen, as evidenced by several recent polls.

9) **rural** [ˋrurəl] (a.) 鄉村的
Crime rates are generally low in rural areas.

10) **urban** [ˋɝbən] (a.) 城市的
The country's urban population continues to grow.

補充字彙

* **lurk** [lɝk] (v.) 潛藏，埋伏
The little girl thought there was a monster lurking under her bed.

* **full-blown** [ˋfulˋblon] (a.) 全面爆發的，成熟的，（花）盛開的
(a.) blown 膨脹的，（花）盛開的
The government is worried that the recession will turn into a full-blown depression.

* **herald** [ˋhɛrəld] (n.) 報信者，先驅（常用於報紙名稱）
Robins are heralds of spring.

Crisis Averted? 化險為夷？

課文朗讀 MP3 160　單字朗讀 MP3 161　英文文章導讀 MP3 162

The New Face of Hunger

An alarming report ²⁾**released** in 2008 by the United Nations Food and Agriculture Organization warned of an ³⁾**escalating** food crisis threatening the world's poor. For
5　much of that year it seemed that ©the report may not have been alarming enough. There were food ⁴⁾**riots** in Mexico, Egypt, Haiti and Somalia; Australia's worst ⁵⁾**drought** in a century ⁶⁾**reduced** the nation's wheat crop by 60%; and average food prices worldwide were 75% higher than in
10　2000. Although the situation has improved in 2009, and for an unexpected reason, a collection of independent forces still *lurks in the shadows, ready to drag the world into a *full-blown food crisis.

Most people expect a food crisis to have an agricultural
15　problem at its roots, yet the ⁷⁾**looming** crisis is mainly a problem of global economics. This is ⁸⁾**evidenced** by the

fact that in many places people are going hungry not because there is no food to eat, but because they can't afford to buy it. As the World Food Program's Greg Barrow explained in an interview in Scotland's *Sunday *Herald*, "As well as being 9)**rural**, the profile of the new hungry poor is also 10)**urban**, which is new. There is food available in the markets and shops—it's just that these people can't afford to buy it. This is the new face of hunger."

20

Translation 中

飢餓新風貌

聯合國糧食及農業組織於二○○八年公布了一份令人警惕的報告，報告中警告，全球貧民正面臨愈來愈嚴重的糧食危機。綜觀二○○八年大致的情況，這份報告恐怕還不夠叫人警惕。墨西哥、埃及、海地和索馬利亞等地皆發生糧食暴動；澳洲百年來最嚴重的乾旱使該國小麥作物減產百分之六十；全球糧食平均價格比二○○○年高出百分之七十五。雖然情況在二○○九年已有所改善，而且是基於某個意想不到的原因，但是一堆個別因素仍然潛伏在暗處，準備把世界捲入全面性的糧食危機。

大多數人都以為糧食危機的起因會是農業問題，但此迫在眉睫的危機主要是全球經濟問題使然。這點可由下列事實得到印證：許多地方的人們不是因為沒東西可吃而挨餓，而是因為買不起。誠如世界糧食計畫組織的葛瑞格巴羅在接受蘇格蘭《週日先驅報》訪談時所說：「除了鄉村居民，新增加的飢餓貧民還包括城市人，這是前所未見之事。市場和商店都有食物可買——只是這些百姓買不起而已。這是飢餓的新面貌。」

Grammar Master

may / might have p.p. 表對過去事情的推測：「當時也許是……」

may、might、should、must 等助動詞 + 原 V
→ 現在或未來的事情

may、might、should、must 等助動詞 + have + p.p.
→ 過去情況的推測或和過去事實相反的言論

注意 must 原本是「必須……」的意思，但接 have p.p. 時則是「當時一定是……」的意思。

例 ● No one answered the phone. They may / might have left the office.
沒有人接聽電話，他們可能離開辦公室了。（表示推測）

● You shouldn't have bought those expensive shoes.
你不該買那雙昂貴鞋子的。（表示已買但不該買的馬後炮）

● Sam was late this morning. His car must have broken down again.
山姆今天早上遲到，他的車一定又拋錨了。（表示推測）

Vocabulary Bank

1) **unprecedented** [ʌnˋprɛsə͵dɛntɪd] (a.) 史無前例的，空前的
The team has enjoyed unprecedented success this season.

2) **industrialization** [ɪn͵dʌstrɪələˋzeʃən] (n.) 工業化
China's rapid industrialization has led to serious environmental problems.

3) **sector** [ˋsɛktə] (n.) 部門，產業
The financial crisis has affected all sectors of the economy.

4) **urbanization** [͵ɝbənɪˋzeʃən] (n.) 都市化
Urbanization has both positive and negative effects on the environment.

5) **raw** [rɔ] (a.) 生的，未加工的
Some vegetables are poisonous if eaten raw.

6) **petroleum** [pəˋtrolɪəm] (n.) 石油
Gasoline is a by-product of petroleum.

7) **fertilizer** [ˋfɝtḷ͵aɪzə] (n.) 肥料
Organic vegetables are grown without chemical fertilizers.

8) **harvest** [ˋhɑrvɪst] (v.) 收割，採收
The grapes at our vineyard are harvested by hand.

補充字彙

* **downside** [ˋdaʊn͵saɪd] (n.) 不利條件，缺點；「優點」則為 upside
What are the upsides and downsides of this plan?

* **populous** [ˋpɑpjələs] (a.) 人口稠密的，人口眾多的
Tokyo is the world's most populous city.

* **quadruple** [kwɑˋdrʊpl] (v.) 成為四倍
Exports are expected to quadruple over the next five years.

* **exponentially** [͵ɛkspoˋnɛnʃəlɪ] (adv.) 以指數方式
The price of long-distance calls has fallen exponentially.

* **downturn** [ˋdaʊn͵tɝn] (n.)（經濟）衰退
Michael lost his job in the economic downturn.

* **respite** [ˋrɛspɪt] (n.) 暫時緩解（痛苦），喘息
A walk through the park provides a respite from the city's busy streets.

課文朗讀 MP3 163　單字朗讀 MP3 164　英文文章導讀 MP3 165

The *Downside of Economic Growth

©Over the last few decades, the world has experienced 1)**unprecedented** economic growth. Increased 2)**industrialization**, booming manufacturing 3)**sectors** and rapid 4)**urbanization** (especially in India and China, the world's two most *populous countries) have all led to higher demand for energy and 5)**raw** materials. And when demand goes up, so do prices.

Take petroleum, for example. The cost per barrel of oil *quadrupled between 2001 and 2008. Now consider the fact that 6)**petroleum** products are used at all stages of food production. Even if food isn't grown using petroleum-based 7)**fertilizers**, petroleum is used indirectly, in 8)**harvesting**, processing, distribution and packaging. Put simply, oil is used at practically every step of the food production process, from the farm to the dinner plate. When the price of oil rises, food prices rise as well, and because oil is used in so many stages of food production, prices can rise *exponentially.

This brings us to the unexpected reason the greater crisis of 2008 was averted: the global economic *downturn. When recession hit the world's major economies, demand for oil fell and so did its cost. Cheaper oil meant cheaper food, and some of the pressure on the world's poor was relieved. The *respite, however, wouldn't last long.

Grammar Master

in over during	+ the past / last（一段時間）+ 現在完成或現在完成進行式

in、over、during 接 the past / the last + 一段時間（如 week、three days、five years 等），指的都是「在過去的……時間裡」，是算到現在為止，所以要用表示從以前持續到現在的現在完成式 (have/has p.p.)，或現在完成進行式 (have/has been Ving)。

例
● I haven't seen him in the last two weeks.
  過去的兩周裡我都沒有見到他。

● Over the past year, Mary has been on a strict diet.
  在過去一年中，瑪麗進行嚴格的飲食控制。

● We have been working on this project during the past three months.
  過去三個月裡，我們一直在做這個專案。

中 Translation

經濟成長的負面效應

過去幾十年來，全球經歷了前所未有的經濟成長。工業化程度提升、製造業蓬勃發展，以及都市化快速（特別是印度和中國，世界人口最多的兩個國家）皆導致能源及原料的需求增高。而需求增加的時候，價格也水漲船高。

以石油為例。每桶石油價格在二○○一至二○○八年間上升了三倍之多。現在再想想下面這個事實：食物生產的各個階段都會用到石油製品。就算不用石化肥料來耕種，石油也會間接使用於收割、加工、配銷和包裝。簡單來說，食物生產過程幾乎每一個步驟，從耕種到上桌，都會用到石油。當石油價格上升，食物價格也會上揚，而因為食物生產有這麼多階段都要用到石油，價格可能呈指數倍增。

於是出現了一個意想不到的原因，避免掉二○○八年一場更嚴重的糧食危機：由於全球經濟下滑。當經濟衰退襲擊世界各大經濟體，對石油的需求便降低，油價也隨之下跌。石油變便宜了，意味著糧食價格也變得比較便宜，全世界貧窮民眾的部份壓力頓時解除。然而，暫時的喘息持續不了太久。

Language Guide
各種倍數的表達法

1.5倍 +50%

rise/increase/grow...50%
Gas prices rose 50% in the summer of 2006.
油價在 2006 年夏天上漲 50%。

rise/increase/grow...by half
Obesity is expected to increase by half over the next decade.
肥胖症人數預計在未來十年會是現在的一點五倍。

3倍

triple (v.)
Unemployment has tripled in some areas.
一些地區的失業率已上升兩倍。

triple (a.)
The police are investigating a triple homicide.
警方正在調查一起三屍命案。

be three times as...as...
Men are three times as likely to die from injuries as women.
男性受傷死亡的人數約為女性的三倍。

threefold (a.)
I made a threefold return on my investment.
我的投資賺到三倍的報酬。

2倍

cheeseburger   double cheeseburger

doubled (v.)
The city's population has doubled over the past decade.
該城市人口十年來已增加一倍。

doubled (a.)
I'd like a double scoop of strawberry ice cream.
我想要雙球的草莓冰淇淋。

(be) twice as many/much as
Facebook has twice as many users as MySpace.
Facebook 的用戶是 MySpace 的兩倍。

Cigarettes are twice as expensive as they used to be.
香菸的價格是過去的兩倍。

V + twofold (adv.)
The price of many vegetables increased twofold after the typhoon.
許多蔬菜的價格在颱風過後上漲一倍。

4倍

latte   quadruple latte

quadruple (v.)
The national debt quadrupled in five years.
國債金額於五年內變為四倍。

quadruple (a.)
The surgeon performed a quadruple bypass.
外科醫生進行了一場四重繞道手術（編註：心臟三條動脈及一條分支全部阻塞）。

fourfold (a.)
The company expects a fourfold increase in sales.
該公司期待銷售業績能成長四倍。

have/has four times...
China has four times the population of the United States.
中國的人口是美國的四倍。

這幾倍，不必背……

右邊這些知道就好，平常幾乎用不到，不必特別去記。

5倍
quintuple
fivefold

8倍
octuple
eightfold

6倍
sextuple
sixfold

9倍
nonuple
ninefold

7倍
septuple
sevenfold

10倍
decuple
tenfold

exponentially 以指數方式成長

所謂「指數」，就像銀行以複利計算，一段固定期間會以固定指數連本帶利翻一次，引申為「急遽朝同一方向變化」。

The demand for oil is increasing exponentially.
石油需求急遽增加。

若要明確說出翻升的比例（即指數），可以這樣說：

The company's revenues are growing (at) 50% a/per year.
該公司的營收以每年增加 50% 的幅度成長。

Vocabulary Bank

1) **obvious** [ˋɑbvɪəs] (a.) 明顯的
The answer to that question is obvious.

2) **inability** [ˌɪnəˋbɪlətɪ] (n.) 不能，無能
The man's inability to read and write made it difficult for him to find work.

3) **prevent** [prɪˋvɛnt] (v.) 預防，防止
(phr.) prevent from 阻止，妨礙
Parents should teach their children how to prevent fires.

4) **renew** [rɪˋnju] (v.) 重新開始；
更換（執照），續訂，續約
Are you going to renew your lease?

5) **summarize** [ˋsʌməˌraɪz] (v.) 總結，概述
Can you summarize your findings for us?

6) **compound** [kəmˋpaʊnd] (v.) 加重，
使惡化，混合
Borrowing money to pay off debts will just compound the problem.

7) **famine** [ˋfæmɪn] (n.) 饑荒
Thousands of people died in the famine.

8) **commonplace** [ˋkɑmənˌples] (a.) 司空見慣
的，平凡的
Cell phones have become commonplace in most countries.

補充字彙

* **call in** [kɔl ɪn] (phr.) 正式要求歸還
If you miss a payment, the bank has the right to call in your mortgage.

* **foreclose** [forˋkloz] (v.) 取消贖回抵押品的權
利，查封房產
The bank is threatening to foreclose on our home.

* **interconnectedness**
[ˌɪntəkəˋnɛktɪdnɪs] (n.) 相互連接的性質
inter 表「互相」＋ connected ＋ ness 表
「性質、狀態」
Some believe that the increasing interconnectedness among countries makes war less likely.

課文朗讀 MP3 166　單字朗讀 MP3 167　英文文章導讀 MP3 168

1 What One Hand Giveth....

The higher food prices of 2006 and 2007 had led many farmers around the world to borrow money in order to expand their farming operations. At the time, it
5　ᴳseemed like an 1)**obvious**, safe investment. But when the credit crisis hit in 2008, many banks, especially those in developing countries, *called in the loans, often *foreclosing on farms and farm equipment.

Furthermore, the banks' 2)**inability** to lend to
10　farmers 3)**prevented** many from buying the seeds and fertilizers needed to plant new crops. So just as the drop in the price of oil relieved pressure, the *escalation of the credit crisis 4)**renewed** it. In an interview with UPI, Josette Sheeran, executive director of the U.N. World
15　Food Program, 5)**summarized** the situation, "I think the world would like to focus on one crisis at a time, but we really can't afford to. These are not separate crises. The food crisis and the financial one are linking and 6)**compounding**. I'm really putting out the warning that
20　we're in an era now where supplies are still very tight, very low and very expensive."

Indeed, it's the *interconnectedness of global food markets that is at the heart of the problem. Yet ❷ **by the same token**, without this degree of interconnectedness, local shortages a nd 7)**famines** would be far more 8)**commonplace**. It's clearly a crisis with no simple solution, and it's one that affects us all.

25

中 Translation

一手給⋯⋯

二〇〇六及二〇〇七年糧食價格居高不下，驅使全球許多農民借錢來擴大農業經營。這在當時似乎是理所當然又安全的投資。但等到二〇〇八年爆發信貸危機後，許多銀行要求收回貸款（特別是開發中國家的銀行），常常是取消農田與農作設備的贖回權。

此外，由於這些銀行無法借錢給農民，許多農民便無法購買耕種新作物所需的種子和肥料。所以，就在油價下跌紓解壓力的同時，擴大的信貸危機卻又使壓力死灰復燃。聯合國世界糧食組織執行長喬塞特席蘭在接受合眾國際社（UPI 即 United Press International）訪談時，總結了這種情況：「我認為世界會想一次聚焦於一種危機上，但我們真的無能為力。這些並非各自獨立的危機，糧食危機和金融危機是相互牽連且彼此加劇的。我真的必須大聲疾呼，我們正處於一個供給依舊非常吃緊、非常稀少而且非常昂貴的年代。」

的確，問題的核心正是全球糧食市場相互之間的關聯性。不過同樣地，如果沒有如此密切的關聯性，地方性糧食短缺和饑荒恐怕遠比現在更普遍。這顯然是一個無法用單純方法解決的危機，也是影響我們每一個人的危機。

Tongue-tied No More

❶ What one hand giveth, the other taketh away. 左手進，右手出。

giveth、taketh 都是古英文，這句其實就是 What one hand gives, the other takes away.「左手剛給你，右手就收走」，只能當個過路財神。

A: I just got a raise, but it put me in a higher tax bracket, so Uncle Sam gets to keep most of it.
我才剛加薪，稅級卻升了一級，因此美國政府要把大部分加薪的錢都拿走。

B: What one hand giveth, the other taketh away.
真是左手進，右手出啊。

❷ by the same token 同樣地，反過來說

A: If I buy more of the stock, I'll make more when it goes up.
如果那支股票我多買一點，它上漲時我就會賺更多。

B: Yeah, but by the same token, you'll lose more if it falls.
是啊，但同樣地，它下跌時你會賠更多。

Grammar Master

seem 和 seem like 的比較

seem（似乎）後面接形容詞或不定詞 to V，但若後面有 like（像）時，由於此時的 like 是介系詞，後面就一定要接名詞了，不過可在該名詞前放形容詞。

例 • She doesn't seem **to understand** my question.
她似乎不明白我的問題。

• Marco seems **nice**.
= Marco seems like **a nice person**.
馬可似乎是個好人。

Mini Quiz 閱讀測驗

❶ According to this article, what is the real cause of world hunger?
(A) Lack of sufficient food
(B) Global warming
(C) The global economy
(D) Natural disasters

❷ The recession has hit all kinds of industries, and the IT _____ is no exception.
(A) drought   (B) sector
(C) fertilizer   (D) famine

閱讀測驗解答 ❶ (C) ❷ (B)

Vocabulary Bank

1) **construct** [kən`strʌkt] (v.) 建造
The city plans to construct a new library.

2) **surroundings** [sə`raʊndɪŋz] (n.)
環境，周圍的事物
Simon was too sick to be aware of his surroundings.

3) **air conditioning** [ɛr kən`dɪʃənɪŋ] (n.) 冷氣，空調，可簡寫為 AC 或 a/c
Does your office have air conditioning?

4) **dependence** [dɪ`pɛndəns] (n.) 依賴
Many countries are trying to reduce their dependence on oil.

5) **solar** [`solɚ] (a.) 利用太陽光的，太陽的
There's a new cell phone that runs on solar power.

6) **panel** [`pænl] (n.) 鏡板，壁板
The walls of the living room were covered with wood panels.

7) **generate** [`dʒɛnə,ret] (v.) 產生（光、熱、電）
Waves can be used to generate power.

8) **conserve** [kən`sɝv] (v.) 節省，保存
We take shorter showers now to conserve water.

9) **soil** [sɔɪl] (n.) 泥土，土壤
Did you know that you can grow vegetables without soil?

進階字彙

10) **pleasing** [`plizɪŋ] (a.) 令人愉快的，討喜的
The orchestra gave a pleasing performance.

11) **muggy** [`mʌgɪ] (a.) 悶熱的
The weather in Houston is muggy in the summer.

12) **insulation** [,ɪnsə`leʃən] (n.) 隔熱（材質），（電）絕緣體
You can lower your heating bills by putting insulation in your attic.

13) **ventilation** [,vɛntə`leʃən] (n.) 通風，空氣流通
There's a fan in the bathroom for ventilation.

14) **runoff** [`rʌn,ɔf] (n.) 未被土壤吸收的雨水；廢水
Runoff from the storm caused the river to flood.

Green Architecture 綠建築

課文朗讀 MP3 169　單字朗讀 MP3 170　英文文章導讀 MP3 171

　　With all the bad news about the environment these days, green architecture is becoming an increasingly popular way to [1]**construct** new buildings. The goal of green architecture is to build offices and homes

5　that use less energy, need less maintenance, and have less impact on their natural [2]**surroundings**. Green buildings are also designed to be healthier and more [10]**pleasing** to the eye. So how can you tell if a building is green? If it's [11]**muggy** without [3]**air**

10　**conditioning** and dark without artificial lighting, then it's a traditional non-green building. A green building, on the other hand, is comfortable by day even without electricity because [12]**insulation** and [13]**ventilation** ©keep the temperature just right, while its larger

15　windows let in lots of sunlight.

　　Green architecture also cuts [4]**dependence** on natural resources. It reduces power needs by placing [5]**solar** [6]**panels** on roofs to [7]**generate** electricity and putting insulation in walls to keep

20　temperatures comfortable. Another interesting green technology is the

solar panels

"rainwater harvesting system." It collects the

rain that falls on roofs, which can then be used to wash

25 clothes, flush toilets and water plants. Another way to

8)**conserve** energy is to buy local building materials

instead of foreign materials shipped in at great cost.

Green projects also try not to pollute local rivers and

streams by keeping water 14)**runoff** from leaving the

30 construction site. And then there are green roofs, which

have a layer of 9)**soil** and plants on top. The soil provides

insulation, and the plants help clean the air.

華沙大學圖書館的green roof

Language Guide

何謂綠建築?

一聽到「綠建築」,許多人腦中浮現的都是大窗、木造、裝太陽能發電板等建築外觀形式,以及省水、省電、無毒的室內設施。但其實營造綠建築是從建案規劃、設計之初即開始,建築生命週期約 40-50 年,期間施工、使用、管理,一直到最終拆除,都以「消耗最少地球資源、使用最少能源、製造最少廢棄物」為目標,並積極保護環境、追求居住者舒適、謀求與自然調和的健康生活,才是真正的綠建築。

位於波蘭的華沙大學圖書館 (The Warsaw University Library) 所及地區是極富盛名的大面積綠建築案例。

Grammar Master

keep + 受詞 + 受詞補語
使保持某種狀態

keep 這類動詞在接了受詞後,會再加上受詞補語,以補充說明受詞的狀態。可以做為受詞補語的有分詞、形容詞片語、介系詞片語等。

● 受詞補語為**分詞**

例 I am sorry to have **kept** you waiting.
抱歉讓你久等了。

● 受詞補語為**形容詞片語**

例 I wore an overcoat to **keep** myself warm.
我穿上大衣來保暖。

● 受詞補語為**介系詞片語**

例 How long are you going to **keep** my grandfather in the hospital?
你們要我爺爺在醫院裡住多久呢?

其他類似 keep 這類用法的動詞還有 find、catch 和 leave 等。

例 The police **found** the dead **in a run-down shack**.
警察在一個破舊的屋子裡發現了屍體。

例 The teacher **caught** Claire cheating on the final exam.
老師抓到克萊兒期末考作弊。

例 The earthquake **left** thousands of people **homeless**.
這場地震使數千人無家可歸。

Translation

近年來,環境方面的壞消息頻傳,使得綠建築逐漸成為新建築的新寵。綠建築的目標在於打造出使用較少能源、較不須維修、對自然環境的衝擊也較輕微的辦公大樓和住家。綠建築的設計也較健康,較賞心悅目。那麼,要如何判斷是不是綠建築呢?如果沒有冷氣就會悶熱,沒有人造燈光就會陰暗,那它就是傳統的非綠建築。反過來說,綠建築在白天即使沒發電也相當舒適,因為隔熱及通風設備能讓溫度保持適中,較大的窗戶則能讓大量陽光灑進來。

綠建築還能減少對天然資源的依賴。綠建築藉由在屋頂放置太陽能板來發電,以及在牆內安裝隔熱素材來保持舒適的溫度,降低了用電的需求。另一項有趣的綠色科技是「雨水收成系統」。這套系統可以收集降在屋頂的雨水,然後用來洗衣、沖馬桶和灌溉植物。另一種節約能源的方式是購買當地的建材,捨棄運費昂貴的進口原料。綠色建案也會盡可能避免廢水流出工地而污染當地河川。再來是綠屋頂,它們會覆蓋一層土壤,還在上頭種植物。土壤能提供隔熱,植物則有助於清淨空氣。

Vocabulary Bank

1) **skyscraper** [ˋskaɪˏskrepə] (n.) 摩天樓
Manhattan is famous for its skyscrapers.

2) **district** [ˋdɪstrɪkt] (n.) 地區，行政區
Which district of the city do you live in?

3) **dominate** [ˋdɑməˏnet] (v.) 聳立於
The tall mountain dominates the landscape.

4) **shaft** [ʃæft] (n.) 通風井，井狀通道；礦井
A man fell down the elevator shaft and broke his leg.

5) **purify** [ˋpjʊrəˏfaɪ] (v.) 淨化
The water must be purified before drinking.

6) **pedestrian** [pəˋdɛstrɪən] (n.) 行人，步行者
Drivers should always watch out for pedestrians.

7) **foundation** [faʊnˋdeʃən] (n.) 地基
The house has a concrete foundation.

8) **magnificent** [mægˋnɪfəsənt] (a.) 宏偉的，壯觀的
The scenery in New Zealand is magnificent.

9) **survey** [ˋsɚˏve] (n.)（意見）調查
(v.) survey [sɚˋve]
Would you like to participate in our survey?

進階字彙

10) **skyline** [ˋskaɪˏlaɪn] (n.)（建築群以天空為背景襯出的）天際線
Chicago has a beautiful skyline.

11) **aerodynamic** [ˏɛrodaɪˋnæmɪk] (a.) 流線型的，空氣動力學的
The sports car has an aerodynamic shape.

12) **left over** [lɛft ˋovɚ] (phr.) 剩餘下來
Did you have any money left over after your trip?

13) **plaza** [ˋplæzə / ˋplɑzə] (n.) 廣場
Let's meet by the fountain in the plaza.

課文朗讀 MP3 172　單字朗讀 MP3 173　英文文章導讀 MP3 174

30 St Mary Axe is one of Europe's first green [1]**skyscrapers**. It opened in 2004 in London's financial [2]**district**, and at 40 stories high it [3]**dominates** the city's [10]**skyline**. Shaped like a giant glass bullet, the

5　skyscraper's green design allows it to use 50 percent less energy than most buildings its size. Gaps in each floor create six huge [4]**shafts** that serve as a natural ventilation system, with gardens on every sixth floor to [5]**purify** the air. The shafts move hot air out of the

10　building in the summer, and use solar energy to heat the building in the winter. All of this is done, amazingly, without electric heaters or fans. The shafts also allow sunlight to pass through the building, creating a pleasant working environment and keeping lighting

15　costs down.

Although 30 St Mary Axe is all curves, only [G]one piece of curved glass was used to make it. None of the rest of the glass had to be specially made, saving money and conserving natural resources. The [11]**aerodynamic** shape

20　of the building allows air to flow smoothly around it, making it safer in storms. This shape also allows more sunlight—and less wind—to reach street level, so walking nearby is more comfortable for [6]**pedestrians**. And

25　as the building [7]**foundation** is small and round, there was plenty of space [12]**left over** to create a beautiful [13]**plaza** for public use. In December 2005, this [8]**magnificent** green skyscraper was voted the most

30　admired new building in a [9]**survey** of the world's largest architecture firms.

Translation 中

倫敦聖瑪麗斧街三十號是歐洲第一批綠色摩天大樓之一。它於二〇〇四年在倫敦金融區啟用，樓高四十層，高聳於這座城市的天際線。這座外形宛如巨型玻璃子彈的摩天樓拜綠設計之賜，使用的能源只有大多數同等大小建築的一半。每一樓層的間隙形成六座巨大的通風井，作為天然的通風系統，每六層樓還闢有花園來淨化空氣。這些通風井會在夏天把熱空氣排出大樓，冬天則用太陽能來暖化整棟建築。令人驚奇的是，以上功能完全不需電熱器或風扇。通風井也讓陽光得以穿透大樓，創造宜人的工作環境並降低照明成本。

雖然聖瑪麗斧街三十號的外觀全是弧線，但其實只用了一片有弧度的玻璃，其餘玻璃皆不必特別製造，既省錢又節省天然資源。這棟建築的流線外型讓空氣得以暢通無阻地在周圍流動，使它在暴風雨中更安全。這種形狀也會讓更多陽光——以及較少的風——可以觸及街面，因此行經附近的路人感覺更為舒適。而因為建築地基小而圓，四周留下有充足空間可以打造美麗的廣場供大眾使用。二〇〇五年十二月，在一項以全球各大建築事務所為受訪對象的調查中，這棟壯觀的綠色摩天大樓獲票選為最受推崇的新建築。

30 St Mary Axe

Language Guide

綠建築標章九大指標（一）

內政部審查頒發「綠建築標章」涵蓋九大指標，我們可以從中一窺綠建築的全貌：

一、生物多樣化指標

「無蟲、無菌」並非綠建築的追求，除了廣植花草樹木，還要保存大量蚯蚓、蟻類、細菌、菌類等最基層生物，以及昆蟲、蜥蜴、青蛙等初級生物消費者的生存環境，才能使高級生物有豐富的食物基礎，營造生物多樣化的環境，提升整個建築基地的綠地生態品質。

二、綠化指標

綠化的目的在於讓植物行光合作用、減少空氣中的二氧化碳，減緩地球暖化。除了在建築基地自然土層種植大型喬木，也要利用屋頂、陽台、外牆等人造物上栽種各類植物。

三、基地保水指標

提升建築基地自然土層及人工土層涵養水分及貯留雨水的能力，除了有利於土壤內微生物的活動，進而改善土壤之活性，維護建築基地內之自然生態環境平衡，也能發揮土地自然調節氣候的功能。

四、日常節能指標

空調與照明佔建築物總耗能源的絕大部分，利用遮蔭、通風、隔熱來降低對空調的依賴；利用開窗、屋頂導光來改善照明，並採用太陽能熱水系統與太陽能電池，即能得到顯著的節能效果。

五、二氧化碳減量指標

指建築主體結構建材（不包括水電設備、裝潢及室外工程的材料）生產過程中所使用的能源而換算出來的二氧化碳排放量。透過鋼構造（而非砂石、水泥、鋼筋、磚塊）及金屬帷幕外牆使結構輕量化、減少花俏的造型結構、採用寒帶林木為材料，可減少二氧化碳的排放量。

Grammar Master

計算「不可數名詞」的方式

英文裡有許多不可數名詞（例如：glass、news），這類名詞與可數名詞不同，它們不能直接加複數字尾 -s。當我們想計算不可數名詞時，通常會借助量詞（例如：piece）來達成。

● 不可數名詞為單件時：

a/one + 量詞 + of + 不可數名詞

例 a bag of flour 一袋麵粉

a grain of sand 一粒沙

a pair of jeans 一條牛仔褲

● 不可數名詞為多件時：

數字 + 量詞-s + of + 不可數名詞

例 two pieces of glass 兩片玻璃

five bottles of wine 五瓶酒

Know it ALL 英文閱讀

Vocabulary Bank

1) **stained** [stend] (a.)（玻璃、木材等）染色的
   (v.) stain [sten]（玻璃、木材等）染色
   The church has beautiful stained glass windows.

2) **exterior** [ɪk`stɪrɪə] (n.) 外部，外觀
   The exterior of the building is covered with tile.

3) **era** [`ɛrə] (n.) 歷史時期，年代
   She was the most successful singer of her era.

4) **sloping** [`slopɪŋ] (a.) 傾斜的
   The car has a sloping hood and large windows.

5) **eco** [`iko] (n.) 生態環境，為 ecology [ɪ`kɑlədʒɪ] 的縮寫。eco-friendly 即「對生態環境無害的，環保的」
   We stayed at an eco-resort in Costa Rica.

6) **termite** [`tɝmaɪt] (n.) 白蟻
   It's a myth that termites can eat through concrete.

7) **architect** [`ɑrkə,tɛkt] (n.) 建築師
   We hired an architect to design our new house.

8) **partially** [`pɑrʃəlɪ] (adv.) 局部，部分
   (a.) partial [`pɑrʃəl] 局部的，部分的
   The church was partially damaged in the fire.

9) **collect** [kə`lɛkt] (v.) 採集，收集
   Solar panels collect sunlight and turn it into electricity.

10) **consume** [kən`sum] (v.) 消耗，消費
    The U.S. consumes more oil than any other country.

11) **conscious** [`kɑnʃəs] (a.) 意識到的
    常用來構成複合字「有…意識的」，energy-conscious 即「有考慮到能源重要性的」
    Our company sells eco-conscious products.

進階字彙

12) **photovoltaic** [,fotovɑl`teɪk] (a.) 光電的；
    photovoltaic cell 即「光電蓄電池」
    photo 表示「光」的字首 + voltaic 電流的
    The government is building a photovoltaic power plant.

口語補充

13) **high-tech** [`haɪ`tɛk] (a.) 高科技的，高科技感的（設計），也寫做 hi-tech
    Robert wants to work for a high-tech firm after he graduates.

For an example of green architecture right here in Taiwan, look no further than the Beitou Branch of the Taipei Public Library. The library's [1)]**stained** wood [2)]**exterior** is quite beautiful, and at first glance you may think it is a Japanese [3)]**era** building. However, a closer look reveals an unusual [4)]**sloping** roof and large windows, which were designed to make the building [G5)]**eco**-friendly. Using wood is a challenge in Taiwan, with its humid climate and [6)]**termites**. The easy thing to do would be to use harmful chemicals to protect it, but the [7)]**architects** used natural wood oils to do the job instead. And the large window area lets in lots of sunlight and provides natural ventilation, which means electric lights and air conditioning don't get turned on so often.

Now back to that sloping roof—it's [8)]**partially** covered with [12)]**photovoltaic** cells to turn sunlight into electricity, and the rest is topped with a thick layer of dry soil for insulation. This keeps the heat in when the weather's cold, and keeps it out when it's hot. The roof also [9)]**collects** rainwater, which is used for the library's

toilets. And the building even has a system that displays the electricity being generated and [10]**consumed**, plus humidity levels and room temperatures. Last but not least, the library was built close to public transportation so you don't need

25　to drive to get there. The Beitou Library and 30 St Mary Axe prove that green architecture isn't just energy-[11]**conscious** and [13]**high-tech**, but also people-friendly and easy on the eyes.

中 Translation

至於台灣本地的綠建築，最好的例子莫過於台北市立圖書館北投分館。該館的染色木外觀相當漂亮，乍看下你或許會以為那是日據時代的建築。但趨近一看，獨特的斜屋頂和大面窗便映入眼簾，這些是設計來讓建築比較環保的。由於氣候潮濕、白蟻多，在台灣使用木材是一大挑戰。最簡單的方式是用有害的化學物質來防護，但建築師選擇使用天然樹油來做這項工作。而大面積的窗戶可以讓大量陽光灑入，並提供自然通風，這代表電燈和冷氣不必那麼常開。

回來談談那個斜屋頂——它有一部分是覆蓋著光電蓄電池，用來將陽光轉變成電力，其餘部分則覆上厚厚一層乾土來隔熱，天冷時可以留住熱氣，天熱時可以排掉熱氣。該館的屋頂也能收集雨水，用於館內盥洗室。這棟建築甚至有一個系統，可以顯示正在製造及消耗多少電力，還有濕度和室溫顯示。最後但並非最不重要的一點是，該館的位置緊鄰大眾運輸，所以你不必開車去。北投分館和聖瑪麗斧街三十號的例子證明，綠建築不僅具有能源意識和高科技，也相當平易近人、賞心悅目。

圖片提供：台北市立圖書館北投分館

Language Guide

綠建築標章九大指標（二）

六、廢棄物減量指標
廢棄物是指建築營造及最終拆除過程所產生的棄土、廢棄建材、及逸散揚塵等破壞環境衛生及人體健康的物質。

七、水資源指標
透過雨水與生活雜用水循環再利用、採用省水器材，可達到節約水資源的目的。

八、污水與垃圾改善指標
雨污水分流、垃圾集中場改善、生態濕地污水處理與廚餘堆肥，可達到污水、垃圾減量目的。

九、室內健康與環境指標
評估一棟建築「適合人居」的程度，包括隔音、採光、通風狀況。此外也要求減少室內裝修量，採用生態塗料、接著劑與建材，以減低有害氣體逸散。當然建材也要求低污染、可循環利用。

Grammar Master

複合形容詞

英文的形容詞除了平時我們熟知的單個形容詞（good、red、tall）以外，還可以自行創造新的形容詞。這種經由結合兩個以上單字所組合而成的形容詞，就叫做「複合形容詞」。複合形容詞的形成方式如下：

● 名詞 + 形容詞
例 user-friendly 容易使用的
　 eco-conscious 具有生態意識的
　 duty-free 免稅的
　 water-resistant 防水的

● 名詞 + V-ing / V-pp
例 easy-going 平易近人的
　 time-consuming 耗時的
　 open-ended 開放式的
　 middle-aged 中年的

Mini Quiz 閱讀測驗

❶ Which of the following is NOT true about 30 St Mary Axe?
(A) It uses plants to clean the air.
(B) It is made out of curved glass.
(C) It is an enjoyable place to work.
(D) It is located in England.

❷ The boy was caught _____ a candy bar at the corner store.
(A) steal　　　　(B) stolen
(C) stealing　　(D) stole

Mini Quiz 解答：❶ (B) ❷ (C)

Ⓥ Vocabulary Bank

1) **melt** [mɛlt] (v.) 融化
The ice began to melt in the warm sunshine.

2) **pour** [por] (v.) 灌，倒，注
Can I pour you a drink?

3) **percentage** [pɚˋsɛntɪdʒ] (n.) 百分比，部分
A large percentage of voters support the president.

4) **coastal** [ˋkostl] (a.) 沿海的，海岸的
(n.) coast [kost] 沿海地區，海岸
(n.) coastline [ˋkost͵laɪn] 海岸線
The coastal areas were hardest hit by the typhoon.

5) **leave behind** [liv brˋhaɪnd] (phr.) 拋下，留下
The little boy left his toy behind on the bus.

6) **abandon** [əˋbændən] (v.) 丟棄，遺棄
Many villagers abandoned their homes during the war.

7) **global** [ˋglobl] (a.) 全世界的，global warming 即「全球暖化」
There are increasing signs that the global recession is over.

8) **glacier** [ˋgleʃɚ] (n.) 冰河
(a.) glacial [ˋgleʃəl] 冰河的
This canyon was created by a glacier millions of years ago.

9) **cork** [kɔrk] (n.) 軟木塞，軟木
Bob pulled the cork out of the wine bottle.

10) **interior** [ɪnˋtɪrɪɚ] (n.) 內陸，內部
The interior of the country is very dry.

11) **contribute** [kənˋtrɪbjut] (v.) 提供，出力
(phr.) contribute to 促成
All the players contributed to the team's success.

12) **flooding** [ˋflʌdɪŋ] (n.) 淹水，洪水
The heavy rains caused severe flooding.

進階字彙

13) **thaw** [θɔ] (v.) （冰雪）融化，解凍
The ground thaws as winter turns into spring.

14) **in turn** [ɪn tɝn] (phr.) 既而，因而
Smoking makes your mouth dry, which in turn causes bad breath.

Ice, Ice, Baby
無冰的世界

課文朗讀 MP3 178　單字朗讀 MP3 179　英文文章導讀 MP3 180

It's an amazing fact that if all the ice in Greenland, a vast island in the Arctic Circle, were to ¹⁾**melt**, enough water would ²⁾**pour** into the ocean to raise sea levels by at least seven meters. If even a significant ³⁾**percentage** of that ice melted,
5　it would put major ⁴⁾**coastal** cities all over the planet under water and force hundreds of millions of people to flee and ⁵⁾**leave** their homes **behind** forever. And that's not counting the world's largest ice sheet in Antarctica. If the Antarctic ice sheet ¹³⁾**thawed**, most of the world's cities would have to be
10　completely ⁶⁾**abandoned**. That means London, Tokyo, New York and Taipei would no longer exist. And life as we know it would be changed forever.

左圖為格陵蘭島，若島上所有的冰都融化，海平面會上升至少七公尺

Russia

Greenland

Scandinavia

Scientists used to think that our ice sheets would remain stable over the coming centuries even with the rising

15 temperatures caused by man-made [7)]**global** warming. But more recent studies have revealed that the pace at which [8)]**glaciers** in Greenland and Antarctica are sliding into the oceans has increased rapidly in recent decades. According to researchers, this is caused by the loss of floating ice shelves

20 along the [4)]**coasts**. These ice shelves act like a [9)]**cork** in a bottle, keeping glaciers from flowing into the sea. As they disappear [G]due to warming sea water, ice from the [10)]**interior** flows out at a much faster rate. That, [14)]**in turn**, [11)]**contributes** to a rise in sea levels, and puts coastal areas around the world

25 at risk of [12)]**flooding**.

中 Translation

這是一個驚人的事實：如果格陵蘭──北極圈裡一座面積廣大的島──所有的冰都融化了，灌入海洋的水量，將足以讓海平面上升至少七公尺。甚至只要有相當比例的冰融化，就可能讓全球各地重要沿海城市沒入水中，迫使數億民眾永遠逃離家園。而這還沒把南極那塊世界最大的冰原計算在內。萬一南極冰原解凍了，世界絕大部分的城市勢必完全遭到離棄，那表示倫敦、東京、紐約和台北將不復存在，而我們所知的生活也將永遠改變。

科學家過去認為，即使人為全球暖化造成氣溫上升，我們的冰原在未來幾世紀都還是能保持穩定。但近年來的研究卻顯示，格陵蘭和南極冰河滑落海洋的速度，在近二、三十年來迅速加快。研究人員指出，這是在沿岸漂浮的冰架崩解所致。這些冰架的作用就像瓶中的軟木塞，能阻止冰河流進大海。一旦冰架因海水溫度升高而消失，內陸的冰就會以遠高於以往的速度流出，繼而造成海平面升高，讓世界各地沿海地區陷入水患之危。

Earth Sciences 101
地球科學小學堂

 Language Guide

Ice, Ice, Baby

本文標題是借用 *Ice, Ice, Baby* 這首美國白人饒舌樂手 Vanilla Ice 的成名曲，一九九〇年全美發表之後一炮而紅，成為史上第一首登上告示牌排行榜 (Billboard Charts) 榜首的嘻哈單曲 (hip-hop single)，對於將 hip-hop 介紹給主流市場功不可沒，在此之前 hip-hop 都被視作黑人音樂。

Arctic、Antarctic，哪個是北極？

公布答案之前，先來認識一下 Arctic [ˈɑrktɪk] 這個字。Arctic 源自希臘文的熊 (bear)，指的是天上的小熊星座（Ursa Minor，Little Bear 的意思，中文星象稱做北斗七星），而位於小熊尾巴的就是北極星 (Polaris)。如此一來，大家應該就很容易記住 Arctic 是「北極（的）」，而 Antarctic [ænˈtɑrktɪk] 其實就是 anti- （對立，反）+ arctic，北極正對過去當然就是「南極（的）」。

Arctic

Antarctic

另外，Antarctic 和 Antarctica 這兩個字也很容易搞混。Antarctica 是指「南極洲」這塊世界第五大陸，你只要記得世界各大洲 Asia（亞洲）、Africa（非洲）、North America（北美洲）、South America （南美洲）都是 a 字尾，就不會搞混 Antarctic 和 Antarctica 這兩個字了。

Grammar Master

due to 用法

due to 中文翻譯為「因為」，其後只能接名詞或名詞片語，然而中文解釋為「因為」的用法有很多，例如: since、as、for、because、because of 等等，又該怎麼區別呢？

● **since、as**：常用於商業書信中，後接表示原因的名詞子句
句型：Since/As +子句..., S+V....
　　　子句... since/as S+V....

例 **Since** she loves music so much, Carrie decided to become a musician.
因為凱莉熱愛音樂，所以她決定要當個音樂家。

例 **As** it was getting late, we decided to head home.
因為時間已晚，我們決定回家。

● **because**：同樣譯為「因為」，句型與 since 和 as 相同，可放於句首或句中

例 **Because** I worked fast, I was able to finish early.
因為我做得很快，所以能提早完成。

例 I didn't go to the gym **because** I was too tired.
我沒有去健身房，因為我太累了。

because of 和 due to 其後只能接名詞或名詞片語（而非子句）。

例 The game was postponed **because of** bad weather.
由於天候不佳，比賽延遲舉行。

例 The accident was **due to** poor visibility.
這起意外肇因於視線不良。

● **for**：也譯為「因為」，不可放在句首
句型：S+V..., for 子句....

例 Jake told the truth, **for** he had nothing to lose.
亞克說了實話，因為他已經豁出去了。

Arctic 北極，北極的
泛指地球北極周圍的地區（大致為北緯 66 度 33 以北），涵蓋北冰洋 (Arctic Ocean) 及加拿大北部、格陵蘭（丹麥屬地）、俄羅斯、美國阿拉斯加州、冰島 (Iceland)、挪威 (Norway)、瑞典 (Sweden) 和芬蘭 (Finland) 等地

Arctic Circle 北極圈
北緯 66 度 33 圈內的範圍

North Pole 北極
分為北半球的地理北極 (Geographic North Pole) 及地磁北極 (Magnetic North Pole)

Antarctic 南極，南極的
泛指地球南極周圍的地區（大致為南緯 60 度以南），涵蓋南極匯流圈 (Antarctic Convergence) 以南的南冰洋 Southern Ocean 及南極洲大陸

Antarctica 南極洲

Antarctic Circle 南極圈
南緯 66 度 33 圈內的範圍

South Pole 南極

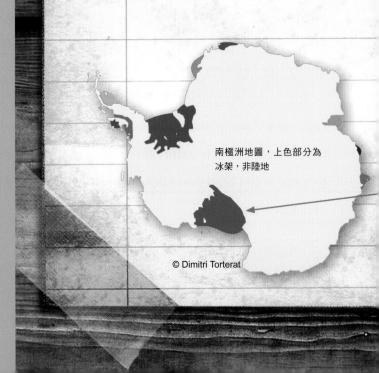

南極洲地圖，上色部分為冰架，非陸地

© Dimitri Torterat

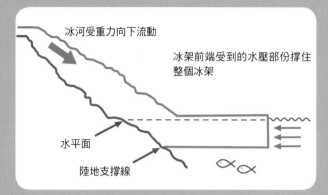

ice cap

ice sheet 冰原
面積大於五萬平方公里、
長期覆蓋於大陸的冰層，
位於南極洲及格陵蘭

ice cap 冰帽
面積小於五萬平方公里，覆蓋
於高地

glacier 冰河

ice shelf 冰架
冰原和冰河受重力影響，
會慢慢由陸地滑入海中，
底部已脫離陸地的冰層
即為冰架

iceberg 冰山
冰河或冰架斷裂崩入
海中的浮冰

glacier

南極的 Ross 冰架

冰架融化崩解過程

1 穩定的冰河與冰架

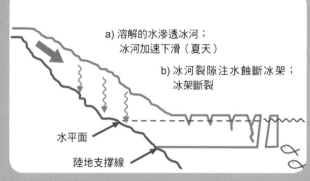

冰河受重力向下流動

冰架前端受到的水壓部份撐住
整個冰架

水平面

陸地支撐線

2 較溫暖的氣候造成兩種影響

a) 溶解的水滲透冰河；
　　冰河加速下滑（夏天）

b) 冰河裂隙注水蝕斷冰架；
　　冰架斷裂

水平面

陸地支撐線

3 冰架崩落後，冰河前端不穩

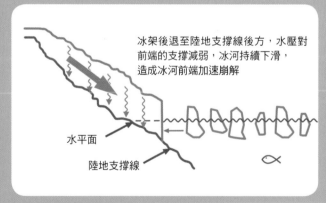

冰架後退至陸地支撐線後方，水壓對
前端的支撐減弱，冰河持續下滑，
造成冰河前端加速崩解

水平面

陸地支撐線

4 冰河加速

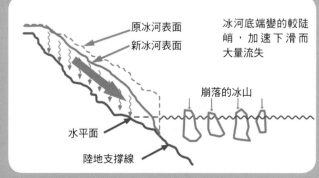

原冰河表面
新冰河表面

冰河底端變的較陡
峭，加速下滑而
大量流失

崩落的冰山

水平面

陸地支撐線

© wiki_ZoeFari

Vocabulary Bank

1) **vanish** [ˋvænɪʃ] (v.) 消失
Wetlands are vanishing at a rapid rate.

2) **reflect** [rɪˋflɛkt] (v.) 反射，反映
A mirror reflects light.

3) **exactly** [ɪgˋzæktlɪ] (adv.) 完全地，確切地
(a.) exact [ɪgˋzækt] 精確的，確切的
This apartment is exactly what I'm looking for.

4) **capture** [ˋkæptʃɚ] (v.) 捕捉，捕獲
The assassination of President Kennedy was captured on film.

5) **layer** [ˋleɚ] (n.) 層
The wedding cake had four layers.

6) **breeze** [briz] (n.) 微風，和風
A soft breeze blew through the trees.

7) **harmful** [ˋhɑrmfəl] (a.) 有害的
Smoking is harmful to your health.

8) **atmosphere** [ˋætməsˏfɪr] (n.) 大氣，空氣
Mars has a very thin atmosphere.

9) **bubble** [ˋbʌbḷ] (v.) 冒泡，源源不絕冒出
(phr.) bubble up 往上冒泡，冒出
Air from the divers bubbled up to the surface.

10) **not to mention** [nɑt tə ˋmɛnʃən] (phr.) 更不用說，更何況
The new treatment is expensive, not to mention risky.

進階字彙

11) **murky** [ˋmɝkɪ] (a.) 陰暗的，朦朧的
The dust storm turned the sky a murky yellow.

12) **worrisome** [ˋwɝrɪsəm] (a.) 令人煩惱的
The child's bad behavior was worrisome to his parents and teachers.

But the problems don't end there. As the ice [1)]**vanishes**, it leaves behind the dark blue-green waters of the northern oceans. ©While ice [2)]**reflects** most of the sun's energy back into space, the polar waters do [3)]**exactly** the opposite. They absorb the sun's light and heat. And because the northern oceans tend to be [11)]**murkier** than the tropical oceans, the sun's energy is [4)]**captured** near the surface, causing the top [5)]**layer** of water to heat up more rapidly. The warmed [6)]**breezes** coming off these waters then heat the surrounding lands of Arctic North America, Northern Europe and the vast Russian coastline.

And this is where things get really [12)]**worrisome**: on land. This is where you have something that you really don't want to warm up—the tundra. The soil beneath the tundra usually stays frozen throughout the year, which is a good thing, because when it thaws it starts pumping out not just carbon dioxide, but also methane, the king of greenhouse gases. Methane is 35 times more [7)]**harmful** to

snowy owl

caribou

musk ox

the [8]**atmosphere**

20 than CO₂, and it's

already starting to [9]**bubble**

up from the beds of Arctic lakes,

which are thawing due to global warming. [10]**Not to mention**

that the bottoms of the shallow Arctic seas are producing

25 more methane as they warm up too. If we don't put a stop to

this soon, we'll be faced with several hundred years of greatly

increased greenhouse gas levels.

甲烷從解凍的湖底冒出

中 Translation

但問題不是到這裡就沒了。隨著冰層消失，北端的海洋將露出深藍綠色。冰會將大部分的太陽能反射回太空，但極地海域卻恰恰相反，它們會吸收太陽的光和熱。而因為地球北端海洋普遍比赤道海域來得陰暗，太陽能會在水面附近被吸收，而使海水上層熱得更快。接下來，從這些海域吹來的暖風會使極圈內北美、北歐及廣闊俄羅斯沿岸的附近陸地溫度上升。

而這才是真正令人擔心之處：陸地。這地方有著最好不要變熱的東西——凍原。凍原地表下的土壤通常終年結凍，而這是好事，因為一旦它解凍，釋放出的不只是二氧化碳，還有甲烷，溫室氣體之王。甲烷對大氣層的危害是二氧化碳的三十五倍，而它已經開始從北極地區受全球暖化影響而解凍的湖底汩汩而出了。更別說北極較淺海域的海床隨著溫度上升不斷釋放甲烷。如果我們不趕快加以遏止，往後數百年溫室氣體的排放勢將愈演愈烈。

polar bears

Language Guide

黃色為北極凍原
分布區域

tundra 凍原

tundra [ˈtʌndrə] 是分佈在南、北極和高海拔地區的生態群落，受到氣候嚴寒的影響，這種地方的土壤長期冰凍，樹木難以生存，只有稀疏的灌木、野草和苔蘚能夠生長，因此也稱做「苔原」。

北極凍原的動物主要為北美馴鹿 (caribou)、麝香牛 (musk ox)、北極雪兔 (arctic hare)、北極雪狐 (arctic fox)、雪鴞 (snowy owl)、北極旅鼠 (lemming)，最接近北極的地區則有北極熊 (polar bear)。

南極洲因為跟其他大陸相隔極遠，陸地哺乳動物無法抵達，因此當地只能見到海洋哺乳類動物如海豹 (seal) 及海鳥如企鵝 (penguin)。

greenhouse gases 溫室氣體

溫室氣體分佈於地球大氣底層，能夠吸收地表散發出來的輻射熱（即「紅外線」infrared radiation），再將所吸收的熱傳回地表。若是缺少溫室氣體，地球表面溫度估計會比現在低攝氏三十三度。但反之，若是溫室氣體過多，則會促發全球暖化。溫室氣體最主要成分為：

• water vapor 水蒸氣
• carbon dioxide 二氧化碳
• methane 甲烷
• nitrous oxide 氧化亞氮（笑氣）
• ozone 臭氧

Grammar Master

while 的不同用法：

● **while** 為「雖然」，與 although 用法相同（文章第 3 行），可放在句首或句中
例 **While** old cars are cheaper, new cars are more reliable.
= New cars are more reliable, **while** old cars are cheaper.
雖然舊車比較便宜，但新車還是比較可靠。

● **while** 為「然而」，同 whereas 用法
例 Some couples argue all the time, **whereas** others rarely argue.
= Some couples argue all the time, **while** others rarely argue.
有些夫妻終日爭吵不斷，然而有些夫妻卻很少吵架。

● **while** 為「當……的時候」，可以放在句首也可以放在句中，但放在句中時 while 前不加逗點。
例 Did you go surfing **while** you were in Hawaii?
你去夏威夷有衝浪嗎？

● **while** 當名詞時，解釋為「一會兒、一段時間」，常見用法為 for a while
例 It hasn't rained **for a while**.
已經好一陣子沒下雨了。

Vocabulary Bank

1) **soak** [sok] (v.) 吸收
   (phr.) soak up 吸起
   Heather used a sponge to soak up the spilled wine.

2) **dissolve** [dɪ`zɑlv] (v.) 融化，溶解
   Sugar and salt dissolve in water.

3) **shrink** [ʃrɪŋk] (v.) 變小，變少
   The sweater shrank in the wash.

4) **naive** [nɑ`iv] (a.) 天真的，輕信的，也可寫作 naïve
   It's naive to believe everything you read in the papers.

5) **majestic** [mə`dʒɛstɪk] (a.) 雄偉的
   Nepal is famous for its majestic scenery.

6) **crown** [kraun] (n.) 頂端，王冠，冠狀的東西
   It took an hour to reach the crown of the hill.

7) **threaten** [`θrɛtn̩] (v.) 可能發生或變成（負面的狀況）；威脅
   The storm threatened to turn into a hurricane.

進階字彙

8) **seep** [sip] (v.) 滲漏
   Water seeped in through cracks in the wall.

9) **lubricant** [`lubrɪkənt] (n.) 潤滑劑
   Lubricants are necessary to keep motors running.

10) **oblivion** [ə`blɪvɪən] (n.) 被遺忘，消失無蹤
    A nuclear war would send the world into oblivion.

11) **indigenous** [ɪn`dɪdʒənəs] (a.) 土著的，本地的
    Many governments set aside land for indigenous peoples.

Language Guide

carbon footprint 碳足跡

carbon footprint 是指「一個產品、組織或活動的溫室氣體總排放量」，原本是 ecological footprint（生態足跡），但為了簡化其概念以利宣導，經常只以二氧化碳 (carbon dioxide) 排放量來計算，因此稱做 carbon footprint。

課文朗讀 MP3 184　單字朗讀 MP3 185　英文文章導讀 MP3 186

If present warming trends continue, the Arctic sea ice will totally disappear during the summer months within the next few decades. And in Greenland, there's so much runoff that it's creating lakes on the ice sheets. Because the lakes are darker in color than the ice they cover, they [1]**soak** up the sun's heat and make the ice [2]**dissolve** even faster. Even worse, this water [8]**seeps** to the bottom of glaciers, where it acts as a [9]**lubricant**, causing them to slide into the sea even faster. All of this [G]contributes to [3]**shrinking** ice sheets and rising sea levels. And you'd be [4]**naive** to think this is just a problem at the ends of the earth. Everywhere you go, the ice is disappearing. Over in Africa, [5]**majestic** Mt. Kilimanjaro, famous for its beautiful ice cap, is about to lose its white [6]**crown** forever. While over in the Himalayas, the glaciers are [7]**threatening** to melt into [10]**oblivion** too.

融化的水在冰上形成湖泊，顏色比水深

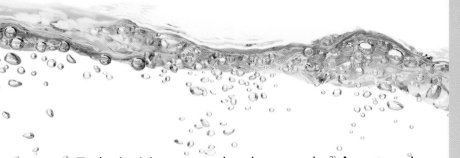

Today's rising ocean levels not only [7]**threaten** the residents of coastal cities, but also [11]**indigenous** peoples like those living on small Pacific islands. As ocean levels rise, their homes will be the first to go under. And indigenous peoples

20 living on small farms in highland areas or river deltas depend upon glacial melt water to grow crops and wash their clothes. When the glaciers melt away, many of the poorest people of Peru and Chile, Pakistan and India, will lose their water supplies. And this is the greatest tragedy of all: the

25 problems caused by melting ice will have the greatest impact on the people with the smallest carbon footprint.

中 Translation

如果現今的暖化趨勢持續下去，未來二、三十年內，北極海冰將在夏季完全消失，而在格陵蘭，融化的水已經多到在冰原上形成湖泊。因為湖泊的顏色比所覆蓋的冰來得深，湖泊會吸收太陽的熱量，讓冰融得更快。更糟的是，這些水會向冰河底部滲漏，在那裡形成潤滑劑的作用，致使冰河更迅速地滑入海中。以上種種都會促成冰原萎縮、海平面上升。如果你以為這只是地球南北極的問題，那你就太天真了。無論你走到哪裡，冰都在消失中。在非洲，以美麗的冰帽聞名、高峻雄偉的吉力馬札羅山，就快要永遠失去它雪白的王冠了。而在喜馬拉雅山脈，冰河也有融盡之虞。

今天海平面上升的情況不僅威脅沿海城市的居民，也危及世居太平洋小島等地的原住民。當海平面上升，他們的家園將會首當其衝沒入水中。住在高地或河流三角洲以小農地維生的原住民，皆仰賴冰河的融水來種植農作和洗滌衣物，一旦冰河融化殆盡，秘魯、智利、巴基斯坦和印度等地許多最貧窮的百姓將失去他們的供水。而最大的悲劇莫過於：受融冰問題衝擊最烈的，將是製造最少碳足跡的人。

Mt. Kilimanjaro

G Grammar Master

contributing to 的用法

contributing to 在本文中表示「促成」，也就是成就某事的推手之一。

例 Deforestation **contributes to** global warming.
濫伐森林促成地球暖化。

要注意別把 contributing to 和 lead to、bring about、result in 這些片語搞混了，這些片語是表示「導致，造成……的後果」。

● lead to
例 Drunk driving often **leads to** fatal accidents.
酒駕常造成致命意外。

● bring about
例 Financial reform **brought about** great changes in the economy.
財政改革導致經濟劇變。

● result in
例 Advances in technology have **resulted in** safer airplanes.
科技進步造就出更安全的航機。

而 contribute to 除了「促成」之外，還有其他用法：

● contribute to 捐助、幫助
例 The company **contributed** funds **to** both political parties.
這間公司贊助資金給兩派政黨。

● contribute to 為……寫稿
例 The writer **contributes** articles **to** a number of journals and magazines.
這位作家為許多期刊和雜誌寫稿。

Mini Quiz 閱讀測驗

❶ Which of the following are NOT threatened by rising sea levels?
(A) Indigenous peoples on Pacific islands
(B) Residents of coastal cities
(C) Indigenous peoples in highland areas
(D) People in London, Tokyo, New York and Taipei

❷ Kevin missed a day of work _____ he was sick.
(A) due to
(B) because
(C) for
(D) because of

❸ Be sure to see the Eiffel Tower _____ you are in Paris.
(A) during
(B) whereas
(C) though
(D) while

閱讀測驗解答 1 (C) 2 (B) 3 (D)

V Vocabulary Bank

1) **occasionally** [əˈkeʒənˌlɪ] (adv.) 有些時候，偶爾
(a.) occasional [əˈkeʒənḷ]
We only eat out occasionally.

2) **format** [ˈfɔrmæt] (n.) 出版品的開本，版面樣式
The publisher is thinking of changing the format of the magazine.

3) **review** [rɪˈvju] (n./v.) 評論；寫評論，複審
(n.) reviewer [rɪˈvjuə] 評論者
Does this paper have movie reviews?

4) **circle** [ˈsɜkḷ] (n.)（共同興趣或利益的人所形成的）圈子
The author is well known in literary circles.

5) **rural** [ˈrurəl] (a.) 鄉間的，農村的
The typhoon caused heavy flooding in rural areas.

6) **existence** [ɪgˈzɪstəns] (n.) 問世，存在
The baseball team has been in existence for five years.

7) **prop** [prɑp] (v.) 支撐，頂住
(phr.) prop up
Kevin leaned back in his chair and propped his feet up on the desk.

8) **thereafter** [ðɛrˈæftə] (adv.) 之後（一般用於書寫，不用於口語）
Rita graduated from college and shortly thereafter found a good job.

進階字彙

9) **dining** [ˈdaɪnɪŋ] (n.) 用餐
(phr.) fine dining 頂級餐飲，包含選用上等食材、高雅用餐環境，及無微不至的服務
The town offers many fine dining choices.

10) **compilation** [ˌkɑmpəˈleʃən] (n.) 選輯，編輯成品
The book is a complication of the writer's newspaper columns.

11) **service station** [ˈsɜvɪs ˈsteʃən] (n.) 休息站，服務站
Let's fill the tank at the next service station.

12) **bumpy** [ˈbʌmpɪ] (a.) 崎嶇不平的，顛簸的
After a long, bumpy bus ride, we finally arrived at the village.

13) **workbench** [ˈwɜkˌbɛntʃ] (n.)（修車技師、木匠、珠寶鑲嵌師等的）工作台
The carpenter's workbench was covered with tools.

MICHELIN
the Last Word on Fine Dining
米其林
頂級餐飲它說了算

© 2008 Michelin North America, Inc.

課文朗讀 MP3 187　單字朗讀 MP3 188　英文文章導讀 MP3 189

The Michelin series of guidebooks is the world's oldest, most respected and, [1)]**occasionally**, most feared series of restaurant and hotel guides. First published in 1900 by André Michelin, the guide began as a [10)]**compilation** of travel information related to **motor** touring. It offered localized information for motorists in France, telling them where to find restaurants, hotels, and [11)]**service stations**. The content and [2)]**format** of the series has changed significantly over the years, but its [3)]**reviews** still **1** **carry a lot of weight**. In many [4)]**circles** it has become **2** **the last word** **on** the world's finest fine dining establishments.

André Michelin, together with his brother Édouard, founded the Michelin **Tyre** Company in 1888 in Clermont-Ferrand, a small city in central France. André created the first Michelin guide as a way to promote motor touring, encouraging more **automobile** owners to get out and explore the country. It was a very clever marketing move. By helping motorists navigate the [12)]**bumpy** roads of [5)]**rural** France, André was in effect helping ensure a steady supply of customers for new **tires**.

For the first two decades of its [6)]**existence**, the guide was available free of charge at service stations around France. But after discovering a pile of guides being used to [7)]**prop** up a [13)]**workbench** in a garage, the brothers realized that a free guide would not be taken seriously. [8)]**Thereafter**, they began charging a small price for it. At the same time, they also introduced the now famous Michelin Star to indicate establishments of the highest quality.

中 Translation

米其林指南系列是全世界歷史最悠久、最受推崇，有時也最令人畏懼的餐廳和旅館指南。這部一九〇〇年由安德烈米其林首次出版的指南，一開始是汽車旅遊相關的旅行資訊選輯，為法國的汽車旅遊者提供地區性的資訊，告訴他們上哪找餐廳、旅館和服務站。這個系列的內容和版面多年來已大幅改變，但它的評鑑仍極具份量。在許多圈子裡，它已經成為全球最佳美食餐廳最權威的意見。

安德烈米其林和兄弟艾德華一八八八年於法國中部的小城市克萊蒙費朗創辦米其林輪胎公司。安德烈創造出第一本米其林指南，是為了推廣汽車旅遊，鼓勵更多車主外出探索這個國家。這是非常聰明的行銷手法。透過協助車主馳騁於法國鄉村崎嶇不平的道路，安德烈其實是鞏固了新輪胎的穩定客源。

米其林指南推出後的頭二十年，在法國各地的服務站都可免費拿取。但自從在一家修車廠看到一大疊指南被用來支撐工作台，兄弟倆便認清免費指南不會被認真看待的事實。此後，他們開始收取小額費用。在此同時，他們也採用如今鼎鼎大名的米其林星級來標示最高品質的餐廳。

 Language Guide

英美用字大不同

motor = automobile

motor [`motə] 是英式英文的「汽車」，文中的 motor touring 是指「開車旅遊」，motorist 是指「駕駛，開車旅行的人」。而美語會用 automobile [`ɔtə,əmobɪl] 這個字表示汽車。

tyre = tire

文中「米其林輪胎公司」Michelin Tyre Company 的 tyre 是英式英文的「輪胎」，美語則拼成 tire，發音都是 [taɪr]。

Tongue-tied No More

1 carry (a lot of) weight (with...) 對……（很）有影響力

carry a lot of weight with... 表示對某個人或某個團體有很大的影響力。

A: If I want a raise, why do I need to get Eric on my side?
如果我想要獲得加薪，為什麼需要得到艾瑞克的支持？

B: Because his opinions carry a lot of weight with the boss.
因為他的意見對老闆有舉足輕重的影響。

2 the last word 最權威的評論，最後決定權

本文標題及第一段的 the last word on... 表示「關於……最權威的評論」。the last word 有「最後決定權」的意思，當我們要表示「最後要由某人做決定」，會說 someone has the last word。若後面的介系詞換成 in，則表示「在某方面是最好的」。

A: I can recommend a great hotel to stay at—it's the last word in luxury.
我可以推薦一間很棒的飯店——其奢華無人能敵。

B: Uh, actually we're looking for something that won't break the bank.
呃，其實我們在找不會害我們破產的。

Grammar Master

talk/discuss on + 明確的主題

about 和 on 雖然都能接主題，但 about 討論的範圍較籠統，且通常為較輕鬆地討論；on 則是態度較認真地探討某議題。

例 ● The farmers sat on the porch talking **about** the weather.
農夫坐在前廊聊天氣。
（天氣是一個隨便聊的話題）

● The government recently published a report **on** emerging markets in Asia.
政府最近發表了一份亞洲新興市場的報告。（對某議題的研究分析）

© 2008 Michelin North America, Inc.

2009 米其林指南

1900年創刊的Michelin Guide於 2009 年發行第 100 期，從單一地區版本演變成涵蓋澳洲 (Australia)、比利時及盧森堡 (Belgium and Luxembourg)、法國 (France)、德國 (Germany)、愛爾蘭及英國 (Ireland and the UK)、義大利 (Italy)、荷蘭 (the Netherlands)、西班牙及葡萄牙 (Spain and Portugal)、瑞典 (Switzerland) 等國家，及紐約市 (New York City)、舊金山 (San Francisco)、洛杉磯 (Los Angeles)、拉斯維加斯 (Los Vegas)、東京 (Tokyo)、香港及澳門 (Hong Kong and Macau) 等城市，共十四個版本。

米其林指南發行 100 期大事記

1900	創刊。指南內容主要是如何修理輪胎等汽車資訊、全法國加油站、修車廠、旅館名單及地圖，當時全法國只有不到三千輛汽車在路上跑
1904	發行第一本國外版 Michelin Guide Belgium （比利時）
1908	成立 the Bureau of Itineraries（旅遊行程詢問處），提供免費旅遊諮詢服務
1920	米其林兄弟發現指南被拿來墊高工作台，從此下定決心必須以販售方式發行
1921	因世界大戰停刊一期
1922	恢復發行，售價七法郎
1926	第一顆星誕生
1929	指南開始附「滿意度問卷」，邀請讀者評論指南所選出的餐廳

1931	第二顆及第三顆星誕生
1936	三星等的評判標準訂定，沿用至今
1945	戰後復刊（第二次世界大戰期間停刊）
1997	指南上加入「Bib特選餐廳」，介紹物超所值的平價餐廳 米其林寶寶的名字是 Bibendum，暱稱為 Bib
2003	指南上加入「Bib特選旅館」，介紹物超所值的平價旅館
2005	首次跨越大西洋，發行紐約版
2007	推出東京版
2008	推出香港及澳門版
2009	發行第 100 期（資料來源：http://www.viamichelin.co.uk/）

© 2008 Michelin North America, Inc.

© 2008 Michelin North America, Inc.

米其林星級評選標準

❀❀❀
Exceptional cuisine, worth a special journey
絕佳美食，值得專程前來

❀❀
Excellent cuisine, worth a detour
出色美食，值得繞路過來

❀
A very good cuisine in its category
同類型餐廳中的美饌佳餚

Bib Gourmand Bib 特選餐廳
Inspector's favorite for a good value
評鑑員的最愛，物超所值

對古董級米林指南有興趣？
請至 🌐 http://www.nxtbook.com/nxtbooks/michelin/theinspectors/#/0

米其林級美味，台灣也享受得到！

台灣第一間米其林餐廳——侯布匈（Joel Robuchon）2009 年 9 月登陸台北東區新開幕的頂級購物中心 BELLAVITA。餐廳主持人 Joel Robuchon 被譽為「全世界最會摘星的主廚」，他在世界各地開的餐廳都有得到米其林指南的星星。

© 2008 Michelin North America, Inc.

V Vocabulary Bank

1) **refer** [rɪˋfɝ] (v.) 論及，談到
(phr.) refer to
Which report are you referring to?

2) **rank** [ræŋk] (v./n.) 評等
How would you rank the album on a scale of one to ten?

3) **sightseeing** [ˋsaɪt͵siɪŋ] (n./a.) 觀光（的），遊覽（的），sightseeing spot 即「觀光景點」
I didn't have time for sightseeing on my trip.

4) **staff** [stæf] (n.) 工作人員（統稱）
The staff at the hotel was very helpful.

5) **advance** [ədˋvæns] (a.) 預先的，事先的
(phr.) in advance 預先，事先
If you want to get a seat on the train, you should buy your ticket in advance.

6) **random** [ˋrændəm] (a.) 隨機的，任意的，無規則的
The results of this survey are based on a random sample of college students.

7) **rating** [ˋretɪŋ] (n.) 評分，評價
(v.) rate [ret] 給分，對⋯做評價
That hotel has a two-star rating.

8) **pioneer** [͵paɪəˋnɪr] (v.) 開創，倡導
The doctor pioneered a new form of heart surgery.

9) **astronomer** [əˋstrɑnəmɚ] (n.) 天文學家
The comet was named after the astronomer who discovered it.

10) **critic** [ˋkrɪtɪk] (n.) 評論家，持批評態度的人
(n.) criticism [ˋkrɪtə͵sɪzəm] 批評，指責
The new restaurant is popular with critics.

11) **award** [əˋwɔrd] (v.) 給予，授予
Anthony Hopkins was awarded an Oscar for his performance in *The Silence of the Lambs*.

12) **mere** [mɪr] (a.) 僅僅
Entrance to the museum costs a mere two dollars.

進階字彙

13) **frugal** [ˋfrugl] (a.) 儉省的，節制花用的
My parents taught me to be frugal.

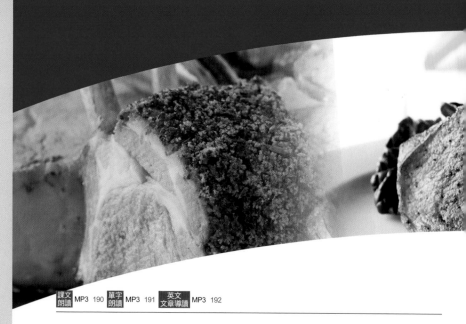

課文朗讀 MP3 190　單字朗讀 MP3 191　英文文章導讀 MP3 192

When people ¹⁾**refer** to the Michelin guide, they are usually talking about the Red Guide—the Michelin series with red covers that focuses on restaurants and hotels. The company also publishes
5 the Green Guide, a series with green covers that ❶ **places more emphasis on** travel and tourism. These guides ²⁾**rank** ³⁾**sightseeing** spots by degree of interest and importance, and also provide cultural
10 and historical information.

© 2008 Michelin North America, Inc.

But it's the Michelin Red Guide that has made the company famous. Restaurants are chosen by Michelin's ⁴⁾**staff** and then reviewed, with no ⁵⁾**advance** notice, at a ⁶⁾**random** time. The reviewers do not make themselves
15 known to the restaurant staff, which ensures that the meal they review is prepared just as it would be for any other diner. The company claims to revisit all the restaurants they cover once every 18 months to ensure that their ⁷⁾**ratings** are current. It's not uncommon for a
20 restaurant to lose or gain a star after the first review.

The Michelin guides deserve credit for ⁸⁾**pioneering** the use of stars to ⁷⁾**rate** restaurants. Nowadays, many

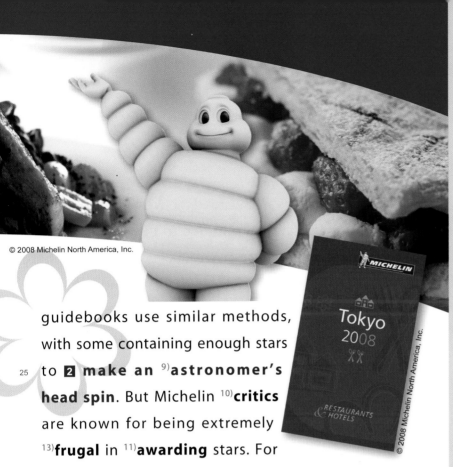

© 2008 Michelin North America, Inc.

Tokyo 2008

MICHELIN

RESTAURANTS & HOTELS

© 2008 Michelin North America, Inc.

guidebooks use similar methods, with some containing enough stars

25 to **2 make an** [9]**astronomer's head spin**. But Michelin [10]**critics** are known for being extremely [13]**frugal** in [11]**awarding** stars. For example, the 2008 Tokyo Red Guide awarded only nine

30 restaurants with their highest three-star rating—that's a [12]**mere** nine out of the city's total of over 150,000 restaurants! But since so few restaurants are selected for review, many chefs [G]consider it an honor just to be included in the guide in the first place.

中 Translation

人們提到米其林指南時，通常指的是紅色指南——紅色封面、聚焦於餐廳和旅館的米其林系列。該公司另外還出版綠色指南，綠色封面、較著重旅遊和觀光的系列，以受人喜愛及重要程度為觀光景點排名，也提供文化和歷史資訊。

但讓該公司揚名立萬的是米其林紅色指南。餐廳是由米其林員工選定，然後在未事先通知的情況下突擊評鑑。評鑑人員不會讓餐廳員工知曉他們的身份，以確保他們評鑑的餐點跟餐廳提供給其他顧客的一樣。該公司聲稱每十八個月會重新造訪指南收錄的所有餐廳一次，讓他們的評分維持最新。一家餐廳在首次評鑑後失去或獲得一顆星並不是什麼稀奇的事。

米其林指南堪稱以星星來評定餐廳等級的先驅。現在，許多指南都採用類似的方法，其中有的星星多得足以令天文學家眼冒金星。但米其林評審是出了名的惜「星」如金，比方說，二〇〇八年東京紅色指南就只給了九家餐廳他們最高等級的三顆星——東京總共超過十五萬家餐廳只有區區九家獲得青睞！但正因只有少數餐廳能獲選參與評鑑，許多主廚都覺得，只要能被納入指南就是一種榮耀了。

Tongue-tied No More

1 place emphasis on...
將重點擺在……，著重於……
emphasis [ˈɛmfəsɪs] 是「強調的重點」的意思，也可以說 lay emphasis on... 或 lay stress on...。
A: What do you think I should talk about in my speech on globalization?
你認為我的全球化演講該說些什麼？
B: I think you should place emphasis on the negative effects of globalization.
我覺得應該把重點放在全球化的負面影響上。

2 make one's head spin
讓某人頭昏腦脹
make one's head spin 也可以說 make one's head swim。spin 是「旋轉」，swim 是「搖晃」，這兩種動作都會讓人頭昏，因此都引申為「暈眩」的意思。make one's head spin/swim 除了表示真的頭昏（如搭雲霄飛車），也表示「令人非常困惑」或是「令人吃不消」。
A: Today's calculus lesson really made my head spin.
今天的微積分課實在讓我一頭霧水。
B: Me too—and this is just the second week of class!
我也是——這還只是第二週的課程耶！

Grammar Master

consider 的用法
consider 和 think 雖然都有「認為」的意思，但 think 的後面可以接完整子句，而 consider 卻不能接子句。consider 的用法有兩種：
● consider + A (to be) B
→ 視 A 為 B
例 We consider this (to be) an insult.
我們認為這是一種侮辱。
● consider + A + 形容詞
→ 認為 A 是……的
例 Do you consider Rita pretty?
你認為莉塔漂亮嗎？

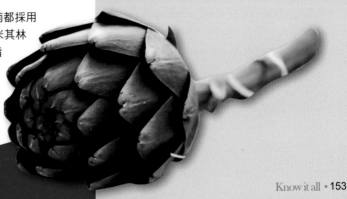

Vocabulary Bank

1) **cuisine** [kwɪˋzin] (n.) 菜餚，烹飪
   Thailand is famous for its spicy cuisine.

2) **atmosphere** [ˋætməs͵fɪr] (n.) 氣氛，氛圍
   The place doesn't have much atmosphere, but the food is great.

3) **luxurious** [lʌgˋʒurɪəs] (a.) 奢華的，非常舒適的
   The tycoon only stays in the most luxurious hotels.

4) **exceptional** [ɪkˋsɛpʃənl] (a.) 優秀的，罕見的
   I only leave a large tip when the service is exceptional.

5) **graphic** [ˋgræfɪk] (a.) 圖解的，圖畫的
   Anna studied graphic design in college.

6) **summary** [ˋsʌmərɪ] (n.) 總結，摘要
   At the end of the lecture, the professor made a summary of the main points.

7) **long-standing** [ˋlɔŋˋstændɪŋ] (a.) 存在已久的
   Eating turkey on Thanksgiving is a long-standing tradition in America.

8) **assure** [əˋʃur] (v./n.) 確定，保證；保證金，抵押
   The taxi driver assured us that we wouldn't miss our flight.

9) **guarantee** [͵gærənˋti] (v.) 保證，擔保
   The refrigerator is guaranteed for two years.

進階字彙

10) **haute** [ot] (a.) 時髦優雅的
    haute cuisine 即「烹飪藝術界」
    haute couture 即「高級女時裝業」
    Paris is the capital of haute couture.

11) **saucy** [ˋsɔsɪ] (a.) 帥氣的；莽撞的，在此指「醬汁多的」，因法國菜以淋醬、沾醬很多聞名（為非正式用法）
    The woman wore her hat at a saucy angle.

口語補充

12) **shortchange** [ˋʃɔrtˋtʃendʒ] (v.) 欺騙，找錢時少給
    I think I got shortchanged at the bar.

13) **stellar** [ˋstɛlə] (a.) 極佳的，無與倫比的
    The orchestra gave a stellar performance.

While the stars are awarded for a restaurant's 1)**cuisine**, the guides also award from one to five "knife and fork" symbols for a restaurant's overall quality and 2)**atmosphere**. All restaurants in each guide receive knife and fork ratings, with one indicating a "quite comfortable" restaurant and five a "3)**luxurious**" restaurant. They also use other special symbols for restaurants with reasonably priced menus (coins) and restaurants with 4)**exceptional** wine lists (grapes). Apart from their 5)**graphic** reviews, the guides also include very short 6)**summaries** (usually two to three sentences) of the reviewer's dining experience.

Michelin reviews are highly regarded in the world of 10)**haute** cuisine. They're taken so seriously, in fact, that they can often make or break a restaurant. But the reviews are Ⓖnot without their critics. The most 7)**long-standing** criticism of the guides is that they place too much emphasis on the French style of cooking. Restaurateurs in other countries often feel 12)**shortchanged** by reviews that seem to ❶ **turn their noses up at** anything not 11)**saucy** enough to be considered French. Several chefs in Tokyo

received media attention when they refused to allow Michelin to rate their restaurants, on the grounds that foreigners were not fit to judge Japanese cuisine.

25　But all criticism aside, diners at Michelin-rated restaurants are [8]**assured** a dining experience of the highest quality. A restaurant with a Michelin star is almost [9]**guaranteed** to be nothing short of [13]**stellar**.

中 Translation

除了星星是授予餐廳美食的榮耀，米其林指南也以一至五副「刀叉」的符號來評定一家餐廳的整體品質和氣氛。每本指南裡的每一家餐廳都有刀叉的評分，一副代表「相當舒適」，五副即代表「豪華」餐廳。米其林還使用其他特殊符號來代表餐廳菜單上的價位合理（銅板）和酒單出色（葡萄）。除了圖解式的評鑑外，米其林指南也會以非常簡短的摘要（通常是兩、三句話）總結評鑑人的用餐經驗。

米其林的評鑑在烹飪藝術界極受重視，事實上，它們被看重的程度常可成就或毀滅一家餐廳。但米其林的評鑑並非無人批評。其中存在最久的批評便是，該指南太過強調法國料理方式。其他國家的餐廳常會有被虧待的感覺，因為米其林的評鑑似乎瞧不起任何醬汁不夠多而稱不上法式的餐點。東京有好幾位主廚引起媒體的注意，就是因為他們拒絕米其林給他們的餐廳評分，理由是外國人不宜評斷日本料理。

但撇開所有批評不談，到米其林評等餐廳用餐的客人，一定能享受到最高品質的用餐體驗。擁有一顆米其林星星的餐廳，幾乎已經保證其明星地位了。

Tongue-tied No More

1 turn one's nose up at...
拒絕……，看輕……

這句話是在描述一種動作：抬高鼻子把頭轉開，一副不想聞到怪味道的表情。引申為「拒絕……、對……嗤之以鼻」的意思。

A: I'd never eat ceviche—it's made with raw fish!
我從來不吃墨西哥海鮮盤——那是用生魚做的！

B: Hey, you shouldn't turn you nose up at something you've never tried before.
嘿，你不該對你沒試過的東西嗤之以鼻。

Grammar Master

雙重否定：not（名詞）without...
雖然一般來說在寫作或說話時最好不要用雙重否定的句型，但有時為了強調或求句型變化，會用 not（名詞）without...（不是沒有……）的句型。

例 ● She is **not** (a woman) **without** intelligence.
她並不是個笨女人。

● Though selfish, he is **not without** compassion.
他雖然自私，但還是有同情心的。

Mini Quiz 閱讀測驗

❶ Why did the Michelin brothers start charging for their guide?
(A) Because they wanted to make more money
(B) Because they wanted more people to buy it
(C) Because they wanted people to take it seriously
(D) Because their tire business was losing money

❷ Do you consider _____ good teacher?
(A) Mr. Rogers is a
(B) Mr. Rogers be a
(C) that Mr. Rogers is
(D) Mr. Rogers to be a

❸ When we get together, we usually drink beer and talk _____ sports.
(A) about　　(B) on
(C) over　　(D) for

Vocabulary Bank

1) **evolve** [ɪˋvɑlv] (v.) 逐步發展、演變
The English language is constantly evolving.

2) **revolve around** [rɪˋvɑlv əˋraʊnd] (phr.) 以…為中心
Mary's life revolves around her children.

3) **occasion** [əˋkeʒən] (n.) 場合，時刻，重大活動
Emma only drinks on special occasions.

4) **ceremony** [ˋsɛrə͵monɪ] (n.) 儀式，典禮
The wedding ceremony was held at a small church.

5) **initiate** [ɪˋnɪʃɪ͵et] (v.)（通過儀式）接納，吸收（新成員）
Many new members were initiated into the church.

6) **milestone** [ˋmaɪl͵ston] (n.) 里程碑
Reaching a million dollars in sales was a major milestone for the company.

7) **lawn** [lɔn] (n.) 草坪，草地
Michael mows the lawn every Saturday.

8) **rely on** [rɪˋlaɪ ɑn] (phr.) 依賴，依靠
Taiwan's economy relies on international trade.

9) **expose** [ɪkˋspoz] (v.) 使接觸到，使暴露於
The goal of the program is to expose students to art.

進階字彙

10) **fraternity** [frəˋtɝnətɪ] (n.) 大學兄弟會，常簡稱為 frat [fræt]
Kyle is thinking of joining a fraternity.

11) **sorority** [səˋrɔrətɪ] (n.) 大學姊妹會，婦女聯誼會
Cynthia's sorority is having a party this Saturday.

口語補充

12) **dorm** [dɔrm] (n.) 宿舍，為 dormitory [ˋdɔrmə͵torɪ] 的簡稱
Would you rather live in the dorms or rent an apartment?

Party
美國大學生的派對文化
IN THE U.S.A.
COLLEGE STYLE!

Hollywood isn't the only place in the U.S. that knows how to party. College students across the country can hold their own when it comes to letting loose and
5 getting down!

College party culture in America has [1] **evolved** over the years. College parties [G] used to [2] **revolve around** important [3] **occasions** during the school year. They
10 would often be held after school dances and events like homecoming games and graduation [4] **ceremonies**. [10] **Fraternities** and [11] **sororities** held parties to [5] **initiate** new members and mark other important
15 [6] **milestones** throughout the school year.

Although college students still party for the same reasons they did in the past, 21st century college parties can happen anytime, anywhere, for any reason. While
20 party cultures vary from school to school, they normally range from small parties in [12] **dorm** rooms to fraternity and sorority parties, [7] **lawn** parties and block parties. Some colleges have even developed
25 reputations as being "party schools." These campuses boast the biggest and best parties around!

Besides giving students the chance to forget about school and just have fun,
30 parties are also a great way to meet new people. Most college students are living away from their families and the friends they had in high school. Since they're on their own for the first time in their
35 lives, it's important for them to develop a new circle of friends they can [8] **rely on** for support. College parties also give students the opportunity to meet people from different majors, [9] **exposing** them
40 to new ideas and helping them make connections that will be useful to them in their future careers.

homecoming games

beach party

lawn party

中 Translation

好萊塢不是美國唯一知道如何開派對狂歡的地方。說到隨心所欲和縱情享樂,全美各地的大學生可是毫不遜色!

這麼多年下來,美國大學的派對文化已逐步演化。以往大學派對都是為學年中的特別場合而舉行,通常是在學校舞會和球隊返校比賽及畢業典禮等活動後舉辦。兄弟會和姊妹會也會在學年中開趴來招募新成員及慶祝其他重要的里程碑。

時至今日,雖然大學生仍會拿過去那些理由來開派對,但二十一世紀的大學生派對隨時隨地、任何理由都可以辦。儘管派對文化因學校而異,但一般可分為在宿舍內的小派對、兄弟會和姊妹會派對、露天草坪派對和封街派對等等。有些學校甚至博得「派對學校」之名,這些校園號稱有最盛大、最精采的派對!

除了提供學生忘掉學業及找樂子的機會,派對也是認識新朋友的絕佳途徑。多數大學生都離鄉背井,遠離家人和高中朋友。因為這是他們這輩子第一次獨立生活,發展一個可以依賴且尋求支持的新交友圈分外重要。大學派對也給學生機會認識不同科系的人,讓他們接觸新的思維,幫助他們建立人脈,未來對他們的事業會很有用。

Language Guide

兄弟會、姊妹會

兄弟會 (fraternity) 和姊妹會 (sorority) 這兩個字是由拉丁語演變而來,frater 和 soror 分別代表兄弟 (brother) 和姊妹 (sister) 之意,現在則是指美國大學裡的一種學生組織,類似台灣的社團,不同的是,成員通常都會一起住在「會館」fraternity/sorority house,成員就像一個大家庭,除了舉辦派對,兄弟姊妹會還會舉辦運動比賽和募款等活動,讓成員從中培養溝通、領導等能力。

Grammar Master

used to + V 過去常做某事

used to 這個片語常與過去式連用,表示「以前常做某事,但現在沒有了」。構成否定句時,必須用過去式助動詞 did,並使用原形動詞 use。

例 I **used to** go to the movies a lot, but I never have the time now.
我以前常去看電影,但現在根本沒時間了。

例 I'm surprised to see you drinking. You **didn't use to**.
看見你喝酒我很驚訝,你以前滴酒不沾。

常見派對類型

派對類型千奇百怪,有的是以特殊服裝造型為主題,例如軍裝派對 (GI Joes and Army Hoes)、天使與魔鬼派對 (angels and devils)、警察與強盜派對 (cops and robbers)、牛仔派對 (cowboys and Indians)……等,或者是以節慶為名義舉辦的萬聖節派對 (Halloween party)、聖誕節派對 (Christmas party),其他常見的派對還有:

Beach Party 海灘派對

別以為海灘派對一定要在海灘邊舉辦,美國大學生會把地下室或私人住所佈置成海灘來開趴,現場甚至有沙地和泳池!主辦者如此費力,參加者當然也要身著清涼泳裝配合演出,常見的遊戲有水槍大戰、沙灘排球……等。

Graffiti Party 塗鴉派對

graffiti [græˋfitɪ] 是義大利文「壁畫」的意思,現在則引申為「即興創作」。塗鴉派對現場備有各式畫筆和顏料,身著白色上衣的參加者可以盡情在別人衣服上作畫和留言,大膽發揮創意和想像力。

Mardi Gras Party 嘉年華派對

早期天主教徒為了迎接復活節、淨化自身,會於復活節前夕進行齋戒,而 Mardi Gras [ˋmɑdɪ grɑs] 即為齋戒開始前大吃大喝的狂歡日,演變至今,Mardi Gras 儼然已成為嘉年華會的代名詞,裝扮成各式人物的遊街慶祝活動、派對更是少不了。參加嘉年華派對的男士一定要記得多帶幾串珠子 (breads), 因為珠子象徵著財富和榮耀,當女生對你猛拋媚眼時,別忘了送她一串珠子當報酬。

Rubik's Cube Party 魔術方塊派對

玩魔術方塊的目標是要把六面都轉成同一個顏色,而魔術方塊派對則是把方塊換成人,參加者的衣物配件須盡可能包含魔術方塊上有的顏色(紅、白、藍、黃、綠、橘),到了派對現場,再想盡辦法跟別人交換,讓身上服飾只有一種顏色,優勝者通常會獲頒小禮物。

炒熱氣氛的喝酒遊戲

說到美國的大學派對,就絕對少不了便宜又方便清理的「桶裝酒」keg,而喝酒遊戲則是助興的重要活動之一,常見的喝酒遊戲有:

beer pong 啤酒乒乓球

長桌兩端分別擺上六杯裝滿的啤酒,接著派出兩名代表,輪流試著將乒乓球以彈跳方式投入對方酒杯中,若順利進球,對方就必須喝光那杯啤酒,以此類推,直到最後一杯酒喝完為止。此遊戲也可增加酒杯數量或調整規則(例如未以彈跳方式就直接投進杯中不算)以增加遊戲難度。

flip cup 啤酒接力

在長桌兩端擺上裝滿的啤酒數杯,兩邊各派出隊員站在酒杯後方,哨聲響起,排在最前頭的隊員必須以最快的速度將第一杯酒喝光,然後把空酒杯倒扣在桌面上,下一個人要等酒杯放下的那瞬間才能拿起第二杯開始喝,先喝完全部啤酒的那方即獲勝。

quarters 彈錢幣遊戲

遊戲規則很簡單,只要將錢幣彈進酒杯中,對方就得乾一杯,但可別小看這小小一枚硬幣,想要百發百中,可是需要一些技巧的。

Kings 國王遊戲

參加者輪流翻撲克牌,翻到的每個數字都代表不同指令(遊戲前先講好規則,例如翻到 A,全場的人就必須乾杯,規則可自定),遊戲進行到四張老 K 都抽完或全部牌翻完即結束。

wizard staff 巫師魔法杖

這遊戲不適用於桶裝啤酒,因為魔法杖是利用啤酒空罐製成,參賽者必須先喝下大量啤酒,再將喝完的空罐以膠帶固定,一個接一個串連,而魔法杖的高度取決於啤酒罐的多寡,喝的越多,魔法杖就越高。完成魔法杖後,就能開始揮舞手中魔杖,展開廝殺了。

參加派對注意守則

- **Don't complain about paying $5 to drink all night.**
  不要喝了整晚的酒還抱怨要付五塊的酒錢。
  派對的酒可不是免費喝到飽的,參加的賓客都要分攤一點酒錢。

- **Don't bring your jacket to a college party.**
  參加大學派對別帶外套。
  並非所有派對場地都設有衣櫥供賓客放置外套,而隨手拿著外套又相當不方便,故出席派對時,帶越少東西越好。

- **Don't argue or fight with the people running the party.**
  不要和派對主人起爭執。
  酒酣耳熱之際,難免會發生衝突,此時要盡量保持冷靜,化解糾紛。

- **Watch what shoes you wear.**
  慎選合宜鞋子。
  若派對是在骯髒的地下室舉辦,不妨穿著較舊的鞋子前往。若是穿著涼鞋出席派對,則要注意足部保養和美容。

- **Pre-game with your friends before you go out.**
  參加前和朋友喝個幾杯。
  與朋友喝得微醺後再結伴一同到派對續攤。

資料來源:http://www.collegetips.com/

wizard staff

Vocabulary Bank

1) **cramped** [kræmpt] (a.) 狹窄的
The seats on the bus were cramped and uncomfortable.

2) **quarters** [ˋkwɔrtɚz] (n.) 住所，住處
The company moved to larger quarters last year.

3) **regulation** [ˌrɛgjəˋleʃən] (n.) 規章，規定
Students are expected to follow school regulations.

4) **consumption** [kənˋsʌmpʃən] (n.) 飲用，食用
There is no link between coffee consumption and heart disease.

5) **inevitable** [ɪnˋɛvɪtəbl] (a.) 不可避免的，必然（發生）的
Death and taxes are inevitable.

6) **theme** [θim] (n.) 主題
What is the theme of your essay?

7) **accordingly** [əˋkɔrdɪŋlɪ] (adv.) 照著，相應地
You're an adult now and should act accordingly.

8) **sandal** [ˋsændl] (n.) 涼鞋（常為複數形）
We're not allowed to wear sandals to work.

9) **entertain** [ˌɛntɚˋten] (v.) 娛樂；招待，請客
It's hard to keep kids entertained.

進階字彙

10) **keg** [kɛg] (n.) 桶裝啤酒，小酒桶。kegger 即「啤酒派對 (keg party)」
How many kegs are you getting for the party?

11) **toga** [ˋtogə] (n.)（古羅馬人的）寬外袍
That frat throws a wild toga party every year.

12) **unwind** [ʌnˋwaɪnd] (v.) 放輕鬆，紓解壓力
What do you do to unwind after work?

口語補充

13) **crash** [kræʃ] (v.) 闖入，無票進入
Let's go crash that kegger tonight!

14) **hangover** [ˋhæŋˌovɚ] (n.) 宿醉
Brian woke up with a nasty hangover on New Year's Day.

With the [1)]**cramped** [2)]**quarters** and strict [3)]**regulations** of dormitories, most major parties take place at and around the frat and sorority houses. While some of these parties are invitation only, others are open to all. And even if you're not

5　invited, you can always [13)]**crash** the party! Needless to say, good looking girls are always welcome. When the weather's nice, parties are held on lawns, and sometimes the whole block is closed off and you can party in the street!

Essential to the modern-day college party is the [10)]**keg**.

10　This is because they're big, convenient (plastic cups are much easier to clean up than broken bottles!) and are the cheapest way to buy large quantities of beer. Drinking games **❶ go hand in hand** with keg parties, and often lead to over-[4)]**consumption** and the [5)]**inevitable** next day [14)]**hangover**.

frat house

PI KAPPA ALPHA

15　　　　Some fraternity
and sorority house parties
involve more planning than
the typical ¹⁰⁾**kegger**. A ⁶⁾**theme**
is chosen, and guests are asked to dress ⁷⁾**accordingly**.
20　Popular theme parties include ¹¹⁾**toga** parties, where guests
wear ᴳnothing but white sheets and ⁸⁾**sandals**, and decade
parties like "'70s Disco," where guests wear styles from the
'70s like bell-bottoms and platform shoes. Hosts decorate
the house to suit the theme and plan games and contests
25　to ⁹⁾**entertain** guests.

　　　　Whether in a dorm, outdoors, or at a frat or sorority
house, American college students are sure to find a great
way to ¹²⁾**unwind** after a hard week at school at one of the
many parties on campus. If parents only knew why most
30　students would rather attend college away from home!

中 Translation

由於宿舍空間狹小、規定嚴格，多數大型派對都會在兄弟會或姊妹會的會館舉辦。有些派對僅限受邀者出席，有些則對外開放。就算沒被邀請，也可以不請自來！不用說，漂亮的女孩永遠受歡迎。如果天氣好，派對會在草地上舉行，有時甚至會封閉整個街區，讓你在街上趴個過癮！

現代大學派對有項不可或缺的要素：桶裝啤酒。因為桶裝啤酒大又方便（塑膠杯比被砸破的酒瓶容易清理多了！），也是購買大量啤酒最划算的方式。跟啤酒派對密不可分的喝酒比賽，常常會讓人喝太多，隔天免不了要宿醉。

有些兄弟會和姊妹會的會館派對比一般的啤酒派對更有規劃。主題選定後，客人會被要求依主題打扮。受歡迎的主題派對包括古羅馬造型派對（客人什麼都沒穿，只有披上白床單、穿涼鞋），還有年代派對，例如「七〇年代迪斯可派對」（客人的穿著須符合七〇年代的風格，如喇叭褲、厚底鞋）。主辦人會裝飾屋子以符合主題，並規劃遊戲和比賽來娛樂嘉賓。

不論是在宿舍、戶外或兄弟姊妹會館舉辦，美國大學生在學校辛苦一週後，必定會在琳瑯滿目的校園派對中找到好方式來紓解身心。要是爸媽明白，為什麼多數學生寧可選擇離家念大學就好了！

Tongue-tied No More

❶ go hand in hand
連在一起，相伴而來

想形容事情交互影響、相互伴隨，有 A 即有 B，就可以用 go hand in hand 這句話來表示。
A: Why is there so much crime in this neighborhood?
　為什麼這一區的犯罪率這麼高？
B: Crime and poverty go hand in hand.
　犯罪和貧窮總是伴隨而來。

Grammar Master

與 but 有關的片語
but 除了作為連接詞，表示「但是，可是」的意思，還可以充當介系詞使用，常用的 but 介系詞片語如下：
● **nothing but = only** 只是，只有
例 She does **nothing but** complain all day long.
　她成天都在埋怨。
● **anything but = not…at all** 絕不是，一點也不
例 Aron is **anything but** a fool
　亞隆一點都不傻。
● **all but = almost completely** 幾乎
例 Their screams of excitement **all but** drowned out the music.
　他們興奮的尖叫聲幾乎淹沒了音樂聲。

Mini Quiz 閱讀測驗

❶ Which of the following is NOT true about college parties?
　(A) They can happen anytime and anywhere.
　(B) They can have different themes.
　(C) They are usually held on important occasions.
　(D) They are a good way for students to relax.

❷ Christine _____ wear skirts, but now she wears them all the time.
　(A) didn't used to
　(B) didn't use to
　(C) didn't get use to
　(D) didn't get used to

❸ It's time to buy new batteries; these ones are _____ dead.
　(A) anything but
　(B) nothing but
　(C) all about
　(D) all but

Vocabulary Bank

1) **cosmetic** [kɑzˋmɛtɪk] (a./n.) 美容的；（常用複數）化妝品
   Dr. Cohen runs a cosmetic clinic in Los Angeles.

2) **procedure** [prəˋsidʒɚ] (n.) 療程，手術
   Liposuction is a simple and safe procedure.

3) **surgery** [ˋsɝdʒərɪ] (n.)（外科）手術
   Most back pain can be treated without surgery.

4) **enhance** [ɪnˋhæns] (v.) 提高（價值），增進（品質）
   The government is working to enhance water quality.

5) **to date** [tə det] (phr.) 至今
   The author's latest novel is his best work to date.

6) **involve** [ɪnˋvɑlv] (v.) 需要，包含
   Does the job involve a lot of overtime?

7) **significant** [sɪgˋnɪfɪkənt] (a.) 大量的，大幅度的
   There has been a significant increase in crime over the past decade.

8) **invasive** [ɪnˋvesɪv] (a.) 侵入性的（醫療程序）；侵略性的（疾病）
   (v.) invade [ɪnˋved] 侵入
   Researchers are developing less invasive medical tests.

9) **therapy** [ˋθɛrəpɪ] (n.) 療法，治療
   The cancer patient is receiving radiation therapy.

10) **alter** [ˋɔltɚ] (v.) 改變
    We may have to alter our plans.

11) **drastically** [ˋdræstɪklɪ] (adv.) 極度地，極端地
    (a.) drastic [ˋdræstɪk]
    The government drastically cut spending to reduce the deficit.

12) **alternative** [ɔlˋtɝnətɪv] (n.)（替代）選擇，選項
    If you don't want to drive, taking the train is a good alternative.

13) **diversity** [dɪˋvɝsətɪ/daɪˋvɝsətɪ] (n.) 多樣性
    New York is a place of great cultural diversity.

14) **popularity** [ˌpɑpjəˋlærətɪ] (n.) 普及，流行，廣受歡迎
    The popularity of video games continues to grow.

Tongue-tied No More

1 break the bank 花大錢

break the bank 這個說法本來用在賭博上，指一個人所贏得的錢超過「莊家」banker 所能支付的，這裡的 bank 是指「莊家的賭本」，後常被用來形容人「花大錢；花費很多」的意思。

A: I heard that restaurant is really expensive.
   我聽說那家餐廳很貴。

B: Well, it's not exactly cheap, but it won't break the bank.
   是不便宜啦，不過也不至於要花上大錢。

A New Wave of Cosmetic Procedures
美容整型新風潮

課文朗讀 MP3 202　單字朗讀 MP3 203　英文文章導讀 MP3 204

To look good these days, wearing fashionable clothes and having great hair just isn't enough. At one time, [1]**cosmetic** [3]**surgery** was only available to the rich and famous. Thanks to recent advances in medical technology, however, cosmetic [2]**procedures** have become safer and more affordable. And with so many images of beautiful people in the media, people are under ever greater pressure to look their best. So it's no surprise that cosmetic surgery is becoming an increasingly popular and acceptable option for those who want to [4]**enhance** their looks.

The most common cosmetic surgeries in the United States [5]**to date** are liposuction, breast enlargement and cosmetic eye surgery. While these procedures can improve a person's appearance, they also [6]**involve** a [7]**significant** amount of recovery time and a certain amount of risk. But new technologies are giving rise to a new and affordable type of procedure known as non-surgical cosmetic treatment. These non-[8]**invasive** procedures can be used to reduce fine lines, puffiness around the eyes and unwanted body hair. Treatments like Botox injections, IPL [9]**therapy** and mini facelifts may not [10]**alter** a person's appearance [11]**drastically**, but they require very little recovery time and are an affordable

[12)]**alternative** for people who want to look good without **1 breaking the bank**.

Many doctors are predicting a dramatic increase in the [13)]**diversity** of patients receiving cosmetic treatment in the next few years. Furthermore, it is likely that as new cosmetic products and techniques become available, non-surgical and minimally invasive procedures will continue to rise in [14)]**popularity**.

30

Mini Quiz 閱讀測驗

❶ Which of the following is NOT an invasive procedure?
(A) IPL therapy
(B) liposuction
(C) cosmetic eye surgery
(D) breast enlargement

中 Translation

這年頭,要漂亮,光靠穿流行服飾和剪時髦髮型是不夠的。曾經,整型美容手術只有富人名流做得起。然而,拜近來醫療技術發展之賜,整型手術已變得更安全、更負擔得起了。由於媒體充斥著俊男美女的畫面,人們正受到愈來愈大的壓力,要展現自己最好的一面。因此,毫無意外地,對於那些希望變得更美的人來說,整型手術正成為日漸風行且可接受的選項。

如今在美國最常見的整型手術是抽脂、隆乳及眼部美容。儘管這些手術可美化一個人的外表,但也需要相當長的復原時間,也隱含一定程度的風險。但新的技術造就了一種全新且索價不高的療程,稱為非手術美容治療。這些非侵入性的療程可用來減少皺紋、眼袋和你不想要的體毛。肉毒桿菌注射、脈衝光療法(編註:IPL 為 Intense Pulsed Light 的簡稱)及微拉皮等療法或許不會大幅改變一個人的容貌,但需要的復原時間極短,對於想變美又不想花大錢的人來說,也是另一種負擔得起的選擇。

許多醫師預期,未來幾年接受整型美容治療的病患將會愈來愈多元。另外,隨著全新的美容產品及技術問世,非手術及侵入性極低的療程也可望愈來愈受歡迎。

Ⓥ Vocabulary Bank

1) **itch (for/to)** [ɪtʃ] (v./n.) 渴望
I'm itching to play the latest *Grand Theft Auto* game.

2) **save up** [sev ʌp] (phr.) 存錢
Phil is saving up to buy a car.

3) **visa** [ˋvizə] (n.) （護照上等的）簽證
They won't let you on board an international flight without a visa.

4) **program** [ˋprogræm] (n.) 計畫，方案；課程
Our school has a good financial aid program.

5) **available** [əˋveləbl] (a.) 可用的，可得的
This phone is available in three colors.

6) **lead** [lid] (v./n.) 領導，指導，榜樣
If you're not sure what to do, just follow my lead.

7) **requirement** [rɪˋkwaɪrmənt] (n.) 規定，必要條件
Previous experience is a requirement for the job.

8) **vary** [ˋvɛrɪ] (v.) 呈多樣化，有差異
The age at which children begin to speak varies.

9) **insight** [ˋɪn͵saɪt] (n.) 深入的理解，見解
The scholar's work shows great insight.

10) **extended** [ɪkˋstɛndɪd] (a.) 長期的，持久的
I'm planning on taking an extended vacation.

11) **imply** [ɪmˋplaɪ] (v.) 意味著，暗示
Are you implying that I need to lose weight?

12) **valid** [ˋvælɪd] (a.) 有效的，合法的
It's illegal to drive without a valid driver's license.

Working Holiday
打工度假不是夢

課文朗讀 MP3 205　單字朗讀 MP3 206　英文文章導讀 MP3 207

Are you [1]**itching** for a long vacation but don't have enough money [2]**saved up**? Would you like to experience living and working in another culture? If so, then a working holiday may be just the thing for you. When most people think of working holidays, ⒢Australia is usually the first country that comes to mind. Australia was the first country to offer working holiday [3]**visas**—its working holiday [4]**program** was established in 1975—and it's still the most popular destination. Originally open to young people from Great Britain, the Republic of Ireland and Canada, the visa is now [5]**available** to young people from 18 different countries, and the list keeps growing.

Over the years, many other countries have followed Australia's [6]**lead**. From Argentina to Austria, from Singapore to Switzerland, 26 countries around the world now offer working holiday visas. [7]**Requirements** and restrictions [8]**vary** from country to country, but the basic concept is the same: to promote international understanding by allowing young people to gain in-depth understanding of the cultures and customs of other countries. And what better way to gain [9]**insight** into another culture than living and working in a foreign country for an [10]**extended** period of time. As the name [11]**implies**, working holiday visas, which are usually [12]**valid** for 1 year, allow the holder to both work and travel during their stay. Some countries, like Australia, even allow visa holders to enroll in short-term study [4]**programs**.

中 Translation

你很想度個長假，卻存不夠旅費嗎？你想要體驗在另一個文化生活和工作的感覺嗎？如果是的話，打工度假就剛好很適合你。大多數人一想到打工度假，第一個想到的國家通常是澳洲。澳洲是第一個提供打工度假簽證的國家——它的打工度假方案早在一九七五年就成立——而且至今仍是最受歡迎的地方。原本只開放給英國、愛爾蘭及加拿大的年輕人，如今已經擴增為十八個國家，且名單仍繼續增加中。

這些年來，其他許多國家也跟隨澳洲的腳步。從阿根廷到奧地利，從新加坡到瑞士，目前世界上共有二十六個國家提供打工度假簽證。申請條件和限制隨著每個國家不同而有所差異，不過基本理念都是相同的：讓年輕人得以深入了解異國文化和風俗，進而促成國際觀。有什麼方法能比得上在異國居住、工作一段時間，更能對該國文化獲得深入了解呢？顧名思義，通常期限為一年的打工度假簽證持有人獲准在停留期間一邊工作、一邊旅行。某些國家，例如澳洲，甚至允許簽證持有人報名短期學習課程。

G Grammar Master

the + 序數（+ 名詞）to V
第……個做某事的……

表達「第……個做某事的……」時，在 the 的後面接 first、second、third、last 等序數，後面的名詞可省略，再接 to V。

例 ● Emily was the first (person) to arrive.
　　愛蜜莉是第一個到的人。

　● We were the last (ones / people) to know about this.
　　我們是最晚知道這件事的人。

　● Josh was the second (student) to hand in the answer sheet. 喬許是第二個交答案卷的學生。

Language Guide

認識打工度假

打工度假其實就是海外工讀，相當適合預算有限又嚮往異國生活的年輕人，他們能於旅途中打工賺取旅費以支應所需，並透過旅行的方式來開拓視野，體驗不同的民俗風情。

「打工度假」在國外已實行長達三十年以上，包含台灣在內，世界上有超過二十個國家有此政策，目前與台灣簽訂的國家有澳洲、紐西蘭，以及今年六月剛開始的日本。經過一趟長途旅程的洗滌歷練，往往能讓人有所成長，故許多國家都對此政策抱持正面積極的態度，鼓勵年輕人多多出國增長見聞。

但海外工讀的種類與方式，往往會因國家與計畫類型而有所差異，故名稱也有所不同，以下列舉較熱門的海外工讀地點提供參考：

美國 Work and Travel

美國暑期工讀旅遊計畫（Work and Travel，簡稱 WAT）是 美國政府國務院旗下的一個學生交流計畫，引進台灣已有十年之久，參加者須為 18～28 歲之在學大專生或應屆畢業生，且持有 J-1 簽證（Exchange Visitor Visa，交換訪客簽證。必須先透過由美國國務院審核的合法承辦機構協助申請 DS-2019 表格文件，通過之後才能順利取得 J-1 簽證），計畫期間為六月至十月初，每人最長工作期限不得超過四個月。通常在工作結束、簽證時效尚未到期前，會有約一個月左右的旅遊時間。

依各家機構規定不同，報名之後會有語言能力測驗或是雇主來台面試。因為暑假正值旅遊旺季，故大部分工作都與觀光服務業相關，如餐廳、遊樂園等，工作地點的分配則以學生報名的先後順序、個人特質、英文溝通能力及可工作的時間等作為評斷標準來分發，平均時薪約為六～八美元之間。機構和雇主並無免費提供住宿的義務，但多數雇主會協助安排，學生只要支付低額的住宿費用即可。

英國 Study and Work

到英國海外工讀比較類似所謂的帶薪實習 (Study and Work)，與所謂的實習 (internship) 有所不同，internship 無薪資給付，但在工作安排上較彈性多元，可依個人需求及興趣來安排，而 Study & Work 則為一種可支薪的專業「課程」，工作性質大多以服務業為主，如餐飲、飯店、醫護等工作。基本上必須先就讀一定時數的語言課程以及相關基礎課程，之後再由學校依個人程度與課程所學來安排合適工作，待工作結束後，還要回到原學校修習最後的結業課程，這樣階段式的學習模式被稱為「三明治課程」，不但兼顧理論與實務，且為日後就業奠定穩固基礎。

只要年齡介於18～30歲，不論身份為學生或社會人士皆可報名參加，課程時間因學校不同而有所差異，通常為三個月至一年不等。完成此課程不但可以拿到英語課程的結業證書、雇主推薦函，還有機會獲得英國劍橋大學所頒發的 UCLES（University of Cambridge Local Examinations Syndicate，英國劍橋大學實習工作經驗證書），替未來求職加分。

加拿大 Study and Work

到加拿大海外工讀其實比較偏向遊學計畫的延伸，與英國一樣須持有學生簽證，在念完語言課程後，由學校協助安排一些簡單的工作，如房間打掃、餐廳清潔等勞務工作，但並非所有學校都有這種工讀課程的安排，出發前務必先做確認。

澳洲 **Working Holiday**

打工度假計畫 (Working Holiday) 是澳洲與台灣政府共同協商簽訂的互惠計畫，適用年齡為 18～30 歲之間，主要目的為旅遊，工作只是為了資助旅費。澳洲打工度假簽證效期為一年，申請者必須提供來回機票以及至少澳幣五千元的財力證明，以證明即使在當地找不到工作，也有財力負擔旅費，不至於滯留澳洲。初審通過後，還必須進行健康檢查，身心狀態正常者才算符合資格，英文只要具備基本會話能力即可。原本一生只能申請一次的打工度假簽證，於 2005 年底放寬規定，將次數增加為兩次，故在澳洲停留時間可能長達兩年。前三個月為訓練課程，之後便進入正式工作，但不得受雇於同一個雇主達六個月以上。這類提供給外國年輕人的工作，不外乎以採收水果及農耕等勞務性工作為主。此外，澳洲打工度假簽證持有人可以修習四個月的語言課程。

紐西蘭 **Working Holiday**

紐西蘭打工簽證的規定和澳洲相去不遠，有效期限同樣為一年，同樣須出示財力證明，但受雇時間縮短至三個月，語言進修也縮至三個月。較為不同的是，紐西蘭政府多出一項規定，停留在紐西蘭期間，必須持有醫療及全額住院保險，由此可見紐西蘭對於社會福利的重視。

日本 **Working Holiday**

繼紐西蘭、澳洲後，日本於今年開跑成為第三個開放台灣青年打工度假的國家，申請時間分成六月及十一月兩個梯次，每梯次將開放一千人的名額，簽證效期為一年，除了有年齡的限制之外（18～30 歲），申請者還必須身體健康、無犯罪紀錄，並附上打工度假計畫書及台幣八萬元以上的存款證明，但學歷及語言程度不拘。

除了打工度假簽證之外，透過申請日本的語言學校基本上也能完成在當地打工賺錢的夢想，因為就讀語言學校的學生就可申請「資格外許可」的證明在日本當地打工，而申請學校並沒有名額限制，只要年滿十八歲且高中畢業就能提出申請。

打工度假海外遊學

遊學簡而言之就是邊玩邊學，沒有身分和年齡限制，也沒有申請正式入學的高門檻、不必拘泥於文憑的取得，對於經濟能力不足卻又想出國開開眼界和練英文的人是很不錯的入門選擇。若不想花太多時間蒐集資料，坊間有許多代辦中心會貼心地從住宿、課程甚至是旅遊規畫全為你安排妥當。遊學時間為一個月至一年不等，不過以一趟為期兩個月的自助遊學來評估，大約需花費台幣二十萬左右。

相較於遊學，海外工讀對於有經濟預算考量，卻苦無機會出國的人而言可說是一大福音。在國外盛行多年的海外工讀，向來是歐洲學子最熱門的暑期活動，尤其是一些經濟條件較差的國家，學生就能把握此機會在工讀地點拚命兼差賺飽荷包。但與遊學相較之下，海外工讀除了美國有學生身分限制外，大部分國家多半有年齡限制。

總而言之，遊學活動有較大的自主空間，例如可以選擇地點、課程、時間長短，適合獨立性低、無打工經驗、想體驗國外學生生活的人；但海外工讀則受制於雇主，且往往有時間及年齡限制，適合獨立自主、勇於接受挑戰者。出國前，務必審慎考慮自身經濟狀況、旅遊目的和個人特質，才能有一趟不虛此行的異國之旅。

.Know itALL 英文閱讀

V Vocabulary Bank

1) **eligible** [ˋɛlɪdʒəb!] (a.) 合乎資格的
With your grades, you should be eligible for a scholarship.

2) **off-limits** [ˋɔfˋlɪmɪts] (a.) 禁止進入的
This area is off-limits to hotel guests.

3) **round-trip** [ˋraʊndˋtrɪp] (a.) 來回的，雙程的
How much is round-trip airfare to Japan?

4) **breeze** [briz] (n.)（口）輕而易舉的事
Setting up your own blog is a breeze.

5) **quota** [ˋkwotə] (n.) 定額，限額
The U.S. has strict immigration quotas.

6) **applicant** [ˋæpləkənt] (n.) 申請人
Applicants will be notified when their applications have been received.

7) **representative** [rɛprɪˋzɛntətɪv] (a./n.) 代表的；代表
Our company is sending a representative to the convention.

8) **issue** [ˋɪʃu] (v.) 核發，發行
How long does it take to issue a new passport?

9) **agriculture** [ˋægrɪ͵kʌltʃə] (n.) 農業
Agriculture was invented around 10,000 years ago.

10) **hospitality** [͵hɑspɪˋtælətɪ] (n.) 餐旅（業）
Michael has a degree in hospitality management.

11) **broaden** [ˋbrɔdn̩] (v.) 使…變寬闊
Going to college will broaden your mind.

12) **horizon** [həˋraɪzn̩] (n.)（知識、經驗等的）範圍，眼界，視野
The horizons of human knowledge are constantly expanding.

13) **perspective** [pəˋspɛktɪv] (n.) 觀點，角度
You should try to see things from my perspective.

課文朗讀 MP3 208　單字朗讀 MP3 209　英文文章導讀 MP3 210

But if you're from Taiwan, you're probably thinking, "This sounds great, but am I [1)]**eligible**?" The answer is yes! While most of the world's working holiday programs are [2)]**off-limits** to R.O.C. passport holders, Australia and New

5　Zealand welcome young people from Taiwan with open arms. As long as you're 18-30 years old, in good health, and have sufficient funds (enough to buy a [3)]**round-trip** ticket and cover the initial part of your stay), applying is a [4)]**breeze**. And while New Zealand has a [5)]**quota** for

10　[6)]**applicants** from Taiwan (600 per year, so be sure to apply early), the [G]Australian [7)]**representative** office in Taipei predicted that over 10,000 working holiday visas would be [8)]**issued** to Taiwanese applicants this year!

And if you're looking for something a little closer

15　to home, you're in luck! The Japanese working holiday program, which started in 1980, is now open to Taiwanese applicants. Requirements are similar to the Australian program, and you don't need to be fluent in Japanese to apply. So what are the benefits of a working holiday? In

20　addition to honing your foreign language skills—wouldn't "fluent in English" (or Japanese) look nice on your résumé?—you can also gain valuable

international work experience in your career field.
Although many people choose to do seasonal work in
25 9)**agriculture** or 10)**hospitality** (i.e. picking fruit or working
at hotels), you're free to look for work in your field of study.
Even more importantly, living, working and traveling in
another country will 11)**broaden** your 12)**horizons** and give
you the international 13)**perspective** that will help you get
30 ahead in the globalized world of the 21st century.

中 Translation

如果你是台灣人，你大概會想：「聽起來很吸引人，但是我符合申請資格嗎？」答案是可以！雖然世界上大多數打工度假方案都將中華民國護照持有人排除在外，澳洲和紐西蘭卻是敞開雙臂歡迎台灣年輕人前往。只要你的年紀在十八歲到三十歲之間，身體健康，有足夠的資金（夠買一張來回機票，並付得起剛開始在當地居留的生活費），申請程序簡單得很。雖然紐西蘭對台灣申請人有限制人數（每年六百人，因此務必提早申請），不過台北的澳洲代表處表示，今年預計發放超過一萬張打工度假簽證給台灣申請人！

如果你要找離家近一點的地方，你走運了！日本從一九八〇年開始實施的打工度假計畫，現在已開放給台灣人申請。申請條件和澳洲的方案相似，而且日文不流利也能申請。那麼，打工度假的好處究竟在哪？除了能夠磨練你的外語能力之外——履歷表上若寫著「英（日）文流利」看起來不是很讚嗎？——你還能在你的職業生涯中獲得寶貴的國際工作經驗。儘管許多人選擇從事季節性的農業或餐旅業工作（例如摘水果或到飯店上班），你還是可以依照自己所學來找工作。更重要的是，在異國居住、工作、旅行能夠讓你開拓視野，帶給你國際觀，讓你在二十一世紀這個全球化世界中獲得成功。

Grammar Master

時態的一致性

有時一個句子裡可能會提到過去和未來兩個不同時間的事，比如「他昨天說他明天會來」。在較嚴謹的文法規則裡，句子後半部的時態要和前半部一致，也就是說整句話的時態要以前半部為主。

例 ● He said yesterday that he would come tomorrow.
他昨天說他明天會來。

● I thought Jenny was your younger sister.
我原本以為珍妮是你的妹妹。

Mini Quiz 閱讀測驗

❶ According to the article, which of the following is NOT one of the benefits of going on a working holiday?
(A) You can gain insight into a foreign culture.
(B) You can improve your foreign language skills.
(C) You can pursue a career in another country.
(D) You can gain international perspective.

❷ Bob told me he _____ a doctor.
(A) was
(B) is
(C) isn't
(D) hasn't

❸ Perry was _____ at the meeting.
(A) the last one arrive
(B) the last arriving
(C) the last to arrive
(D) last person to arrive

閱讀測驗解答 1 (C) 2 (A) 3 (C)

Flash Mobs 快閃族
Not Just *a Flash in the Pan

© Duncan Rawlinson
http://thelastminuteblog.com

課文朗讀 MP3 211　單字朗讀 MP3 212　英文文章導讀 MP3 213

Vocabulary Bank

1) **warehouse** [ˋwɛr͵haʊs] (n.) 倉庫
The company's warehouse is located near the harbor.

2) **flood** [flʌd] (v.)（大量）湧入
Thousands of fans flooded into the stadium for the big game.

3) **applaud** [əˋplɔd] (v.) 鼓掌，喝采
The audience applauded enthusiastically at the end of the play.

4) **poke** [pok] (v.) 用手指戳
My dad poked me in the ribs when I fell asleep in church.

5) **fad** [fæd] (n.) 一時的流行風潮
Tracy always follows the latest fads.

6) **disperse** [dɪˋspɝs] (v.) 解散，驅散
The police fired teargas to disperse the crowd.

7) **participation** [pɑr͵tɪsəˋpeʃən] (n.) 參與
(v.) participate [pɑrˋtɪsə͵pet] 參與
(n.) participant [pɑrˋtɪsəpənt] 參與者
Class participation will account for ten percent of your grade.

8) **like-minded** [ˋlaɪkˋmaɪndɪd] (a.) 志趣相投的，看法一致的，也拼作 likeminded
Joining a club is a great way to meet like-minded people.

9) **commentary** [ˋkɑmən͵tɛrɪ] (n.) 評論，表達意見
The magazine contains news and commentary on culture and politics.

補充字彙

* **a flash in the pan** [ə flæʃ ɪn ðə pæn] (phr.) 一時的流行
Some people think Twitter is just a flash in the pan.

* **unison** [ˋjunəsn̩] (n.) 一致
(phr.) in unison 同時，一起
The fans cheered for their team in unison.

* **backfire** [ˋbæk͵faɪr] (v.) 產生與預期相反的結果
I hope our plan doesn't backfire.

The first flash mob was created in Manhattan in early 2003 by Bill Wasik, senior editor of *Harper's Magazine*. ⓒHe got a bunch of people to gather around an expensive rug at a Macy's department store. When
5　approached by sales assistants, they all gave the same story: they lived together in a 1)**warehouse** and were shopping for a "love rug." Another time, 200 people 2)**flooded** the lobby of a Hyatt hotel and 3)**applauded** in *unison for 15 seconds. Wasik says he did this as
10　a sort of social experiment to ❶4)**poke fun at** people who think of themselves as being hip and who try to be individuals by joining the latest fad. But it seems to have *backfired and launched a new 5)**fad**.

For those not in the know, a flash mob is a group
15　of strangers who appear suddenly in a public place, do something weird but harmless for a few minutes, and then quickly 6)**disperse**. They might repeat a phrase over and over, stare at something for no good reason, or even have a pillow fight. Flash mobs are arranged
20　over the Internet through e-mail or social media sites

like Twitter or Facebook, and [7]**participation** is open to anyone with a heartbeat. It's a sort of street theater where the actors are performing more for their own entertainment than for an audience. While the purpose

25 is usually to have fun and meet [8]**like-minded** people, sometimes flash mobs are used as a mild form of social [9]**commentary** or protest.

中 Translation

快閃族——絕非一閃即逝的風潮

二○○三年初，第一群快閃族由《哈潑雜誌》資深編輯比爾瓦席克於曼哈頓所組成。他找了一群人聚集在梅西百貨一塊昂貴的毯子周圍，當銷售人員上前詢問，他們全都口徑一致：他們一起住在一個倉庫裡，想買一條「愛毯」。還有一次，兩百人湧入一家凱悅飯店的大廳，一起鼓掌十五秒鐘。瓦席克說，他這麼做是在進行一種社會實驗，以取笑那些自以為新潮又想透過趕時髦來突顯自我的人。但這種做法似乎產生反效果，並帶動一股新的風潮。

先說一聲，以防有人不知道：快閃族是一群突然出現在公共場所的陌生人，做某件怪異但無傷大雅的事，幾分鐘後便一哄而散。他們可能會一再重複同樣的話，莫名瞪著某樣東西，甚至打枕頭仗。快閃族是在網路上透過電子郵件或 Twitter、Facebook 等社交媒體網站集結，只要是有心跳的人都可參加。這是一種街頭戲劇，只不過演員的表演是為了讓自己開心，而非給觀眾欣賞。雖然快閃族的目的通常是找樂子和認識志同道合的人，但有時也被當作一種溫和的社會評論或抗議形式。

❄ Language Guide

International Pillow Fight Day 國際枕頭仗日

目前全球最大規模的快閃活動要算是 International Pillow Fight Day 了，人們透過網路彼此串連，全球在同一時間展開枕頭大戰。2009 年的 International Pillow Fight Day 是在 4 月 4 日舉行，想見識枕頭揮舞、羽毛滿天的瘋狂景象，可至 🌐 http://www.break.com/usercontent/2009/4/Pillow-Fight-Day-Los-Angeles-2009-698259.html 一窺洛杉磯活動的盛況。

International Pillow Fight Day 是 The Urban Playground Movement（「都市遊樂場」活動組織）號召的活動之一，他們的目標是要為各大都市的公共空間帶來片刻歡愉，讓人群不再是受到某種商業或政治宣傳而被動聚集。在他們為 International Pillow Fight Day 設置的網站 🌐 http://www.pillowfightday.com/ 可以看到他們建議各地自行號召活動的方法：

Rules for a Pillow Fight 枕頭仗規則

Soft pillows only! 只能使用軟枕頭！

Swing lightly—many people will be swinging at once.
輕輕甩，因為會有很多人同時甩。

Don't swing at people without pillows or with cameras.
不要攻擊手上沒有枕頭，或是拿照相機的人。

Remove glasses beforehand! 事先摘下眼鏡。

The event is free and appropriate for all ages.
本活動免費，老少咸宜。

Wait until the signal to begin.
等信號響起再開戰。

This event is more fun with feathers!
本活動用羽毛枕比較好玩！

最後他們不忘提醒大家要自備清潔工具，玩完之後要清潔環境、恢復原狀！

Ⓖ Grammar Master

get + 受詞 + to V
使／命令……去做……

例 ● The manager **got Rita to type** that report.
經理叫莉塔打那份報告。

Know it ALL 英文閱讀

Vocabulary Bank

1) **large-scale** [ˋlɑrdʒˋskel] (a.) 大規模的
The government is launching a large-scale investigation into police corruption.

2) **disco** [ˋdɪsko] (n.) 舞廳，迪斯可音樂
We went dancing at a disco last night.

3) **underground** [ˋʌndɚˏɡraund] (n./a.) 地下（的），首字母大寫 Underground 則為「倫敦地下鐵」
Did you ride the Underground when you went to London?

4) **tune** [tun] (n.) 旋律，曲調
Becky hummed a tune while she washed the dishes.

5) **bizarre** [bɪˋzɑr] (a.) 怪異的
Jake's hippie parents are always wearing bizarre clothes.

6) **spray** [spre] (v.) 噴灑
Water sprayed from the broken pipe.

7) **simultaneously** [ˏsaɪməlˋtenɪəslɪ] (adv.) 同時，同步
(a.) simultaneous [ˏsaɪmlˋtenɪəs] 同時的，同步的
Two students answered the teacher's question simultaneously.

8) **limp** [lɪmp] (v./n.) 跛行
The injured player limped off the field.

9) **satisfying** [ˋsætɪsˏfaɪɪŋ] (a.) 心滿意足的
(v.) satisfy [ˋsætɪsˏfaɪ]
That was the most satisfying meal I've had in a long time.

補充字彙

* **bystander** [ˋbaɪˏstændɚ] (n.) 旁觀者，路過的人
Several innocent bystanders were killed in the gun battle.

* **squirt** [skwɝt] (v./n.) 噴射，squirt gun 即「水槍」
The lemon squirted in my eye when I cut it open.

* **nuts** [nʌts] (a.) （俚）發瘋的，傻里傻氣的
My friends thought I was nuts to get married so soon.

* **spoof** [spuf] (v.) 嘲弄，開玩笑
The students spoofed the teacher when he left the classroom.

* **spontaneity** [ˏspɑntəˋneətɪ] (n.) 自發性，自然發生
The couple tried to put the spontaneity back in their relationship.

課文朗讀 MP3 214　單字朗讀 MP3 215　英文文章導讀 MP3 216

　　One of the earliest 1)**large-scale** flash mobs was London's "Silent 2)**Disco**" in 2006. People gathered in 3)**Underground** stations and began dancing to music on their iPods. The idea was to ⊙have people dancing to 4)**tunes** that only they
5　could hear, which would naturally look pretty 5)**bizarre** to *bystanders. More than 4,000 "mobsters" showed up at Victoria Station, and were eventually dispersed by police. In 2007, Vancouver hosted the first "Vancouver Water Fight." Everyone brought *squirt guns and 6)**sprayed** each
10　other for several minutes. Sound *nuts? The next year, 5,000 people showed up. And in March 2008, the world's largest pillow fight took place 7)**simultaneously** in 25 cities around the world. According to the *Wall Street Journal*, 5,000 people turned out in New York City alone.

15　　Another interesting kind of flash mob is the Zombie Walk. Hundreds or even thousands of people dress up like zombies and 8)**limp** through shopping malls. The idea is to *spoof shoppers and suggest that they too are zombies because they purchase name brand products
20　after being told what to do by TV commercials. Of course, people taking part in flash mobs are also told

what to do by others. So who's the real zombie? Then again, if
25 you've been chained to a desk all day, going out the door and doing something silly and harmless is a fun way to socialize and **1 blow off steam**. In the words of one recent participant: "I can't believe how 9)**satisfying** that was!" It looks like this form of
30 organized *spontaneity is here to stay.

中 Translation

最早的大規模快閃族之一是二〇〇六年倫敦的「無聲迪斯可」。人們群集地鐵站，開始一邊聽自個兒 iPod 播放的音樂，一邊跳舞。當時的構想是，讓人們隨著只有自己能聽到的旋律起舞，這在旁人看來當然相當怪異。當時共有超過四千名快閃族在維多利亞車站現身，最後被警方驅離。二〇〇七年，溫哥華舉辦第一屆「溫哥華水仗」，每個人都帶了玩具水槍，互相掃射幾分鐘。聽起來很瘋狂嗎？次年共有五千人與會。而二〇〇八年三月，世界最大的枕頭仗在全球二十五個城市同時開打。據《華爾街日報》報導，光是紐約市就有五千人參加。

另一種有趣的快閃族是「殭屍遊行」。數百人甚至上千人化裝成殭屍的模樣，在購物中心蹣跚而行。用意是要戲弄購物者，暗指購物者也跟殭屍沒兩樣，因為電視廣告叫他們買什麼品牌的產品，他們皆唯命是從。當然，參加快閃族的人也是照別人的話行事，所以誰才是真正的行屍走肉呢？不過話又說回來，如果你已經綁在辦公桌前一整天，出門做些愚蠢又無傷大雅的事，也是參與交際和紓解壓力的有趣方式。套用最近一位快閃族成員的話：「想不到那竟然會讓我這麼心滿意足！」看來這種「有組織的自發性」將會留存下去了。

Language Guide

-ster 字尾構成的名詞

文中用 mobster 這個字表示「參與快閃 (flash mob) 活動的人」，但 mob 這個字原本是「幫派」的意思，mobster 也就帶有「幫派份子」的貶義。

英文中有許多字尾是 -ster 的字眼，用來代表「與……有關的人」、「有……品性的人」。例如：

gang 幫派	→	gangster 幫派份子
hip 趕時髦的	→	hipster 愛趕時髦的人。衍生出「嬉皮」hippie 一字
prank 胡鬧，惡作劇	→	prankster 愛惡作劇的人
pun 說雙關語，俏皮話	→	punster 愛說俏皮話的人
trick 哄騙，戲弄	→	trickster 騙子
young 年輕的	→	youngster 年輕人

Tongue-tied No More

1 blow off steam 紓解壓力

壓力鍋如果一直加熱卻不釋放裡面的蒸汽 (steam)，最後鍋子就會爆炸 (blow)。但在這裡 blow 並不是爆炸，而是「吹氣」的意思，blow off 表示「把氣吹出來」，壓力解除之後也就不會爆炸囉。

A: How come you like to play ice hockey so much?
你為什麼那麼愛玩冰上曲棍球？

B: It's a great way to blow off steam.
那是紓解壓力的好方法。

Grammar Master

have + 受詞 + V / Ving
使 / 命令……去……

例 ● My mom **had me do** the dishes.
= My mom **had me doing** the dishes.
我媽媽要我洗碗。

● The pilot **had everyone fasten** their seatbelts.
= The pilot **had everyone fastening** their seatbelts.
飛機駕駛要大家繫好安全帶。

Mini Quiz 閱讀測驗

❶ Why did Bill Wasik create the first flash mob?
(A) to make fun of people who follow fads
(B) to launch a new fad
(C) to thank a hotel for good service
(D) to purchase a carpet

❷ The professor _____ everybody open their textbooks to Chapter Two.
(A) told   (B) said
(C) had   (D) got

V Vocabulary Bank

1) **wardrobe** [ˈwɔrdrob] (n.)（一人的全部）衣服、服裝
They each bought a new wardrobe for their European vacation.

2) **assume** [əˈsum] (v.) 以為，認為
I assumed you wouldn't be coming to the meeting.

3) **immigrant** [ˈɪməgrənt] (n.) 移民，僑民
(v.) immigrate [ˈɪməˌgret] 遷入
The immigrant is slowly learning to speak English.

4) **wholesale** [ˈholˌsel] (a./adv.) 批發的，成批售出的；批發
Store owners buy wholesale, so they can earn a decent profit.

5) **durability** [ˌdurəˈbɪlətɪ] (n.) 耐久性
(a.) durable [ˈdurəbl] 持久耐用的
Toyota cars are known for their durability.

6) **fabric** [ˈfæbrɪk] (n.) 織品，布料
Most of this fabric is made in India.

7) **fund** [fʌnd] (v./n.) 出資；資金，基金
Because he is so rich, Bill Gates is often asked to fund new ideas.

8) **patent** [ˈpætn̩t] (n./a./v.) 專利
The patent for this device is owned by Apple.

9) **copper** [ˈkɑpɚ] (n./a.) 銅；銅製的
Copper is often used to make electric wire.

10) **overalls** [ˈovɚˌɔlz] (n.) 工作褲
The workers wear overalls because they last a long time.

11) **overnight** [ˈovɚnaɪt] (adv./a.) 一夜間，突然
You can't expect to succeed overnight.

12) **rebellion** [rɪˈbɛljən] (n.) 反叛，叛逆
(v.) rebel [rɪˈbɛl] 造反，反抗
The government sent in troops to put down the rebellion.

補充字彙

13) **rivet** [ˈrɪvɪt] (n./v.) 鉚釘；固定，釘牢
The metal frame is held together by rivets.

14) **denim** [ˈdɛnɪm] (n.) 丹寧布，牛仔布
Blue jeans are made of denim.

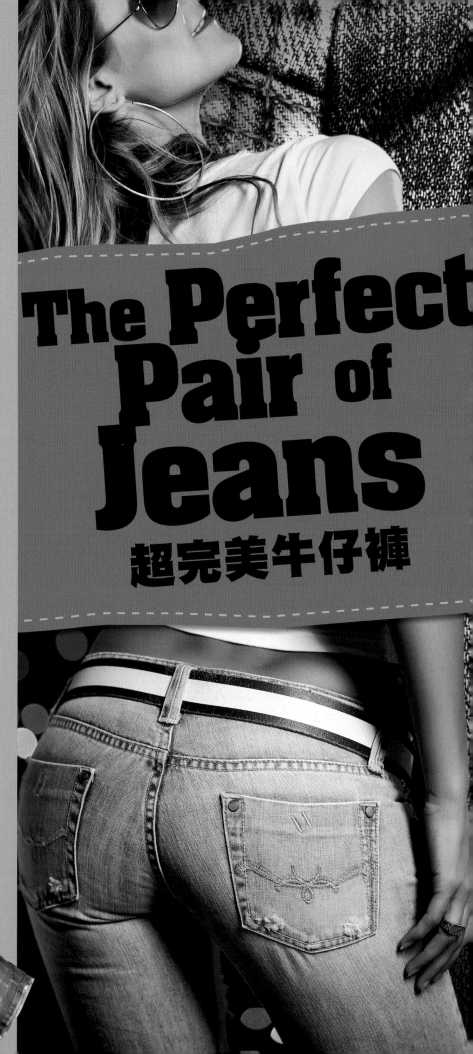

The Perfect Pair of Jeans
超完美牛仔褲

課文朗讀 MP3 217　單字朗讀 MP3 218　英文文章導讀 MP3 219

Jeans, that perfect and comfortable part of one's [1]**wardrobe** that no one can live without, have a history that is interesting yet mostly unknown. Most people [2]**assume** that Levi Strauss ⓖinvented the "blue jean," but he actually only had a hand in the process.

During the Gold Rush of California, Levi Strauss, a 24 year-old [3]**immigrant**, moved to San Francisco to start a [4]**wholesale** business that sold clothes. It was then he met a tailor named Jacob Davis who came up with the idea to use metal [13]**rivets** to hold pockets to pants for added [5]**durability**. At the time, [14]**denim** was a [6]**fabric** worn by workers, who needed something more [5]**durable** and practical. Davis asked Strauss to [7]**fund** the [8]**patent** for his idea, and soon after [9]**copper**-riveted "waist [10]**overalls**," as jeans were then called, were being sold with the Levi Strauss label.

In 1891, Strauss' patent went public and riveted clothing was sold by several companies in the U.S. Two other famous companies began cashing in on the sale of jeans—Lee's and Wrangler. In the forties and fifties, famous Western movie stars gave jeans new fame by wearing them in movies. The most significant was James Dean, who appeared in *Rebel without a Cause* (1955) wearing [14]**denim**. Almost [11]**overnight**, the youth of American had to have a pair of "jean pants," and they became a symbol of youth, freedom and [12]**rebellion**.

中 Translation

牛仔褲——每個人生活必備的衣飾中最完美、舒適的那件——有著一段饒富趣味但多數人都不知曉的歷史。許多人以為是李維史特勞斯發明「藍色牛仔褲」，但他其實只有參與其過程而已。

在加州淘金熱潮期間，二十四歲的李維史特勞斯搬到舊金山展開成衣批發業。他在那時遇到名為雅各戴維斯的裁縫師，戴維斯提出用金屬鉚釘把口袋固定在長褲上以增加耐用度的想法。當時，丹寧布是工人穿的布料，他們需要較耐用又實用的東西。戴維斯請史特勞斯出資為他這個構想申請專用權，不久，釘了銅釘的「齊腰工作褲」——牛仔褲當時的名稱——就以李維史特勞斯為品牌上市銷售了。

一八九一年，史特勞斯公開專利後，美國數家公司便販售起鉚釘服飾。兩家知名公司，Lee 和藍哥開始因賣牛仔褲大發利市。四○及五○年代，穿牛仔褲的西部片明星讓牛仔褲有了嶄新的聲名。其中最重要的莫過於詹姆士狄恩，他在一九五五年的《養子不教誰之過》裡身穿牛仔褲，幾乎一夕之間，美國年輕人都非要有一件牛仔褲不可，牛仔褲也成為青春、自由和叛逆的象徵。

ⓖ Grammar Master

invent/create/discover 的用法

雖然 invent、create、discover 這三個字都有「無中生有」之意，但 invent 與 create 是指創造出「原本不存在的事物」，而 discover 則是發現「原本早已存在，但不為人知的事物」。

例 ● Who **invented** the steam train?
誰發明蒸汽火車？（蒸汽火車原本不存在，有人發明了它）

● Julie **created** a hyper little monster by giving her son too much candy.
茱莉給兒子吃太多糖而創造出一個超級好動的小怪物。

● Alexander Fleming accidentally **discovered** the antibiotic substance penicillin from fungus.
亞歷山大佛萊明意外從黴菌中發現抗生物質盤尼西林。
（盤尼西林本來就存在，後來被人發現）

Vocabulary Bank

1) **demand** [dɪˋmænd] (v./n.) 要求，請求
The union is demanding higher pay for workers.

2) **canvas** [ˋkænvəs] (n.) 油畫布，帆布
The boat's sail is made of canvas.

3) **creativity** [ˌkrieˋtɪvətɪ] (n.) 創造力
(a.) creative [kriˋetɪv] 有創意的
The band's creativity is what gained them so many fans.

4) **communist** [ˋkɑmjuˌnɪst] (a./n.) 共產黨的；共產黨員，共產主義者
(n.) communism [ˋkɑmjuˌnɪzəm] 共產主義
There are very few communist countries left in the world.

5) **surpass** [səˋpæs] (v.) 勝過，優於
The amount of rainfall this month has surpassed last year's record.

6) **significance** [sɪgˋnɪfəkəns] (n.) 重要性，重要
(a.) significant [sɪgˋnɪfəkənt]
The significance of the government's report cannot be underestimated.

7) **stylish** [ˋstaɪlɪʃ] (a.) 時髦的，流行的
That shop sells stylish clothing and accessories.

補充字彙

8) **embroider** [ɪmˋbrɔɪdə] (v.) 繡花，刺繡
The dress was embroidered with colorful flowers.

9) **flared** [flɛrd] (a.) 喇叭形的
(v.) flare [flɛr]
Dana likes to wear shirts with flared sleeves.

10) **capitalistic** [ˌkæpətəˋlɪstɪk]
(a.) 資本主義的
(n.) capitalism [ˋkæpətəˌlɪzəm]
The financial crisis has caused people to question the capitalistic system.

11) **decadence** [ˋdɛkədəns] (n.) 衰微，墮落
The movie highlights the decadence of the 1980s.

12) **coveted** [ˋkʌvɪtɪd] (a.) 夢寐以求的
The coveted prize is rarely awarded.

13) **accentuate** [ækˋsɛntʃuˌet] (v.) 凸顯，襯托
The color of your dress really accentuates your eyes.

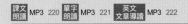

課文朗讀 MP3 220　單字朗讀 MP3 221　英文文章導讀 MP3 222

As young people continued to rebel and [1]**demand** more freedom of expression during the 60s, jeans acted as the [2]**canvas** for their [3]**creativity**. New [8]**embroidered**, painted and dyed jeans were designed to match the current styles of clothing. Bell bottom jeans ([9]**flared** at the bottom) and hip-huggers (low-waisted) became hugely popular when the famous singers Sonny and Cher wore them on TV. Jeans were viewed as an important part of the hippie counterculture.

Jeans gained popularity overseas. In the 70s, jeans represented [10]**capitalistic** [11]**decadence** in [4]**communist** countries such as China and Russia. They were sold at high prices on the black market and were highly prized for decades. By the late 80s, jeans became common around the world and countries began making their own labels.

Since the late 90s, jeans have ©taken their place in the world of high fashion. Top designers such as Donna Karan, Versace and DKNY turned high priced, high-quality jeans into [12]**coveted** items among brand worshipers. The average price for a pair now ranges from fifteen dollars to three hundred. Today, jeans can be found to fit every size and shape and are no longer made only of denim, but from an array of fabrics. A woman searches for that "perfect pair" of jeans to [13]**accentuate** the qualities of

her figure and display her individual style. [5)]**Surpassing** even the "little black dress" in [6)]**significance**, the perfect pair of jeans is now the basis of the modern wardrobe

30 and an expression of a relaxed, yet [7)]**stylish** lifestyle.

中 Translation

六〇年代，年輕人繼續反叛且要求更多表達自由，牛仔褲成為他們發揮創意的畫布。新的刺繡、繪畫和染色的牛仔褲應運而生，用來搭配當時的衣著風格。拜知名歌手珊妮和雪兒在電視上穿著之賜，喇叭褲（褲腳呈喇叭型展開）和低腰褲（腰線較低）大受歡迎。牛仔褲被視為嬉皮反文化的重要元素。

牛仔褲在海外日益風行。七〇年代，牛仔褲在中、俄等共產國家代表著資本主義的腐敗，在黑市以高價販售，價格高昂不下有數十年之久。到八〇年代晚期，牛仔褲已遍及世界各地，各國也開始發展自己的品牌。

自九〇年代晚期開始，牛仔褲便在高級時尚圈占有一席之地。唐娜凱倫、凡賽斯及DKNY 等頂尖設計師將高價、高品質的牛仔褲變成崇尚名牌者夢寐以求的商品。現在一條牛仔褲的平均售價從十五美元到三百美元不等。現有合適各種尺寸和體型穿著的牛仔褲，原料也不再限於丹寧布，而是取材於各式各樣布料。女性尋找「完美」的牛仔褲來凸顯自己的身材特色及展現個人風格。完美牛仔褲的重要性甚至超越「黑色小洋裝」，現已成為摩登服飾的基本品，也表達出一種隨意但時髦的生活風格。

Grammar Master

與 的用法

- take place→ 發生；舉行
- take one's place→ 取得自己的席位

在文中，take one's place 引申為牛仔褲在時尚界裡儼然「佔有一席之地」。值得注意的是，在句子中當 take sb's place 的人稱代名詞 與主詞不一致時，則表示「取代某人」。

例 ● When will the wedding ?
婚禮何時舉行？

● The actors on the set.
演員在拍片現場就定位了。

● No one could ever my mother's .
沒有人可以取代我媽媽的地位。

Mini Quiz 閱讀測驗

❶ According to the article, when did jeans first become a must-have among young people?
(A) during the Gold Rush
(B) after James Dean wore them in a movie
(C) when they gained popularity overseas
(D) when they took their place in the world of high fashion

❷ The conference began after everyone _____.
(A) took its place
(B) took the place of theirs
(C) took place
(D) took their places

❸ Thomas Edison is most famous for _____ the light bulb.
(A) inventing
(B) discovering
(C) producing
(D) selling

閱讀測驗解答 ❶ (B) ❷ (D) ❸ (A)

Vocabulary Bank

1) **heel** [hil] (n.) 鞋跟，高跟鞋（多為複數形）
The heels on her shoes are really high.

2) **elegant** [ˋɛləgənt] (a.) 優雅的，漂亮的
The woman is known for her elegant fashion sense.

3) **flatter** [ˋflætɚ] (v.) 讓…更好看，使出色
Those glasses really flatter your eyes.

4) **versatile** [ˋvɝsətl̩] (a.) 多功能的
He chose this laptop because it's very versatile.

5) **cuff** [kʌf] (v./n.) 捲起褲腳或袖口；褲腳，袖口
You should cuff those pants, so they don't drag on the ground.

6) **loose** [lus] (a./v.) 寬鬆的；鬆開
This shirt is a little too loose in the shoulders.

7) **faded** [ˋfedɪd] (a.) 褪色的
Jessica looks sexy in her faded blue jeans.

補充字彙

8) **puckered** [ˋpʌkɚd] (a.) 有皺褶的，皺起的
(v.) pucker [ˋpʌkɚ] 有皺褶，皺起
The blouse was made from a puckered fabric.

9) **blazer** [ˋblezɚ] (n.)
休閒西裝外套，獵裝
He's required to wear a tie and blazer to work.

Shopping for Jeans
買牛仔褲實用對話

課文朗讀 MP3 223　單字朗讀 MP3 224　英文文章導讀 MP3 225

Dialogue 1

Customer: I'm looking for some jeans to fit this pair of five-inch [1])**heels**.

Salesperson: Why don't you try this skinny boot cut and this [8])**puckered** slim fit.

Customer: I like the way this puckered one fits around the heel. You can still see the shoe.

Salesperson: That's a sexy look. Now try the skinny boot cut.

Customer: Wow! This pair makes my legs look much longer!

> **對話一**
> 顧　客：我想找件牛仔褲來搭這雙五吋高跟鞋。
> 售貨員：何不試這件合身靴型褲，還有這件抓皺的修身褲？
> 顧　客：我喜歡這件抓皺的褲子蓋住鞋跟周圍的感覺，還看得到鞋子。
> 售貨員：這樣很性感。現在來試試合身靴型褲。
> 顧　客：哇！這件讓我的腿看起來長多了！

Dialogue 2

Customer: Do you have a boot-cut jean that doesn't flare too much?

Salesperson: This pair is just wide enough for a boot, but still looks [2])**elegant**.

Customer: I think the waist is too low for my taste.

Salesperson: This pair may suit you better then; it's got a high waist with a slight boot cut.

Customer: Now this is a pair I can wear to work with my [9])**blazer**.

> **對話二**
> 顧　客：你們有喇叭沒那麼大的靴型褲嗎？
> 售貨員：這件剛好夠寬可以蓋住靴子，不過看起來還是很優雅。
> 顧　客：以我的品味看來，我覺得這件太低腰了。
> 售貨員：那這件可能會比較適合你，高腰又有一點點靴型剪裁。
> 顧　客：這是條我可以配西裝外套穿去上班的牛仔褲了。

Dialogue 3

Customer: Do you have any jeans that are form-fitting?

Salesperson: This pair is made with denim, cotton and Lycra.

Customer: Wow! These stretch really well.

Salesperson: They [3)]**flatter** any figure and are the most comfortable pair we have.

Customer: And they look more formal than denim. These make me look slimmer!

Salesperson: They're really durable too. We call them the perfect pair of jeans.

對話三
顧　客：你們有緊身牛仔褲嗎？
售貨員：這件是丹寧、棉和萊卡布料製成的。
顧　客：哇！彈性真好。
售貨員：它適合任何身形，而且是我們最舒服的一件。
顧　客：而且看起來比丹寧褲正式，讓我看起來比較苗條！
售貨員：它還很耐穿。我們都稱它是最完美的牛仔褲。

Dialogue 4

Customer: What pair do you recommend for traveling to a tropical island?

Salesperson: You'll want something that's [4)]**versatile** yet comfortable. This button-fly 501 boyfriend cut in white is ideal.

Customer: Cute!

Salesperson: Wear it [5)]**cuffed** or rolled for walking on the beach. It's a [6)]**loose** fit with a straight leg.

Customer: I think I'll take a white pair and a [7)]**faded** blue pair.

對話四
顧　客：去熱帶島嶼旅行，你會推薦哪件褲子？
售貨員：你應該會想要一件多功能又舒適的褲子。這件 501 排扣設計的男孩風白色寬版褲很適合。
顧　客：太好了！
售貨員：在海邊散步時可以把褲管反摺或捲起來。這件是寬版的直筒褲。
顧　客：我想買一條白色和一條褪色藍的。

Language Guide

想買牛仔褲，這樣說就對了……

I'd like to buy a pair of
樣式 / 顏色 褲款.

vintage/old-fashioned 復古的

distressed/destroyed 破破爛爛的，有破洞的

dark/light wash 深 / 淺刷色

stonewashed 石洗

indigo 靛藍色

beige 米黃色，灰棕色

sheen 帶有光澤感的

褲款
low/mid/high waist jeans 低 / 中 / 高腰褲
依腰的位置不同來做區分，是牛仔褲最基本的分類，低腰褲也稱 hip huggers。

straight (leg) jeans 直筒褲
褲筒上下一樣寬，是最受歡迎的經典褲款。

bell bottom/flared jeans 喇叭褲
褲子下襬呈喇叭形狀展開，能修飾腿型。

boot-cut jeans 靴型褲
靴型褲就是所謂的小喇叭褲，大腿部位合身，膝蓋以下有略為開展的弧度，之所以被稱為靴型褲，是因為它微微開展的弧度剛好可以蓋住鞋子。

boy cut/boyfriend jeans 男孩風寬版褲
褲子的版型較寬，就像女生穿男朋友褲子般，故得名。

cuff jeans 反摺褲
褲筒寬度特別設計，讓反摺後的褲腳不會往上縮，保持自然平直。

ankle jeans 九分褲
長度到腳踝左右的褲款。

baggy jeans 垮褲
寬大鬆散的褲筒，是許多年輕人喜歡的款式。

skinny/slim fit jeans 合身褲
因褲子超合身，腿部纖細且高挑的女生穿起來會更加修長。

legging jeans 緊身牛仔褲
適合纖瘦的人穿或是當內搭褲。

carpenter jeans 木匠褲
顧名思義是做給木匠穿的，所以褲型寬鬆且大腿側邊多設計有大口袋。

loose jeans 寬版褲
腰合身，但褲管鬆的褲子

jean shorts 牛仔短褲

Vocabulary Bank

1) **contrast** [ˈkɑntræst] (n.) 對比
(phr.) in contrast to/with… 與…形成對比
In contrast with his brother, Robert is quite tall.

2) **conviction** [kənˈvɪkʃən] (n.) 信念，信仰
What are your religious convictions?

3) **refreshing** [rɪˈfrɛʃɪŋ] (a.) 提神的，神清氣爽的
There's nothing like a refreshing glass of lemonade on a hot day.

4) **reintegrate** [riˈɪntɪˌgret] (v.) 重新融入
It's difficult for prisoners to reintegrate into society.

5) **networking** [ˈnɛt.wɜkɪŋ] (n.) 建立關係網絡，social networking site 即「社群網站」
(n./v.) network [ˈnɛt.wɜk] 關係網絡，社群；建立、經營人脈
Megan found her job through networking.

6) **crop** [krɑp] (n.) 農作物，一次收穫（量）
Many farmers lost their crops in the flood.

7) **aspect** [ˈæspɛkt] (n.) 方面，觀點
We must consider the various aspects of the problem.

進階字彙

8) **coin** [kɔɪn] (v.) 創造（新詞彙、說法）
New words are being coined all the time.

9) **underage** [ˌʌndəˈedʒ] (a.) 未成年的
The bar was fined for serving alcohol to underage drinkers.

10) **(out) on the town** [ɑn ðə taʊn] (phr.)
到鬧區酒吧等娛樂場所玩
Did you enjoy your night on the town?

11) **veganism** [ˈvigəˌnɪzəm] (n.) 純素主義
（只吃植物產品，也只使用非動物製品）
(n./a.) vegan [ˈvigən] 嚴守素食主義者／的
(a./n.) vegetarian [ˌvɛdʒəˈtɛrɪən] 素菜的，素食的／者
Carla is thinking of becoming a vegan.

口語補充

12) **pesky** [ˈpɛskɪ] (a.) 麻煩的，討厭的
These pesky mosquitoes are driving me crazy!

What's In with American Teens?

美國青少年潮流

課文朗讀 MP3 226　單字朗讀 MP3 227　英文文章導讀 MP3 228

Trends constantly change. Looking back on old photos, even the trendiest people think to themselves, "What was I thinking?" And nobody is more aware of changing trends than teenagers, especially American ones, who [8]**coined** the
5　phrase, "That's so five minutes ago." To find out what's hip, let's take a look at what's in with American teens these days.

Although [9]**underage** Americans can't legally enjoy alcoholic beverages, that doesn't mean they can't pretend to! Dressing up and going out [10]**on the town** wouldn't

be complete without a trip to the bar for some mocktails. Mocktails, as the name suggests, are cocktails without alcohol. Drinking virgin daiquiris, piña coladas and mojitos makes teens feel like adults, but without any of the [12)]**pesky** responsibility.

Moving from beverages to food, [11)]**veganism** is another trend becoming popular with American teens. In [1)]**contrast** to committed [11)]**vegans** who choose to give up animal products based on personal [2)]**convictions**, these trendy teens simply want to try something new. Giving up hamburgers may be hard at first, but most find that switching to salads and soy milk can be [3)]**refreshing**. While some may decide to remain vegans, most eventually [4)]**reintegrate** into carnivore society.

More trends can be seen in [G] how young Americans spend their time. Many teens use their Facebook accounts to play FarmVille, the most popular game on this social [5)]**networking** site, with over 82.7 million active users. FarmVille allows players to plant and harvest [6)]**crops**, pick fruit, raise animals, and buy farm equipment and seasonal decorations. The ability to give gifts to friends and visit their farms adds a social [7)]**aspect** to the game.

FarmVille

中 Translation

潮流時時在變。回頭看那些老照片,即便是最趕時髦的人都會想:「那時我到底在想什麼?」而沒有人比青少年更能察覺不斷變化的潮流,特別是創了「那已是五分鐘舊的事了」這句話的美國青少年。要了解什麼正夯,且讓我們看看美國青少年最近流行什麼。

雖然未成年的美國人不能合法暢飲酒精飲料,但並不代表他們不能假裝一下!盛裝去享受夜生活,如果沒上酒吧喝點仿雞尾酒,就不夠圓滿。顧名思義,仿雞尾酒就是不含酒精的雞尾酒。喝不含酒精的戴吉利、鳳梨可樂達和墨西多會讓青少年覺得自己像大人,但又沒有任何討人厭的責任。

從飲料講到食物,吃純素是另一個在美國青少年間日益流行的潮流。不同於那些基於個人信念而選擇捨棄動物類食品的忠誠純素者,這些時髦的青少年只是想嘗試新鮮的玩意兒。放棄漢堡一開始或許很難,但大多數人發現改吃生菜沙拉和豆漿別有一番滋味。雖然有些人可能決定繼續當純素者,多數人最終仍重回肉食社會。

看美國年輕人如何打發時間,可以了解更多潮流。很多青少年用 帳號玩這個社群網站最受歡迎的遊戲「開心農場」,目前使用者超過八千二百七十萬人。開心農場讓玩家種植及收割農作、採收水果、飼養家畜,還有購買農具和季節飾品。送禮物給朋友和造訪朋友的農場,這些功能為這個遊戲增添了社交層面。

G Grammar Master

名詞子句

文中裡的後面所引導的子句便是名詞子句,作為介系詞 的受詞。「名詞子句」顧名思義就是具有名詞的功能,大多會以、、來引導。

● 名詞子句當主詞
  Ben skipped class
  班蹺課讓他的父母大為震驚。

● 名詞子句當主詞補語
  she skipped class茱蒂犯的錯在於她蹺課。

● 名詞子句當動詞的受詞
  Jason was able to go to work when he was so sick
  我真不知道傑森怎麼能病得那麼重還去上班。

● 名詞子句當介系詞的受詞
  what Mary said瑞克沒聽瑪麗說的話。

● 名詞子句當同位語
  what career path he should follow
  該走哪一行是喬治難以解決的難題。

MOCKTAIL COCKTAIL 比一比

mocktail 仿雞尾酒

mock 當形容詞是「假的，模擬的」；cocktail 則為糖、水、果汁、酒調成的飲料。mock + cocktail 形成 mocktail 表示「不含酒精的雞尾酒」，會以 virgin「純粹的，什麼都不加的」這個字來形容，「不摻酒的戴吉利」是 virgin daiquiri，「不摻酒的墨西多」是 virgin Mojito。

接下來，我們一起來看看對話中三種雞尾酒飲料摻酒及不摻酒的作法，順便學學調酒食譜的英文。為了讓大家以後能看懂各家各派食譜的寫法及用字，總編特別從六個不同網站蒐集以下食譜：

Daiquiri

Ingredients:
- 1 1/2 oz light rum
- 3/4 oz lime juice
- 1/4 oz sugar syrup

Steps:
1 Pour the light rum, lime juice and sugar syrup into a shaker with ice cubes
2 Shake well
3 Pour into a chilled cocktail glass.

材料：
- 1 又 1/2 盎司淡味蘭姆酒
- 3/4 盎司萊姆汁
- 1/4 盎司糖漿

步驟：
1 將淡蘭姆酒、萊姆汁、糖漿倒入調酒器，加入冰塊
2 搖勻
3 倒入冰鎮過的雞尾酒杯
http://cocktails.about.com

Virgin Strawberry Daiquiri

Ingredients:
- 2 large strawberries, hulled
- 1/4 cup white sugar
- 1 tbsp lemon juice
- 3/4 cup chilled lemon-lime soda
- 4 ice cubes

Steps:
1 Combine the strawberries, sugar, lemon juice and lemon-lime soda in a blender
2 Add the ice and blend until smooth
3 Pour into a fancy glass to serve

材料：
- 2 個大草莓，把蒂去掉
- 1/4 杯白砂糖
- 1 大匙檸檬汁
- 3/4 杯冰鎮過的檸檬萊姆汽水
- 4 個冰塊

步驟：
1 將草莓、糖、檸檬汁和檸檬萊姆汽水倒入果汁機中混合攪拌
2 加入冰塊攪打至細滑無顆粒
3 倒入漂亮的杯子即可端出
http://allrecipes.com

Piña Colada

Ingredients:
- 3 oz light rum
- 3 tbsp coconut cream
- 3 tbsp crushed pineapple

Steps:
1 Put all ingredients into blender with 2 cups of crushed ice
2 Blend at a high speed for a short length of time
3 Strain into a Collins glass and serve with a straw

材料：
- 3 盎司淡味蘭姆酒
- 3 大匙椰奶
- 3 大匙碎鳳梨果肉

步驟：
1 將全部材料放進果汁機，加入兩杯碎冰
2 以高速攪打一下
3 過濾倒入柯林斯玻璃杯，插上吸管即可端出
http://www.drinksmixer.com

Virgin Piña Colada

Ingredients:
- 4 oz cream of coconut
- 4 oz pineapple juice
- 2 cups ice
- 2 pineapple slices
- 1 maraschino cherry

Steps:
1 Add the cream of coconut, ice, and pineapple juice to the blender
2 Blend until ice is crushed
3 Pour into two 8 ounce glasses
4 Garnish with 2 pineapple slices and a maraschino cherry

材料：
- 4 盎司椰奶
- 4 盎司鳳梨汁
- 2 杯冰
- 2 片鳳梨肉
- 1 顆酒釀櫻桃

步驟：
1 將椰奶、冰、鳳梨汁倒入果汁機
2 攪拌至冰塊打碎
3 倒入容量 8 盎司的玻璃杯。
4 用 2 片鳳梨片、1 顆酒釀櫻桃裝飾
http://www.wikihow.com

Mojito

Ingredients:
- 2-3 oz light rum
- Juice of 1 lime (1 oz)
- 2 tsp sugar
- 2-4 mint sprigs
- soda water

Steps:
1 Muddle the mint and sugar with a splash of soda water in a mixing glass until the sugar dissolves and you smell the mint
2 Squeeze the lime into the glass, add rum and shake with ice
3 Strain over cracked ice in a highball glass
4 Top with soda water, garnish with mint sprig and serve

材料：
- 2 至 3 盎司淡味蘭姆酒
- 一顆萊姆的果汁（一盎司）
- 2 茶匙糖
- 2 至 4 枝薄荷葉
- 蘇打水

步驟：
1 薄荷、糖及小量汽水一起放入攪拌杯輕輕攪拌，直到糖融化，薄荷味散發出來
2 將萊姆汁擠入杯中，加入蘭姆酒及冰塊一起搖勻
3 過濾倒入裝有碎冰的長型玻璃杯
4 淋上汽水，以薄荷葉裝飾即可端出
http://supercocktails.com

Virgin Mojito

Ingredients:
- 1.5 oz of rum (Don't worry, it's not going in your drink — check out step 1.)
- 2 tsp sugar
- 1/2 of one lime, cut into pieces (this is more lime than a normal mojito to make up for the lack of rum)
- 6 large mint leaves
- ice
- soda water

Steps:
1 Give the rum to someone who drinks
2 Put the lime, mint, and sugar in a glass and muddle
3 Fill cup with ice about 3/4 full
4 Top off with soda water
5 Stir with a spoon
6 Garnish with fresh sugar cane if you can get some

材料：
- 1.5 盎司蘭姆酒（別擔心，這不會進到你的飲料裡——看步驟 1。）
- 2 茶匙糖
- 1/2 個萊姆，切成小塊（這個量比一般 mojito 多，以補沒加蘭姆酒之不足）
- 6 片大薄荷葉
- 冰
- 蘇打水

步驟：
1 把蘭姆酒拿給喝酒的人
2 將萊姆、薄荷和糖放進玻璃杯中輕輕地攪拌
3 在杯中裝 3/4 杯滿的冰塊
4 倒入蘇打水至杯滿為止
5 用湯匙攪拌
6 如果找得到新鮮甘蔗，就拿來裝飾
http://www.slashfood.com

KE$HA

課文朗讀 MP3 229　單字朗讀 MP3 230　英文文章導讀 MP3 231

　　While enjoying these trendy activities, American teens can be found listening to the latest pop music by artists like Lady Gaga, Ke$ha and Justin Bieber. Lady Gaga's bizarre clothing, [12)]**erratic** [1)]**behavior** and electronic dance music drive
5　people wild, while party girl Ke$ha, with her [2)]**carefree** [3)]**attitude** and half-spoken, half-sung lyrics brings a smile to everyone's face. [G] In contrast, 16-year-old Canadian Justin Bieber, who was discovered on YouTube, brings his [4)]**listeners** back to a time of [5)]**innocent** first love, [6)]**seducing**
10　listeners with his [7)]**earnest** music and open smile.

Justin Bieber

Lady Gaga

183

V Vocabulary Bank

1) **behavior** [bɪˋhevjɚ] (n.) 行為，舉止
The prisoner was released early for good behavior.

2) **carefree** [ˋkɛrˏfri] (a.) 輕鬆愉快的，無憂無慮的
Trey misses the carefree days of college.

3) **attitude** [ˋætətjud] (n.) 態度，意見
I try to start each day with a positive attitude.

4) **listener** [ˋlɪsənɚ] (n.) 聽眾，傾聽者
比較：listener 指（單一）聽眾；audience 為集合名詞，泛指（整群）聽、觀眾，讀者
The DJ takes requests from listeners on his show.

5) **innocent** [ˋɪnəsənt] (a.) 純真的，無辜的，無罪的
The soldiers were accused of murdering innocent children.

6) **seduce** [sɪˋdus] (v.) 吸引，引誘
The audience was seduced by the singer's beautiful voice.

7) **earnest** [ˋɝnɪst] (a.) 誠摯的
Kevin is an earnest and hardworking young man.

8) **fascination** [ˏfæsəˋneʃən] (n.) 著迷，強烈興趣
Mark's fascination with airplanes led him to become a pilot.

9) **broom** [brʊm] (n.) 長柄刷，掃帚
The old man swept the floor with a broom.

10) **grab** [græb] (v.) 拿，抓
The woman screamed when the mugger grabbed her purse.

11) **last** [læst] (v.) 持久，維持
How long will these batteries last?

進階字彙

12) **erratic** [ɪˋrætɪk] (a.) 古怪的，反常的
The man was stopped by the police for erratic driving.

口語補充

13) **take off** [tek ɔf] (phr.) 快速受到歡迎，突然蔚為風潮，一夕成名
The star's career took off after he was nominated for an Oscar.

A final trend, one that comes back every four years, is the [8)]**fascination** with Olympic sports. Vancouver's recent
15 Winter Olympic Games left young Americans once again excited about skiing, snowboarding and ice hockey. One new winter sports trend to really [13)]**take off** this time around is curling, which is like a colder version of shuffleboard. This game
20 involves two teams of four players and is played on a sheet of ice. [9)]**Brooms** are used to curve the path of stones that team members slide towards a target at the far end of the ice. Across America, teens are [10)]**grabbing** their brooms and picking up this trendy winter sport.

25 While these trends may be hot right now, the only guarantee is that they won't [11)]**last** forever. That's why the important thing is being trendy—not the trends themselves. For American teens, and teens
30 everywhere, being trendy never goes out of style!

ice hockey

snowboarding

shuffleboard

中 Translation

享受這些時髦的活動時，美國青少年也會聆聽諸如女神卡卡、惡女凱莎和賈斯汀比伯等藝人最新的流行音樂。女神卡卡的奇裝異服、古怪行徑和電子舞曲讓人們瘋狂，跑趴女孩惡女凱莎無憂無慮的態度和半說半唱的歌詞令人莞爾。相形之下，在 YouTube 被發掘的十六歲加拿大男孩賈斯汀比伯則將聽眾帶回純真的初戀時光，以他誠摯的音樂和開朗的笑容吸引眾生。

最後一項潮流——每四年就會捲土重來——是對奧運的狂熱。最近的溫哥華冬季奧運讓美國年輕人重燃對滑雪、滑雪板和冰上曲棍球的熱情。這次真正走紅的冬季運動新潮流是冰壺，它就像推圓盤遊戲的寒冷版。對戰雙方各派四位選手，在一片冰上競賽。選手用刷子刷出路徑來引導石壺前進，而石壺則是由隊友朝遠端的標靶向前推擲。在全美各地，青少年紛紛抓起長柄刷，玩起這種時髦的冬季運動。

雖然這些潮流現在或許正夯，但唯一可以保證的是，不會永遠這麼夯。所以，跟上潮流才是重點——而非潮流本身。對美國青少年和世界各地的青少年來說，只要跟上潮流就永遠不褪流行。

Language Guide

curling 冰壺比賽

冰壺運動 (curling) 源於十六世紀的蘇格蘭，一九二四年成為奧林匹克觀摩項目，一九八八年成為奧林匹克正式項目。奧運冰壺運動一場共有十局 (end)，場上兩隊各五名球員（一次派四名上場），每個球員有兩球的機會輪流從發球架 (hack) 滑出花崗石壺（curling stone 或稱 rock），朝冰壺場 (curling sheet) 另一端的靶 (house) 滑行，石壺推出之後，兩名球員會持冰壺刷 (curling broom) 為石壺開道，但抵達彼端的欄線 (hog line) 就要讓石壺自由滑行，直到在靶內停下來為止（停在靶外不計分），愈靠近靶心（button 或稱 tee）得分愈高，十局總分較高的一隊獲勝。

球員將手中的石壺滑出之後，除了其他石壺之外，石壺不可以碰到任何東西，包含冰壺刷及邊線 (outline)。球員可藉由撞擊將對手的石壺撞離靶心，並透過控制石壺停留的位置阻擋對手的石壺前進至有利位置，或避免對手將本隊已在靶中的石壺撞開。

文中提到類似的 shuffleboard（推圓盤比賽）則是在平滑地板上進行，是用稱為 cue 的棒子推稱為 puck 的圓盤進入對面的計分區中。

Grammar Master

連接副詞

in/by contrast「與……相比」是連接副詞，即具有連接功能的副詞。常見的連接副詞有 as a result、therefore、however、in addition、on the contrary 等等。連接副詞常置於句首，後面接一個逗號。

例 Jimmy stayed up late last night. **As a result,** he missed the bus to school this morning.
吉米昨晚熬夜。結果，他今早錯過了上學的校車。

連接副詞也可以連接兩個獨立的句子，但要注意標點符號的用法：連接副詞置於兩個子句當中，與前子句間會有分號，其後再加上逗號。

例 The economy hasn't improved in the past two years; **on the contrary,** it's gotten worse.
過去這兩年經濟非但沒有好轉，相反地，情況愈來愈糟了。

Mini Quiz 閱讀測驗

1 According to the article, which of the following teen trends is most likely appear again in the future?
(A) Listening to Justin Bieber
(B) Drinking mocktails
(C) Interest in Olympic sports
(D) Veganism

（C）❶ 答案與解析見網路

Vocabulary Bank

1) **peer** [pɪr] (n.) 同輩，同儕
   It's hard for teens to resist peer pressure.

2) **embrace** [ɪm`bres] (v.) 接受，採納
   We need a leader who is willing to embrace new ideas.

3) **urban** [`ɜbən] (a.) 都市的，居住在城市的
   Urban areas are usually more dangerous than rural areas.

4) **announce** [ə`naʊns] (v.) 宣布，發佈
   The winners will be announced at the end of the show.

5) **reference** [`rɛfərəns] (n.) 提及，暗示，影射
   (v.) refer [rɪ`fɝ] 論及…，提及…
   The movie is full of pop culture references.

6) **lens** [lɛnz] (n.) 鏡片，鏡頭
   Gina scratched one of the lenses when she dropped her glasses.

7) **anonymity** [ˌænə`nɪmətɪ] (n.) 匿名，不被注意的狀態
   The retired star enjoyed a life of anonymity in the small town.

8) **thrift store** [θrɪft stor] (n.) 二手商店，
   (n.) thrift 節儉
   You can find lots of bargains at that thrift store.

9) **rip** [rɪp] (v.) 撕裂，扯破
   The boy fell and ripped his trousers.

進階字彙

10) **chic** [ʃik] (a./n.) 時髦（的）
    Have you seen Carla's chic new haircut?

11) **throwback** [`θro͵bæk] (n.) 復舊，回溯
    The singer's new album is a throwback to '60s soul music.

12) **media-saturated** [`midiə `sætʃə͵retɪd] (a.) 被媒體包圍的
    (v.) saturate 充滿，飽和
    It's difficult to avoid advertising in our media-saturated society.

13) **hobo** [`hobo] (n.) 遊民，流浪者
    The hobo travels from town to town on freight trains.

14) **dreadlocks** [`drɛd͵lɑks] (n.) 雷鬼頭（長而細的髮串，源自牙買加）
    Bob Marley wore his hair in dreadlocks.

口語補充

15) **nerd** [nɝd] (n.) 書呆子，笨蛋
    It's hard to believe that Jason was a nerd in high school.

美國青少年
Hip and Chic [10)]

潮服

課文朗讀 MP3 232　單字朗讀 MP3 233　英文文章導讀 MP3 234

    While clothes may not make the man, these days they definitely do make the teen. For American teens today, looking hip can make the difference between being "in" and "out" among their [1)]**peers**. Here are a few fashion trends that
5　young Americans are currently [2)]**embracing**.

    Scarves were originally intended to keep wearers' necks warm in winter, but now teens can be seen wearing them year-round. Whether it's a [11)]**throwback** to the glamorous Hollywood look of the 1920s or a nod to the bundled up
10　[3)]**urban** chic look, scarves of all colors and patterns are appearing around the necks of teens across the country. A scarf added to a nice T-shirt or light sweater [4)]**announces** that a teen knows what looks good.

    A second [5)]**reference** to the Hollywood lamour
15　of the past is the return of oversized glasses, whether sunglasses or corrective [6)]**lenses**. Giant black sunglasses

give today's [12] **media-saturated** teens an air
of [7] **anonymity**, while at the same time crying
out, "Look! I'm a star." And while only [15] **nerds**

20   wore thick black frames in the past, hip teens
today know that these glasses are very much in style.

    [G] In contrast to the above trends, a third fashion trend
is making teens look like homeless people. To achieve this "[13]
hobo chic" look, teens are buying their clothes in [8] **thrift stores**,

25   wearing [9] **ripped** jeans, loose sweaters and leather boots, and
even wearing their hair in [14] **dreadlocks**. While hobo chic may
be cheap, it's not always popular with teens' parents.

中 Translation

服裝或許沒辦法成就一個人，但這年頭服裝絕對可以成就青少年。對當今美國青少年來說，外表時髦與否就是在同儕間判定誰「流行」、誰「落伍」的標準。下面是美國年輕人目前奉為圭臬的一些流行趨勢。

圍巾原本的功用是在冬天保持脖子溫暖，但現在可以看到一年到頭都披著圍巾的青少年。不管是彷一九二〇年代迷人好萊塢風格的復古款，或是崇尚多層次穿搭的都會流行風，各色各樣的圍巾正出現在全美各地青少年的脖子上。一件好看的T恤或薄毛衣加上一條圍巾，等於宣布這個青少年知道什麼叫好看。

第二種沿襲好萊塢昔日風情的元素是，超大尺寸的眼鏡回來了，不論太陽眼鏡或矯正眼鏡皆然。超大黑色墨鏡帶給現今成天浸淫於媒體的青少年一種保持低調的氛圍，同時又大聲宣告：「看！我是明星。」而儘管以往只有書呆子會戴厚重黑色鏡框，但今日時髦的青少年也知道這種眼鏡很夯。

有別於上述趨勢，第三種時尚趨勢要讓青少年看來像無家可歸的流浪漢。為了達成這種「遊民風」，青少年到二手店買衣服，穿破爛的牛仔褲、鬆垮的毛衣和皮靴，甚至把頭髮編成雷鬼頭。遊民風或許不用花什麼錢，但青少年父母不見得喜愛。

名人談衣著

古諺有云：「佛要金裝，人要衣裝」，「衣冠禽獸」卻也所在多有。就像本文第一句引用古羅馬時的一句諺語 The clothes make the man.「人要衣裝」（拉丁原文為：Vestis virum reddit），但其實有不少人持相反意見。一起來看看大文豪、時尚達人及絕頂聰明的人，對衣著有哪些見解吧。

Language Guide

bundled up 混搭風，多層次穿搭

bundle up 原本是指天冷穿衣時多捆一條圍巾、戴一頂帽子、裹一層大衣……把人包得密不透風，因為看起來披披掛掛、層層疊疊，被稱做「多層次穿搭」。這種保暖的穿衣方式成為一種時尚之後，就變成利用大量配件、相異質感素材的混搭流行風格。

nerd 的刻板形象

描寫美國青少年的電影中都會有 nerd，這種男孩會戴粗框大眼鏡（因為被欺負時眼鏡經常折斷，有時鏡架還會用膠帶黏著固定）、戴牙套 (braces)、褲頭拉得老高，更慘一點的還滿臉青春痘（acne）。他們常被描繪成不擅長體能活動、死讀書、喜歡下棋的社交障礙者，一般都是白種或亞裔。

nerd 和另一個字眼 geek [gik] 所描述的人造型很像，但 geek 更強調他們只顧著鑽研科學、電腦、科技的生活方式。

Grammar Master

in contrast to 與……相比

in contrast to 譯為「與……相比」、「與……相反」，用來表示與前文或前者相反，是轉折語 (transition term) 的一種，如果轉折語使用得當，可以讓文章變得更通順。

句型 In contrast to + N. , S. + V....（注意介系詞 to 之後接的是名詞或名詞片語，而非子句）或 In contrast, S. + V. ...

例 **In contrast to** Malaysia, Singapore is much more stable.

= **In contrast,** Singapore much more stable than Malaysia.
和馬來西亞相較之下，新加坡要來得穩定的多。

Clothes make the man.
Naked people have little or no influence on society.
~Mark Twain

人要衣裝。裸體的人對社會幾乎毫無影響力。

—馬克吐溫

The finest clothing made is a person's skin, but, of course, society demands something more than this.
~Mark Twain

做得最好的服裝是人的皮膚，但是，當然啦，社會的要求不僅如此。

—馬克吐溫

bundled up

nerd

Be careless in your dress if you will, but keep a tidy soul.
~Mark Twain

衣服可以隨便穿，只要你高興就好，但靈魂一定要保持整潔。

—馬克吐溫

Dress is at all times a frivolous distinction, and excessive solicitude about it often destroys its own aim.
~Jane Austen

衣服總是大同小異，過度在意衣著常會適得其反。
一珍奧斯汀

Any man may be in good spirits and good temper when he's well dressed. There ain't much credit in that. ~Charles Dickens

衣冠楚楚的人或許興高采烈、心情愉快，但不見得是好事。
一查爾斯狄更斯

It's always the badly dressed people who are the most interesting.
~Jean Paul Gaultier

最有趣的人總是穿得很糟。
一尚保羅高堤耶

Adornment is never anything except a reflection of the heart.
~Gabrielle "Coco" Chanel

裝飾打扮只不過是內心狀態的投射。
一可可香奈兒

If most of us are ashamed of shabby clothes and shoddy furniture, let us be more ashamed of shabby ideas and shoddy philosophies.... It would be a sad situation if the wrapper were better than the meat wrapped inside it.
~Albert Einstein

倘若大多數人因為衣著寒酸、家具簡陋而感到羞恥，那就更該為思想卑鄙、人生觀低劣而感到羞恥……。金玉其外、敗絮其中是很悲哀的事。
一愛因斯坦

V Vocabulary Bank

1) **ridiculous** [rɪˋdɪkjələs] (a.) 可笑的，荒謬的
Ted looks ridiculous in that green hat.

2) **glance** [glæns] (n./v.) 一瞥
A glance at his watch told him he was late.

3) **lounge** [laʊndʒ] (v./n.)（懶洋洋地）倚靠
（躺），休息室
The couple spent the evening lounging on the couch and watching TV.

4) **worshipper** [ˋwɜʃɪpɚ] (n.) 禮拜者，也可寫作 worshiper
(v.) worship [ˋwɜʃɪp] 禮拜，敬仰
The worshippers walked quietly into the church.

5) **depict** [dɪˋpɪkt] (v.) 描寫，描述
The new book depicts the president as a puppet and a liar.

6) **tanner** [ˋtænɚ] (n.) 仿曬劑、仿曬用品，sunless tanner 即「不需要日曬即可變成古銅肌膚的用品」
(v./n.) tan [tæn] 曬成古銅色；古銅色
(a.) tanning [ˋtænɪŋ] 曬成古銅色的
Can you recommend a good tanner for my skin type?

7) **momentum** [moˋmɛntəm] (n.) 氣勢，動力
The politician's campaign is gaining momentum.

8) **stance** [stæns] (n.) 立場，態度
What is the president's stance on abortion?

9) **staple** [ˋstepl̩] (n.) 主要成分，要素
Reality shows are a prime-time staple.

進階字彙

10) **snug** [snʌg] (a.) 舒適的，溫暖的
The baby, safe and snug in his crib, drifted off to sleep.

11) **mania** [ˋmenɪə] (n.) 瘋狂，狂熱
Harry Potter mania intensifies with the release of each new movie.

12) **delve** [dɛlv] (v.) 探究，探索
The documentary delves into the history of World War II.

13) **noteworthy** [ˋnot.wɜðɪ] (a.) 顯著的，值得注意的
The doctor made noteworthy contributions to cancer research.

14) **fleece** [flis] (n.) 刷毛，羊毛
This fleece jacket will keep you warm and dry in any weather.

口語補充

15) **comfy** [ˋkʌmfɪ] (a.) 舒服的，為 comfortable [ˋkʌmfɚtəbl̩] 的簡稱
These new socks are really comfy!

課文朗讀 MP3 235　單字朗讀 MP3 236　英文文章導讀 MP3 237

One of the hottest and most unexpected recent trends is the Snuggie. This blanket ⊙with sleeves may look [1)]**ridiculous** at first [2)]**glance**, but it was one of the most popular gifts for teens this past holiday season. As teens [3)]**lounge on** the sofa
5　wrapped up in their Snuggies, they can **❶ rest assured** that they're not only [10)]**snug** and [15)]**comfy**, but also on the cutting edge of fashion.

Summer may already be here, but vampire [11)]**mania** may limit the number of sun [4)]**worshippers** this year.
10　As teens [12)]delve deeper into the world of vampires—as [5)]**depicted**, for example, in the Twilight movies—they're embracing darker clothing and paler skin. Sunless [6)]**tanners** and [6)]**tanning** salons may be on their way out as pale replaces [6)]**tan**. Bronze may be the color of the gods, but pale is the color
15　of today's fashion-forward teen.

A final [13)]**noteworthy** trend that's been gathering [7)]**momentum** is the anti-fur [8)]**stance** adopted by many teens. While some embrace faux fur in their coats and cold-weather gear, most have **❷ turned their backs on**
20　the entire concept. Fur has been a [9)]**staple** of the fashion world for centuries, but like the petticoat, it may have taken its last walk down the runway.

So put on your scarf, oversized glasses and thrift-store sweater, throw out that old fur coat and wrap yourself up

25 in a soft [14]**fleece** Snuggie. **❸ Take a page from** trendy American teens and prepare to be admired!

中 Translation

近來最火熱也最出人意外的一股風潮是「懶人袖毯」。這種有袖子的毛毯乍看之下或許有些滑稽，但它是上個耶誕假期最受青少年歡迎的禮物之一。當青少年裏著懶人袖毯，懶洋洋地窩在沙發上，他們可以放一百二十個心：他們不僅溫暖舒適，還走在時尚流行尖端。

夏天或許已經來臨，但吸血鬼熱潮可能會大幅減少今年曬太陽的人數。青少年愈深入地探索吸血鬼的世界──例如《暮光之城》系列電影所描繪──他們也就欣然接受更暗沉的服裝和更蒼白的皮膚。隨著蒼白膚色取代古銅色，仿曬乳和日曬膚沙龍可能正逐漸退燒。古銅或許是神明的顏色，但蒼白才是今年崇尚時髦的青少年膚色。

最後一個值得一提、日趨擴大的趨勢是許多青少年採取的反皮草立場。固然有些青少年會接受外套或禦寒衣物中含有人造皮草，但多數人堅拒這整個概念。皮草幾世紀以來一直是時尚世界的必需品，但就像襯裙（編註：petticoat [`pɛtɪ͵kot] 是指西方古代女人綁在腰間撐起裙子的皺褶襯裙，皺褶會依所需求的蓬度增加層次及皺褶多寡）一樣，或許已經登不上伸展台了。

所以，披上你的圍巾，穿戴超大眼鏡和二手店毛衣，扔掉過氣的皮草外套，把自己裏進柔軟的刷毛懶人袖毯，仿效時髦的美國青少年，準備接受誇獎吧！

美國大學生穿印有學校隊徽的 Snuggie 到球場當啦啦隊

© wiki_aaronisnotcool of ShaggyBevo.com

🎓 Grammar Master

with 的不同用法
with 除了有「和」的意思，還可以表示「帶有著……」。
用法： A + with + （形容詞）+ B
例 a rabbit **with** long ears　一隻有長耳朵的兔子
例 a mini-skirt **with** exquisite lace
　　一件有精緻蕾絲的迷你裙

🔊 Tongue-tied No More

❶ rest assured 放心
A: We're really counting on you to seal the deal, Marcus.
　馬可仕，我們要拿下那筆生意全要靠你了。
B: Rest assured—I'll get the job done.
　放心——我會搞定的。

❷ turn one's back on 放棄，拋棄
turn one's back on sb./sth. 可以表示字面上的意思「轉身背對」，也可如同課文中引申為「背棄」。另一個相似的片語是 turn one's nose up at... ，則是表示「拒絕……，看輕……」的意思。
A: Did you hear? Robert ran off with his secretary.
　你聽說了嗎？羅伯特跟他的祕書私奔了。
B: How could he turn his back on his wife and kids like that?
　他怎麼可以就這樣拋妻棄子？

❸ take a page from (one's book)
效法，模仿
字面上是「從別人的書上照抄一頁」，引申為「模仿他人的行為或作法」，也可以說 take a page/leaf out of one's book。
A: Wow, the living room looks really nice!
　哇，客廳好漂亮！
B: Thanks, I took a page from Mom's book and had it decorated.
　謝了，我是學媽媽的方法，然後請人來裝潢。

📝 Mini Quiz 閱讀測驗

❶ ___ What does the article say about fur?
　(A) It's quite popular, like the petticoat.
　(B) It's been used sparingly in fashion for centuries.
　(C) It is no longer allowed on the runway.
　(D) It may be on its way out.

❷ ___ What's your _____ on dating coworkers?
　(A) approach　(B) stance
　(C) location　(D) reference

答案測驗閱讀 ❶ (D) ❷ (B) ❸ (C)

Vocabulary Bank

1) **necessity** [nə`sɛsətɪ] (n.) 必要性，必需品
The company will hire new staff when the necessity arises.

2) **invention** [ɪn`vɛnʃən] (n.) 發明，創造
(n.) inventor [ɪn`vɛntə] 發明家
The kite is a Chinese invention.

3) **blunder** [`blʌndə] (n.) 大錯，愚蠢的錯誤；犯（大）錯
The new tax was a major political blunder.

4) **compile** [kəm`paɪl] (v.) 彙整，編輯
Steven is busy compiling information for his presentation.

5) **notorious** [no`torɪəs] (a.) 惡名昭彰的
Al Capone was Chicago's most notorious gangster.

6) **pesticide** [`pɛstɪ.saɪd] (n.) 殺蟲劑
The farmer sprayed pesticide on his crops.

7) **brittle** [`brɪt]] (a.) 易碎的，脆的
Your bones become brittle as you age.

8) **prey** [pre] (n.) 獵物，被捕食的動物
Snakes swallow their prey whole.

9) **brink** [brɪŋk] (n.) （懸崖、危險、絕種等的）邊緣
The two countries are on the brink of war.

10) **alternative** [ɔl`tɜnətɪv] (n.) 選擇，替代方案
What are the alternatives to this treatment?

進階字彙

11) **mosquito** [mə`skito] (n.) 蚊子
Malaria is transmitted by mosquitoes.

12) **neurological** [.nurə`lɑdʒɪkəl] (a.) 神經（學）的
(n.) neurology [nu`rɑlədʒɪ] 神經醫學
(n.) neurologist [nu`rɑlədʒɪst] 神經學家
Exposure to lead can cause neurological damage.

13) **decompose** [.dikəm`poz] (v.) 分解，腐爛
The dead bodies decomposed in the heat.

The 50 Worst Inventions

50 大最爛發明

DANGEROUS IDEAS

課文朗讀 MP3 238　單字朗讀 MP3 239　英文文章導讀 MP3 240

　　¹⁾Necessity is the mother of invention, and great **²⁾inventors** like Leonardo Da Vinci, Thomas Edison and Nikola Tesla have all made the world better through their innovative inventions. ⓖNot every invention, however, is

5　necessary, and sometimes they can be a huge mistake. *Time* magazine examined some of these **³⁾blunders** and **⁴⁾compiled** a list of the 50 worst inventions of history. Let's take a look at a few of the most **⁵⁾notorious**.

　　One of the world's worst inventions seemed wonderful

10　at first. The chemical **⁶⁾pesticide** DDT was discovered in 1873 and effectively used against **¹¹⁾mosquitoes** from 1942 to 1972. After over a billion pounds of the chemical was pumped into the environment, the U.S. government discovered that DDT leads to **¹²⁾neurological** and fertility

15　problems in humans, and causes birds to lay **⁷⁾brittle** eggs. DDT pushed the bald eagle and other birds of **⁸⁾prey** to the **⁹⁾brink** of extinction. This goes to show that inventions should be thoroughly researched before they're put to use.

20　　　Another invention that's harmful to the environment

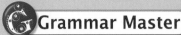
came about as a cheap and convenient [10)]**alternative** to paper bags. The plastic grocery bag came into use in the 1970s, and now accounts for 80% of the bags used in the U.S. While millions of trees have been saved, 500 million

25 plastic bags are thrown away each year. While paper bags [13)]**decompose**, plastic bags take hundreds of years to break down. So what should you do? Bring a reusable bag with you next time you go grocery shopping!

中 Translation

需要為發明之母，達文西、愛迪生和尼古拉特斯拉（編註：發明交流電發電機以及無線電）等偉大發明家全都透過他們創新的發明讓世界變得更好。然而，不是每一件發明都有其必要，有時它們反而可能鑄成大錯。《時代雜誌》檢視了其中一些紕漏，彙整出史上五十大最爛發明的清單。讓我們看看其中最惡名昭彰的幾樣吧。

有一項世界最爛的發明一開始似乎很棒。化學殺蟲劑 DDT（編註：學名為 Dichlorodiphenyltrichloroethane 雙對氯苯基三氯乙烷）發明於一八七三年，在一九四二年至一九七二年間被有效地用來撲滅蚊蟲。在超過十億磅的這種化學藥劑流入環境之後，美國政府發現 DDT 會導致人體神經和生殖系統的病變，也會使鳥類生下易碎的蛋。DDT 將禿鷹及其他食肉鳥類推向絕種的邊緣。可見得，發明應先經徹底研究再付諸使用。

另一項有害環境的發明問世時儼然是購物紙袋既便宜又方便的替代品。塑膠購物袋在一九七〇年代開始使用，現在占了美國百分之八十的袋類使用。雖然拯救了數百萬棵樹木，每年卻有五億的塑膠袋遭到丟棄。紙袋會腐爛，但塑膠袋卻要花上數百載光陰才能分解。所以你該怎麼做呢？下次去超市購物時，隨身帶個可重複使用的袋子吧！

50 大最爛發明節選
除了文章提到的幾種爛發明外，還有哪些「夭壽」發明呢？以下內容節錄自 TIME 網站，欲知完整內容請到 http://www.time.com/time/specials/packages/completelist/

- **Segway** 賽格威電動車
  推出時以「都會區交通革命」為號召造成轟動，但價格實在太高，銷售成績奇差。雷聲大雨點小的爛發明。

- **Clippy Word** 小幫手
  Office 97 加入這個一打開 Word 文件就會在頁面上跳來跳去的小幫手很雞婆，例如只要在文件打入 Dear 就會自動變成「信件模式」——根本沒有人在寫信了啦！真是惹人生氣的爛發明。

- **Agent Orange** 橘劑
  越戰期間美軍為了突破越共的叢林游擊戰，而傾灑大量含有戴奧辛的落葉劑。至今，胡志民市人民血液戴奧辛含量仍是一般人的 200 倍，許多越戰老兵也成癌症受害者。

☯ Grammar Master

however 的用法

1. **然而，但是，相對地**：此用法下，however 可置於句中或句首來連接前後兩個子句，後面務必加上逗點。放在句中時，若前面為完整子句，however 前面需要再加上分號，若是直接插入句中，則前後都是逗號。

   故文中第 4 行的這句也可以寫成
   However, not every invention is necessary.

   例 The first test was quite easy. The second, **however,** was much more difficult.
   = The first test was quite easy; the second, **however,** was much more difficult.
   第一份考卷很容易，但是第二份就難多了。

2. **不管，無論如何（方式）**

   例 At our company, we're allowed to dress **however** we like.
   在我們公司，不管穿什麼衣服上班都可以。

3. **不管，無論如何（程度）**

   例 **However** much we disagree with other people's views, we should still respect them.
   不論我們有多不認同其他人的觀點，我們仍應尊重。

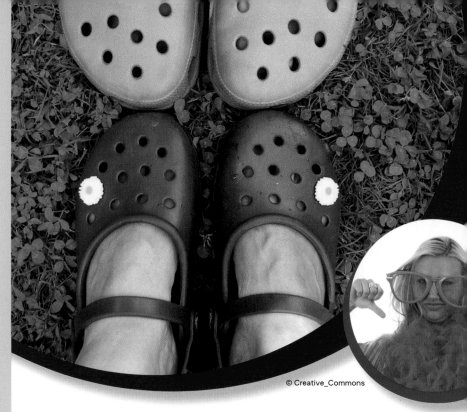

© Creative_Commons

Vocabulary Bank

1) **demand** [dɪˋmænd] (v./n.) 要求
The union is demanding higher pay for workers.

2) **formula** [ˋfɔrmjələ] (n.) 配方，公式，方法
The speaker shared his formula for success with the audience.

3) **fake** [fek] (a.) 偽造的，假冒的
Alex bought a fake Rolex in Hong Kong.

4) **imaginary** [ɪˋmædʒə͵nɛrɪ] (a.) 幻想的，虛構的
(n.) imagination [ɪ͵mædʒə͵neʃən] 想像力，創作力
The movie is set in an imaginary world.

5) **virtual** [ˋvɝtʃʊəl] (a.) 虛擬的
Steve hired a virtual assistant to help him set up his online business.

6) **decoration** [͵dɛkəˋreʃən] (n.) 裝飾品，裝潢
Where did you buy the decorations for your Halloween party?

7) **resource** [rɪˋsors] (n.) 資源
The country's greatest resource is its skilled workforce.

8) **immune** [ɪˋmjun] (a.) 不受影響的，免疫的
Few people are immune to criticism.

9) **plague** [pleg] (n.) 禍害，惱人的人事物
New laws are being passed to fight the plague of identity theft.

10) **suicide** [ˋsuə͵saɪd] (n./v.) 自殺
The man committed suicide by jumping off a bridge.

進階字彙

11) **diehard** [ˋdaɪ͵hɑrd] (n.) 死忠的，頑固的
Only diehard England fans think their team can win the World Cup.

12) **feedback** [ˋfid͵bæk] (n.) 意見，反應
Jim asked for feedback from the audience after his presentation.

口語補充

13) **tacky** [ˋtækɪ] (a.) 俗不可耐的
Did you see the tacky outfit Jill has on?

課文朗讀 MP3 241 　單字朗讀 MP3 242 　英文文章導讀 MP3 243

Sometimes a dumb invention reinvents something that's fine just the way it is. In 1985, executives at Coca Cola decided to replace the original drink with a sweeter version. People initially liked the taste, but [11]**diehard** Coke fans [1]**demanded** a return to their favorite flavor. After a wave of negative [12]**feedback**, the company brought back the original [2]**formula**, rebranding it as Coca-Cola Classic. They'd learned an important lesson: ❶ **if it ain't broke, don't fix it!**

Internet users also face countless new inventions each year, and one of the worst is the Facebook game FarmVille. More than 10% of Americans have played this game, wasting their precious time planting [3]**fake** crops and milking [4]**imaginary** cows. Some even waste real money buying [5]**virtual** houses and [6]**decorations**. ❷As the game grows in popularity, and each user's farm grows, more and more time, effort and money is being spent growing food that can't even be eaten. Talk about wasted [7]**resources**!

The world of fashion hasn't been [8]**immune** to the [9]**plague** of bad inventions either. Crocs, a brand of rubber clog, were introduced to the world in 2002 and **② spread like wildfire**. These [13)]**tacky** shoes are now available in high heels and loafers, and while they may be comfortable, they're uglier than ever. It may be true

25 that Crocs are convenient, durable and easy to clean, but wearing them is a form of fashion [10)]**suicide**. Rubber shoes belong on the beach, at the pool or in the laundry room— never anywhere else.

中 Translation

有時一個愚蠢的發明反而會弄巧成拙。一九八五年，可口可樂的高層決定以較甜的版本來取代原來的飲料。人們一開始滿喜歡這個口味，但死忠的可口可樂粉絲要求恢復他們喜愛的口味。在一片負面聲浪後，公司回歸原有配方，並重新定名為「可口可樂經典口味」。他們學到一個重要的教訓：東西如果沒壞就不要修！

網路族每年也都會面對排山倒海的新發明，而其中最爛的一個便是臉書的開心農場遊戲。超過十分之一的美國人玩過這個遊戲，浪費他們寶貴的時間種植假的農作物，替幻想中的母牛擠奶。有些人甚至浪費真鈔購買虛擬的房舍和裝潢。隨著這款遊戲愈來愈受歡迎，每一名使用者的農場愈開愈大，便有愈來愈多時間、精力和金錢花在種植根本不能吃的糧食上。真是浪費資源！

時尚圈也不能倖免於爛發明的禍害。橡膠鞋品牌卡駱馳在二〇〇二年問世，迅速蔓延走紅。這些俗不可耐的鞋子現在也出了高跟鞋和懶鞋，或許穿來舒適，卻比原來更醜。卡駱馳便利、耐穿和容易清洗或許是事實，但穿這種鞋等於是一種「時尚自殺」。橡膠鞋屬於海灘、泳池畔或洗衣間──絕對不該出現在其他地方。

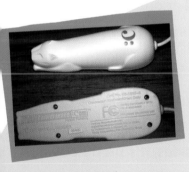

50 大最爛發明節選

● **CueCat 條碼掃描機**
對著條碼掃瞄後即可進入特定網站，但這有比直接用滑鼠選點選網址方便嗎？廠商對此疑問一直無正面回覆。多此一舉的爛發明。

● **Subprime Mortgages 次級房貸**
銀行亂借錢給信用不佳民眾，造成房屋查封潮，成為金融海嘯罪魁禍首。

● **Crinoline 大蓬裙**
維多利亞時期流行搭配馬甲的大蓬裙，直徑可達 2 公尺，讓女性連要走出門口都有困難。比起來高跟鞋在實用功能上壓倒性勝出。

● **Nintendo Virtual Boy 任天堂第五代**
因可產生類似 3D 電影的立體影像，取名 Virtual Boy（虛擬男孩），外型醜陋卻要價不斐，上市僅六個月，為任天堂壽命最短的遊戲機種。

☞ Tongue-tied No More

❶ If it ain't broke, don't fix it.
別弄巧成拙，別多此一舉。

這是一句好用的英文諺語，意思是說「沒壞的東西不要修」。本來東西好好的卻把它拆開來修理，或是將它加油添醋一番，最後反而把東西弄壞了。中文可以翻譯成許多不同的版本，簡單來說就是告誡別人「別沒事找事做」！

A: Why do they keep changing the YouTube layout? It's really annoying!
為什麼他們老是一直更換 YouTube 的使用頁面，真的很煩耶！

B: I know. If it ain't broke, don't fix it!
對啊。真是沒事找事幹！

❷ spread like wildfire
（消息等）迅速傳開

此用法常見於報導、文章當中，字面上意思是「像野火般迅速蔓延」，意同中文「不脛而走」，都是形容某件事情不需推廣就馬上散播開來。

例 The rumor spread like wildfire over the Internet.
這謠言在網路上不脛而走。

⏱ Grammar Master

As + S + V, S + V + 比較級
隨著……而愈來愈……

此句型常與形容詞或副詞的比較級一起用，如課文中這句，as 引導出的子句說明「愈來愈如何」的起因。

例 **As** the sun rose in the sky, it got hotter and hotter outside.
當太陽從天空升起，外頭就愈來愈熱。

這樣的句型也可與表示變化的動詞 become、get、turn、grow 連用：

例 **As** the teacher entered the classroom, the students became quiet.
= The students became quiet **as** the teacher entered the classroom.
當老師一進教室，學生就安靜了。

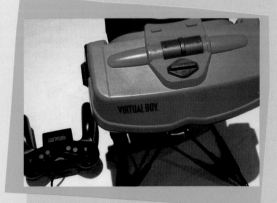

Ⓥ Vocabulary Bank

1) **ultraviolet** [ˌʌltrəˈvaɪəlɪt] (a./n.)
紫外（線）的；紫外線（簡稱UV）
Ultraviolet light is invisible to the human eye.

2) **radiation** [ˌrediˈeʃən] (n.) 輻射，放射
Microwave ovens use radiation to cook food.

3) **tanning** [ˈtænɪŋ] (n.)（皮膚）曬黑
(v./n.) tan [tæn] 曬黑；古銅色
Shelly got her tan at a tanning salon.

4) **steadily** [ˈstɛdəlɪ] (adv.) 穩定地
(a.) steady [ˈstɛdɪ]
Prices have risen steadily over the past year.

5) **addicted** [əˈdɪktɪd] (a.) 上癮的，入迷的
(n.) addiction [əˈdɪkʃən] 成癮，入迷
Samantha is addicted to chocolate.

6) **skip** [skɪp] (v.) 略過，跳過
I woke up late and had to skip breakfast.

7) **spray** [spre] (n./v.) 噴霧，噴液；噴灑
What brand of hair spray do you use?

8) **buck** [bʌk] (n.) 美元
Can you loan me five bucks?

9) **spice** [spaɪs] (n.) 香料
The curry contains dozens of different spices.

10) **summary** [ˈsʌmərɪ] (n.) 總結，摘要
At the end of the lecture, the professor made a summary of the main points.

11) **step back** [stɛp bæk] (phr.) 停下來（思考）
We need to step back and consider our options.

進階字彙

12) **shell out** [ʃɛl aʊt] (phr.) 付（大）錢
I had to shell out 200 bucks for a concert ticket!

Ⓖ Grammar Master

副詞的位置

文中的副詞是屬於放在句首修飾全句的用法。副詞還可以放在：

● 動詞後：用來修飾動詞

例 If we <u>drive</u> **fast**, we can get there before dark.
如果我們開快一點，天黑之前就可抵達。

● 形容詞前：用來修飾形容詞

例 The man was **barely** <u>conscious</u> when he arrived at the hospital.
這名男子到達醫院時幾乎沒有意識。

● 副詞前：副詞也可以用來修飾副詞

例 The Japanese economy grew **very** <u>slowly</u> in the 1990s.
一九九〇年代，日本經濟成長非常緩慢。

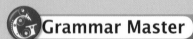

課文朗讀 MP3 244　單字朗讀 MP3 245　英文文章導讀 MP3 246

Each year in the United States, over 2 million people get skin cancer and approximately 12,000 die from it. While it is widely known that [1)]**ultraviolet** [2)]**radiation** causes skin cancer, [3)]**tanning** beds have been used in
5 the U.S. since the late 70s and have [4)]**steadily** grown in popularity. These death machines are especially popular among teenagers. ⒼInterestingly, recent studies have shown that people can become [5)]**addicted** to tanning beds just like they can to alcohol or drugs. This invention
10 kills people, so [6)]**skip** it and try a [7)]**spray** [3)]**tan**.

And last but not least, the fake ponytail. Fake hair never looks real. And even if you [12)]**shell out** the big [8)]**bucks** and buy a ponytail made from real hair, you're not going to fool anybody. And besides, it's pretty obvious
15 when you have short hair one day and a long ponytail the next. While growing your hair out may be a pain, 🔢 **good things come to those who wait**. And you can sport different hairstyles at every length along the way. Remember, 🔢 **variety is the** [9)]**spice of life**!

20   This has been a short 10)**summary** of just a few of the 50 worst inventions named by *Time*. And because inventors all around the world are working overtime to come up with more, there's sure to be a steady stream of terrible inventions in the future. So 11)**step back** and think

25 twice before you buy something that should never have been invented in the first place.

中 Translation

在美國，每年有超過兩百萬人罹患皮膚癌，而約有一萬兩千人因此喪命。雖然紫外線會導致皮膚癌是眾所皆知之事，美國仍自七〇年代晚期開始使用助曬機，並日益普及。這些致命機器尤其深受青少年歡迎。有趣的是，近來有研究顯示，人們使用助曬機也會成癮，就像是酒癮或毒癮一樣。這種發明會要人命，所以別用了，試試噴霧仿曬劑吧！

最後一項但並非最不爛的是：假馬尾。假髮怎麼看也絕不會像真的，即使花大把鈔票買真髮做成的馬尾，也騙不了任何人。另外，如果今天是短髮，明天留著長長的馬尾，真相更是昭然若揭。雖然把頭髮留長或許很辛苦，但好東西值得等待。何況在留長的過程中，每一種長度都可以展示不同髮型。別忘了，變化是生活的調味料！

以上只是《時代雜誌》所選的五十大爛發明其中幾項簡短摘要。由於全球各地的發明家都在夙夜匪懈努力想出更多新發明，未來一定還會有源源不絕的爛發明出現，所以要購買任何原本不該發明的東西之前，請三思而後行。

50 大最爛發明節選
- **Parachute Jacket** 降落傘夾克
  1912 年問世，第一次在巴黎鐵塔頂試跳時，傘沒開，人也掛點了。
- **Electric Facial Mask** 電子面膜
  想要裝扮成殺人魔又同時享有年輕的肌膚嗎？買這個就對了。
- **Smile Checks** 微笑探測裝置
  日本人發明測試微笑的裝置，指數由 0 到 100，連微笑都要被打分數，日本人真是「賣勾假」啦！

Tongue-tied No More

1 Good things come to those who wait.
好酒沈甕底，好事多磨。

這是一句英文諺語，字面上意思是「好東西只給有耐心的人」，期待有最好的結果，通常都需要耐心等待。中文翻譯可以有很多說法，譬如「皇天不負苦心人」、「耐心等待，好事終會降臨」、「好事多磨」等。

A: Why is our food taking so long? I'm starving!
我們的菜怎麼弄這麼久啊？我快餓死了！
B: Good things come to those who wait.
好酒沈甕底嘛！

2 Variety is the spice of life.
人生多變才精彩。

這也是一句英文諺語，意思是說變化才有驚喜，甚至可成為人生中的轉捩點。一成不變的生活就像沒有調味過的菜，枯燥無味，所以才說「變化是人生的調味料」，有變化的人生比較精彩。

A: When are you going to get a steady girlfriend?
你什麼時候才要交個固定的女朋友？
B: I'm not in any hurry. Variety is the spice of life!
我可一點都不急。人生多變才精彩嘛！

Mini Quiz 閱讀測驗

1   Which of the following is NOT on *Time*'s list of the worst inventions in history?
(A) A chemical pesticide
(B) Plastic shopping bags
(C) Coca-Cola Classic
(D) A brand of rubber clog

2   _____ you look at the data, the relationship between smoking and lung cancer is obvious.
(A) How
(B) However
(C) How much
(D) However

3   The people at the next table were talking _____.
(A) quite loudly
(B) very loud
(C) extremely noisy
(D) very noise

閱讀測驗解答 1 (C) 2 (D) 3 (A)

Vocabulary Bank

1) **annual** [ˋænjʊəl] (a.) 一年一次的
He won the annual tennis tournament three years in a row.

2) **stunt** [stʌnt] (n.) 驚險動作，特技
Evel Knievel was famous for his daring motorcycle stunts.

3) **contestant** [kənˋtɛstənt] (n.) 參賽者
Four contestants were eliminated from the competition on Friday.

4) **flip** [flɪp] (n.)（跳水、體操等表演的）空翻
The rider won the event after performing a double flip.

5) **participant** [pɑrˋtɪsəpənt] (n.) 參與者
How many participants have signed up for the activity?

6) **aggressive** [əˋgrɛsɪv] (a.) 有衝勁的，
aggressive inline skating為「特技直排輪」
This skatepark is designed for aggressive skaters.

7) **grind** [graɪnd] (v., n.) 磨，發出刺耳嘎嘎聲。
grind在直排輪運動中是指用輪鞋底部滑過欄杆或石塊的邊緣
Steve broke his arm trying to do a grind on a railing.

8) **artificial** [ˌɑrtəˋfɪʃəl] (a.) 人造的
Some ski resorts use artificial snow to extend their ski seasons.

9) **foam** [fom] (n.) 泡棉，泡沫塑膠
This hockey helmet has a foam lining for added protection.

10) **cushion** [ˋkuʃən] (v.) 緩衝
Boxers wear mouth guards to cushion blows to the face.

補充字彙

* BMX是Bicycle Mountain Cross（或Bicycle Moto Cross）的縮寫，直譯為「腳踏車土堆飛躍賽」，原本是一種要在高低起伏的土坡跑道上進行競速的單車運動，現在BMX已經用以泛指所有使用20吋輪徑的腳踏車，以及用這種腳踏車進行的比賽，因為輪徑較一般腳踏車小，常被稱作「小輪車」

* adrenaline [æˋdrɛnəlɪn] (n.) 腎上腺素

* wakeboarding [ˋwekˋbordɪŋ] (n.) 花式短板滑水

* street luge [strit.luʒ] (n.) 旱地雪橇

* bouldering [ˋboldərɪŋ] (n.) 抱石攀岩，boulder為「巨岩」

The X Games
—Your Ticket to Thrills!

課文朗讀 MP3 247　單字朗讀 MP3 248　英文文章導讀 MP3 249

The X Games are an [1)]**annual** sports competition with an emphasis on extreme sports. What are extreme sports? Generally, extreme sports are more dangerous than traditional sports and often involve spectacular [2)]**stunts**. These include sports like skateboarding, freestyle *BMX biking, skiing and snowboarding. In the extreme sport events included in the X Games, the [3)]**contestants** often do different tricks to gain points, many of which are invented by the contestants themselves. Here's the extreme part: contestants get points mainly for leaving the ground with their vehicle and doing [4)]**flips**, twists and turns. These stunts can be quite dangerous, and [5)]**participants** are often injured in competition or while practicing.

*Adrenaline is also a common factor in X Game events, and sports like [6)]**aggressive** inline skating, bungee jumping, *wakeboarding, *street luge and *bouldering are sure to get the blood pumping. Aggressive inline skating is a lot like skateboarding and includes performing tricks in the air and [7)]**grinding**, or sliding on rails. The different kinds of tricks have odd names like *soul*, *acid*, *makio* and *royale*. Wakeboarding is a lot like waterskiing, but instead of a long ski, the rider stands on a shorter board and performs flips and rolls. Bouldering is rock climbing without a rope, but is limited to short climbs to avoid serious injuries. It's typically performed on large boulders or [8)]**artificial** rock faces. Climbers use powdered chalk to keep their hands dry and a crash pad—a thick [9)]**foam** pad placed on the ground to [10)]**cushion** falls.

.Know itALL 英文閱讀

✦ Language Guide

sport還是sports？

本文第一段出現了兩個 sports，an annual sports competition 這邊的 sports 是形容詞「運動的」。

The championship game is going to be held at the local sports arena.
冠軍賽將在本地的運動場舉行。

with an emphasis on extreme sports 這邊的 sports 是 sport 的複數，當名詞「運動」。

A: What's your favorite sport?
你最喜歡的運動是什麼？

B: I like all kinds of sports.
我各種運動都喜歡。

sport 當名詞還有「輸得起的人，有運動精神的人」的意思：

Jim used to be a sore loser, but now he's a good sport.
吉姆以前是個輸不起的傢伙，但現在他很有運動精神了。

聊聊extreme sports

Aren't people who do extreme sports afraid of pain?
玩極限運動的人都不怕痛嗎？

I'm afraid to try kitesurfing—it sounds really dangerous.
我不敢玩風箏衝浪——聽起來超危險的。

I couldn't even stand up after I put the inline skates on.
我穿上直排輪之後根本站不起來。

I took a rock climbing class, but my whole body was sore for days afterwards.
我上過一次攀岩課，但接下來全身痠痛好幾天。

I went bungee jumping last weekend, and I screamed the whole way down.
我上週末去玩高空彈跳，墜下去時一路都在慘叫。

中 Translation

極限運動大賽——這樣才叫驚險刺激！

極限運動大賽是一年一度的運動賽事，以極限運動為主。極限運動是什麼？一般說來，極限運動比傳統運動更危險，通常帶有驚人的特技。這類運動包括滑板、自由式小輪車、滑雪與滑雪板等運動。包括在極限運動大賽內的極限運動賽事中，參賽者通常會使出各種不同的招式來得分，其中有許多是參賽者自創。極限之處在於：參賽者的得分關鍵主要是，要將坐騎騰空離地，做翻轉、扭動和迴旋的動作。這些特技相當危險，參賽者經常在比賽或練習中受傷。

腎上腺素也是極限運動大賽的共同要素，而特技直排輪、高空彈跳、花式短板滑水、旱地雪橇、抱石攀岩，這些運動無一不讓人血脈賁張。特技直排輪很像滑板，在空中表演招式以及磨行也就是在欄杆上滑行，不同種類的招式有奇怪的名稱，像靈魂、酸、瑪其歐和羅躍。花式短板滑水很類似一般滑水，只是選手不是用長長的滑水板，而是站在比較短的滑水板上表演翻轉、側翻。抱石攀岩就像一般的攀岩，只是不繫安全繩，不過只限於短距攀爬，以免嚴重傷害。通常是在大岩石或人造石面上攀爬，攀爬者以岩粉保持雙手乾燥，並在地上鋪一塊厚實的海綿墊，緩衝墜落的力道。

課文朗讀 MP3 250　單字朗讀 MP3 251　英文文章導讀 MP3 252

Skysurfing is probably one of the most dangerous of the extreme sports. The contestant jumps out of an airplane and "surfs" on a snowboard-like board, performing a number of tricks like flips and twists before ¹⁾**deploying** a ²⁾**parachute** and landing. Street luge involves lying feet-first on a large *fiberglass or plastic board with wheels and speeding downhill. While street luge doesn't involve any tricks, it's still exciting to watch because riders can reach speeds of up to 70 miles per hour.

The X Games has ³⁾**numerous** ⁴⁾**sponsors** and is ⁵⁾**broadcast** on ESPN and ABC Sports. The "X Fest" is hosted at the same time as the games and features live music and interactive activities. The X Games has also worked to promote environmental issues by focusing on reducing waste at their functions. For example, the shuttle buses at the Games use *bio-diesel fuel, and fans who recycle their garbage are awarded ⁶⁾**tokens** that can be used for credit at gift shops. The Summer X Games, which started in 1995, take place in Southern California (usually Los Angeles or San Diego) and have an average ⁷⁾**attendance** of 200,000. The Winter X Games, which ⁸⁾**kicked off** in 1997, are hosted mostly in Colorado (except for the years 2000 and 2001, when they took place in Vermont) and have an average attendance of around 50,000.

Vocabulary Bank

1) **deploy** [dɪ`plɔɪ] (v.) 展開
The airplane crashed on the runway after its landing gear failed to deploy.

2) **parachute** [`pærə͵ʃut] (n.) 降落傘
The skydiver successfully deployed his reserve parachute after his main chute failed to open.

3) **numerous** [`njumərəs] (a.) 很多的
I've surfed at that beach numerous times.

4) **sponsor** [`spɑnsə] (n.) 贊助者
The sailor is looking for sponsors to fund his round-the-world trip.

5) **broadcast** [`brɔd͵kæst] (v.) 播送，廣播
動詞三態：broadcast, broadcasted, broadcast
The finals will be broadcast live on national television.

6) **token** [`tokən] (n.) 代幣
Do you have any slot machine tokens left?

7) **attendance** [ə`tɛndəns] (n.) 出席人數
Record attendance is expected at this year's festival.

8) **kick off** [kɪk ɔf] (phr.)（口）開辦，開始
The festival will kick off with a fireworks display.

補充字彙

* fiberglass [`faɪbə͵glæs] (n.) 玻璃纖維

* bio-diesel fuel [`baɪo͵dizl `fjuəl] 生質柴油燃料，以回收的廢食用油製成

Language Guide

speed的動詞和名詞用法

本日第一段出現兩次 speed，Street luge involves...speeding downhill這邊是動詞，常用動名詞，表示「快速疾駛」。speeding 也可以當名詞，表示「開快車」、「超速」。

Boys on sleds were speeding down the slope.
坐雪橇的男孩們高速滑下斜坡。

Dave go two speeding tickets last month.
達夫上個月收到兩張超速罰單。

下一句riders can reach speeds of up to 70 miles per hour，這邊的speed就是名詞，表示「速度」。

Many swimmers and cyclists shave their legs for speed.
許多游泳選手和自由車選手會刮腿毛來增加速度。

聊聊extreme sports

I'd never go parachuting.
我絕對不會去玩跳傘。

What if I jumped out of the plane and my parachute didn't open?
萬一跳下飛機降落傘卻沒打開怎麼辦？

How come so few women are involved in extreme sports?
玩極限運動的女生怎麼那麼少啊？

You'd have to be crazy to try base jumping.
你一定是瘋了，才會去玩定點跳傘。

Mini Quiz 閱讀測驗

❶ What do climbers use crash pads for?
   (A) To keep their hands dry
   (B) To protect themselves when they fall
   (C) To rest on after climbing
   (D) To keep themselves from falling

❷ How often are the X Games held?
   (A) Once every two years   (B) Twice a year
   (C) Every other year   (D) Once a year

閱讀測驗解答 ❶ (B) ❷ (D)

中 Translation

空中衝浪大概是最危險的極限運動之一，參賽者從飛機躍下，站在類似滑雪板的板子上，表演一些翻轉扭動的招式，然後才開啟降落傘、落地。旱地雪橇的參賽者頭上腳下，躺在裝有輪子的大片玻璃纖維或塑膠板上，急速滑下坡。雖然旱地雪橇並沒有什麼招式，看起來還是很刺激，因為參賽者時速可高達70英里。

極限運動大賽有眾多贊助商，並且在ESPN和美國廣播公司的運動頻道播出。大賽期間，同時也舉辦了「極限音樂節」，有現場音樂表演和互動活動。極限運動大賽也努力宣揚環保議題，致力降低舉辦活動所製造的廢棄物，例如，賽會接駁車使用生質柴油，回收垃圾的運動迷也可獲得代幣，可在禮品店消費時扣抵現金。夏日極限運動大賽於1995年開始在南加州舉行（通常是在洛杉磯或聖地牙哥），平均參與人次高達20萬人。冬季極限運動大賽於1997年開始主要在科羅拉多州舉行（除了2000與2001年是在佛蒙特州），平均參與人次大約五萬。

Bring on Some Cheer!

活力四射
啦啦隊

1) **cheer** [tʃɪr] (n./v.) 隊呼（長呼）；喝采，加油打氣
(n.) cheerleading [ˈtʃɪrˌlidɪŋ] 啦啦隊運動
The cheers of the fans filled the stadium.

2) **chant** [tʃænt] (n.) 隊呼（短呼）；口號，吟誦
Have you memorized the new chants yet?

3) **cheerleader** [ˈtʃɪrˌlidɚ] (n.)（美）啦啦隊員
My mom was a cheerleader in high school.

4) **attainable** [əˈtenəbḷ] (a.) 能達到的
Do you think my dream of becoming a singer is attainable?

5) **uniquely** [juˈniklɪ] (adv.) 獨特地，獨一無二地
Guilt is a uniquely human emotion.

6) **invention** [ɪnˈvɛnʃən] (n.) 發明，創造
The kite is a Chinese invention.

7) **deck out** [dɛk aut] (phr.) 裝飾，打扮
The Christmas tree was decked out in lights and ornaments.

8) **boost** [bust] (v.) 提升，促進
The tax cut is supposed to boost the economy.

9) **pro** [pro] (a.) 專業的，為 professional 的簡稱。pro 若當名詞，則表示「贊成的論點」
Stan likes to watch pro wrestling.

10) **routine** [ruˈtin] (n.) 一套固定的舞步或動作
We need to practice our routine for the dance contest.

11) **rank** [ræŋk] (v.) 列為
Jack ranks at the top of his class.

12) **gear** [gɪr] (n.) 器材，用具
Will all our camping gear fit in the trunk?

補充字彙

* **integral** [ˈɪntəgrəl] (a.) 不可或缺的
Internet marketing is integral to the success of our company.

* **gymnastic** [dʒɪmˈnæstɪk] (a.) 體操的
(n.) gymnastics [dʒɪmˈnæstɪks] 體操
We added some gymnastic moves to our dance routine.

* **athletically** [æθˈlɛtɪkḷɪ] (adv.) 運動上地
(a.) athletic [æθˈlɛtɪk] 運動的
My brother is more athletically gifted than I am.

課文朗讀 MP3 253　單字朗讀 MP3 254　英文文章導讀 MP3 255

　　"Five, six, seven, eight…who do we appreciate?" Almost every American girl knows this [2])**chant**, and many dream of becoming one of two things in life: a princess or a [3])**cheerleader**, the latter of course being the more [4])**attainable** goal.

5　Cheerleading is a [5])**uniquely** American [6])**invention** and, ironically, wasn't invented by a girl at all. It was started by Johnny Campbell, a student at the University of Minnesota, in 1898. He "cheered on" the home team by yelling out a chant to the crowd that is still used at U of

10　M football games today. And thus, the cheerleader—a person who stands in front of the crowd at a sporting event, [7])**decked out** in team colors, leading them in "cheers" that [8])**boost** team spirit—was born.

Cheerleading has since become an *integral part of
15 American sports and pop culture. Today, you can't attend
any high school, college or 9)**pro** football or basketball
game without seeing cheerleaders cheering on the
sidelines and performing during halftime. Although
most cheerleaders are female, males are necessary for
20 competitive teams as they assist in the *gymnastic feats
that cheerleaders perform. Cheerleading has also become
ᴳ**so** *athletically challenging and competitive that it's
now considered a sport in its own right. Cheerleaders often
take part in local and national competitions, where they
25 perform 10)**routines** that are both strenuous and dangerous.
In fact, cheerleading has been recently 11)**ranked** as the most
dangerous sport in U.S. high schools and colleges. Unlike
football players, cheerleaders wear no protective 12)**gear**, and
are thrown high in the air in death-defying stunts that wow
30 audiences.

中 Translation

「五、六、七、八……我們認為誰最棒？」幾乎每個美國女孩都熟悉這一句口
號，也有許多女孩夢想一輩子能達成以下兩件事其中之一：成為公主或是啦啦隊
員。當然，後者是比較容易達成的目標。啦啦隊是美國獨一無二的產物，但弔詭
的是，創始人並不是女生。啦啦隊是 1898 年由明尼蘇達大學學生強尼坎柏創始
的，他在為自己學校的球隊加油時，喊出明尼蘇達美式足球隊比賽至今仍在使用
的一句口號。於是，啦啦隊員——在運動比賽中站在觀眾前面，以球隊的代表顏
色為裝扮，帶領群眾歡呼，鼓舞球隊士氣的人，因而誕生。

啦啦隊後來成為美國運動與大眾文化不可或缺的一部分。現在，不管你觀賞高
中、大學、職業美式足球或籃球賽，都會看到啦啦隊在場邊歡呼，並在中場休息
時間表演。雖然啦啦隊成員大多是女生，但男生也是啦啦隊競賽隊伍必要的角
色，因為他們可以協助完成高難度的體操動作。啦啦隊至今已經變得運動難度
高、競爭激烈，因此現在也被視為一項運動項目。啦啦隊員經常參加地方性和全
國性的比賽，在比賽中表演費勁又危險的動作。事實上，啦啦隊近來已被列為美
國高中與大學最危險的運動。有別於美式足球員，啦啦隊員沒有穿戴護具，被高
高拋到空中做一些挑戰死神的特技動作來讓觀眾驚呼連連。

🇬🇧 Language Guide

一定要會的啦啦隊英文

cheerleading squad 啦啦隊	flag 旗幟
squad captain 啦啦隊長	mascot 吉祥物
pep rally（運動比賽前的）啦啦隊表演	routine 一套舞步
judge 裁判	choreography 編舞
coach 教練	stunt 特技
sidelines 場地邊線	toss 拋擲
championship 錦標賽	shoulder stand 肩膀站立
trophy 獎盃	back handspring 後手翻
cheer 隊呼（長呼）	high kick 踢腿
chant 隊呼（短呼）	tumble 翻騰
uniform 制服	cradle 搖籃式抱接
megaphone 大聲公	toe touch 劈腿
pom-pom 綵球	pyramid 金字塔隊形，疊羅漢

flyer/top person 上層人員，指被拋向空中的隊員

base 基層人員，負責支撐及拋擲隊友的人

spotter 保護人員，站在底部和上層後方的隊員，負責保護上層人員安全，並分擔基層人員的負重

I'm interested in joining the squad—do you accept guys?
我想加入啦啦隊，你們收男生嗎？

Where are the cheerleading tryouts being held? 啦啦隊甄選在哪舉辦？

We need to come up with a better routine if we want to win the competition.
我們必須想出更棒的舞步才能贏得比賽。

That's an illegal stunt. 那個特技動作違規。

ᴳ Grammar Master

so that 的不同表達法

so/too + adj./adv.＋that... 「如此……以至於
……」用來表達因果關係。
例 ● It's so dark that I can't see anything!
　 = It's too dark, so I can't see anything.
　　 這裡太暗，以至於我什麼都看不到

常常和 so...that...not 混淆的是 too...to「太……
以至於不能」，但 too...to 已有否定的意思，所
以不必加 not。
例 ● He's so tall that he can't fit in the car.
　 = He's too tall to fit in the car.
　　 他太高，以至於擠不進車裡。

...so that...「為了……」用來表達目的，也就是 in
order to... 或 so as to... 的意思。若要變為否定「為
了不……」，只要把 not 放在 to 的前面即可。
例 ● He practices baseball every day so that he
　 can become a baseball player.
　　 他每天練習籃球，為了能成為籃球員。

課文朗讀 MP3 256　單字朗讀 MP3 257　英文文章導讀 MP3 258

Vocabulary Bank

1) **rewarding** [rɪˋwɔrdɪŋ] (a.) 獲益良多的，有報酬的，感到充實的
Going to college was a very rewarding experience.

2) **superior** [səˋpɪrɪɚ] (a.) 優越的
Scholarships are available to students with superior grades.

3) **discipline** [ˋdɪsəplɪn] (n.) 紀律，毅力
The new teacher had trouble maintaining discipline in the classroom.

4) **squad** [skwɑd] (n.) 小隊，小組 cheerleading squad 即為「啦啦隊」
The bomb squad was called in to defuse the bomb.

5) **synonymous** [sɪˋnɑnəməs] (a.) 同義的
Picasso's name is synonymous with modern art.

6) **reputation** [ˏrɛpjəˋteʃən] (n.) 名譽，名聲
The scandal destroyed the senator's reputation.

7) **achiever** [əˋtʃivɚ] (n.) 成功的人
Low achievers at the school were placed in a special class.

8) **status** [ˋstætəs] (n.) 地位，身分
Luxury cars are status symbols.

補充字彙

* **pom-pom** [ˋpɑmˏpɑm] (n.)（啦啦隊表演用）綵球
At the end of the cheer, the cheerleaders threw their pom-poms in the air.

Grammar Master

介系詞 to？還是不定詞 to+V？

in addition to... 表示「除……以外，還有……」是片語 in addition 和介系詞 to 形成的介系詞片語，後面接名詞或動名詞，而不是接原形動詞形成不定詞。以下是使用 to 當介系詞的常用動詞或片語：

in addition	
(be) committed	
(be) devoted	to＋ 動名詞 (Ving) / 名詞
(n.)	
(be) used	
look forward	

例 ● In addition to going to school, Michael is also working part-time.
除了去上學，麥可還兼職工作。

● In addition to furniture, we also sell rugs and curtains.
除了家具，我們還有賣地毯和窗簾。

Sound like something you'd like to do? Cheerleading is an exciting and [1)]**rewarding** sport, but not all people are born to be cheerleaders. It takes [2)]**superior** athletic ability, [3)]**discipline**, an outgoing personality, and also good

5　grades to make it onto a cheerleading [4)]**squad**. And for that reason, cheerleaders have become [5)]**synonymous** with success for many young Americans. [G]In addition to their [6)]**reputations** as high [7)]**achievers**, cheerleaders also enjoy higher social [8)]**status**—becoming a cheerleader

10　automatically makes you a member of the "popular crowd." But these benefits don't come easily. It's not only tough to make it on the squad; it's also tough to stay on the squad. One bad grade and a few missed practices, and you'll be asked to turn in your *pom-poms.

15　Let's say you are one of the lucky and talented few who make it in the world of cheerleading. What can it do for your future? Outstanding high school cheerleaders can qualify for college scholarships and cheer at the college level. And those

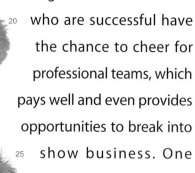

20　who are successful have the chance to cheer for professional teams, which pays well and even provides opportunities to break into

25　show business. One

example is Paula Abdul, who started out as a cheerleader for the Los Angeles Lakers. After being discovered by The Jacksons at a Lakers game, she went on to become a famous choreographer and pop singer. Other famous people with
30 cheerleading pasts include Halle Berry, Madonna, and even presidents Eisenhower, FDR and George W. Bush!

中 Translation

你也想試試看嗎？啦啦隊是個刺激又讓人備感充實的運動，但不是每個人都是天生的啦啦隊員。要擠進啦啦隊，不但要有超人的運動能力、毅力、外向的個性，還要有好成績。也因為如此，啦啦隊員對許多美國年輕人來說已經是成功的同義詞。除了贏得佼佼者的名聲，啦啦隊員也享有較高的社會地位——只要當上啦啦隊員，就自動成為「受歡迎的人」。但是這些好處得來不易。要擠進啦啦隊不但很難，要待在隊伍中也不簡單。只要成績不佳、漏掉幾次練習，你就會被要求交出綵球了。

假設你是少數幸運又有天賦的人，成功踏入啦啦隊世界，對你的未來有什麼幫助呢？傑出的高中啦啦隊員有資格拿到大學獎學金，可以加入大學啦啦隊，表現優異的隊員將有機會成為職業球隊的啦啦隊員，不但薪資優渥，甚至有機會進入演藝圈。寶拉阿巴杜就是一例。她一開始是洛杉磯湖人隊的啦啦隊員，在湖人隊比賽中被傑克森家族合唱團發掘之後，一路成為知名的編舞家與流行歌手。其他曾經擔任啦啦隊員的名人還包括：荷莉貝瑞、瑪丹娜，甚至美國前總統艾森豪、小羅斯福以及布希！

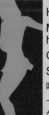

V Vocabulary Bank

1) **resume** [rɪˋzum] (v.) 重新開始，繼續
The game resumed after a two-hour delay.

2) **derive (from)** [dɪˋraɪv] (v.) 衍生，
（從……）取得
Chocolate is derived from the beans of the
cacao tree.

3) **obstacle** [ˋɑbstək!] (n.) 障礙（物）。
obstacle course 即「障礙訓練場」
The road to success is full of challenges
and obstacles.

4) **civilian** [sɪˋvɪljən] (a./n.) 平民的；平民
Recruits aren't allowed to wear civilian
clothing at any time during basic training.

5) **objective** [əbˋdʒɛktɪv] (n./a.) 目的，
目標；客觀的
(n.) object 目標，物體
My objective this semester is to improve
my grades.

6) **conquer** [ˋkɑŋkɚ] (v.) 克服，征服
Sheldon was finally able to conquer his
fear of heights.

7) **imposing** [ɪmˋpozɪŋ] (a.) 壯觀的，宏偉的
The courtyard is surrounded by tall,
imposing buildings.

進階字彙

8) **daredevil** [ˋdɛr͵dɛv!] (a./n.) 不怕死的；愛冒
險的人
A daredevil skateboarder leaped over the
Great Wall of China.

9) **protagonist** [proˋtægənɪst] (n.) 主角，主要
人物
The protagonist is killed in the third act of
the play.

10) **unscathed** [ʌnˋskeðd] (a.) 毫髮無傷的
The driver walked away from the accident
unscathed.

11) **intrigue** [ɪnˋtrig] (v.) 使好奇，使著迷
Clara was intrigued by the idea of starting
her own business.

12) **pigeonhole** [ˋpɪdʒən͵hol] (v./n.) 歸類；分
隔，小隔間
Over the years, Bruce Willis became
pigeonholed as an action hero.

13) **martial art** [ˋmɑrʃəl ͵ɑrt] (n.) 武術
Tae kwon do is the most popular martial
art in the world.

14) **agility** [əˋdʒɪlətɪ] (n.) 敏捷，靈活
Gymnastics requires great balance and
agility.

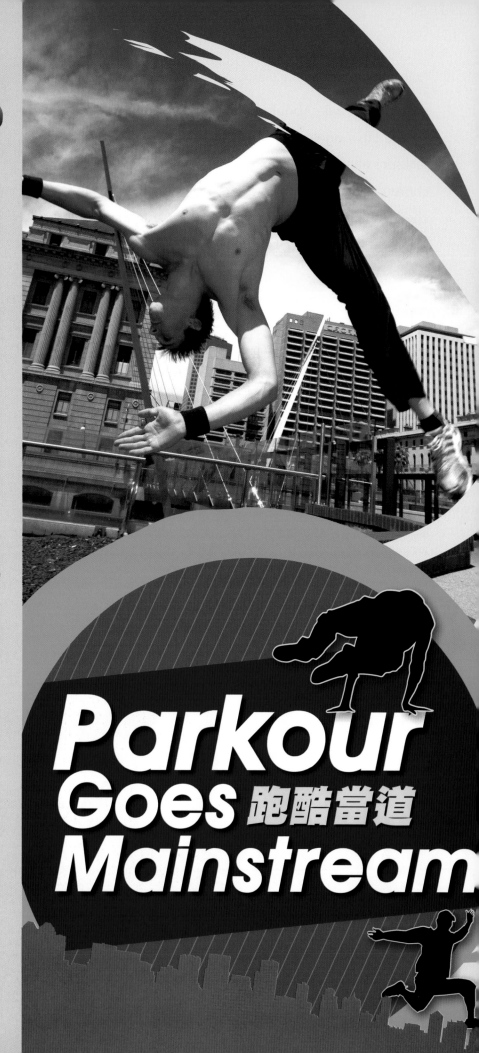

Parkour Goes 跑酷當道 Mainstream

課文 朗讀 MP3 259 單字 朗讀 MP3 260 英文 文章導讀 MP3 261

Moviegoers worldwide were first introduced to parkour in the 2001 film *Yamakasi*, by French director Luc Besson. The [8]**daredevil** [9]**protagonists** in the movie **risk**
5 **life and limb** running though the streets of Paris, climbing walls, launching themselves from one rooftop, and rolling as they land on another. After all that, they get up, mostly [10]**unscathed**, and [1]**resume** running.
10 Audiences were [11]**intrigued**, to say the least. So, while it's clear that *Yamakasi* helped launch parkour's star, what exactly is it?

Parkour is rather difficult to [12]**pigeonhole**. The invented word is [2]**derived** from the French
15 term *parcours du combattant*, the [3]**obstacle**-course training method used in the military, but parkour is strictly a [4]**civilian** activity. To accomplish the leaps, vaults and rolls that make up parkour, one must be very athletic,
20 but the lack of competition or performance suggests that it's not really a sport. Perhaps it's best thought of as a discipline similar to a [13]**martial art**, but instead of the fight, parkour is concerned more with the flight.

25
The [5]**objective** of parkour is to move from one place to another in the smoothest and most efficient way possible. This often means overcoming obstacles—like a three-meter-high concrete wall—that may lie in
30 your path. To accomplish this, traceurs, as those who practice parkour are known, rely on [14]**agility**, strength, sense of balance, and quick thinking. Traceurs believe that any [5]**object**, [G]whether physical or mental, can
35 be [6]**conquered**, no matter how [7]**imposing** it may seem.

中 Translation

在法國導演盧貝松二○○一年的《企業戰士》一片中，全世界影迷第一次見識到跑酷。片中不怕死的主角冒著生命危險跑過巴黎街道、攀越牆壁、從一座屋頂騰空躍起，落到另一座屋頂時翻滾，然後站起來，毫髮未傷，繼續向前狂奔。觀眾無不著迷——這是最輕淡寫的說法了。那麼，雖然跑酷能這般引人矚目顯然是拜《企業戰士》所賜，但，跑酷究竟是什麼呢？

跑酷滿難歸類的，這個新造的詞源自法語，軍方使用的障礙訓練方式，但跑酷百分之百是一項平民活動。要完成跑酷所需的跳躍和翻滾，玩家必須身手矯健，但由於跑酷缺乏競賽和表演，並不算是真正的運動。或許把它視為一種類似武術的訓練是最恰當的，但跑酷與打鬥無關，反倒與逃跑比較相關。

跑酷的目標是以最順暢、最有效率的方式從一地移動到另一地，通常這意味著必須克服沿路的障礙——這例如前方路上三公尺高的混凝土牆。要做到這點，跑酷玩家（練習跑酷的人被稱為）須仰賴敏捷度、力量、平衡感和迅速的思考。跑酷玩家相信任何事物——這無論是實體的或精神的——這都可以征服，不管它看起來有多儡人。

Know it ALL 英文閱讀

Tongue-tied No More

1 risk life and limb 冒生命危險

limb [lɪm] 指的是手和腳,而 risk life and limb 字面上的意思是「冒著失去性命和手腳的危險」,其實就是「很危險」。

A: How about renting a car when we get there?
我們到那邊時去租車如何?

B: No way! I'm not gonna risk life and limb driving in L.A.
千萬不要!我不想冒著生命危險在洛杉磯開車。

Grammar Master

用(不論……)為首的插入語

要補充說明句子中的某個名詞「不論是……」時,可在後面加逗點,插入以 whether 開頭的片語,然後再用一個逗點,把插入語和所修飾的名詞後面原本該接的字隔開。

例 ● All citizens male or female are protected by the law.
所有公民,不論男女,皆受法律保護。

● Outgoing mail domestic or international should be placed in the green box.
欲寄出的郵件,不論目的地為國內或國外,都應放在綠色的信箱裡。

Language Guide

跑酷簡介

跑酷此名稱取自 parkour [pɑ`kur] 的音譯,有人稱它為 free running、freerun、urban ninja [`ɝbən `nɪndʒə] 或是簡稱為 PK,而跑酷玩家則被稱為 traceur [træ`sɝ]。這項源自法國的運動,透過網路分享,現在已普及全球,甚至也開始在中國蔓延發燒。動作片中不時能看到跑酷的畫面,身為跑酷發起人之一的大衛貝爾 (David Belle) 為了推廣跑酷文化,還曾多次參與電影演出,如《企業戰士》 Yamakasi、《暴力特區》 Banlieue 13、《巴比倫密碼》 Babylon A.D. 等。跑酷有別於一般運動,沒有既定規則也沒有競爭對手,而是把整座城市當作運動場,恣意地穿梭其間,因此與其說跑酷是項極限運動,倒不如說它是一門生活哲學來得貼切,因為進行跑酷時,必須先克服內心的恐懼以主宰心智,並透過敏捷速度來增進自身的應變能力,對初學者而言是項極困難的考驗。

跑酷常見基本動作
roll 翻滾

一般都先從側翻開始,做完翻滾動作後要盡量回到原位。

land 著地

準確從一個目標跳到另一個目的地,落地時只利用雙腿來緩衝。

balance 保持平衡

行走在欄杆或牆邊時需要絕佳的平衡感。

tic-tac 交叉跳躍

利用腳蹬牆的反作用力越過障礙物或是抓取東西。

gap jump 大跳躍

從 A 處移到 B 處或是橫跨一個缺口就需要大跳躍，此項動作常與翻滾連用。

wall run 走壁

無法攀爬時，跑酷玩家便會以走壁方式行進，大約走三至四步至牆的最高點再翻牆而過。

cat leap 貓式跳躍

顧名思義就是學習貓的跳躍動作，從一面牆跳到另一面牆，雙手抓住牆的上端，腳在牆上滑兩步做為緩衝再翻越過去。

cat to cat 貓式接力

連續使用攀爬抓牆方式行進。

palm spin 掌心翻轉

以手掌壓樹或桌子等物品當支點，進行翻轉動作。

king kong vault 猩猩跳躍

有時也被簡稱為 kong vault 或 kong，是跑酷常見的基本招式，在奔跑的過程中以雙手按著障礙物然後雙腳打開跨過去，類似跳箱。

若想進一步認識跑酷的酷炫招式，可至 http://tc.parkour.us/ 或是 http://www.metacafe.com/tags/yamakasi/ 一窺跑酷英姿。

談論跑酷 實用句

Do you know what parkour is?
你知道什麼是跑酷嗎？

I saw parkour in *Casino Royale*.
我有在《007 首部曲：皇家夜總會》裡看過跑酷。

Parkour is about overcoming obstacles to get from point A to point B as quickly as possible.
跑酷就是盡可能快速穿越障礙物，從 A 地移動到 B 地。

I want to take up parkour and test my limits.
我想加入跑酷，挑戰自己的極限。

Are there any parkour groups in Taiwan?
台灣有跑酷團體嗎？

What equipment do you need for parkour?
參加跑酷需要什麼裝備？

Parkour seems like a pretty dangerous activity.
跑酷好像是滿危險的活動。

Parkour requires great strength and agility.
跑酷必須具備過人的體力和敏捷。

I saw in the news that lots of people get injured doing parkour.
我在新聞上看到不少人在跑酷時受傷。

You need to be really careful when you're doing parkour.
跑酷時務必要注意安全。

There's no way my parents will let me take up parkour.
我父母絕對不會答應讓我參加跑酷。

Vocabulary Bank

1) **founder** [ˈfaʊndə] (n.) 創立者，創辦人
Jigoro Kano was the founder of judo.

2) **spur (on)** [spɜ] (v.) 鞭策，鼓勵
The cheering crowd spurred the team to victory.

3) **fulfill** [fʊlˋfɪl] (v.) 完成（任務等），執行（命令等）
The manager was fired for failing to fulfill his duties.

4) **exploit** [ˈɛksplɔɪt] (n.) 功績，英勇事蹟（常用複數 exploits）
We learned about the exploits of Napoleon in history class.

5) **pursuit** [pəˋsut] (n.) 消遣，職業
Photography was once a pursuit for the rich.

6) **virtually** [ˈvɝtʃʊəlɪ] (adv.) 幾乎，差不多
The city was virtually destroyed during the war.

7) **specific** [spɪˋsɪfɪk] (a.) 特定的，特有的，明確的
The air conditioning turns on when a specific temperature is reached.

8) **decent** [ˈdisənt] (a.) 像樣的，還不錯的
Where can I get a decent meal around here?

9) **grip** [grɪp] (n.) 緊握，抓（地）力
My new tires have good grip.

進階字彙

10) **valor** [ˈvælə] (n.) 英勇，勇氣
The soldier received a medal for valor.

11) **practitioner** [prækˋtɪʃənə] (n.) 從事者
The number of yoga practitioners in Taiwan is growing.

12) **slab (of)** [slæb] (n.) 厚板，厚片
The slab of marble was too heavy to lift.

13) **bale (of)** [bel] (n.) 大包，大捆
The truck was loaded with bales of cotton.

One of parkour's ¹⁾**founders** is David Belle, a 36-year-old Frenchman who comes from a family of firefighters. Growing up, Belle pursued an interest in gymnastics and physical education, ²⁾**spurred** on by stories of his father's ¹⁰⁾**valor** and heroism **1 in the line of duty**. At the age of 15, Belle moved to Lisses, a suburb of Paris, to ³⁾**fulfill** his national service. ᴳWhile there, he **2 fell in with** a group of teenagers who shared his passion for physical activity. Together, they developed the discipline they called parkour, and formed the Yamakasi that inspired Luc Besson's movie.

Today, parkour has spread in large part thanks to the Internet, with ¹¹⁾**practitioners** posting videos of their ⁴⁾**exploits** online and sharing techniques on message boards. Groups have popped up in cities around Europe and North America, where members practice in parking garages and empty buildings. Indeed, parkour is more of an urban ⁵⁾**pursuit**, with traceurs preferring ¹²⁾**slabs** of concrete to ¹³⁾**bales** of hay—not that they would **3 pass up the chance** to do a "kong vault" over one, of course.

⑤While popular with teenagers and twenty-somethings, parkour can be practiced by ⁶⁾**virtually** anyone. Some shoe companies have even come out with parkour-⁷⁾**specific** lines, but all you really need is some light clothing and tennis shoes with ⁸⁾**decent** ⁹⁾**grip**. Details on parkour groups in your area are just a few mouse clicks away, and there's no better time to hit the streets and get moving. After trying parkour, you'll never look at your city the same way again.

20
25
30

Translation

跑酷的發明人之一是法國人大衛貝爾，現年三十六歲的他出身消防家庭。成長期間，貝爾深受父親英勇的出勤事蹟影響，而去追求他對體操和體育的喜好。十五歲的時候，貝爾搬到巴黎郊區里塞服役。他在那裡碰到一群和他一樣熱愛體能活動的青少年，他們一起發展出這種他們稱之為跑酷的訓練，並且成立日後激發盧貝松拍片靈感的團體「Yamakasi（源於非洲班圖語，意為「強壯的身心，強壯的人」）」。

如今，在網際網路推波助瀾之下，跑酷已經傳播開來，玩家紛紛把他們英勇表現的影片貼到網路上，並在留言板分享技巧。跑酷團體在歐美城市如雨後春筍冒了出來，成員們在停車場和無人建築裡練習。跑酷確實較適合在城市裡進行，跑酷玩家喜歡混凝土板更勝於乾草包——當然啦，如果碰上能用「猩猩跳躍」方式凌空越過乾草包的機會，他們可是不會放過的。

跑酷固然深受青少年和二十幾歲人的歡迎，但幾乎人人都可進行。有些製鞋公司甚至推出跑酷專用系列，但其實只需要輕便的衣著和抓地力強的球鞋就可以。你只要按幾下滑鼠鍵就能搜尋到住家附近跑酷團體的詳細資料，如果你想上街動一動，現在就是最好的時機。嘗試過跑酷之後，你看待自己城市的眼光將再也不一樣了。

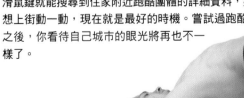

Triathlon
三項全能賽

Vocabulary Bank

1) **competition** [ˌkɑmpəˋtɪʃən] (n.) 競賽；競爭
(n.) competitor [kəmˋpɛtɪtə] 競爭者，參賽者
Evan won second prize in the design competition.

2) **athlete** [ˋæθlit] (n.) 運動員
Michael Phelps is the world's most famous Olympic athlete.

3) **endurance** [ɪnˋdʊrəns] (n.) 耐力
Running in a marathon takes great endurance.

4) **personnel** [ˌpɜsəˋnɛl] (n.) 工作人員（總稱）
All personnel are required to attend the meeting.

5) **attendance** [əˋtɛndəns] (n.) 參與，在場
Attendance at the meeting is required.

6) **administer** [ədˋmɪnəstə] (v.) 施行，給予
The doctor can't administer medical treatment without the patient's consent.

7) **accomplished** [əˋkɑmplɪʃt] (a.) 熟練的，有造詣的
Professor Adams is an accomplished scholar.

8) **household** [ˋhaʊsˌhold] (a.) 家喻戶曉的，眾所皆知的
Global warming has become a household term.

進階字彙

9) **first aid** [fɜst ed] (phr.) 急救（護理）
We always take a first aid kit when we go camping.

10) **dehydration** [ˌdihaɪˋdreʃən] (n.) 脫水
The lost hiker died from dehydration.

11) **set in** [sɛt ɪn] (phr.) 開始
If the wound isn't cleaned, infection may set in.

課文朗讀 MP3 265　單字朗讀 MP3 266　英文文章導讀 MP3 267

    A triathlon is a ¹⁾**competition** in which ²⁾**athletes** swim, cycle and run. They do this without stopping for a break at any time, which makes it ⁶one of the toughest ³⁾**endurance** events in the world. The most famous triathlon, the Ironman, is among the most difficult and takes at least ten hours to complete. The athletes swim 3.8 km, then cycle 180 km and finish off by running a full 42 km marathon. Other triathlons, like those here in Taiwan, are usually much shorter. One of the most popular is the Olympic distance triathlon, in which ¹⁾**competitors** swim for 1.5 km, cycle for 40 km and end with a 10 km run. It's still quite challenging, especially in hot, humid places like Taiwan, so there are usually trained medical ⁴⁾**personnel** in ⁵⁾**attendance**, ready to ⁶⁾**administer** ⁹⁾**first aid** if necessary.

Language Guide

triathlon 三項全能運動

triathlon [traɪˋæθlɑn] 包含游泳、自行車、路跑三項運動（「三項全能選手」為 triathlete [traɪˋæθlit]），依賽程總長分為以下幾種（距離視各場地狀況而有些微差異）：

	Swim	Bike	Run
Sprint distance 短距離 大部分國際比賽採用	0.75 km	20 km	5 km
Intermediate distance 中距離 奧運會賽程	1.5 km	40 km	10 km
Long Course 長距離 被稱為「半鐵人三項」Half Ironman	1.9 km	90 km	21.1 km
Ultra Distance 極限距離 被稱為「鐵人三項」Ironman triathlon	3.8 km	180 km	42 km 馬拉松距離

游泳接自行車、自行車接路跑處設有兩個銜接區 (transition area)，選手可預先在銜接區放置下一個賽程需要的裝備。由於 triathlon 是計時賽，且選手在銜接區逗留的時間也被計入，因此設法縮短更衣、穿鞋的速度，就成了很重要的參賽技巧。

Grammar Master

數量表達中 of 的用法

介系詞 of 可用來表達數量，它常與某些數量用語搭配使用。不過，有時候這些數量用語可以單獨使用，不一定要有 of 出現。

all (of)	many/much (of)	one (of)	some (of)
most (of)	a few/little (of)	two (of)	any (of)

判別 of 出現的時機，可檢視 of 後面的名詞片語是否為限定用法。當名詞為限定用法，數量用語要加上 of（如課文中第 3、第 9 行）。

限定用法 1：
所有格（my、your、his 等）＋ 名詞
例 One **of her** books is written in Spanish.（○）
One her books is written in Spanish.（X）
她的書裡面有一本是西文書。

限定用法 2：
限定詞（the、these、those 等）＋ 名詞
例 Two **of the** students in his class are Japanese.（○）
Two the students in his class are Japanese.（ X ）
他班上有兩個學生是日本人。

當名詞為非限定用法（即名詞前沒有所有格或限定詞）時，則數量用語不需要加 of（如課文中第 25 行）。
例 **Many Taiwanese** are addicted to Facebook.（○）
Many of Taiwanese are addicted to Facebook.（X）
許多台灣人很迷 Facebook。

---

15   A famous example of how tough the races and the competitors can be happened at the 1982 Hawaii Ironman. Julie Moss was a college student who entered the competition because she was doing research on exercise and wanted to gain firsthand experience of a triathlon. An [7)]**accomplished**
20 athlete, she made excellent time and approached the finish line all set to win first place in the women's event. But suddenly severe fatigue and [10)]**dehydration** [11)]**set in**, and she collapsed just meters away from the finish line. One competitor passed her, winning the race. But Moss didn't give
25 up. She crawled across the finish line to win second place. This stunning performance was broadcast worldwide, making Ironman the [8)]**household** name that it is today.

Translation

三項全能運動是一項競賽，參賽運動員必須游泳、騎自行車、賽跑，中間沒有任何休息時間，所以是世上最艱難的耐力賽事之一。最著名的三項全能運動──鐵人三項──是最困難的賽事，至少要十小時才能完成。參賽者要先游泳三點八公里，接著騎自行車一八○公里，最後再跑全程四十二公里的馬拉松。其他三項全能運動，例如台灣本地舉辦的，路程通常短得多。其中之一最常見的是奧運距離的三項全能，參賽者先游泳一點五公里、騎車四十公里，最後再跑十公里，仍然相當具挑戰性，特別是在台灣這種濕熱的地方，因此一般都有受過訓練的醫療人員在場，準備在必要時提供急救護理。

這項競賽到底有多艱難，參賽者又是多麼不屈不撓，有個著名的例子可以說明，發生於一九八二年的夏威夷鐵人三項。茱莉摩斯是位大學生，她之所以參賽是因為當時她正在做運動方面的研究，想親身體驗三項運動。她是個技術高超的運動員，花很短的時間就接近終點線，眼看就要贏得女子組冠軍，不料，她突然出現嚴重的疲勞和脫水症狀，在距離終點線僅僅幾公尺處倒下。另一名選手超越她贏得冠軍，但摩斯並沒有放棄，她爬過終點線，奪得亞軍。這驚人的表現播送到全世界，讓鐵人三項這個名稱成為如今這般家喻戶曉。

Know itALL 英文閱讀

V Vocabulary Bank

1) **historian** [hɪsˋtorɪən] (n.) 歷史學家
The history textbook was written by a renowned historian.

2) **canoe** [kəˋnu] (v./n.) 划 / 乘獨木舟；獨木舟
It took an hour to canoe across the lake.

3) **middle-aged** [ˋmɪdlˋedʒd] (a.) 中年的
The show is targeted at middle-aged housewives.

4) **sleeveless** [ˋslivlɪs] (a.) 無袖的
sleeve 袖子 + -less 「無」的形容詞字尾
Michelle wore a sleeveless dress to the party.

5) **flexible** [ˋflɛksəbl] (a.) 有彈性的，柔軟的
Ballet dancers must be very flexible.

進階字彙

6) **craze** [krez] (n.) 風潮，一窩蜂
Interactive video games are the latest craze.

7) **catchy** [ˋkætʃɪ] (a.) 動聽易記的
That show has a catchy theme song.

8) **headway** [ˋhɛd‚we] (n.) 前進，進展
Little headway has been made in the negotiations.

9) **rubbery** [ˋrʌbərɪ] (a.) 橡膠似的，（四肢）發軟 / 不穩的
The medication made my legs feel rubbery.

課文朗讀 MP3 268　單字朗讀 MP3 269　英文文章導讀 MP3 270

Although most people think of America when they hear the word triathlon, [1]**historians** say the earliest triathlons took place in France. In the early 1900s, there were events in which competitors would run, cycle
5 and [2]**canoe**. In the 1920s, the triathlon as we know it was born. Called "Les Trois Sports" (The Three Sports), it featured a 3 km run, a 12 km bike ride and then a swim across the river Marne. But the first truly modern triathlon was held at Mission Bay, San Diego in 1974. The jogging
10 [6]**craze** was at its peak and Americans everywhere were ❶ **getting back into shape**. Two [3]**middle-aged** joggers who belonged to a track club were looking for something a little more challenging, and decided to create an event that combined running, cycling and swimming. They'd never
15 heard of Les Trois Sports, so they came up with a [7]**catchy** new name: triathlon.

Because triathlons are so physically challenging, athletes have developed more efficient ways to swim, cycle and run. They use the dolphin kick and swim underwater to
20 make [8]**headway** against waves, and bodysurf to use wave energy when coming back to shore. Athletes also wear wetsuits to [G]help them swim faster and stay warm, and there are even special [4]**sleeveless** suits for use in warmer water. Triathlon bikes
25 are designed to rest the muscle groups needed for running, and

athletes often cycle faster at the end to keep their muscles loose and 5)**flexible**. If they don't do this, the sudden change from cycling to running can cause 9)**rubbery** legs and serious pain.

30

中 Translation

雖然多數人一聽到三項全能運動就會想到美國，但史學家表示，最早的三項全能運動在法國舉辦。一九〇〇年代初期，法國已有結合賽跑、自行車和獨木舟的競賽。一九二〇年代，我們所熟悉的三項運動誕生。當時名為 Les Trois Sports（法文，意即「三項運動」）的三項全能運動包含三公里的賽跑、十二公里的自行車和游泳橫渡馬恩河。但第一場真正的現代三項全能賽事於一九七四年在美國聖地牙哥的教會灣舉行。當時慢跑熱潮正值巔峰，到處都有美國人在重建強健體魄。兩個同屬某個徑賽俱樂部、熱愛慢跑的中年人想找比較有挑戰性的事情做，於是決定創立一個結合賽跑、自行車和游泳的賽事。他們從沒聽過 Les Trois Sports，因而想出一個好聽好記的新名字：triathlon。

由於三項全能運動對體能是極大的考驗，運動員已發展出更有效率的方式來游泳、騎車和長跑。他們採取海豚式打水、在水面下游泳以利破浪前進，游上岸時則採取人體衝浪法來利用海浪的能量。運動員也會穿防寒潛水衣，幫助他們游得更快及保持溫暖，甚至還有特製的無袖潛水衣可以用於較溫暖的水域。三項全能運動的自行車設計能讓賽跑所需的肌肉群獲得休息，而且運動員通常會在接近終點時騎得比較快，讓肌肉保持放鬆及彈性。如果不這麼做，從騎車突然轉換到跑步，可能會導致腿軟和劇烈疼痛。

Language Guide

dolphin kick 海豚式打水

dolphin kick [ˈdɑlfɪn kɪk] 是模仿海豚尾鰭動作，雙腿併攏在水面下做波浪擺動，如此在水中的阻力比起一般交錯踢腿減少許多，能有效超越競爭者。操作 dolphin kick 需要非常高超的技巧，奧運金牌名將菲爾普斯 (Michael Phelps) 就是在出發及轉身時運用 dolphin kick 到了出神入化的境界，成為許多專業游泳人士討論的話題。觀看 dolphin kick 動作可至 http://www.youtube.com/ 鍵入 training dolphin kick 搜尋。

bodysurfing 人體衝浪運動

bodysurfing [ˈbɑdɪˌsɜfɪŋ] 是一種不使用衝浪板的衝浪運動，衝浪者要靠完美的流線型體態 (streamline position) 乘上浪頭、在浪中翻滾。文中提到三項運動選手上岸時採用的 bodysurfing 技巧稱做 dolphin pop（海豚出水），是指回岸時在淺水處趁海浪即將上升到最高點之勢跳出水面。

Tongue-tied No More

1 in shape 鍛鍊體能

in shape 經常有人以為是指「（前凸後翹）身材好」，其實應該是「有經過鍛鍊的好體能」的意思。get (back) in (to) shape 即「恢復體能」，表示透過運動來達到體適能的健康標準。

A: I really need to get back into shape.
  我很需要重拾強健體魄。
B: You should come to my yoga class.
  你該來上我的瑜伽課。

Grammar Master

help 的使用

不論是在書面或是口語，help 都是高頻率用字，運用範圍也很廣。當我們想表達「幫助某人某事」時，可以選用下面任一種句型：

● help + 人 + V
● help + 人 + with + 事

例 I **helped** <u>him fill out</u> the application form.
= I **helped** <u>him with the application form</u>.
  我幫他填寫申請表。

例 Can you **help** <u>me wash</u> the dishes?
= Can you **help** <u>me with the dishes</u>?
  你能不能幫我洗碗？

help 另一種常見用法為 can't/couldn't help + Ving，意指「忍不住做某事、不能停止做某事」，與原先的「幫助」相去甚遠。使用時，請注意要使用 V-ing 的型式。

例 She **can't help crying** whenever she hears that song.
  她每次聽到那首歌都會忍不住哭泣。

例 I **couldn't help laughing** when the man slipped and fell.
  那個人滑倒的時候，我忍不住笑了出來。

Know it ALL 英文閱讀

Vocabulary Bank

1) **footage** [ˈfʊtɪdʒ] (n.) 影片片段，連續畫面
The man sold his footage of the protest to CNN.

2) **trigger** [ˈtrɪɡɚ] (v.) 觸發，引起
The beating of the protester triggered a riot.

3) **medal** [ˈmɛdl] (n.) 獎牌，獎章
The swimmer won three gold medals in the competition.

4) **increasingly** [ɪnˈkrisɪŋlɪ] (adv.) 漸增
(v.) increase [ɪnˈkris] 增加
People are increasingly relying on cell phones to communicate.

5) **elsewhere** [ˈɛls.wɛr] (adv.) 在別處，其他地方
The store sells items that are hard to find elsewhere.

6) **handicapped** [ˈhændɪ.kæpt] (a.) 殘障的，visually handicaped 即「視障的」
(n./v.) handicap [ˈhændɪ.kæp] 障礙；妨礙
Rob got a ticket for parking in a handicapped zone.

進階字彙

7) **grueling** [ˈɡruəlɪŋ] (a.) 讓人極度勞累的
Digging ditches is grueling work.

Tongue-tied No More

1 conquer the odds
克服萬難

odds 是「成功的機會」（固定加 s），conquer 是「征服，戰勝」，加在一起就是獲勝，而且是「突破萬難終獲成功」，因此都用在一開始不被看好的事情。相同意思的說法還有 beat the odds、against (all) the odds、against all odds。

A: Doesn't Celia know how hard it is to make it in show business?
希莉雅不知道要進入演藝圈有多難嗎？

B: Yeah, but she thinks she can beat the odds.
知道啊，但她覺得自己能克服萬難。

While the early California triathlons were small events, this all changed ⓖwhen one of the participants moved to Hawaii. Once there, he successfully combined three popular endurance events on the island of Oahu into the triathlon that became known as the Ironman. It was so 7)**grueling** that only twelve men completed the first one in 1978, and only thirteen men and one woman the following year. But television 1)**footage** of Julie Moss crawling across the finish line in 1982 2)**triggered** an explosion of interest in triathlons across the world. Triathlon events were added to international sports competitions like the Pan American Games in the 1990s, and the triathlon became a 3)**medal** sport at the 2000 Olympic Games in Sydney.

Triathlons are becoming 4)**increasingly** popular in East Asia too, and there are now Ironman competitions in Japan, Malaysia and China. Here in Taiwan, there is already a tradition of triathlons going back more than a decade. The 1995 President Cup International Triathlon

Championship, held on Shanyuan Beach near Taidong,

25 attracted 420 participants from Taiwan, Japan, the United States and 5)**elsewhere**. By 2008, the Uni-President sprint triathlon held at Sun Moon Lake attracted over a thousand participants. Even the 2009 Deaflympics in Taipei featured a triathlon for visually 6)**handicapped** youngsters. The

30 triathlon is no longer just a test of strength and endurance for hardcore athletes, but an inspiration for active people everywhere to test their own limits and ■ **conquer the odds**. As they say, just completing a triathlon makes you a winner!

中 Translation

雖然早期在加州的三項全能是小型比賽，但一名參賽者移居夏威夷後，一切全然改觀。一搬到那裡，他便將歐胡島上三種廣受歡迎的耐力競賽成功結合成後來眾所皆知的鐵人三項。那比賽實在太累人了，一九七八年第一屆賽事只有十二位男性賽完全程，次年也只有十三位男性和一位女性完成。但一九八二年茱莉摩斯爬過終點線的電視轉播畫面激發了全世界對三項全能運動的興趣。一九九〇年代，泛美運動會等各大國際體育賽事陸續增設三項全能運動，三項全能運動也成為二〇〇〇年雪梨奧運的奪牌運動。

三項全能運動也在東亞愈來愈受歡迎，目前，日本、馬來西亞和中國都有鐵人賽事。在台灣這裡，三項全能運動已經有十多年的歷史。一九九五年，在台東杉原海水浴場舉行的統一盃鐵人三項國際邀請賽，吸引了來自台、日、美等地共四二〇位選手參賽。二〇〇八年，在日月潭舉行的統一盃鐵人賽更吸引了一千多名參賽者。連二〇〇九年台北聽障奧運也有一場年輕視障選手的三項全能賽事。三項全能運動不再只是考驗死忠運動員的體力和耐力，而是成為激勵人心的活動，讓各地熱愛活動的民眾可以測試自身極限、克服萬難。正如他們所說，只要能完成三項全能賽事，就是贏家！

Language Guide

Pan American Games 泛美運動會

pan- 這個字首表示「全部」all、「（某族群）全體」，因此 Pan American 就表示「全美洲的」。Pan American Sports Organization（PASO，泛美運動組織）總部設於墨西哥市。Pan American Games 為四年一度的國際運動會，於各屆奧運開幕前一年由各美洲城市輪流主舉辦。

Ironman Triathlon 鐵人三項

鐵人三項有很嚴格的時間限制，所有參賽者比須在十七個小時內抵達終點。早上七點準時開始比賽，必須於兩小時二十分內完成游泳項目；下午五點半前抵達自行車終點；最後一段的「馬拉松」marathon [ˈmærə͵θɑn] 路跑須於當天午夜十二點前跑完。

Grammar Master

過去簡單式中 when 的使用

when 作為表示時間的連接詞，表示「當……之時」。當句子中出現連接詞 when，且兩個子句均為過去簡單式時，由 when 引導子句的動作先發生，例如：

例 Dan moved out of his parents' house **when he got a job**. 先發生
丹找到工作後就搬離父母家。

≠ Dan got a job **when he moved out of his parent's house**. 先發生
丹搬離父母家之後就找到工作。

Mini Quiz 閱讀測驗

1 According to historians, where did the triathlon originate?
(A) America
(B) France
(C) Taiwan
(D) Japan

2 Martha used to help her Mom _____ the housework.
(A) for
(B) make
(C) on
(D) with

3 下列句子請根據需要填入 of，或打「X」表示免填
(A) China has the most _____ people of any country in the world.

(B) One _____ those books is mine.

(C) I know several _____ Jack's friends.

(D) I bought a few _____ books yesterday.

閱讀測驗解答 1 (B) 2 (D) 3 (X, of, of, X)

Vocabulary Bank

1) **export** [ˋɛksport] (n./v.) 輸出，出口。import 為「進口」
Coffee is one of Costa Rica's main exports.

2) **athlete** [ˋæθlit] (n.) 運動員
Michael Phelps is the world's most famous Olympic athlete.

3) **headline** [ˋhɛd͵laɪn] (n.) 新聞（大）標題，頭條新聞
Did you read the headline in today's paper?

4) **championship** [ˋtʃæmpɪən͵ʃɪp] (n.) 錦標賽；冠軍稱號
The team won a stunning victory in the championship.

5) **title** [ˋtaɪtl] (n.) 冠軍
The boxer has a good chance of winning the heavyweight title.

6) **serve** [sɝv] (n./v.) 發球（權）
Andy Roddick is known for his powerful serve.

7) **match** [mætʃ] (n.) 比賽，競賽
Did you watch the tennis match on TV last night?

8) **dedicate (to)** [ˋdɛdɪ͵ket] (v.) 以⋯獻給
The director dedicated his Oscar to his parents.

9) **reveal** [rɪˋvil] (v.) 揭曉，透露
The winner of the contest will be revealed tonight.

10) **awful** [ˋɔful] (a.) 可怕的，嚇人的
The food at that restaurant is awful.

11) **rank** [ræŋk] (v.) 排名，把⋯分級
(n.) ranking [ˋræŋkɪŋ] 等級，地位
Martin ranks among the top students in his class

進階字彙

12) **leaguer** [ˋligɚ] (n.) 聯盟成員。little leaguer 即「少棒聯盟選手」
The player's greatest goal is to become a major leaguer.

13) **agility** [əˋdʒɪlətɪ] (n.) 敏捷，靈活
Gymnastics requires good balance and agility.

口語補充

14) **crowd favorite** [kraʊd ˋfev(ə)rɪt]
(n.) 萬人迷，受人愛戴者
The young pitcher is a crowd favorite.

Taiwan's Rising Stars
台灣體育之光

課文朗讀 MP3 274　單字朗讀 MP3 275　英文文章導讀 MP3 276

No Longer Chasing Chickens

There was a time not too long ago when Taiwan's little [12)]**leaguers** were the island's most famous sporting [1)]**export**. Today, three young [2)]**athletes** with connections to Taiwan are making [3)]**headlines** both at home and abroad. Who are these rising stars?

5　　When Lu Yen-hsun defeated American Andy Roddick in the fourth round of last summer's Wimbledon [4)]**Championships**, he shocked the tennis world. After all, Roddick had become a [14)]**crowd favorite** after losing to Roger Federer in an epic final the year before, and many expected him to challenge for the [5)]**title** again. With patient play, however, the 26-year-old Lu finally broke Roddick's [6)]**serve** in the fifth set, and went on to win the biggest [7)]**match** of his young career. In his post-match interview, which he gave in English, Lu [8)]**dedicated** his victory to his family and his father, who had

15 recently passed away. "I did it for my father," he said, "I did it for myself also. I did it for all the people who support me."

Long before Lu was playing on Wimbledon's famous grass courts, he was chasing chickens on a farm in Taoyuan, where he grew up. As a boy, he would wake up early to help his father catch

20 the chickens, which was no easy task. "It's very tough work," Lu [9)]**revealed**. "They're always working between one in the morning to six in the morning, very early." [G]While neither the hours nor the [10)]**awful** smell appealed to him, the job gave him the speed and [13)]**agility** he displays on the tennis court today. Lu, [11)]**ranked** 39th

25 by the ATP, surely has a bright future ahead of him.

Mini Quiz 閱讀測驗

❶ ▮▮▮▮ **According to the article, which of the following is true about**
Lu Yen-hsun?
(A) He won Wimbledon last summer.
(B) He lost to Roger Federer at Wimbledon.
(C) He beat Andy Roddick at Wimbledon.
(D) He made it to the finals at Wimbledon.

❷ ▮▮▮▮ **How did working on a chicken farm help Lu become a better**
tennis player?
(A) It trained him to wake up early in the morning.
(B) The tough work made him stronger.
(C) It gave him time to practice his tennis.
(D) It made him faster and more nimble.

中 Translation

告別追雞的日子

不久之前有一段時間，台灣少棒選手曾是本島最有名的運動輸出品。如今，有三位和台灣有關聯的年輕運動員，已占據國內外的頭條新聞。這些明日之星到底是何方神聖？

去年夏天的溫布頓錦標賽第四輪比賽，盧彥勳打敗美國選手安迪羅迪克的時候，震撼了整個網球界。 畢竟，羅迪克前年在史詩般慘烈的決賽中輸給羅傑費德勒之後，他就成為眾人的寵兒，很多人期待他今年再度挑戰冠軍頭銜。不過，靠著耐心地穩紮穩打，二十六歲的盧彥勳最後在第五盤破了羅迪克的發球局，接著贏得他年輕職業生涯的最大比賽。在賽後訪問中，他全程以英文回答，並將這項勝利獻給他的家人和剛剛過世的父親。「這是為了我父親，」他說：「也是為了我自己，還有為了所有支持我的人。」

早在盧彥勳踏上溫布頓著名的草地球場打球之前，他在桃園的農場上追著雞跑，這就是他長大的地方。他還是個小男孩的時候，會每天早起幫忙父親抓雞，這可不是簡單的工作。「這是很難的工作，」盧彥勳說道：「他們總是在凌晨一點到六點工作，非常早。」儘管這份工作對他來說時間不對，味道也難聞，但是這份差事造就了他今日在網球場上展現的速度和靈敏。盧彥勳，男子職業網球排名第三十九名（編註：此排名統計截自二○一○年十月中旬），未來的前途肯定是一片光明。

✦ Language Guide

ATP 男子職業網球

ATP 全名為 Association of Tennis Professionals（職業網球球員協會），是世界男子職業網球選手的自治組織機構，性質類似球員工會，成立於一九七二年。主要任務是協調職業運動員和賽事之間的夥伴關係，並負責組織和管理職業選手的積分、排名、獎金分配，以及制定比賽規則和給予或取消選手參賽資格等工作。

世界四大網球公開賽

常常聽說的「大滿貫」grand slam 就是將世界網球四大公開賽的冠軍全部抱回的大贏家。四大公開賽分別為：

©Rg030

Australian Open
澳洲網球公開賽
每年的一月在澳洲舉行，是唯一參賽選手必須同時在草地球場跟硬地球場上比賽的賽事。

©Arnaud25

French Open
法國網球公開賽
每年五月底到六月初舉行是四大公開賽中唯一的紅土球場 (clay court)。

©Albert Lee

The Wimbledon Championships
溫布頓網球公開賽
每年六月底到七月初舉行，是四大公開賽中歷史最悠久，也是唯一的草地球場 (grass court)。

©Darylsam

U.S. Open 美國網球公開賽
每年的八月底至九月初舉行，場地為硬地球場 (hard court)，也是四大賽中唯一一保持男女同酬獎金制度的賽事。

G Grammar Master

用 while 連接兩個對比的事件

句型 While S+V, S+V. 或 S+V, while S+V.
在英文中 while 和 whereas 都可以表示前後兩句直接的對比，順序可以對調，不影響意義。注意 while 子句不論在前或在後，兩個子句中間都會用逗號隔開來表示對比和停頓。whereas 通常出現在比較正式的書寫中，while 則比較常用。

例 While a used car would be cheaper, a new car would be more reliable.
= A used car would be cheaper, while a new car would be more reliable.
二手車雖然比較便宜，但新車比較靠得住。

閱讀測驗解答 **❶** (C) **❷** (D)

Vocabulary Bank

1) **tournament** [ˋtɝnəmənt] (n.) 錦標賽，聯賽
The chess player has won many tournaments.

2) **stroke** [strok] (n./v.) （高爾夫球、網球、撞球等的）擊球，打法
My tennis coach is helping me work on my stroke.

3) **identify** [aɪˋdɛntə͵faɪ] (n./v.) 確認，識別，發現
The police identified the suspect by his tattoo.

4) **profile** [ˋprofaɪl] (n.) （人物）簡介
There's an author profile at the back of the book.

5) **historic** [hɪˋstɔrɪk] (n.) 歷史上著名的、有重大意義的
The town is filled with historic buildings.

6) **domestically** [dəˋmɛstɪklɪ] (adv.) 在國內
(a.) domestic [dəˋmɛstɪk] 國家的，國內的
Most of the company's products are domestically produced.

7) **delight** [dɪˋlaɪt] (v.) 使高興，取悅
The magician delighted the kids with his tricks.

8) **assembled** [əˋsɛmbld] (a.) 聚集的，集合的
The principal spoke to the assembled students.

9) **swing** [swɪŋ] (v.) （運動）揮（桿、棒等）
The batter swung at the ball and missed.

進階字彙

10) **impression** [ɪmˋprɛʃən] (n.) 印象
(v.) impress [ɪmˋprɛs] 給…極深的印象
What was your impression of Jennifer's boyfriend?

11) **overjoyed** [͵ovɚˋdʒɔɪd] (a.) 欣喜若狂的，極度高興的
Carolyn was overjoyed that she won the scholarship.

口語補充

12) **pro** [pro] (a./n.) 職業（選手），
為 professional 的簡稱，turn/go pro
即「晉升職業選手」
The player hopes to go pro next season.

Tongue-tied No More

1 to one's name 屬於某人名下

to one's name 表示「屬於某人名下所有的」，常用於指稱某人名下擁有的資產。

A: Maybe you can borrow the money from Jason.
也許你可以跟傑森借錢。

B: Jason? Are you kidding? He doesn't have a penny to his name.
傑森？你在開玩笑嗎？他身無分文。

©Wojiech Migda

課文朗讀 MP3 277　單字朗讀 MP3 278　英文文章導讀 MP3 279

Sing When You're Winning

Lu Yen-hsun isn't the only athlete from Taiwan to make an [10)]**impression** in the U.K. this year. Yani Tseng, just 21 years old, won the Women's British Open golf [1)]**tournament** in August by a single [2)]**stroke**. ⊙Having already won the Kraft Nabisco
5 Championship earlier in the year and the LPGA Championship in 2008, she's become the youngest female golfer in the modern era to win three major championships.

In her climb up the rankings, Yani Tseng has followed in the footsteps of a number of leading female golfers from Asia,
10 like South Korea's Se Ri Pak. It's hall-of-famer Annika Sorenstam, however, who Tseng [3)]**identifies** as her idol. She carries a note from her hero that says "Trust your ability," and even bought Sorenstam's house outside Orlando, Florida in 2009. According to her [4)]**profile** on LPGA.com, Tseng dreams of owning a
15 Lamborghini. With close to US$4.5 million in prize money **1 to her name** since turning [12)]**pro** in 2007, she could buy a pair!

韓國高球選手补世莉

©Keith Allison
曾雅妮的偶像安妮卡索倫絲坦

In her interview after winning the British Open, an [11]**overjoyed** Tseng reported that she'd been receiving text messages from friends back home and thought that her victory would be "huge in Taiwan." She also expressed her hope that her [5]**historic** win would help grow the sport [6]**domestically**. The shy champion even [7]**delighted** the [8]**assembled** media by singing a few lines from Minnie Ripperton's "Lovin' You," which she said helped her relax on the course. Indeed, it's hard not to love Tseng the way she's been [9]**swinging**—and winning—lately.

Mini Quiz 閱讀測驗

❶ **According to the article, which of the following is true about Annika Sorenstam?**
(A) She is Yani Tseng's hero.
(B) She's a leading female golfer from Asia.
(C) She considers Yani Tseng her idol.
(D) She's more famous than Se Ri Pak.

❷ **When did Tseng start playing golf for a living?**
(A) When she turned 21
(B) In 2007
(C) In 2008
(D) In 2009

中 Translation

唱出勝利樂章

盧彥勳並非今年唯一在英國大放異彩的台灣運動員。年僅二十一歲的曾雅妮,今年八月以一桿之差贏得英國女子公開賽的冠軍。她今年初已經贏得卡夫特納貝斯克錦標賽,也拿下二〇〇八年的美國女子職業高球聯盟冠軍,已成為當代贏得三大賽冠軍的最年輕女子高爾夫球選手。

在她的排名逐漸上升的過程中,曾雅妮一直追隨亞洲許多頂尖女子高爾夫球選手的步伐,例如南韓的补世莉。不過,曾雅妮視為偶像的人,是已經進入名人堂的安妮卡索倫絲坦。她隨身攜帶偶像寫的小紙條,上面寫著「相信自己的能力」,甚至在二〇〇九年買下索倫絲坦位於佛羅里達州奧蘭多外圍的房子。根據她在美國女子職業高球聯盟官方網站上的檔案資料,曾雅妮夢想擁有一台藍寶堅尼跑車。自從二〇〇七年轉戰職業選手至今,她名下的獎金已經累積將近四百五十萬美元,買兩台都沒問題!

贏得英國公開賽的賽後訪問中,欣喜若狂的曾雅妮說她一直收到家鄉朋友的簡訊,她認為她的勝利將會是「台灣的大事」。她也表達了自己的期望,希望她這個歷史性的勝利有助於這項運動在國內的發展。這位害羞的冠軍甚至唱了幾句蜜妮萊普頓的「愛你」來取悅聚集的媒體,她說唱這首歌能幫助她在球場上放鬆。的確,曾雅妮近來的球技和勝利,很難叫人不愛上她。

Language Guide

LPGA 女子職業高爾夫球協會

LPGA 全名是 Ladies Professional Golf Association,其實這個協會世界各國都有,但是名氣最大的是美國的 LPGA,因為他們每年二月到十二月舉辦的 LPGA Tour 聞名於世,是所有女子高爾夫球好手追求的至高榮譽。至於男子高爾夫球的賽事則是 PGA Tour。

世界四大高球公開賽

Masters Tournament 美國名人賽
也稱為 The Masters,每年四月由 Augusta National Golf Club(奧古斯塔球場)舉辦。依照傳統,勝利者會穿上代表名人賽冠軍的綠色外套。

United States Open Championship 美國公開賽
亦簡稱為 U.S. Open,由美國高爾夫協會 (USGA) 於每年的六月主辦,為了避免某些選手因為熟悉場地而造成比賽不公,故比賽隨機任選美國境內球場作為賽地。

The Open Championship 英國公開賽
常稱為 British Open,始於一八六〇年,是四大公開賽中歷史最悠久的賽事,也是唯一在美國境外舉行的高爾夫球公開賽,每年七月由英國的高爾夫球組織 R&A 主辦。

PGA Championship PGA 錦標賽
每年八月在美國舉辦,由於是每年四大公開賽事中最後一項,因此也被戲稱為「光榮的最後一擊」Glory's last shot。

hall-of-famer 名人堂名人
很多種運動都有設名人堂 (hall-of-fame),因為在該運動界中達成的不凡成就,而應邀進入名人堂的選手就是 hall-of-famer。高爾夫球的名人堂就是由二十六個高爾夫球組織所創辦的世界高爾夫名人堂 (World Golf Hall of Fame)。

Grammar Master

Ving 引導的分詞構句

用法 S+V1, S+V2. = Ving ..., S+ V2
當兩個子句的主詞相同,我們可以刪掉 V1 的主詞,把 V1 改成分詞,表示主詞所處的狀態:
例 <u>Sam</u> **is** fluent in French. <u>Sam</u> handles all the company's French clients.
= **Being** fluent in French, <u>Sam</u> handles all the company's French clients.
　山姆的法文很流利,負責接洽公司所有法國客戶。

但如果 V1 的動作比 V2 早發生,那麼先發生的動作則要改成 Having + p.p.。如文章中第 4 行,won the Championship… 比 ...become the youngest female golfer... 還要早發生,就必須改成 **Having** <u>won</u> the Nabisco Championship earlier...
例 **Having** <u>forgotten</u> to bring his camera, Jack didn't take any pictures on his trip.
　因為沒帶相機,傑克在旅程中沒拍任何照片。

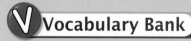

金州勇士隊的主場館
Oracle Arena

Vocabulary Bank

1) **celebrated** [ˈsɛlə͵bretɪd] (a.) 著名的，馳名的
Mark Twain is one of America's most celebrated authors.

2) **emigrate** [ˈɛmɪ͵ɡret] (v.) 移居外地，移民
Kevin's parents emigrated from Hong Kong to America when he was a child.

3) **excel** [ɪkˈsɛl] (v.) 表現優異，勝過他人
Lisa excels at math and science.

4) **draft** [dræft] (n./v.)（職業運動的）選秀
The team added several new players in the draft.

5) **recall** [rɪˈkɔl] (v.) 回想，想起
I can't recall the last time I had a meal this good.

6) **recognize** [ˈrɛkəɡ͵naɪz] (v.) 認出，發現
Yo-Yo Ma's musical talents were recognized early on.

7) **potential** [pəˈtɛnʃəl] (n./a.) 潛力，可能性；潛在的，可能的
Going to university will help you reach your full potential.

8) **assist** [əˈsɪst] (n.)（籃球）助攻
That player holds the season record for assists.

進階字彙

9) **rebound** [rɪˈbaʊnd] (n./v.) 籃板球，（球等）彈回
Who leads the league in rebounds?

Language Guide

Ivy League 常春藤聯盟

Ivy League 是指由位於美國東北部的八所大學組成的名校聯盟，這八所學校都是美國最頂尖、最難進入的大學，也是全世界接受捐款最多的學校，擁有優秀的學生與師資。

八所常春藤盟校依英文首字母排序如下：

● Brown University 布朗大學
● Columbia University 哥倫比亞大學
● Cornell University 康乃爾大學
● Dartmouth College 達特茅斯學院
● Harvard University 哈佛大學
● University of Pennsylvania 賓州大學
● Princeton University 普林斯頓大學
● Yale University 耶魯大學

課文朗讀 MP3 280　單字朗讀 MP3 281　英文文章導讀 MP3 282

A Basketball Ph.D.

Lu and Tseng have joined professional baseball players Kuo Hong-chih and Wang Chien-ming as Taiwan's most 1)**celebrated** athletes, but it won't be long before one more name is added to that list. Jeremy Lin, a 6-foot-3 (191 cm)
5　basketball guard, signed a contract with the Golden State Warriors last summer to become the first American-born Taiwanese to play in the NBA. Although Lin, 22, was born and raised in Palo Alto, California—his parents 2)**emigrated** from Changhua County—©there is no doubt that fans in
10　basketball-mad Taiwan will claim him as one of their own.

After graduating from Harvard University, where he 3)**excelled** both in the classroom and on the basketball court, Lin wasn't selected during the 2010 NBA 4)**Draft**. "People always said you wouldn't be able to make it to the NBA," he 5)**recalls**.
15　He impressed during an NBA summer league, however, and invitations from several teams soon followed, including the Warriors, his favorite. Lin—Ivy League educated and Asian American—isn't your typical professional basketball player, but ©those who know the game 6)**recognize** his high basketball
20　IQ and 7)**potential**. There's no doubt that his every jump shot, 8)**assist**, and 9)**rebound** will be cheered by basketball fans from the Bay Area to Taipei this season.

Whether you're a tennis, golf, basketball or baseball fan, there's a lot to like about Taiwan's star athletes. With their
25　talent and your support, they're sure to reach even greater heights in the years to come.

© 達志影像

NBA 美國職籃

NBA 的全文是 National Basketball Association（國家籃球協會），但一般直接稱 NBA 或美國職籃或 NBA 籃球聯賽，是美國第一大職業籃球賽事。協會一共擁有三十支球隊，分屬東區聯盟 (Eastern Conference) 和西區聯盟 (Western Conference)，而每個聯盟各由三個分區 (division) 組成，每個分區有五支球隊。三十支球隊當中只有一支來自加拿大，其餘都位於美國本土。

NBA 正式賽季於每年十一月開打，分為常規賽 (regular season) 和季後賽 (playoffs) 兩部分。每個聯盟的前八名，包括各個分區的冠軍，有資格進入季後賽。季後賽採用七戰四勝制，共分四輪；季後賽的最後一輪也稱為總決賽 (NBA Finals)，由兩個聯盟冠軍爭奪 NBA 總冠軍。

NBA 台灣第一人？

林書豪是首位正式踏入 NBA 的台裔球員，為什麼強調台裔而不是台灣人，因為林書豪的父母是美國的台灣移民，他沒有台灣護照，從小到大也沒在台灣打過球，只能說是正宗台灣出品。因此真正土生土長，又在台灣打籃球打進 NBA 的球員，至今在紀錄上還是掛零。台灣唯一最接近 NBA 的，應屬現在中國東莞打球的陳信安，他原本是裕隆隊的球員，曾經先後參加沙加緬度國王隊 (Sacramento Kings) 和丹佛金磚隊 (Denver Nuggets) 訓練營，並在熱身賽中出賽。

Mini Quiz 閱讀測驗

❶ ☐ **Why was Jeremy Lin offered a contract by the Warriors?**
(A) Because he excelled in school and on the court
(B) Because he played well in Summer League games
(C) Because he wasn't selected during the 2010 NBA Draft
(D) Because he received invitations from several teams

❷ ☐ **Which of the following is NOT true about Lin?**
(A) He grew up in the United States.
(B) He is the first Taiwanese American to play in the NBA.
(C) He graduated from an Ivy League university.
(D) He's one of Taiwan's most celebrated athletes.

Translation

籃球博士

盧彥勳和曾雅妮已經加入職棒球員郭泓志與王建民的行列，成為台灣最知名的運動員，不過不久之後那張名單又將增添了一個名字。林書豪，六呎三吋（一百九十一公分）的籃球後衛，今年夏天與金州勇士隊簽約，成為首位加入美國職籃的美國出生台灣人。儘管二十二歲的林書豪是在加州帕羅奧多出生長大，但他的父母是從彰化縣移居至此，所以無庸置疑，瘋籃球的台灣球迷會說他也是台灣人。

哈佛大學畢業後（他在課堂上和籃球場上都表現優異），林書豪在二〇一〇美國職籃選秀中鎩羽而歸。他回憶：「大家都說你進不了美國職籃的。」不過，他在美國職籃夏季聯賽中表現出色，好幾支球隊的邀約不久就接踵而至，其中包括他最愛的勇士隊。林書豪，在常春藤盟校念書又是亞裔美國人，並不是典型的職籃球員，但是真正懂籃球的人看出他的高超的籃球智商和潛能。今年球季開始，從灣區到台北的籃球迷無疑都會為他的每次跳投、助攻和籃板而歡呼。

無論你是網球迷、高爾夫球迷、籃球迷或是棒球迷，台灣明星運動員都值得你青睞。他們的天分加上你的支持，他們鐵定會在來年攀上更高的顛峰。

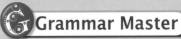

Grammar Master

There is no doubt that S+V
毫無疑問地……

在英文中我們要表示某件事情是「毫無疑問」的，我們可以在 There is no doubt that 後方直接說出這件事情。類似的表達還有：

◆ It is doubtless that...
It goes without saying that...
Needless to say, S+V.
Without a doubt, S+V.

例 **There's no doubt** that the Chinese economy will continue to grow.
中國的經濟無疑會持續成長。

those/people who... 那些……的人

如果形容詞子句要修飾的對象不是那麼確定，在英文中會直接用 those 或 people 來代替。如果 who 是在受格位置，則可以省略。像是社群網站 Facebook 上經常會顯示出 people you may know，這裡的 people 後方就是省略在受格位置的 who(m) (You may know these people.)

例 A parade was held to honor **those who** died in the war.
這場遊行是為了向戰死者致敬。

這種不確定的對象也可以用單數 he/one who... 表示「凡是……的人」，常見於正式用法。

例 **He who** laughs last, laughs best.
最後笑的人笑得才最開心。

閱讀測驗解答 ❶ (B) ❷ (D)

人體進化死角

Evolutionary Dead Ends
—Tonsils and Other Useless Body Parts

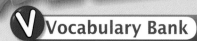

Vocabulary Bank

1) **evolutionary** [ˌɛvəˈluʃənˌɛrɪ] (a.) 進化的
I'm taking a class in evolutionary biology.

2) **bacteria** [bækˈtɪrɪə] (n.) 細菌bacterium [bækˈtɪrɪəm] 的複數
Many bacteria are beneficial to human health.

3) **overwhelm** [ˌovəˈhwɛlm] (v.) 征服，淹沒
(phr.) be/get overwhelmed with…
It's a myth that the immune system can be overwhelmed by vaccines.

4) **infection** [ɪnˈfɛkʃən] (n.) 感染
Most ear infections can be treated with antibiotics.

5) **thus** [ðʌs] (adv.) 因此，從而
Less than 3% of the Earth's water is fresh, and thus suitable for drinking.

6) **subject** [ˈsʌbdʒɪkt] (n.) 話題
(phr.) on the subject of… 談到…
Since we're on the subject of salaries, let's talk about the year-end bonus.

補充字彙

* dead end [dɛd ɛnd] 盡頭，死角

* tonsil [ˈtɑnsl] (n.) 扁桃腺（因左右一對，常為複數）。

* tonsillectomy [ˌtɑnslˈɛktəmɪ] (n.) 扁桃腺切除手術

* considering [kənˈsɪdərɪŋ] (prep.) 考慮到，就…而論

* lymphatic [lɪmˈfætɪk] (a., n.) 淋巴的；淋巴腺的

* microorganism [ˌmaɪkroˈɔrgəˌnɪzəm] (n.) 微生物（常為複數）

* hooky [ˈhʊkɪ] (n.) （美國口語）逃學
(phr.) play hooky

* appendix [əˈpɛndɪks] (n.) 闌尾，同vermiform [ˈvɜːməˌfɔrm] appendix

* cecum [ˈsikəm] (n.) 盲腸

* intestine [ɪnˈtɛnstɪn] (n.) 腸，large intestine即「大腸」

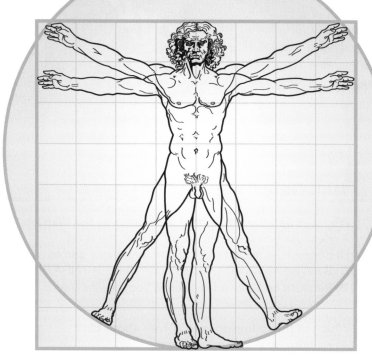

課文朗讀 MP3 283　單字朗讀 MP3 284　英文文章導讀 MP3 285

When we think of useless body parts, *tonsils are usually the first things that come to mind. That's not surprising, *considering the painful *tonsillectomy most of us had as children. Strictly speaking, though, the tonsils
5　aren't exactly useless. Like other organs in the *lymphatic system, tonsils are part of our immune system, and help protect us against 2)**bacteria** and other *microorganisms.

The problem comes when they get 3)**overwhelmed** with bacteria and become targets of 4)**infection**
10　themselves—5)**thus** the tonsillectomy we all remember so well. So while not useless, our tonsils usually end up causing us more harm than good. On the other hand, most of us also

remember all the ice cream we got to eat while recovering from our tonsillectomy, and who'd miss the chance to play
15 *hooky for a few days!

While still on the [6]**subject** of not completely useless parts, the *appendix, or more precisely the *vermiform appendix, is worth a mention. The word "vermiform," which comes from Latin, means "worm-like"—which is a pretty
20 good description of this narrow tube that is attached to the *cecum, a pouch-like structure that forms the beginning of the large *intestine.

Due to the fact that the appendix can cause death through infection, and the general good health of patients
25 who have had their appendix removed, it was long thought that the organ had no useful function in the human body. However, recent experiments have shown that the appendix is rich in infection-fighting lymphatic cells, which suggests that it may play a role in the immune system.

中 Translation

進化的死角——扁桃腺及其他無用的身體部位

當我們想到無用的身體部位，第一個映入腦海的通常是扁桃腺。這並不令人訝異，只要想想我們大多數人小時候所受的扁桃腺切除手術之苦就能明白。但嚴格來說，扁桃腺並非完全無用。就如同淋巴系統其他器官，扁桃腺是免疫系統的一部分，能幫助我們抵抗細菌及其他微生物。

當扁桃腺被細菌擊潰，自己也成為感染的目標時，問題就來了——接著就是我們全都難忘的扁桃腺切除手術。所以儘管並非無用，我們的扁桃腺最終通常還是弊大於利。話又說回來，我們大多數人也記得扁桃腺切除手術復原期間吃的那一堆冰淇淋，而且誰會想錯過好幾天不用上學的機會！

既然還在討論並非完全無用的身體部位，盲腸，或講得更精確一點叫闌尾，就值得一提。vermiform這個字源於拉丁文，意思是「像蟲一樣」——用來形容這截接在盲腸（大腸最前端的袋狀體）上的窄管，倒是相當貼切。

由於盲腸受到感染會導致死亡，而且割除盲腸的病人一般來說都算健康，所以長期以來一直認為這個器官在人體內沒有功能。不過，最近的實驗顯示，盲腸富含可對抗感染的淋巴細胞，代表它可能在免疫系統扮演某種角色。

Language Guide

美國人為何難忘「扁桃腺切除手術」？

美國人接受扁桃腺切除手術的比例相當高，許多人的扁桃腺在兒童時期就「割掉」remove了。難怪文章一開頭說「想到無用的身體部位就想到扁桃腺」，而不是「智齒」wisdom teeth。

扁桃腺位於咽喉上方，手術後若過度吞嚥會造成傷口出血，因此復原期間患者必須吃冷的流質食物，冰淇淋就成了最受歡迎的選擇。接受手術的兒童大多需要在家休息一週讓傷口癒合。

對美國人來說，扁桃腺切除手術就代表一段痛苦、甜蜜與悠哉交織而成的童年回憶。

Have you had your tonsils out / removed?
你的扁桃腺割掉了嗎？

How old were you when you had your tonsils out / removed?
你幾歲的時候割扁桃腺的？

I don't get tonsillitis very often.
我的扁桃腺不常發炎。

Tonsillitis is so painful, I might as well get my tonsils removed.
扁桃腺炎超痛，乾脆去割扁桃腺算了。

Grammar Master

while的用法

while 當名詞用是「一會兒」的意思，但本文中出現幾個 while 的用法，則是當作連接詞來用：

❶ 作「當……的時候」、「在……的同時」來解釋。

...most of us also remember all the ice cream we got to eat while recovering from our tonsillectomy.

While still on the subject of not completely useless parts, the appendix, or more precisely the vermiform appendix, is worth a mention.

❷ 作「雖然」、「儘管」用：

So while not useless, our tonsils usually end up causing us more harm than good.

❸ 作「然而」解釋。在此補充說明本文未提及的「表示上下子句對比關係」的用法：

I enjoy staying at home while my girlfriend prefers going out.

Vocabulary Bank

1) **relate** [rɪˋlet] (v.) 有關
(phr.) be related to 與⋯有關
Scientists have long believed that humans are related to apes.

2) **tend** [tɛnd] (v.) 傾向，易於
(phr.) tend to
Aging brain cells tend to lose their function.

3) **essential** [ɪˋsɛnʃəl] (a.) 必不可少的
Vitamin C is an essential nutrient that the human body is unable to produce.

4) **contract** [kənˋtrækt] (v.) 收縮
Your pupils contract when exposed to bright light.

5) **mammal** [ˋmæmḷ] (n.) 哺乳動物
Bats are the only mammals that can fly.

6) **threaten** [ˋθrɛtṇ] (v.) 威脅
When threatened, blowfish can inflate to several times their normal size.

7) **goose bumps** [gus bʌmps] 雞皮疙瘩
I always get goose bumps when I hear that song.

補充字彙

* mandibular [mænˋdɪbjələ] (a.) 顎的

* molar [ˋmolə] (n.) 臼齒

* chomp [tʃɑmp] (v.) 大聲咀嚼（草料）

* sideways [ˋsaɪd,wez] (adv.) 從旁邊

* halfway [ˋhæfˋwe] (adv.) 不完全地

* extrinsic [ɛkˋstrɪnsɪk] (a.) 外在的

* trio [ˋtrio] (n.) 三個一組

* hone in [hon ɪn] (phr.) 鎖定

* wiggle [ˋwɪgḷ] (v.) 擺動

* erector pili [ɪˋrɛktə ˋpaɪlaɪ] 豎毛肌

* follicle [ˋfɑlɪkḷ] (n.) 小囊

課文朗讀 MP3 286　單字朗讀 MP3 287　英文文章導讀 MP3 288

And now on to the totally useless. Another part that is likely [1)]**related** to an earlier high-plant diet is the *mandibular third *molars, more commonly known as wisdom teeth. While they may have been useful back when
5　we were *chomping on leaves all day, these days only about 5% of the population has a healthy set of wisdom teeth. Because humans have smaller jaws than they used to, wisdom teeth [2)]**tend** to
10　grow in *sideways, grow in *halfway, or not grow in at all. While they may make our dentists pretty happy, they're definitely a big pain for the rest of us.

15　Next on the useless list are the *extrinsic ear muscles. This *trio of muscles allows animals like rabbits and dogs to move their ears independently of their heads so they can *hone in on faraway sounds. But ours are so weak that
20　we can barely manage to *wiggle our ears, and lots of people can't move their ears at all. While learning to wiggle your ears may be good for a few

25 laughs, it's hardly an 3)**essential** skill.

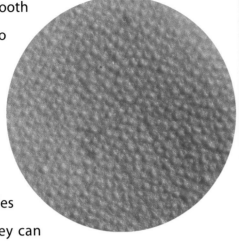

The *erector pili, a smooth muscle fiber attached to hair *follicles that makes hair stand up when it
30 4)contracts, is found in most 5)**mammals**, including humans. Many mammals use these muscles to puff up their fur so they can
35 keep warm in cold weather, and some use them to raise their fur so they appear bigger when they feel 6)**threatened**. Of course, we don't have enough body hair to keep us warm, so all these muscles do for us is give us 7)**goose bumps**.

中 Translation

現在來談一談完全無用的。另一個可能與人類早期吃大量植物有關的器官是下頜第三大臼齒，也就是一般所說的智齒。雖然在人類以前整天大嚼樹葉時它們可能很有用，但時至今日只剩大約5%的人會有一組健康的智齒。因為人類的下頜比以前小，智齒容易長歪、只冒出一半，或是完全不長出來。雖然智齒可能會讓我們的牙醫笑口常開，對我們其他人而言卻絕對很痛苦。

無用名單的下一個是外耳肌肉。這三條一組的肌肉可以讓兔子或狗這類動物不轉頭就能擺動耳朵，讓牠們能鎖定遠處的聲響。但人類的外耳肌肉非常無力，使得我們幾乎無法擺動耳朵，許多人更是完全無法讓耳朵動上一動。練習搖耳朵或許能讓人莞爾一笑，但完全算不上是必要技能。

豎毛肌是附著於毛囊的一條平滑肌，收縮的時候會讓毛髮豎立，大多數哺乳動物身上都有，包括人類在內。許多哺乳動物利用這種肌肉來蓬起皮毛，禦寒保暖；還有些動物在感覺受到威脅時，會利用這種肌肉豎起毛髮，讓自己看起來更大隻。當然啦，我們的體毛不夠多，無法保暖，這些肌肉只會讓我們起雞皮疙瘩。

Language Guide

痛起來要人命！

我們台灣人雖然不時興割扁桃腺，但大都有拔智齒的經驗。智齒大約是在16到24歲之間長出來（或是長不出來），讓我們在高中到大學期間飽受「牙齦發炎」gingivitis / inflammation of the gums 之苦。許多人最後的決定，就是長痛不如短痛，乾脆拔掉！

拔智齒之所以恐怖，在於它不像割扁桃腺要「全身麻醉」general anesthesia / put sb. under，絕大多數人拔智齒都是在神智清楚的情況下，讓牙醫在自己的嘴裡又鋸、又挖、又拔、又縫，接下來一兩天臉還會腫得像豬頭！

All of my wisdom teeth are impacted.
我的智齒全都是阻生牙。

When I was in high school, my wisdom teeth were always getting infected.
我念高中時，智齒老是受到感染。

Everybody says getting your wisdom teeth removed is really scary, so I haven't had the courage to do it.
大家都說拔智齒很恐怖，所以我遲遲不敢去拔。

I didn't get them removed until I was getting ready to study abroad two years ago.
一直到兩年前準備出國念書，我才去拔掉智齒。

Grammar Master

so + adj. +that... 太……以至於……

同樣表因果關係的句型還可以用 such+adj.+n.+that...

My English teacher speaks so fast that I can't understand her.

My English teacher is such a fast speaker that I can't understand her.
我的英文老師講話太快了，以至於我沒辦法聽懂。

課文朗讀 MP3 289　單字朗讀 MP3 290　英文文章導讀 MP3 291

Considering our *primate past, it shouldn't be surprising that a number of our useless parts are *leftovers from our tree-swinging days. The *palmaris longus muscle, a long, slender muscle that stretches from the elbow to the

5　wrist, may have been important in the past for climbing and hanging. It's completely missing in 11 percent of modern humans, and they seem to do fine without it. Another primate leftover is the *plantaris muscle, which runs from the back of the knee to the heel. It was used by

10　our primate ancestors to 1)**grip** things with their feet, and is missing in nine percent of modern humans.

And some useless parts may be leftovers from even further back in our evolutionary past. The third 2)**eyelid**, that small red 3)**patch** in the inner corner of your eye, is a

15　*remnant of the "*nictitating membrane," which is found in animals like chickens, lizards and sharks. While animals use the membrane to protect and

20　clean their eyes, ours just sits there looking like something that got stuck in our eye.

Vocabulary Bank

1) **grip** [grɪp] (v.) 抓牢
Before you swing, you need to learn how to grip the club.

2) **eyelid** [ˋaɪ͵lɪd] (n.) 眼皮
Camels have three eyelids to protect their eyes from blowing sand.

3) **patch** [pætʃ] (n.) 片狀的東西，斑點
Watch out for that patch of ice on the road.

4) **rib** [rɪb] (n.) 肋骨
Men and women both have 12 pairs of ribs.

5) **reptile** [ˋrɛptaɪl] (n.) 爬蟲類
Reptiles are unable to generate their own body heat.

6) **artery** [ˋɑrtərɪ] (n.) 動脈
Arteries carry blood away from the heart.

補充字彙

* primate [ˋpraɪmet] (n.) 靈長類動物

* leftover [ˋlɛft͵ovə] (n.) 殘餘物

* palmaris [palˋmarɪs] (a.) 手掌的，palmaris longus (muscle)即「掌長肌」

* plantaris [plænˋtarɪs] (a.) 腳底的

* remnant [ˋrɛmnənt] (n.) 殘餘，遺跡

* nictitating membrane [ˋnɪktɪ͵tetɪŋ ˋmɛmbren] 瞬膜

* cervical [ˋsɝvɪk!] (a.) 頸部的

* downright [ˋdaʊn͵raɪt] (adv.) 非常地

1 Last but not least, the neck $^{4)}$**rib**, or *cervical rib, which is possibly a leftover from the age of $^{5)}$**reptiles**. Neck

25 ribs are not only useless, but can be *downright dangerous. They often cause $^{6)}$**artery** and nerve problems, and children born with neck ribs are 125 times more likely to develop early childhood cancer than those who don't have them.
2 It's a good thing that they appear in less than one

30 percent of the population.

中 Translation

只要想一想我們過去是靈長類，應該就不會訝異於我們身上好幾個無用部位，都是從我們在樹上盪來盪去的日子遺留下來的。掌長肌是一條從手肘延伸至手腕的細長肌肉，在過去可能是攀爬、懸吊很重要的部位，現代人類有11%的人完全沒有這條肌肉，他們似乎都還過得好好的。另一個靈長類遺跡是蹠肌，這條肌肉從膝蓋後方延伸至腳跟，我們的靈長類祖先用腳抓東西時會用到它，而9%的現代人身上已經找不到了。

有一些些無用部位可能是更早之前的演化遺留物。第三眼瞼，也就是眼睛內側那塊小小的紅色肉墊，那是「瞬膜」的殘跡，瞬膜仍可在雞、蜥蜴和鯊魚等這類動物身上看到。動物會用瞬膜來保護、清潔眼睛，而我們的瞬膜就只杵在那邊，看起來像是什麼東西卡在眼睛裡。

最後一個也不遑多讓，頸肋骨可能是爬蟲類時期的遺跡。頸肋骨不僅無用，而且還可能非常危險。它們經常會引發動脈及神經問題，生下來就有頸肋骨的兒童，罹患早期兒童癌症的機率是沒有頸肋骨兒童的125倍，幸好只有不到1%的人身上會有頸肋骨。

Tongue-tied No More

1 Last but not least,...
　　最後提到的也不差

這個好用句是要讓大家知道「不要以為最後講的就不重要」，只要說出 Last but not least,... 保證讓人拉長耳朵洗耳恭聽，看看還有什麼好東西是你沒說出來的。

Last but not least, I'd like to thank my family for their love and support.
最後提到，但並非最不重要的是，我要感謝家人的愛與支持。

The room has a color TV, a balcony, and last but not least, a king-size bed.
這個房間有彩色電視機、陽台，最後還有個很讚的，一張特大號雙人床。

2 It's a good thing (that)... 幸好

這是一個固定的慣用語，下次碰到需要表示「幸好……」的時候，勇敢在It's a good thing 後面加上一個完整句子就對了！

A: Oh no, it just started pouring outside!
糟了，外面剛剛下起大雨！

B: It's a good thing I brought my umbrella.
幸好我有帶傘。

Grammar Master

Last but not least 的慣用語法以及 which 引導之非限定關係子句

Last but not least使用時句型很簡單，只要把你想說的「不代表最不重要」的那件東西直接放在後面，用個逗號隔開就好了！而什麼是非限定關係子句呢？關係子句也稱做「形容詞子句」，用來補充說明或是描述所提及的名詞，提供讀者對該名詞更詳盡的資訊。「非限定」表示這個補充說明的存在與否，並不影響到主要子句要表達的意思。

所以當你看到這個這麼長的句子正在想；「天啊！到底在說什麼？」的時候，別緊張，找出主要的句子和扮演說明角色的句子，一切就一目了然囉！就像文中這句話其實最重要的只有Last but not least, the neck rib. 這個句子而已，很簡單吧！

Do you know where these useless parts are?

人體無用部位分佈圖

the third eyelid
第三眼瞼

位於兩眼睛的內側，也就是平常會堆積眼屎的部位。

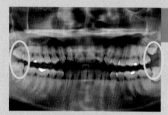

wisdom teeth
智齒

是人類恆齒中的第三對大臼齒(molar)。

tonsils
扁桃腺

位於咽喉上方，左右各一個，因此英文通常以複數形出現。

palmaris longus muscle
掌長肌

位於「前臂」forearm外側。palmaris 這個字要在醫學字典裡才找的到，意思就是 palmar「手掌的」。longus則是拉丁文的 long「長的」。

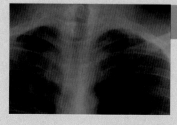

cervical rib
頸肋骨

這根多出來的肋骨長在第七節脊椎骨上，位於一般人的第一對肋骨上方。也有人長出「一對」頸肋骨，但這種病例非常罕見。

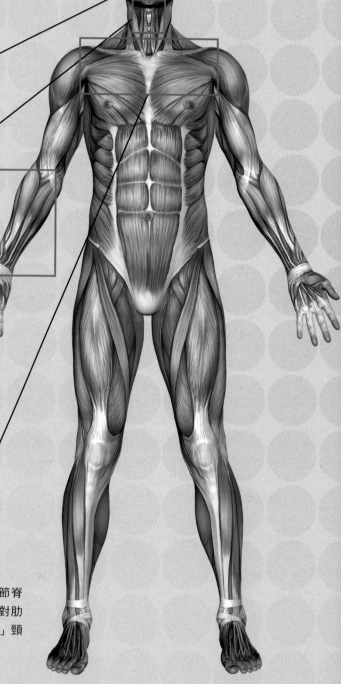

extrinsic ear muscles
外耳肌

長在頭外側的耳朵只是一些皮瓣，extrinsic ear muscles 是指連接這些皮瓣底部的三條肌肉，分別連到頭的上、前、後三個方向，由於這三條肌肉成組運作（其實是不運作……），文中才說 This trio of muscles...。至於「內耳」則是 inner ear。

erector pili
豎毛肌

滿布於全身皮膚，只要會起雞皮疙瘩的地方就有 erector pili。在皮膚的剖面圖中可以看到一小條連接毛囊與表皮的肌肉，那就是 erector pili。

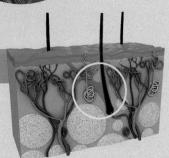

vermiform appendix
闌尾

大腸頭那一段袋狀的部位是「盲腸」cecum。而「闌尾」vermiform appendix 就是掛在盲腸下方那一截細細的管狀物。

文中已經解釋 vermiform 源自拉丁文「像蟲的」worm-like，其實 appendix 也源於拉丁文，意思是「懸掛於」to hang upon。至於 cecum 的拉丁文意思——你猜對了！就是 blind「盲的」。

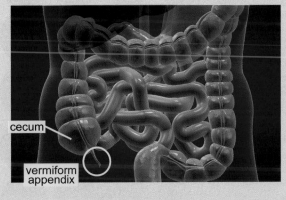

cecum

vermiform appendix

plantaris muscle
蹠肌

plantaris 是醫學用字，其實就是 plantar「腳底的，腳後跟」。

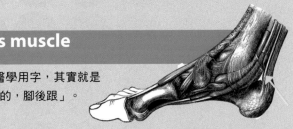

V Vocabulary Bank

1) **capacity** [kə`pæsətɪ] (n.) 能力，理解力
Researchers have found that apes have the capacity to learn language.

2) **horizon** [hə`raɪzn̩] (n.)（知識、經驗的）範圍，視野，intellectual horizons 即智力範圍」
Studying overseas is a great way to expand your horizons.

3) **gasp** [gæsp] (v.) 喘，上氣不接下氣；（因驚訝等）倒抽一口氣
The audience gasped in surprise when the magician made the lady disappear.

4) **deliberately** [dɪ`lɪbərɪtlɪ] (adv.) 刻意地
The boy admitted that he broke the vase deliberately.

5) **strengthen** [`strɛŋθən] (v.) 加強
You should strengthen your English skills if you want to study abroad.

6) **meditation** [ˌmɛdə`teʃən] (n.) 靜坐，冥想
Ken went to Japan to study Zen meditation.

7) **guidance** [`gaɪdn̩s] (n.) 指導，輔導
Young children look to their parents for guidance.

8) **athlete** [`æθlit] (n.) 運動員
Bobby wants to be a professional athlete when he grows up.

9) **enhance** [ɪn`hæns] (v.) 提高，增進
Many women use makeup to enhance their looks.

10) **unpleasant** [ʌn`plɛzn̩t] (a.) 討厭的
The fish market was filled with unpleasant odors.

補充字彙

* **strenuous** [`strɛnjuəs] (a.) 費力的
Digging ditches is strenuous work.

* **comfort zone** [`kʌmfət zon] (phr.) 習慣的生活方式，固定的思考模式
Most people prefer to stay in their comfort zones.

* **visualization** [ˌvɪʒəlɪ`zeʃən] (n.) 想像，視覺化
Visualization techniques can be used to relieve stress.

* **hypnosis** [hɪp`nosɪs] (n.) 催眠
Ben Affleck quit smoking through hypnosis.

* **overeating** [`ovɚ`itɪŋ] (n.) 暴飲暴食
Overeating can lead to serious health problems.

Mental Workout 心智鍛鍊

課文朗讀 MP3 292　單字朗讀 MP3 293　英文文章導讀 MP3 294

When training our physical muscles, we gradually lift heavier weights or do more *strenuous exercise. ⓖSomething similar happens when we train our "mental muscles"—our mental 1)**capacity** increases and our intellectual 2)**horizons** expand. While a one-kilometer run may leave you 3)**gasping** for breath at first, you'll find that by gradually increasing the distance each day, you'll be able to run three kilometers effortlessly after just a month. Similarly, you can 4)**deliberately** do things that are just outside of your *comfort zone to increase your mental capacity.

Just as we use a variety of equipment and exercises to train different muscles, there are all sorts of activities we can participate in to 5)**strengthen** our minds. Techniques such as *visualization, 6)**meditation**

and *hypnosis can be quite useful, but may require professional [7)]**guidance** in order to be effective. They are often used by [8)]**athletes** to [9)]**enhance** their performance under pressure, or by ordinary people to overcome bad
20   habits such as smoking or *overeating.

Here are some examples of how to break out of your comfort zone and give your mind a little extra workout in your daily life. You can simply start by eating at a new restaurant, trying a new kind of food or beverage, buying
25   your groceries at a different store, taking a different route to school or work, or finding the most [10)]**unpleasant** task on your to-do list and tackling it first. You will be surprised at how much you can learn in a short time by making such small changes in your life.

中 Translation

鍛鍊身體肌肉的時候，我們漸進地舉起較重的重量，或是做較耗體力的運動。我們鍛鍊「心智肌肉」的時候，也會有類似的情形發生——我們的心智能量會增加，智力範圍也會擴展。儘管一開始跑步一公里可能會讓你上氣不接下氣，但是你會發現，逐日增加距離，只要一個月後你就能夠毫不費力地跑三公里。同樣地，你也可以刻意做些超乎自己的舒適圈以外的事來增加你的心智能量。

正如我們會運用各種不同的器材和運動來訓練不同的肌肉，我們也可以參與各種不同的活動來加強心智。觀想、打坐以及催眠等方法可能相當有效，但是要達到效果，可能需要專業的指導。運動員經常採用這些方法來加強他們在壓力之下的表現，一般人也會用來克服吸菸或暴食等不良習慣。

以下舉幾個例子，告訴你如何走出自己的舒適圈，並且在日常生活中給你的頭腦來點額外的訓練。你可以簡單地從在不同的餐廳用餐開始、或是嘗試新種類的食物或飲料、在不同的商店採買菜、走不同的路線上課或上班，或者找出待辦事項清單上最討厭的工作、先處理它。你將會驚訝於生活中這些微小的改變，就能讓你在短時間獲益良多。

Language Guide

觀想、靜坐與催眠

大家對於 meditation（靜坐）與 hypnosis（催眠）可能並不陌生，但 visualization（觀想）是什麼呢？

visualization 字面上的意思是「視覺化」，也就是利用「想像力」imagination 在腦中描繪某個概念的具體形象，例如「成功」人人都愛，但到底怎麼樣才算是成功，每個人會有不同的見解，指導自我成長的訓練師就可以運用 visualization 的方法，要人鉅細靡遺地把心之所欲具體想像出來，對運動員來說，成功可能是 2012 年的奧運金牌、抵達終點線的勝利瞬間……，而且要日復一日一再想像，越詳細越好。簡單來說，visualization 就是「正向思考」positive thinking 的一環。

不論是 visualization、meditation 或 hypnosis，都是在探索內心的真實慾望及感受，藉以開發出未知的潛力，相關理論相信藉此能改變「外在世界」the outer world（即境隨意轉），進而獲致圓滿的人生。

Grammar Master

形容詞的後位修飾

要用形容詞修飾 no-、some-、any-、every- 加上 one、body、thing、where、time 所形成的不定代名詞時，形容詞須放在此類名詞的「後面」修飾。

● It wouldn't surprise me if Jimmy did <u>something stupid</u>.

  不管吉米做什麼蠢事都不會令我驚訝。

● She likes <u>everything beautiful</u>.

  她喜歡一切美麗的事物。

V Vocabulary Bank

1) **time-consuming** [ˈtaɪmkənˌsumɪŋ] (a.) 費時的
Raising children is very time-consuming.

2) **massage** [məˈsɑʒ] (n.) 推拿，按摩
Can you give me a foot massage?

3) **cultivate** [ˈkʌltəˌvet] (v.) 培養，陶冶
The school is trying to help students cultivate an interest in science.

4) **stimulate** [ˈstɪmjəˌlet] (v.) 刺激，促進（功能）
Reading stimulates the imagination.

5) **perspective** [pɚˈspɛktɪv] (n.) 觀點，看法
You should try to see things from other people's perspectives.

6) **comprehend** [ˌkɑmprɪˈhɛnd] (v.) 理解，領會
I'll never comprehend why Mark and Ellen got divorced.

7) **accommodate** [əˈkɑməˌdet] (v.) 適應
Carl had trouble accommodating himself to the new environment.

8) **sociable** [ˈsoʃəb!] (a.) 好交際的，和藹可親的
The people in this town are very sociable.

9) **default** [ˈdɪfɔlt] (n.)（電腦）預設值。在對話中是指「不假思索就採取的回應」，亦即不管三七二十一就先說 Yes!
How do I restore the default settings for this program?

10) **initiate** [ɪˈnɪʃɪˌet] (v.) 開始，發動；開口（交談）
The government plans to initiate reforms.

11) **gathering** [ˈgæðərɪŋ] (n.) 聚會
Rick proposed to his girlfriend at a family gathering.

12) **banquet** [ˈbæŋkwɪt] (n.) 宴會
Many foreign leaders attended the White House banquet.

補充字彙

* **study group** [ˈstʌdɪ grup] (n.) 讀書會
Stanley formed a study group with several of his classmates to prepare for the exam.

* **familiarize** [fəˈmɪljəˌraɪz] (v.) 熟悉
The aim of this class is to familiarize students with English literature.

* **rekindle** [riˈkɪnd!] (v.) 重振，重燃
My visit to the museum rekindled my interest in art.

課文朗讀 MP3 295　單字朗讀 MP3 296　英文文章導讀 MP3 297

　　It's widely accepted that learning a new language is one of the most effective ways to train your mind. Yet while language learning can be [1]**time-consuming** and frustrating (it's commonly known that learning a new
5　language becomes more difficult the older you get), people of all ages can certainly benefit from learning new things, such as how to play an instrument, cook, or give [2]**massages**. You can also [3]**cultivate** a new hobby, attend a *study group on a subject you're unfamiliar
10　with, or simply visit somewhere you've never been before.

Learning something new every day helps
*familiarize us with new concepts and ways of doing
things. In doing so, we ⁴⁾**stimulate** our minds and see the
15 world through different ⁵⁾**perspectives**. And the broader
our experience and understanding of the world around
us, the better our minds become at ⁶⁾**comprehending**
novel situations and ⁷⁾**accommodating** sudden changes.

Another effective way to train your mind is to
20 be open and ⁸⁾**sociable**. When someone asks you to
do something, make your ⁹⁾**default** answer "yes," but
don't forget to say "no" when appropriate. Dare to
ask questions—either for help, or simply to ¹⁰⁾**initiate**
conversations with strangers. Try to sit next to someone
25 you don't know at a ¹¹⁾**gathering**, ᴳwhether it's a formal
business conference or a friend's wedding ¹²⁾**banquet**. Or
you can *rekindle a friendship by calling or e-mailing an
old friend you haven't seen in a long time.

中 Translation

普遍認為，學習一種新語言是訓練心智最有效的方法之一。不過，雖然語言學習可能相當耗時又令人挫折（一般人都知道，年紀愈老，學習新語言愈困難），但是各年齡層的人的確能從學習新事物的過程中獲益，例如學習彈奏樂器、烹飪或幫人按摩…等。你也可以培養新的興趣、參加你不熟悉主題的讀書會，或僅僅是造訪某個你過去從未去過的地方。

每天學習新事物，有助於我們熟悉新觀念與做事的新方法。我們藉此可以刺激頭腦並且以不同的角度看世界。我們對週遭環境的體驗和了解愈廣博，我們的頭腦越能夠理解新情勢、適應突發狀況。

另一個訓練智力的有效方法，就是讓自己心胸開闊並且平易近人。當有人要求你做某件事時，將你的回答預設為「好」，但也別忘了在適當的時候說「不」。勇於發問——無論是請求協助，或者只是和陌生人開啟對話。在聚會的場合中，試著坐在你不認識的人旁邊，無論是在正式的商業會議還是朋友的婚宴。或者你也可以打電話或e-mail給一個許久不見的老朋友來重燃友誼。

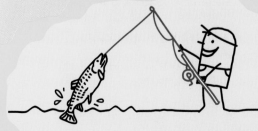

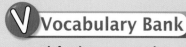

Vocabulary Bank

1) **satisfaction** [ˌsætɪsˈfækʃən] (n.)
滿足，成就感
The company's top goal is to improve customer satisfaction.

2) **occupation** [ˌɑkjəˈpeʃən] (n.) 職業
Please state your name and occupation for the court record.

3) **expressive** [ɪkˈsprɛsɪv] (a.) 表情豐富的，善於表達的
Dance is a very expressive art form.

4) **creativity** [ˌkrieˈtɪvətɪ] (n.) 創造力
Tanya took a painting class to develop her creativity.

5) **embrace** [ɪmˈbres] (v.) 擁抱，欣然接受；把握（機會等）
Robert is always willing to embrace new ideas.

6) **flexibility** [ˌflɛksəˈbɪlətɪ] (n.) 彈性，靈活度
Sharon enjoys the flexibility of working at home.

7) **conventional** [kənˈvɛnʃən!] (a.) 慣例的，傳統的
My fiancée wants to have a conventional church wedding.

8) **nutrition** [njuˈtrɪʃən] (n.) 營養，食物
Good nutrition is essential to good health.

補充字彙

* **like-minded** [ˈlaɪkˈmaɪndɪd] (a.) 志趣相投的
My wife and I are like-minded in many ways.

* **socioeconomic** [ˌsoʃɪoɪkəˈnɑmɪk] (a.) 社會經濟的
All people, regardless of socioeconomic status, deserve access to affordable healthcare.

* **adaptability** [əˌdæptəˈbɪlətɪ] (n.) 適應性
Adaptability is an important quality in today's job market.

課文朗讀 MP3 298　單字朗讀 MP3 299　英文文章導讀 MP3 300

Joining a club or group is a great way to meet *like-minded people. Just think of a subject or hobby you're interested in, and see if there are any related clubs in your local area. Doing volunteer work for a non-profit

5　organization is another excellent choice. You'll not only get to meet interesting people and learn new skills, but also enjoy the ¹⁾**satisfaction** of helping others. As you actively expand your personal contacts in your daily life, you will be exposed to people of different ²⁾**occupations**,

10　*socioeconomic backgrounds, and cultures. Through interaction with a diverse range of people, we can learn from each other and gain a better understanding of our similarities and differences.

15　Ultimately, all these forms of mental training will make you a more open and ³⁾**expressive** person. As you become a better listener and communicator, you'll not only learn more from those around you, but begin to inspire others as well. Your ⁴⁾**creativity**

20　will also blossom, as your mind will learn to

Language Guide

健腦食物

腦細胞所需營養是全面性的。醣類 (carbohydrate) 是腦部最主要的能量來源;脂肪 (fat) 可促進腦細胞及腦神經的發育,是維持智力的必要物質,而攝取卵磷脂 (lecithin)(蛋黃、大豆、堅果中富含)對增強記憶力有幫助。蛋白質 (protein) 中的穀胱甘肽 (GSH, glutathione)(動物肝臟、魚類中富含)可增進腦細胞活力,預防腦細胞老化;鈣 (calcium) 可以抑制腦細胞異常放電,維生素 E (vitamin E) 可預防頭腦疲勞。此外,維生素 B 群 (B complex) 及鐵 (iron)、鋅 (zinc)、硒 (Se, selenium)、銅 (copper) 等礦物質及微量元素(小米、金針花、綠葉蔬菜、豆類、柑桔、胡蘿蔔、黑木耳、動物內臟中富含)也是很重要的健腦營養素。

坊間還有許多宣稱對腦有益的保健食品,如銀杏葉萃取物 (ginkgo leaf extract)、魚油(富含 DHA, docosahexaenoic acid)、海豹油(seal oil,富含 DPA, docosapentaenoic acid),近年來都成為熱門商品。

[5)]**embrace** new possibilities and invent new solutions [6)]when necessary. In the rapidly changing world of today, our chances of success, and even survival, are dependant on [6)]**flexibility** and *adaptability in the face of challenges

25 to our [7)]**conventional** ways of thinking. Maintaining regular mental workout habits can therefore provide our minds with the exercise and [8)]**nutrition** required to keep us healthy and happy.

中 Translation

參加社團或任何團體是遇到志趣相投人們的好方法。只要想一個你有興趣的主題或嗜好,然後找找看你所在地區是否有相關的社團。在非營利組織從事志工是另一個很棒的選擇。你不但可以認識有趣的人並且學習新技能,也可以享受幫助他人的滿足感。當你主動拓展日常生活的人脈,你就會接觸到不同職業、社經背景與文化的人,透過與不同領域的人互動,我們可以相互學習,並且更了解我們彼此的相似與差異。

最後,這所有形式的心智訓練都會使你成為一個心胸更寬闊、更善於表達的人。當你成為更好的聆聽者和溝通者時,你不只會從身旁的人學到更多,你也會開始啟發別人。你的創造力也會變得旺盛,因為你的心智學會接受新的可能性,並且在有需要的時候創造新的解決方法。在今日這個改變迅速的世界,我們成功的機會、甚至是生存的機會,都仰賴我們的傳統思考方式在面對挑戰時的靈活度與適應能力。因此,維持固定的心智鍛鍊習慣,可以提供我們的心智維持健康與快樂所需的練習和養分。

Grammar Master

從屬連接詞 + 形容詞的用法

從屬連接詞 although、though、when、while、if 等後面直接加上形容詞、過去分詞或 Ving,即可形成副詞子句,為從屬子句減化的通則之一,如本段中的 ...when necessary 即為「從屬連接詞+形容詞」的用法,其他常見的還有 if possible、if any 等。

● Though hard-working, he is still short of money. 他雖然努力工作卻還是手頭很緊。

● I'll give you a reply as soon as possible if possible. 可以的話,我會盡快回覆您。

Mini Quiz 閱讀測驗

❶ Which of the following is NOT mentioned as an effective way to train your mind?
(A) visiting new places
(B) talking to people you don't know
(C) always saying yes
(D) getting in touch with old friends

閱讀測驗解答:❶ (C)

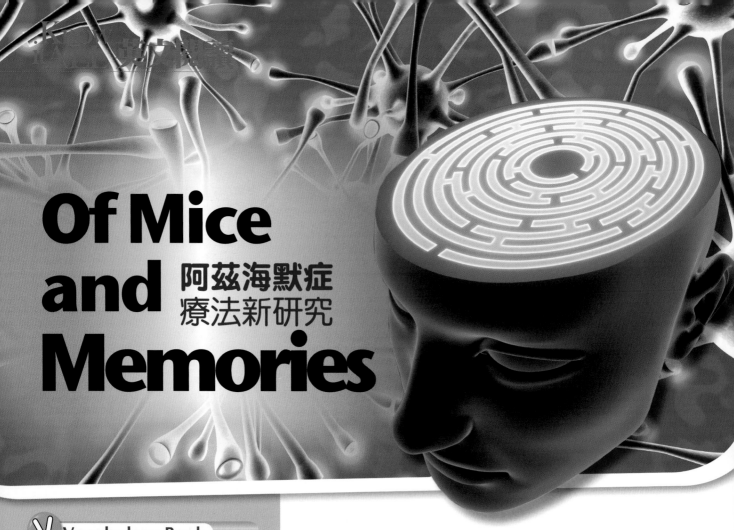

Of Mice and Memories

阿茲海默症療法新研究

V Vocabulary Bank

1) **treatment** [ˋtritmənt] (n.) 治療；處理
The accident victims were sent to the hospital for treatment.

2) **involve** [ɪnˋvɑlv] (v.) 牽涉，連累
How many people were involved in the accident?

3) **inject** [ɪnˋdʒɛkt] (v.) 注射（藥物）
The nurse injected the patient with antibiotics.

4) **aid in** [ed ɪn] (phr.) 有助於，協助
The charity is aiding in the fight against hunger.

5) **cholesterol** [kəˋlɛstəˌrol] (n.) 膽固醇
Eggs are high in cholesterol.

進階字彙

6) **neuron** [ˋnjʊrɑn] (n.) 神經細胞，神經元
There are billions of neurons in the human brain.

7) **spool** [spul] (n.) （紡織）線軸
Could you hand me that spool of thread?

口語補充

8) **golden years** [ˋgoldn jɪrz] (phr.) 退休頤養天年的時光
We plan to spend our golden years traveling around the world.

課文朗讀 MP3 301　單字朗讀 MP3 302　英文文章導讀 MP3 303

Scientists in Germany may be close to finding an effective [1)]**treatment** for age-related memory loss. In a study they performed on aging mice, a group given a special inhibitor performed better on a memory test than a
5　group that didn't receive the inhibitor. This is great news for people who suffer from Alzheimer's disease.

Creating long-term memories [2)]**involves** a complicated process in the brain. To form a memory, electrical signals are sent between neurons in the brain, releasing
10　neurotransmitters that create new connections between nearby [6)]**neurons**. These neurotransmitters are made by the DNA inside cells in a process called transcription. These DNA are wrapped around protein [7)]**spools** called histones. When DNA is wrapped loosely around a spool, transcription happens
15　more easily, producing more of the neurotransmitters that

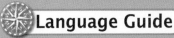
help create memories. When DNA is wrapped too tightly around a protein spool, [G]less of the neurotransmitters are produced, making it harder for memories to form.

20　　So why were the mice able to perform better on the memory test? When scientists [3]**injected** the mice with the inhibitor, the DNA wrapped around the protein spools loosened, creating more of the neurotransmitters that [4]**aid in** memory formation. For now, treatment isn't available for humans, but there are other ways to help keep your

25　memory strong. Eating a low [5]**cholesterol** diet, avoiding heavy drinking and protecting your head from injury (drive safely and avoid contact sports) may help keep your memory young and healthy well into your [8]**golden years**!

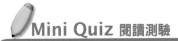

Mini Quiz 閱讀測驗

❶ ____ **What does the inhibitor mentioned in the article do?**
(A) It improves people's memory.
(B) It produces a neurotransmitter.
(C) It loosens DNA wrapped around histones
(D) It cures Alzheimer's disease.

中 Translation

德國科學家可能即將發現一種有效治療與年齡有關之記憶衰退的療法。在一項研究中,他們拿老邁的老鼠做實驗,投以特殊抑制劑的一群老鼠,在記憶測驗中的表現勝過未攝取抑制劑的老鼠。這對深受阿茲海默症所苦的人是一大福音。

大腦創造長期記憶的過程相當複雜。要形成記憶,必須有帶電信號在大腦神經元之間傳送,釋放出神經傳導素,在附近神經元之間產生新連結。這些神經傳導素是透過所謂的轉錄過程,由細胞內的脫氧核糖核酸 (DNA) 製成。這些 DNA 被稱為「組織蛋白」的蛋白線軸纏繞,當 DNA 被纏得較鬆時,傳導就比較容易,進而分泌更多有助於營造記憶的神經傳導素。當 DNA 被蛋白線軸纏得太緊,分泌的神經傳導素就會減少,使記憶較難形成。

那麼,為什麼那些老鼠能在記憶測驗中表現得比較好?當科學家替那些老鼠注射抑制劑,纏繞 DNA 的蛋白線軸便會鬆弛,有助於記憶生成的神經傳導素就分泌較多。現在,這項療法尚未應用在人類身上,但仍有其他辦法能助你保持記憶強健。攝取低膽固醇飲食,避免大量飲酒,以及保護頭部免於受傷(安全駕駛,避免從事肢體碰撞的運動),或許都能助你保持記憶年輕健康,陪你一路走進頤養天年的年代!

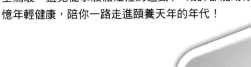

Language Guide

Alzheimer's disease 阿茲海默症
阿茲海默症俗稱為「老年癡呆症」或「老年失智症」,是一種人類腦組織萎縮病變。老化是罹病的因素之一,患者主要為六十歲以上老人。由於女性壽命較長,因此罹患阿茲海默症的女性多於男性。但阿茲海默症並非只發生在老年人身上,少部分家族遺傳患者會在中、壯年即發病。

阿茲海默症罹病初期的症狀是喪失短期記憶(剛發生的事、剛得到的訊息一轉眼就忘記),但因症狀不明顯不會注意到,一直到個性劇烈轉變、突然失去語言能力及空間概念(例如在住家附近迷路),才驚覺已經生病。由於患者無法控制情緒,喪失智力的結果到最後連吃飯、穿衣均無法自理,需要全天候的照護,末期甚至會癱瘓,對親友造成極大的壓力。

histone 組織蛋白
染色體是由 DNA 組成,而組織蛋白內含的數種帶正電的胺基酸會與 DNA 纏繞起來,有助於穩定DNA 的結構。

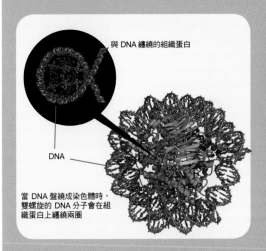

與 DNA 纏繞的組織蛋白

DNA

當 DNA 盤繞成染色體時,雙螺旋的 DNA 分子會在組織蛋白上纏繞兩圈。

G Grammar Master

less of... 較少的……

less of... 表示這件事情的「程度上」是比較少的。less 是 little 的比較級,一般狀況下,less 後方會接不可數名詞,但 less of...「較少的……」後方接可數/不可數名詞均可。

例 Withdrawing cash is **less of** a hassle than it used to be.
提領現金不像以前那麼麻煩了。

翻譯練習
豬流感現在的威脅性沒那麼大了。

(C) ❶
閱讀測驗解答
Swine flu is now less of a threat.
翻譯練習解答
Know it all •241

Nursing
Job Opportunities [1] Abound

工作機會多多的
醫療照護

課文朗讀 MP3 304　單字朗讀 MP3 305　英文文章導讀 MP3 306

As a student, you probably spend a lot of time thinking about what you'll do after you graduate. However, making [2]**career** choices years in advance can be difficult, especially considering how much the job market changes

5　year to year. One [3]**profession** that has a very good [4]**outlook** for many years to come is nursing. Studies have shown that, when compared to other professions, the number of new [14]**job openings** in the nursing industry will grow much faster than average For example, a

10　2009 study by the U.S. [5]**Bureau** of Labor [6]**Statistics** [7]**estimates** that over half a million new nursing [8]**positions** will be created between now and 2018. That's a lot of positions to fill!

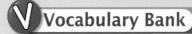

So what kinds of people will most likely be filling these positions? Well, most nurses enter the profession because they have at least a general interest in science. 9)**Biology** is of course the field of science most closely related to medicine, but 10)**chemistry** is also very important. Students who are interested and 11)**excel** in these areas make great 12)**candidates** for careers in nursing.

But nursing is about more than just being well-educated. Many of the best nurses begin with very caring personalities. Of all the people in a hospital 13)**setting**, nurses spend the most one-on-one time with patients. They, and not the doctors, are the ones who communicate important information to the patients, so good communication and 15)**interpersonal** skills are a must.

中 Translation

身為學生的你,大概會花很多時間思考畢業後要做什麼,然而,提前幾年做職涯選擇或許是件難事,尤其如果考慮到就業市場每年都有不小的變化。放眼未來幾年,有一個職業的展望相當不錯:護理。研究已經證實,比起其他職業,護理業新職缺的成長速度將遠高於平均。例如二〇〇九年美國勞動統計局的一份研究就預估,從現在到二〇一八年,護理業創造的新職務將超過五十萬份。職缺真是多!

那麼,什麼樣的人最可能填補這些職缺呢?這個嘛,多數護士進這一行是因為他們對科學大致上算是有興趣。生物當然是與醫學最相關的科學領域,但化學也很重要。喜愛並擅長這些領域的學生就是步入護理生涯的絕佳人選。

但護理工作不只需要受過良好教育,許多最優秀的護士都極富愛心。在醫院環境中,護士和病患一對一相處的時間最久,他們——而非醫師——是向病患傳達重要資訊的人,因此良好的溝通和人際技巧也不可或缺。

V Vocabulary Bank

1) **abound** [əˋbaʊnd] (v.) 大量存在,充足
Business opportunities abound in much of the developing world.

2) **career** [kəˋrɪr] (n.) 職業
Karen plans to pursue a career as a lawyer.

3) **profession** [prəˋfɛʃən] (n.)(受過專門訓練的)職業
Tina has spent her whole life in service industry professions.

4) **outlook** [ˋaʊt.lʊk] (n.) 前景,觀點
The outlook for the economy is improving.

5) **bureau** [ˋbjʊro] (n.) 政府機構的局、署等
This bureau doesn't handle taxation issues.

6) **statistic** [stəˋtɪstɪk] (n.) 統計數字
Statistics show that women in the area live longer than men.

7) **estimate** [ˋɛstə.met] (v.) 估計
I estimate the project will be completed by Tuesday.

8) **position** [pəˋzɪʃən] (n.) 職位,工作
Denise applied for a position at the bank.

9) **biology** [baɪˋɑlədʒɪ] (n.) 生物學
Biology is the study of living things.

10) **chemistry** [ˋkɛmɪstrɪ] (n.) 化學
Brian got a chemistry set for his birthday.

11) **excel** [ɪkˋsɛl] (v.) 表現優異,勝過他人
I knew you'd excel at computer programming!

12) **candidate** [ˋkændɪ.det] (n.) 求職應試者,候選人
The company is looking for candidates with sales experience.

13) **setting** [ˋsɛtɪŋ] (n.) 環境,背景
A Ph.D. is necessary if you want to teach in a university setting.

進階字彙

14) **job opening** [dʒɑb ˋopənɪŋ] (phr.) 職缺
She heard about the job opening through a friend.

15) **interpersonal** [.ɪntəˋpɜsən!] (a.) 人際關係的
Strong interpersonal skills are important for sales professionals.

Vocabulary Bank

1) **adapt** [əˋdæpt] (v.) 適應，改變
Children usually adapt easily to new environments.

2) **trauma** [ˋtrɔmə] (n.)（醫）外傷，傷口
The man suffered head trauma in the accident.

3) **certify** [ˋsɝtə͵faɪ] (v.) 證明
This document has been certified by the court.

4) **qualification** [͵kwɑləfɪˋkeʃən] (n.) 資格，能力
What qualifications does the applicant have?

5) **location** [loˋkeʃən] (n.) 所在地，地點，位置
The resort was built in a beautiful location.

6) **unique** [juˋnik] (a.) 獨特的，獨一無二的
The singer has a unique singing style.

7) **sole** [sol] (a.) 唯一的，專屬的
The sole survivor of the accident was taken to the hospital.

進階字彙

8) **specialization** [͵spɛʃəlɪˋzeʃən] (n.) 專業，主修
This degree offers three fields of specialization.

9) **rehabilitation** [͵rihə͵bɪləˋteʃən] (n.) 復健，康復
The patient spent two weeks in rehabilitation after the surgery.

10) **pediatric** [͵pidiˋætrɪk] (a.)（醫）小兒科的
Shelly wants to become a pediatric nurse.

11) **practitioner** [prækˋtɪʃənə] (n.) 開業者，尤指醫生、律師。nurse practitioner 即「專科護理師」
It takes years of study to become a nurse practitioner.

12) **provider** [prəˋvaɪdə] (n.) 供應者，提供者
This company is a provider of phone and Internet services.

Tongue-tied No More

1 …to name just a few 略舉數例

這裡的 name 是動詞「講出，說出」。to name just a few 是用在約略說出幾個例子之後，表示「這只是其中一小部分」。
A: Who's going to the big game tonight?
誰會去看今晚那場重要比賽？
B: Carson, Steve, Chase, Brenda, to name just a few.
卡森、史帝夫、崔斯、布藍達……這只是其中幾個。

2 The bottom line is… 重點在於

bottom line 原本是帳簿上面寫最後加總的那條線，表示「顯示盈虧的總計金額」，引申為「最重要的事」。
A: I still don't understand the terms of this contract!
我還是搞不懂這個合約上的條件。
B: The bottom line is that you'll pay $65 a month for your phone service.
重點就是你每個月電話費要付六十五元。

課文朗讀 MP3 307　單字朗讀 MP3 308　英文文章導讀 MP3 309

As nurses have taken on increasingly important and specific roles, the industry has continued to [1)]**adapt**. Many nurses now get advanced degrees in various fields of [8)]**specialization**: emergency room and [2)]**trauma**, [9)]**rehabilitation**, [10)]**pediatric** and elderly care, **1 to name just a few**.

5

There's also a type of nurse called a nurse [11)]**practitioner**, or NP. NPs commonly have more advanced degrees. In the United States, NPs are [3)]**certified** by the state in which they practice, so their [4)]**qualifications** can vary depending on [5)]**location**. But what makes NPs [6)]**unique** is that, in many states, they can open their own practices and see their own patients as a primary healthcare [12)]**provider**.

10

2 The bottom line is that nurses now fill many roles that were once the [7)]**sole** responsibility of doctors. And what all this means for you is that, if you're considering a career in nursing, finding a job after graduation isn't something you need to worry about.

15

Translation

由於護士扮演的角色愈益重要且明確，這項行業持續順應這股趨勢。今天許多護士都具備各種專業領域的高等學歷：如急診室及外傷、復建、小兒及老人照護等不勝枚舉。

還有一類護士稱為執業護士，或稱 NP。NP 通常擁有更高的學歷。在美國，NP 是由執業所在地的州來認證，因此其資格可能視地點而異。但 NP 獨特的地方在於，在許多州，他們可以自行開業，以基層醫療提供者的身份照顧病患。

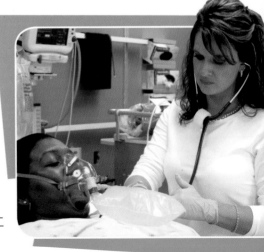

歸根結柢，現在護士填補了許多原本只屬醫師之責的角色。而這對你的意義就是，如果你考慮走護理這一行，畢業後找工作不是什麼需要擔憂的事。

What made you decide to become a nurse?
When I was nine, I came down with pneumonia and was hospitalized for four days. It was my first stay in a hospital and I was too scared to sleep. There was a student nurse there who stayed with me through the night. This left an impression on me, and thereafter I knew I wanted to become a nurse.

問：你怎麼會決定當護士？
答：我九歲時得了肺炎，在醫院住了四天。那是我第一次住院，害怕得不敢睡覺。幸好有一個實習護士整晚陪在我身邊。那讓我留下深刻的印象，之後我便明白，自己想當個護士。

Interview
護理人員怎麼說？
Sato, an Intensive Care nurse at the Round Rock Hospital
受訪者：美國圓岩醫院加護病房護士沙托

What's the hardest part about being a nurse?
Being a patient advocate. For example, when a patient is in a terminal state with no chance of recovery, and their living will states they wish to be removed from life support. Often family members will disagree, yet it's my job to follow the wishes of the patient.

問：當護士最困難的地方是？
答：站在病患這一邊。比如一名病患進入末期，沒有機會痊癒，而生前遺囑表明想移除維生系統，通常他們的家人不會同意，但我的職責是遵從病患的心願。

Is there any advice you'd give to prospective nursing students?
Start volunteering at a hospital as early as possible. This will help you get experience and figure out what specialty or field you'd like to get into. Many people change their minds after a little exposure, and it's better to figure this out early on.

問：對於有意願想念護理的人，你有什麼建議嗎？
答：儘早到醫院擔任志工。這能助你吸取經驗，以及搞清楚你想進入的專業或領域。許多人在短暫接觸後會改變心意，而愈早了解這點愈好。

Did You Know? 護理行業知多少？

• Many colleges and universities in the United States offer nursing programs. The lengths of these programs vary, but all prepare graduates to take one of the required national examinations.

美國許多大專院校都有開設護理課程。課程長短不一，但都足以讓畢業生準備國家資格考試。

• In addition to various state exams, nursing students must take one of the NCLEXs (National Council Licensure Examinations), usually either the NCLEX-PN for Licensed Practical Nurses or the NCLEX-RN for Registered Nurses.

除了各種州考試外，護理生也必須參與國家執照考試：通常不是有照執業護士的 NCLEX-PN，就是合格護士的 NCLEX-RN。

• RNs can expect to receive a salary of between US$38,000 and $50,000 their first year on the job. Pay increases with experience and varies with field of specialization.

合格護士就業第一年的年薪可望在三萬八千至五萬美元之間，薪資會隨著年資增加，並因專業領域而異。

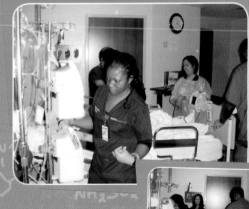

Yoga, A Flexible 瑜伽 Career Choice

高彈性的職涯選擇

課文朗讀 MP3 310　單字朗讀 MP3 311　英文文章導讀 MP3 312

Have you ever noticed how people love to give out advice about choosing careers? "You should look for a job in [1]**technology**. It's still a growing industry." "Why don't you become a lawyer? They're always very well paid." One

5　piece of advice that may [2]**deserve** more attention is that you should find a job doing what you love. That is, find a way to make a living doing something you would do even if you didn't get paid for it. The reasoning behind this advice is that if you

10　make career choices based on your personal interests, then your job will [3]**naturally** be a great fit for you. Today, we'll look at one career that falls into this hobby-turned-profession [4]**category**: teaching yoga.

15 It wasn't too long ago that yoga was considered a [8]**fringe** activity—it wasn't widely popular, and few people knew just [5]**exactly** 20 what it was. Now, all of that has changed. Yoga schools are common in all major American cities, and its practitioners [6]**stretch** from coast to coast (yes, *stretch*). A 2006 study by *Yoga Journal* found that nearly 7% of Americans practice yoga ▮ **on a regular basis**, spending a total of $5.7 billion a 25 year on classes, [7]**equipment**, books and DVDs.

中 Translation

你可曾注意過人們有多喜歡給人選擇職業的建議？「你該去找科技業的工作，那仍是成長中的產業。」「為什麼不當律師呢？律師的待遇向來很好。」有一種建議或許應得到更多關注：你該找一份能做你喜愛的事情的工作。也就是說，想辦法以某種就算沒有收入，你也會去做的事情來維生。其背後的道理是：若你能依個人興趣選擇職業，那麼你的工作自然再適合你不過。今天，我們就要探討一種屬於這類「興趣轉為職業」的職業：教瑜伽。

瑜伽不久前還被視為一種非主流活動——並沒有廣受歡迎，也很少人真的知道它是什麼。現在，一切都不一樣了。瑜伽學校在美國各大城市相當普遍，練瑜伽的人也從東岸延伸至西岸（沒錯，就是延伸）。（編註：stretch 也有「伸展」的意思，瑜珈動作基本上就是在伸展，一語雙關）《瑜伽期刊》在二〇〇六年所做的一份研究發現，有近百分之七的美國人定期練瑜伽，每年總共花費五十七億美元上課及購買瑜珈用品、書籍和影音光碟。

V Vocabulary Bank

1) **technology** [tɛk`nɑlədʒɪ] (n.) 科技，技術
Technology has transformed the way we live and work.

2) **deserve** [dɪ`zɜv] (v.) 應受（賞罰）
I hope that killer gets the punishment he deserves.

3) **naturally** [`nætʃ(ə)rəlɪ] (adv.) 理所當然地，自然地，天生地
Ed was naturally upset when his girlfriend broke up with him.

4) **category** [`kætə,gɔrɪ] (n.) 種類，範疇
The light truck category includes SUVs, minivans and pickup trucks.

5) **exactly** [ɪg`zæktlɪ] (adv.) 完全地，確切地
This apartment is exactly what I'm looking for.

6) **stretch** [strɛtʃ] (v.) 延伸，橫跨；伸展（筋骨）
The beach stretches for miles in each direction.

7) **equipment** [ɪ`kwɪpmənt] (n.) 設備，器材
The new equipment increased the efficiency of the factory.

進階字彙

8) **fringe** [frɪndʒ] (n.) 邊緣，非主流，次要部分
Rugby is a fringe sport in the U.S.

🔑 Tongue-tied No More

▮ **on a regular basis** 定期地……
basis 這個字表示各種事物的「基礎，原則」，on a...basis 就是「以……的原則」。這裡用了 regular，就是表示「定期地……」。這個片語有時候也會以 on the basis of + N 的型態表示同樣的意思，但字句就會稍嫌冗長。

A: Why do I need to get my teeth cleaned on a regular basis?
我為什麼需要定期洗牙？

B: It can help prevent cavities and gum disease.
這可以幫助預防蛀牙和牙周病。

Know it ALL 英文閱讀

V Vocabulary Bank

1) **benefit** [ˈbɛnəfɪt] (n.) 益處，利益
   Exercise has many health benefits.

2) **instruction** [ɪnˈstrʌkʃən] (n.) 教學，講授
   (n.) instructor [ɪnˈstrʌktə] 講師，教練
   Many schools now offer online instruction.

3) **diagram** [ˈdaɪəˌɡræm] (n.) 圖解，圖表
   The teacher drew a diagram of the heart on the blackboard.

4) **occasionally** [əˈkeʒənəlɪ] (adv.) 偶爾
   You should stir the sauce occasionally so it doesn't burn.

5) **qualify** [ˈkwɑləˌfaɪ] (v.) 具有資格，具備合格條件
   A master's degree qualifies you to teach at the university level.

6) **certificate** [səˈtɪfɪkɪt] (n.) 文憑，證書
   You need a copy of your birth certificate to apply for a passport.

7) **enthusiast** [ɛnˈθuziˌɪst] (n.) 熱中者
   Car enthusiasts from all over the world attended the auto show.

進階字彙

8) **hands-on** [ˈhændzˈɑn] (a.) 實際操作的
   （經驗、訓練等）
   The photography workshop provides students with hands-on training.

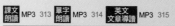

課文朗讀 MP3 313　單字朗讀 MP3 314　英文文章導讀 MP3 315

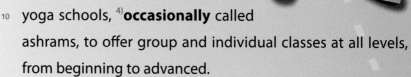

Speaking of classes, yoga is clearly an activity that [1]**benefits** greatly from [8]**hands-on** [2]**instruction**.

5　After all, there's only so much you can learn by looking at [3]**diagrams** in books and watching DVDs. It's common for

10　yoga schools, [4]**occasionally** called ashrams, to offer group and individual classes at all levels, from beginning to advanced.

What [5]**qualifies** a practitioner to become an [2]**instructor**? Mainly practice—years and years of it. Many schools, and a

15　few national and international organizations, issue teaching [6]**certificates** to students who have completed a certain number of class hours. Most organizations require several hundred hours of classroom instruction before a student can be certified as an instructor. This may sound like a lot, but for

20　most yoga [7]**enthusiasts**, this is what they'd be doing with their time anyway. So why not make a career out of it?

中 Translation

說到上課，瑜伽顯然是一種能從親身指導大獲助益的活動，畢竟，光看書中附圖和光碟，你能學會的就只有這麼多。瑜伽學校（有時稱為修行場）一般都提供從入門到進階等各種程度的團體及個人課程。

練瑜伽的人要具備何種資格才能晉升為老師呢？主要透過練習——年復一年的練習。許多學校和一些全國及國際性組織，會核發教學證書給上完一定時數課程的學生。多數組織會要求學生上完數百小時的課堂指導，才會核發老師證書。數百小時聽來或許很多，但對大多數瑜伽愛好者來說，反正那是他們本來就要做的事，所以，何不乾脆以此為職業呢？

Interview

瑜伽老師怎麼說？

Mike Matthews, Ashtanga Yoga Center of Austin

受訪者：阿斯坦加瑜伽中心奧斯汀分校的 麥克馬修斯

What got you interested in yoga?

My sister introduced me to it. At the time I was doing a lot of more traditional exercising, like running and baseball. I found yoga to be a relaxing, calming balance to other sports and life in general.

問：你是怎麼對瑜伽產生興趣？

答：是我姊姊叫我練的。當時我做的都是比較傳統的運動，像是跑步和打棒球，我發現對於其他運動及整體生活而言，瑜伽是種使人放鬆、平靜的平衡。

Why did you decide to become an instructor?

I started teaching yoga as a way to pay for graduate school. I soon found I enjoyed it more than what I was studying in school.

問：你為什麼決定要當瑜伽老師？

答：我開始教瑜伽是為了付研究所的學費。很快我就發現我很喜歡教瑜伽，勝過在學校所學。

What's the most difficult part of being a yoga instructor?

Convincing people that practice must be continual. In our school, it's important to practice six days a week, and I need to convince people to make time for it, no matter how busy they might be.

問：當瑜伽老師最難的地方在哪裡？

答：說服人們相信練習必須持之以恆。在我們這一派，每星期練習六天是很重要的事，而我必須說服大家騰出時間練習，不管他們可能有多忙。

Do you have any advice for aspiring teachers?

Sure. You need to become a good student before you can become a good teacher.

問：對於有志成為瑜伽老師的人，你有什麼建議嗎？

答：有。你必須先當個好學生，才能成為好老師。

Did You Know? 瑜伽知多少？

- There are many different schools of yoga. Though all have similar elements (a focus on breathing and posture), there are also some significant differences. Beginners should do some research before deciding which kind suits them best.

  瑜伽有許多不同派別。雖然有共同的要素（專注於呼吸及姿勢），但各派別之間仍有一些很大的差異，初學者應該先做些研究再決定哪種瑜伽最適合自己。

- Yoga has many proven health benefits. Increased flexibility, lower blood pressure and improved balance and concentration are just a few.

  瑜伽對健康有許多已獲證實的益處。增加柔軟度、降低血壓、改善平衡與專注力，這些只是其中幾項。

- Pay for yoga instructors varies widely, from $25 all the way up to several hundred dollars per hour. Pay is largely dependent on experience and reputation.

  瑜伽老師收取的費用差異甚大，從每小時二十五美元到數百美元都有，主要取決於經驗和聲譽。

- Yoga instructors usually work at established schools, though many choose to start their own schools after gaining sufficient experience.

  瑜伽老師通常會在有規模的學校工作，不過有很多人在吸取充分經驗後選擇自己開業。

NOTES

NOTES

NOTES

NOTES

國家圖書館出版品預行編目 (CIP) 資料

英文閱讀 Know-It-All EZ Talk 總編嚴選閱讀特刊 / EZ 叢書館編輯部 作
– 初版一臺北市：日月文化，2011.12
256 面，21 x 28 公分（EZ 叢書館）
ISBN：978-986-248-229-2（平裝）
1. 英文　2. 讀本
805.18　　　　　　　　　　　　　　　　　　　　　100023566

EZ 叢書館

英文閱讀 Know-It-All EZ Talk 總編嚴選閱讀特刊

作　　者：EZ TALK 叢書館編輯部
副 主 編：陳毅心
文字編輯：陳彥廷 、李明芳
美術設計：管仕豪
版面排版：田慧盈
錄 音 員：Sara Zitter、Michael Tennant、Meilee Saccenti、Jacob Roth

發 行 人：洪祺祥
總 編 輯：林慧美
法律顧問：建大法律事務所
財務顧問：高威會計師事務所

出　　版：日月文化出版股份有限公司
製　　作：EZ 叢書館
地　　址：台北市大安區信義路三段 151 號 8 樓
電　　話：(02)2708-5509
傳　　真：(02)2708-6157
網　　址：www.heliopolis.com.tw
客服信箱：service@heliopolis.com.tw
郵撥帳號：19716071 日月文化出版股份有限公司

總 經 銷：聯合發行股份有限公司
電　　話：(02)2917-8022
傳　　真：(02)2915-7212
印　　刷：禾耕彩色印刷股份有限公司
初　　版：2011年12月
初版十三刷：2017年2月
定　　價：350元
Ｉ Ｓ Ｂ Ｎ：978-986-248-229-2

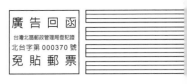

日月文化集團
HELIOPOLIS
CULTURE GROUP

客服專線 02-2708-5509
客服傳真 02-2708-6157
客服信箱 service@heliopolis.com.tw

廣告回函
台灣北區郵政管理局登記證
北台字第 000370 號
免貼郵票

日月文化集團 讀者服務部 收

10658 台北市信義路三段151號8樓

對折黏貼後，即可直接郵寄

日月文化網址：**www.heliopolis.com.tw**

最新消息、活動，請參考 FB 粉絲團

大量訂購，另有折扣優惠，請洽客服中心（詳見本頁上方所示連絡方式）。

日月文化　　　EZ TALK　　　EZ Japan　　　EZ Korea

大好書屋・寶鼎出版・山岳文化・洪圖出版　 EZ叢書館　 EZ Korea　 EZ TALK　 EZ Japan

感謝您購買 **英文閱讀 Know-It-All EZ Talk 總編輯嚴選閱讀特刊**

為提供完整服務與快速資訊，請詳細填寫以下資料，傳真至02-2708-6157或免貼郵票寄回，我們將不定期提供您最新資訊及最新優惠。

1. 姓名：_____　　性別：□男　　　□女

2. 生日：_____年_____月_____日　　職業：_____

3. 電話：（請務必填寫一種聯絡方式）

　　（日）_____（夜）_____（手機）_____

4. 地址：□□□_____

5. 電子信箱：_____

6. 您從何處購買此書？□_____縣/市 _____書店/量販超商

　　□_____網路書店　　□書展　　□郵購　　□其他

7. 您何時購買此書？　　年　　月　　日

8. 您購買此書的原因：（可複選）

　　□對書的主題有興趣　　□作者　　□出版社　　□工作所需　　□生活所需

　　□資訊豐富　　　　□價格合理（若不合理，您覺得合理價格應為 _____）

　　□封面/版面編排　　□其他 _____

9. 您從何處得知這本書的消息：　□書店　□網路／電子報　□量販超商　□報紙

　　□雜誌　□廣播　□電視　□他人推薦　□其他

10. 您對本書的評價：（1.非常滿意 2.滿意 3.普通 4.不滿意 5.非常不滿意）

　　書名 _____　內容 _____　封面設計 _____　版面編排 _____　文/譯筆 _____

11. 您通常以何種方式購書？□書店　　□網路　□傳真訂購　□郵政劃撥　□其他

12. 您最喜歡在何處買書？

　　□_____縣/市 _____書店/量販超商　　□網路書店

13. 您希望我們未來出版何種主題的書？_____

14. 您認為本書還須改進的地方？提供我們的建議？

_____

_____

_____

_____